## ALSO BY LINDA NAGATA

### THE TRIALS

(FORTHCOMING)

### GOING DARK

(FORTHCOMING)

# THE RED

## TRILOGY

# THE RED: FIRST LIGHT

LINDA NAGATA

SAGA PRESS
LONDON SYDNEY NEW YORK TORONTO NEW DELHI

1230 AVENUE OF THE AMERICAS, NEW YORK, NEW YORK 10020



First Saga Press hardcover edition June 2015

SAGA PRESS and colophon are trademarks of Simon & Schuster, Inc.

For information about special discounts for bulk purchases, please contact Simon & Schuster Special Sales at 1-866-506-1949 or business@simonandschuster.com.

The Simon & Schuster Speakers Bureau can bring authors to your live event. For more information or to book an event, contact the Simon & Schuster Speakers Bureau at 1-866-248-3049 or visit our website at www.simonspeakers.com.

The text for this book is set in Adobe Garamond.

Manufactured in the United States of America

First edition

2 4 6 8 10 9 7 5 3 1

CIP data is available from the Library of Congress.

ISBN 978-1-4814-4657-0 (hardcover)

ISBN 978-1-4814-4093-6 (pbk.)

ISBN 978-1-4814-4094-3 (eBook)

# THE RED

# LINKED COMBAT SQUAD

---

## EPISODE 1: DARK PATROL

"There needs to be a war going on somewhere, Sergeant Vasquez. It's a fact of life. Without a conflict of decent size, too many international defense contractors will find themselves out of business. So if no natural war is looming, you can count on the DCs to get together to invent one."

My orientation lecture is not army standard. I deliver it in the walled yard of Fort Dassari while my LCS—my linked combat squad—preps for our nightly patrol. Since sunset the temperature has dropped to ninety-five degrees American, for which we are all grateful, but it's still goddamn hot, with the clinging humidity of the rainy season. Amber lights cast glistening highlights on the smooth, black, sweat-slick cheeks of Sergeant Jayne Vasquez, who arrived by helicopter, along with a week's worth of provisions, just four hours ago.

Like the rest of us, Jaynie Vasquez is wearing a combat uniform, body armor, and the gray titanium bones of her exoskeleton. Her finely shaped eyebrows are set in a skeptical arch as she eyes me from beneath the rim of her brown LCS skullcap. I suspect she's been warned about me—the notorious Lieutenant James Shelley, United States Army—her new commanding officer here at Fort Dassari.

Not a problem. Knowledge is a good thing.

"So how do the DCs go about inventing a war?" I ask her.

She answers in the practical manner of an experienced non-com: "Above my pay grade, sir."

"Worth considering all the same. I imagine it goes like this: All the big defense contractors, the DCs we love to hate, get together—not physically, but in a virtual meeting. At first they're a little cold—that's the nature of a defense contractor—but then one of the DCs says, 'Come on, now. We need someone to host the next war. Any volunteers?'"

"Yes, sir," Specialist Matthew Ransom says with a grin as he presents himself to me for a mandatory equipment check.

"This is serious, Ransom."

"Sorry, LT."

I initiate the check anyway, making an inventory of his gear and confirming that every cinch on his exoskeleton is secure while I pick up the thread of my story.

"'*Any volunteers.*' That's a joke, see? Because a DC will never allow a war in their own country. Rule one: Don't kill off your taxpayers. War is what you inflict on other people."

"That's the truth, sir," Jaynie says in a bitter undertone as she initiates an equipment check for Private First Class Yafiah Yeboah.

Maybe I'm getting through to her.

"Anyway, the joke works, the ice is broken, and ideas start getting tossed around until one of the DCs says, 'Hey, I've got it. Let's do a war in the Sahel. It's good, open terrain. No nasty jungles. It's not quite desert, and we've already got a figurehead in Ahab Matugo.' This sounds pretty good to everybody, so they agree: The next regional war, the one that will keep them in business for another three or four years, or even a decade if things go well, is right here in Africa's Sahel, between the equatorial rain forest and the Sahara."

I reach the last point of inspection, crouched in the mud beside Matt Ransom's left boot where it's strapped into the exoskeleton's floating footplate. Everything looks good, so I slap his thigh strut and tell him, "You're clear."

The frame of my own exoskeleton flexes as I stand. There's a faint sigh from the joints as the struts alongside my legs boost me up with no effort on my part, despite the weight of my eighty-pound backpack. The mechanical joints release a faint, sterile scent of mineral lubricant, barely detectable against the organic reek of mud and dogs.

I turn back to Jaynie. She pauses in her equipment check and asks, "So now the defense contractors have to get the war started, right?"

"First they have to choose sides, but a coin toss will do it. China winds up as primary backer of Ahab Matugo, and an Arab alliance takes the status quo—"

"LT," Ransom interrupts, "you want me to clear you?"

"Yeah. Go ahead." I run my gloved hand over my skullcap as he begins tugging on cinches and checking power levels. I'm remembering the buildup to this war, watching it happen while I served my first combat tour at the tail end of Bolivia. I try hard to keep my voice calm. "So we Americans . . . we don't jump in right away. We have another war to wind up first, so we promise to intervene when humanitarian issues demand it—but we don't discuss what side to come in on because it doesn't fucking matter. Everyone knows we don't understand the local politics and we don't give a shit anyway. There's nothing in this region we want. The only reason we're jumping in is so that our defense contractors can keep their shareholders happy. The

American taxpayers will listen to their hoo-rah propaganda media outlets and pony up the money, blaming the liberals for the bad economy while brain-draining the underclass into the army because hey, it's a job, and even the DCs can't convince Congress to spend ten million dollars each on a combat robot when you can get a fully qualified flesh-and-blood high-IQ soldier for two hundred and fifty thousand."

Ransom steps back. "You're clear, sir."

I ignore him. "And that, Sergeant, is the reason we are here at Fort Dassari, squatting in a country where we're not wanted and we don't belong, and it's why we get to go on a hike tonight and every night through hostile terrain, giving other people who also don't belong here a chance to kill us. We are not here for glory—there isn't any—and there's nothing at stake. Our goals are to stay alive, to avoid civilian casualties, and to kill anyone with an interest in killing us. In nine months, no soldier has died under my command and I'd like to keep it that way. Is that understood?"

Jaynie keeps her face carefully neutral. "Yes, sir, that is understood." And then, because she's not about to be intimidated by a male lieutenant five years her junior and with a quarter of her combat experience, she adds, "Guidance described you as a crazy motherfucker, sir—"

Behind Jaynie, Yafiah claps a hand to her mouth, stifling a snort of laughter.

"—but they promised me, no matter how much of an asshole you are, they won't walk us into an ambush."

I smile pleasantly. "They've come close a few times."

As the most northeastern in a line of remote border forts, we are more exposed than most. The fort itself is our shelter, our base of operations. Its fifteen-foot-high walls enclose the housing unit and a yard just big enough to park two tanks—not that we have tanks, but we do have three ATVs stored under an accordion canopy.

Our mission lies outside the walls. We do interdiction—hunting for insurgents filtering down from the north, while the insurgents go hunting for us. Guidance doesn't always spot them in time, which is one reason we keep a pack of five dogs. They're not official army issue, but the motto of the linked combat squads is *Innovation, Coordination, Inspiration* . . . meaning as an LCS we get leeway to come up with our own strategies.

"One more thing, sir," Jaynie says as I turn away. "Is it true you're cyborged?"

"It's just an ocular overlay." I touch my gloved finger to the corner of my eye. "Like built-in contact lenses, but they receive and display data."

The gold line tattooed along the curve of my jaw is an antenna, and tiny audio buds are embedded in my ears, but I don't mention those.

"You're not linked to the outside world, are you?"

"From a war zone? Not a chance. The only link I'm allowed is to Guidance."

"So you're hooked into Guidance even when you're not wearing the helmet?"

"You got it. Everything I see, everything I hear, gets piped straight upstairs."

"Why is that, sir?"

Not a discussion I want to get into right now, so I turn my attention to the last of our little crew. Private First Class Dubey Lin is standing on the catwalk, nine feet above the ground, peering through a machine-gun port at the surrounding trees. Dubey over-relies on organic sight, but he's always ready to go on time and he never argues. Actually, he never says much of anything at all. "Dubey!" I shout. "Get down here."

"Yes, sir!"

He jumps to the ground, letting the shocks of his

exoskeleton take the impact and startling the dogs, who are so wound up in anticipation of the night's patrol that they lunge at one another. Vicious growls erupt as they spin around in play fights. Ransom gets in on it, launching a few kung fu kicks and chops in Dubey's direction, flexing his exoskeleton's leg and arm struts, but Dubey ignores him, as always.

In the LCS ranks, we've nicknamed the exoskeletons our "dead sisters" because all the parts except the floating footplates look a lot like human bones. Shocked struts with knee articulation run up the outside of the legs to the hips. Across the back, the rig takes an hourglass shape to minimize profile, ending in a shoulder-spanning arch that easily supports both the weight of a field pack and the leverage that can be generated by the slender arm struts.

Packets of microprocessors detect a soldier's movements, translating them to the rig in customized motion algorithms. A soldier in an exoskeleton can get shot dead and never fall down. I saw that in Bolivia. And if there's enough power left in the dead sister, it can walk the body back to a safe zone for recovery. I've seen that too. Sometimes the dead just keep walking, right through my dreams. Not that I'd ever admit that to Guidance.

Jaynie pushes me a little harder. "So if Guidance is listening in on everything you say, sir, why do you keep talking shit?"

"We have to play the game, Sergeant. We don't have to like it. Now, *helmets on*!"

We all disappear behind full-face visors tuned to an opaque black.

Tiny fans vent cool air across my face as I watch an array of icons come up on my visor's display. They assure me I'm fully linked: to my skullcap; to my M-CL1a assault rifle; to each one of my soldiers; to my angel, soaring invisibly high in the night sky; and to my handler at Guidance. "Delphi, you there?"

Her familiar voice answers, "Gotcha, Shelley."

They don't call us a linked combat squad for nothing.

I use my gaze to shuffle through the displays of each soldier in my LCS, confirming that they're linked too.

Technically, every linked combat squad should have nine pairs of boots on the ground, but at Dassari we've never had more than six, and due to personnel transfers, we were down to four before Jaynie got here. The army likes to brag that every LCS soldier is an elite soldier, meeting strict physical and intellectual requirements, with a demonstrated ability to adapt to new systems and circumstances. Translated, this means we're chronically shorthanded, and no one gets a night off.

"Let's all stay awake," I say over gen-com. "It's been too quiet these past few nights. We're due."

"Yes, sir!" Ransom answers like this is good news. Yafiah swears softly. Dubey kicks at the ground in frustration. Only Jaynie doesn't get it.

"You know something we don't?" she asks over gen-com.

"Just a feeling."

Ransom says, "Sometimes God whispers in his ear."

"LT," Yafiah pleads. She knows what's coming, and so do I, but I don't try to rein him in. Ransom is my favorite redneck of all time. He loves everyone, but he'll still kill anybody I tell him to without hesitation. His way of explaining the world may be nonstandard, but his enthusiasms have kept us both alive.

"Ma'am, this here is King David," he informs the sergeant. "Saul don't dare touch a hair of the man's head and Goliath can't get his bullets to fly straight when the lieutenant's around, because James Shelley is beloved of God.

Do what LT tells you and you might live long enough to see Frankfurt one more time."

Ransom is six three. He has a hundred pounds of muscle over Yafiah and a year more experience, but as far as she's concerned, he's the dumb little brother. She turns the blank black face of her visor toward Jaynie and says, "Don't worry none about Ransom, ma'am. He's kind of crazy, but he's good in the field."

Jaynie sounds honestly puzzled when she asks me, "How can you be King David, LT? Because I would have sworn that we were Goliath."

"Goliath," I murmur, using my gaze to select the encyclopedia icon from my overlay, because the truth is, I don't really know the Bible story.

But before I can listen to the abstract of the Goliath entry, Dubey surprises us all by actually speaking. "King David played his own game," he says, his shy voice amplified over gen-com. "And he didn't lose."

Good enough for me.

I whistle at the dogs. The fort's gate swings open. We head out into moonlight, the five of us, Dassari LCS. The fort will defend itself while we're away.

We spread out so we can cover more territory, and so one bomb blast, one rocket, won't take out all of us. The primary weapon we carry is the M-CL1a, also known as the Harkin Integrated Tactical Rifle, yielding an acronym only a gamer could love. The HITR uses AI sights to fire both a 7.62-millimeter round, accurate to five hundred meters, and programmable grenades from the underslung launcher. We're also armed with a handy assortment of hand grenades—frag, flash-bang, smoke. Subtlety is not our talent. We're rigged to hit fast and hard. Powered by the dead sisters, with photomultiplier-based night vision to see where we're going, we're able to make a sweep through the entire district on most nights.

Near the fort the land is flat, and much of it is cultivated, marked off by tall fences that protect sorghum fields and tree farms from roving goats and wandering cattle. But after a couple of kilometers, the farms end. Then it's mostly scattered trees that look a lot like the mesquite I saw in Texas. We're well into the rainy season, so all the trees are leafed out and where there used to be bare red ground between them, wild grass is growing almost head-high. The dogs run through it, hunting for rogue soldiers.

A light wind sighs past, setting the grass swaying around me. I know it's rustling, but my helmet's audio pickups are set to filter out white noise, so I can barely hear it, while more distinct sounds reach me clearly: the panting of the dogs, the lowing of cattle, a bird's piping call.

With the grass so tall I can't see very far, but I keep a map overlaid on my visor with the position of each one of my soldiers marked. The map is constantly updated with data gathered by my angel—a toy drone with a three-foot wingspan, piloted by a semiautonomous AI. The angel watches over us. Everything within range of its camera eyes is recorded, and the raw video *is* boosted to Guidance. In offices in Frankfurt, Charleston, and Sacramento, our handlers scan the raw feed, while Intelligence teams run analytical programs to pick up any bogeys human eyes might miss.

There's always something to see. This is the Old World. People have made their homes here since the beginning of time and they'll probably still be here come the last day—which might not be as far off as we'd like to think.

Yeah, apocalyptic thoughts come a little too easily these days.

Anyway, it doesn't matter how empty this land looks; it *is* inhabited. People live here, raising their children and their livestock, most of them pretending there isn't a war in progress. We don't want to shoot them.

So with the angel's help we've developed a census. We know the name of everyone living within twenty-five kilometers of the fort. We know their facial details, along with their height, weight, gender, posture, and age. We know where they live, what they do for a living, and how they're related to the people around them. Using the census, the angel can ID an individual in low light, with his back turned, from over a kilometer away, and once we've got an ID we go on our way. It's rare that the people here even see us, unless we're on the road.

But if the angel turns up someone who's not in our census? Then we move in.

Not every stranger is an enemy. Smugglers pass through, and so long as they're not carrying weapons or proscribed tech, we let them go. Same for the refugees wandering south out of the Sahara. We talk to them all and add them to our records.

But it's the insurgents we really need to find, before they find us. It's a game of hide-and-seek, and the better the angel gets at spotting people, the better the enemy gets at looking like nothing at all.

So when I get a sudden premonition of danger—a heart-pounding, muscle-tensing certainty that something seriously bad is very near—I visualize a red light. My skullcap picks up the image and displays it on the visors of everyone in my squad. They freeze. Jaynie and Dubey tap into my visual feed right away like they're supposed to. Yafiah and Ransom take a little longer, but within a few seconds we're all looking ahead toward one of our district's rare rocky outcroppings. It's an anomaly in the flat landscape: a wide, irregular formation that rises only a little higher than the low trees around it. I'm pretty sure it's natural, but it looks like it could be the remnant of an ancient pyramid, reduced to a shapeless lump after thousands of seasons of rain.

My handler, Delphi, hasn't said a word since we linked up at the fort, but the moment I break routine she speaks. "What have you got, Shelley?"

I focus on the words "A feeling." It's a phrase I've practiced, so the skullcap picks it up easily and translates it for Delphi.

She tells me what I already know: "The angel's got nothing. I'm bringing it in for a closer look."

"They're in the high ground," I say in the softest of whispers, letting the helmet mic compensate for lack of volume.

Delphi doesn't like my "feelings" because she can't explain them, but she's been with me twice when I've sensed an imminent ambush, so she doesn't argue.

I tap into the angel's infrared feed as it soars on silent wings high above the outcrop. I'm looking for bright points of heat, but I only see our soldiers and our dogs, scattered in an arc on the east side of the mound.

One of our dogs, the cream-colored female we call Pearl, is two meters in front of me. Alerted by my posture, she's standing still, testing the air with her nose. I hiss at her, urging her to move ahead. She trots forward willingly, but then she freezes just short of the mound. My helmet audio enhances her low growl.

"*Fuck*," Yafiah whispers over gen-com. "I want to launch a grenade up there."

So do I, but we can't do it. If it's just a farm kid out on a lark, we could all wind up in prison—and the only reason I'm in this uniform is because I desperately do not want to be in prison.

"Easy," I warn Yafiah.

I wish I could put skullcaps on the dogs. Then I might be able to get an image of what they're sensing. But the defense contractors refuse to outfit strays. They don't want to get fined if the equipment gives false results, so they'll only cap a dog if it's specially bred and trained—and that kind of dog costs twice as much as a soldier. Our LCS isn't authorized.

I hiss at Pearl again, but she lowers her head and looks back at me, refusing to advance any farther.

We'll have to go in ourselves.

I visualize an approach path: me and Yafiah moving directly in, Ransom circling around the back, and Dubey and Jaynie providing cover from opposite sides. Ransom picks it up and takes off fast, staying well back from the mound as he circles around it. Yafiah and I move in, until we have only thirty meters between us as we cautiously advance.

"There it is, Shelley," Delphi says in her businesslike voice. She sends me a still image, with a red circle around a faint heat signature she's spotted in the rocks at the top of the mound.

It's just a gray spot. Its shape doesn't tell me anything, but the thermal signature is a clue to the presence of a ghost soldier, partly camouflaged from the angel's infrared sight by a hooded suit with a thermal coating.

I shift back to angel sight. The heat signature is so repressed I can barely see it until the AI in the angel enhances the image. Then I can see it as a cocked arm, death clutched in its right hand.

"Yafiah!" I shout. "Fall back!"

Powered by her dead sister, she jumps backward four meters, dropping flat in a dense stand of tall grass. The dog, Pearl, whirls around and flees past me as I take aim with my M-CL1a. A glowing, golden point is moving across the screen of my visor. There's no way I could see the grenade on my own, but my tactical AI, using data from the angel and from the helmet cams, has plotted its path for me. An open circle marks my aim. I align the circle with the point, fire a short burst, and drop flat as a concussion booms over my head and lightning flashes. I'm up again as soon as it passes. From the top of the mound an assault rifle chatters and then, his voice low and happy, Ransom says over gen-com, "That's two for me, LT."

We're not done yet.

Delphi finds another ghost about twelve meters away from me, near the bottom of the mound. This one's a gleaming, shapeless blur, much easier to see—probably just someone crouched under a worn-out thermal blanket.

I close the distance, using my dead sister to bound in a crazy zigzag, the joints muttering and my pack creaking against the frame as I go. My target sees me coming. Maybe he panics. Maybe he's just cocky. But he drops his thermal cover and shows himself. I'm all of twenty-three, but in the green glow of night vision he looks to me like a skinny teenage kid as he sights down the barrel of his assault rifle and starts firing.

I'm moving fast. His first bullets don't get anywhere near me, but he shifts his aim and closes the gap while I fire back. I aim from the hip, using the bead in my visor to get the right line. The trigger drops away from my finger as my tactical AI takes over. A single shot, and the kid flies backward, spinning half around before hitting the slope behind him.

"Slam!" Ransom bellows over gen-com.

"Check it out," I warn him.

"Don't worry, LT, there's no one left up top."

"Approaching," Jaynie says.

I spot her on my map. "Gotcha."

She walks out of the tall grass, her weapon aimed at the body of the kid, lying facedown, the back of his head blown out.

"Signs?" I ask.

"No. He's dead."

She crouches beside the body and uses her arm hook to flip it over. There's a bullet hole right between his eyes. "Shit, your AI is good."

I can't feel it directly, but I know my skullcap is working, stimulating my brain to produce a soothing little cocktail, a mix of all-natural brain chemicals that puts an emotional distance between me and what just happened.

I suck fortified water from a tube hooked to a bladder in my pack, while Jaynie searches the body. We're particularly interested in written orders and data sticks. Up above, Ransom searches the two that he killed. I watch the feed from his helmet cam. Both are kids; only one has a thermal suit. That's not a piece of equipment we want to leave lying around, so I send Dubey to help collect it, along with the weapons.

Kids like these are not fighting for Ahab Matugo. He's a modern, secular leader, and they hate him for it. They hate us too, of course. And they hate the people of this district, because those people put up with us. They've been indoctrinated in hate and it wouldn't surprise me to learn that some DC is behind it, encouraging it, financing it, to make sure soldiers like us have something to do. Rumor is, Intelligence broke a similar scheme in Bolivia, but that investigation was iced to save corporate reputations.

I call Yafiah. We whistle for the dogs, and together we make a sweep of the mound, confirming that no one's still hiding.

• • • •

After we distribute the captured weapons between us, we move out, resuming the night's assigned route. Just a few minutes later, the angel picks up a new presence. This one is riding a moped and isn't trying to hide, so we get a quick ID.

"Jalal the gravedigger," Delphi says.

"Did you call him?"

"Checking . . . No. No notification was made. He's come on his own initiative."

"I don't like that much initiative."

Jalal is a local contractor. The army pays him to handle enemy bodies, but he receives notification of a job only after we are away from the vicinity.

"Delphi, how does Jalal know we're not the ones lying dead on the ground?"

"He knows your rep, Shelley. But you're authorized to conduct a field interview."

With a thought, I switch to gen-com. "Converge on my location. Leash the dogs on your way in."

Already I can hear the whine of his moped. Maybe he's following the smell of gunpowder, or maybe he just reasoned from the direction of our gunfire that the mound was the most likely site of the battle.

We take up positions in the grass, eight meters apart, crouched to reduce our profiles—because I don't want to find out too late that Jalal has changed sides. The dogs lie quiet. They're loyal to us. They know where their next meal is coming from.

I watch with angel sight as the moped draws near. Jalal is driving in the dark. Without using any lights, he's weaving around trees and skirting the brush, pushing the moped at a fast clip. I don't see any weapons on him, and the angel doesn't indicate any, but he has a backpack.

I creep through the trees, putting myself in a position to intercept him.

The crunch of the tires is louder than the electric engine. When he's almost on me, I step into the open. My HITR targets his face.

He's so startled he jerks the front tire of the moped. The bike skids and almost goes over. "Shelley! Goddamn!"

Jalal's eyes are veiled by the narrow, gleaming band of his farsights. It's an easy guess that they're capable of night vision, so I'm not surprised he can see me in the dark—but he can't see through my visor, so how the hell does he know it's me?

Shit. I bet he's got his own height and weight profiles.

I say, "You got here quick."

He answers in a local dialect, which my helmet translates in its usual creative fashion. "I am going to the city. Leaving before sunrise. Need to do the job soonest. Right?"

I eye his backpack. It could hold grenades or explosives. It's more likely, though, that it holds shrouds.

"You can't take three bodies on that bike."

He blinks. Then frowns. "Three?"

"Three."

"Okay, then. Long night for me."

"Delphi, send him the map."

There's a glimmer in the screen of his farsights as the data comes in.

"Thank you, Shelley."

He tries to get the bike going again, but I put the foot-plate of my dead sister against his front tire. "Tell me what's going on. What have you heard?"

The surface temperature of his cheeks and forehead jumps a notch. He glances around, trying to figure out where my soldiers are, but he can't see them. When he speaks again, it's in a whisper, though my helmet amplifies it, so it's easy to hear. "Shelley, my uncle, he called my mama. He said twelve soldiers from the north likely coming the next night or two. Seen them at a neighbor farm. Don't know the name."

"To the north?"

"Yes. North. I don't know more."

*Twelve.* No wonder Jalal is out here. He's no fool. He'll bag the bodies, bring them in, bury them long before dawn, and bill the army, and then he'll get the hell out of here, because if the rumor is true there's an excellent chance that when the insurgents come through, they'll target him as a collaborator.

"Work fast," I advise him, taking my foot off the tire and stepping back, out of the way.

"I will, Shelley. Thank you."

As he takes off, I imagine Intelligence engaged in a flurry of activity trying to locate a dozen rogue soldiers just north of our district.

Until they find something, it's not my problem.

Delphi says, "Cleared to continue."

My people reappear. We let the dogs off their leashes and go on our way. No one else tries to kill us.

We get back to the fort just as the last stars are fading in a velvety blue sky. The fort detects us, recognizes us, and opens the gate as we approach. The dogs run to drink water.

I'm tired. We're all tired, but no one talks about it. We clean the dead sisters and our weapons, then plug them into power racks in the bunk room. We restock the bladders in our packs with fortified water, getting them ready to go again. In the village cemetery, the sun will be rising over the fresh graves of three kids younger than I am, by years. I try to feel guilt, remorse, regret . . . but nothing's there. Guidance makes sure of that.

If robots were cheaper, we wouldn't have to be here.

• • • •

There are only two shower stalls and two toilets. My house rule is that the less you get paid, the sooner you get to shower, so Dubey and Yafiah go first. "Five minutes!" I yell at them from the hallway.

Yafiah yells something back. Her voice is muffled, but I'm pretty sure it isn't *Yes, sir.*

I step into the kitchen, pick up five aluminum bowls, and head outside.

The sun isn't quite up, so it's only around ninety in the yard. When I open the door, the dogs are sprawled under their canvas canopy, but as soon as they see me, they're up and swarming. I pop the tops on five cans of dog food, fill the bowls, and become god of the pack as I distribute the day's rations. It takes them about thirty seconds to finish eating. I have my dad send us mange treatments, birth control pills, and pills to knock out their fleas and parasites; their food I buy from a local supplier. It's all worth it.

I take the bowls back in. Jaynie's in the tactical operations center, still in her sweat-encrusted T-shirt and pants. She looks up and nods as I pass by. Command requires the TOC to be staffed at all times when we're not wearing helmets.

Dubey is already done in the shower. He crosses the hall ahead of me, wearing only shorts and his skullcap, disappearing into the bunk room. Ransom has taken over the empty shower stall, while Yafiah is still running water. "Hurry it up, sweetheart," I yell at her.

"I still got thirty seconds, LT."

She probably does. She's pretty obsessive about things like that.

"When you get out, go relieve the sergeant."

I wait for her disgruntled "Yes, sir," and then I take the bowls into the kitchen. By the time I've got them washed, Jaynie is taking a shower, and the second stall is open.

I pitch my clothes into the steam cleaner on top of everyone else's—everything but the skullcap—and I start the load. I'm still wearing the skullcap when I step into the shower. A glance over the partition shows me that Jaynie is still wearing hers too. Good. We're required to wear the skullcaps only when we're rigged, but in a combat zone we're allowed to wear them all the time if that's what we want to do—and I would not trust an LCS soldier who didn't want to.

The skullcap is always working, whether Guidance is riding us or not. The handbook says the brain stimulation it provides is nonaddictive, but I think the handbook needs to be revised. The only time my skullcap comes off is during the ninety seconds in the shower when I have to wash my scalp with a depilatory.

I let the many-times-recycled hot water run over me for almost a minute, working up to the moment. Then I draw a deep breath and slip the skullcap off.

I start counting seconds to distract myself as I rinse it in the shower stream. It's made of a silky fabric with an embedded microwire net, and it's shaped like an athletic skullcap, so it covers from the forehead to the nape of the neck, without covering the ears.

When my count reaches twenty, I hang it on a hook.

I think I psych myself out. It doesn't make sense that my mood can spiral so far downward in just a few seconds . . . but it does anyway. As I grab a shot of depilatory from the dispenser, a hollow black panicky despair is spawning inside my chest.

I rub the depilatory over my head and over my face where a beard would grow if I let it, focusing on my count while hot water sluices over my shoulders. I count so I don't have to think. At seventy, I tilt my head back under the stream, and at ninety I slip the cap back on, pressing it close to my freshly hairless scalp.

I'm safe for another twenty-four hours.

I hated wearing the cap during my initial LCS training—I felt like someone was always looking inside my head—but I don't care anymore. I don't have anything left to hide.

Jaynie's getting dressed when I step out of the shower. I look her over. She's maybe five eight, lean, with small, pretty breasts already hidden under her T-shirt. Her skin is dark, but not as dark as Yafiah's. Mine is brown. Dubey and Ransom are the palefaces around here.

Jaynie looks up, notices my interest, and laughs. "That'll go away soon," she says as she steps into clean pants.

"Shit. Sorry. You know how it is. First day's always awkward."

"Been there," she agrees, buttoning up.

I turn away before I get myself in real trouble—but I've still got an image of her in my head.

Lust is brain chemistry, but so is the way you feel about your sisters and brothers. You might love them, you might die for them, but unless you're a twisted fuck, the last thing you want to do is have sex with your siblings. That's incest revulsion, and though I've never seen it mentioned in a manual, every LCS soldier knows that Guidance has figured out how to mimic the sensation in our heads. It might take a day or two to kick in, but it always happens. We don't live with other men and women, we live with brothers and sisters. I'm an only child, but since I've been in the linked combat squads I've learned what it's like to have siblings. We are a celibate crew.

I've been asleep maybe three hours when I hear Jaynie shouting from the hallway in her best sergeant's voice: "Rise and shine, children!" She hammers on my door. "Command has a new game for us to play. It's called patrol the road and you've got twenty minutes to get under way, so *move*!"

Basic training isn't all that far behind me. I'm on my feet and halfway into my pants before I remember who's in command at our little fort. "What the hell is going on?"

I button up and throw the door open, but Jaynie has already disappeared from the hallway. I can hear Ransom and Yafiah cursing in the bunk room across the hall. Not a word from Dubey, but I'm sure he's up and getting rigged.

The tactical operations center is next to my room. That's where I find Jaynie. "What is it?" I ask, leaning in the door.

She's standing in front of the desk, watching the big monitor as she straps into her dead sister. "A contractor's convoy—they're from Vanda-Sheridan—is due on the western perimeter of our district in ninety minutes or so, bringing in equipment to assemble a new listening station east of us. It's a priority project, and it's up to us to make sure the road is clean."

"*Fuck!*" I stomp over to the desk to review and acknowledge the order. "I hate defense contractors. They're fucking parasites. And Vanda-Sheridan's a fucking beast. When I was in Bolivia, I swear to God their local agent was selling satellite data to the enemy. Vanda-Sheridan is a prime example, Sergeant, of a defense contractor happy to play both sides to prolong a conflict. And now here they are in Africa! Looking after the bottom line."

"Yes, sir," Jaynie says. "Fifteen minutes left before we have to be on the road, sir."

I duck back into my quarters, get my boots and jacket on, and then head for the kitchen, where energy drinks are waiting on the table. Ransom and Dubey are already through their first round. Yafiah must be in the stall. I grab a carton, tip my head back, and empty it in a few swallows.

"Jaynie!" I shout down the hall. "Anybody sniffing around outside during your watch?"

"Just a few goats! I'm shutting down the TOC, sir!"

"Do it!"

I finish my second carton, toss Yafiah out of the stall, deal efficiently with the bodily functions, and then get my armor on.

Delphi starts talking to me through my overlay. "ATVs today, Shelley. We've got no intelligence on insurgents in the neighborhood, but you get to do a ground check anyway."

"As always."

I stomp into the bunk room, get my dead sister off the power rack, and strap in. Even though we're taking the ATVs, you never know when you're going to have to chase somebody down. Ransom checks my rig. Leaving him to clear the two privates, I get my weapon and helmet off the racks, grab my pack, and head outside.

Jaynie's already in the yard, pushing back the accordion canopy of the shed where we keep the ATVs. I help her check batteries, lubricant levels, joint cuffs, and tire wear. "No issues," she says, sounding surprised.

The informality of my LCS tends to confuse the fresh meat. We may not click heels and salute here, but if it matters, we do it and we do it right. "I only win this game if we all get out alive," I remind her.

"Truth."

The ATVs are low-slung, two-passenger vehicles, with the gunner's post elevated behind the driver, and seats specially designed to fit soldiers rigged in bones. They're not the fastest things around, but then there's not a lot of racing competition where we patrol. They're quiet, with four hours of runtime before the battery gives out, rechargeable with photovoltaic mats, and the four-wheel independent suspension makes them agile and stable.

The kids tend to fight over who gets to drive.

"Dibs!" Yafiah yells as she races into the yard carrying her weapon and helmet. "I'm driving. Ransom, you're my gunner."

He comes out behind her, looking confused. "Shit. How come you always—"

Dubey pushes past him. "I want to drive one."

I'm mildly stunned to hear Dubey speak up for himself and I want to encourage him. "Good. You're on. Grab two dogs and put 'em in your gunner's seat. I'll sit behind the sarge. *Helmets on!*"

I confirm my links; I confirm the links of my squad. Then I stand by the gate, holding back the three dogs that aren't going with us while the ATVs roll out. Once I have the dogs safely locked up, I take my seat and we're on our way.

The road runs south for a few kilometers before it reaches the village, and then at the village center another road takes off west. The maps say if you follow that road far enough you'll come to a city. We like to joke about taking off one day to find that city, but it's just a game. The ATVs couldn't get us even a quarter of the way before nightfall, so we'll stay here until the army decrees that we should go somewhere else.

Today we need to cover only the first hundred kilometers or so of the western road. By that time we should find Vanda-Sheridan's convoy. After that, we'll just shadow the trucks until they're out of our district and no longer our concern.

We're running at thirty miles per hour south toward the village, zigzagging to avoid the potholes and the worst of the gullied roadbed. At least it isn't dusty like it would be in the dry season. Each driver keeps the required interval of ninety meters between vehicles. Yafiah and Ransom are in front, me and Jaynie follow them, while Dubey, with the two dogs in his gunner's seat, trails behind. IEDs are rare here, but you never know.

I prefer not to drive, in part because I don't really know how. I grew up in Manhattan, where there was no reason to drive, and I only got my license in Texas because the army required it. But mostly I don't drive because I want to spend my road time looking through the angel's eyes.

I send it ahead to patrol our route, instructing it to follow a wide quartering pattern that surveys terrain on both sides of the road. It's already gone beyond the village. Soon, it'll reach the limit of its range—it's not supposed to ever wander more than ten kilometers from my position—but we'll catch up with it when we get to the other side of the village.

Up ahead, Yafiah slows her ATV to a crawl as she comes up on the edge of the village.

"Visors go transparent," I say over gen-com. Helmets are required wear at all times outside the fort. Normally we keep the visors black to limit the enemy's ability to identify us as individuals and to secure a very effective intimidation factor. But the people of the village are not our enemies, and my soldiers are not faceless demons.

The first few buildings are prefab sheds, but those tend to fall down when the Harmattan wind comes blasting out of the Sahara, so most of the houses are still beautiful red mud brick, with walled courtyards shaded by the spreading branches and feathery leaves of neem trees, or by darker, denser canopies of mango. A cell phone tower stands on the village periphery and dish antennas dot the roofs.

Goats are everywhere, along with chickens and guinea fowl, but only a few people are in sight, mostly grandparents gossiping beside the courtyard walls. Then we pass the school. There's an excited shout, and around twenty kids, ranging in age from six to sixteen, charge out of the school's courtyard, all of them dressed in colorful clothes, laughing and shouting because they don't get to see us very often and they think our ATVs are cool. "Hello, soldiers. Good to see you. Where you going today? Can we come?"

"No way!" Yafiah tells them. "You have to go back to school!"

They run alongside anyway. "Shelley from Manhattan!" they call to me. "Yafiah from California. Dubey from Wash-ing-ton. Matthew from Geor-gi-a!"

Then they realize Jaynie is someone they've never seen before. "Who are you? What's your name?"

"That's Sergeant Jaynie," I tell them.

"Where are you from, Sergeant Jaynie? Where are you from?"

I can't see her face, but I can hear the grin in her voice. "Detroit," she says. "Kansas City, Chicago, Philadelphia, and too many other places for me to remember." And then softly, so the kids won't hear her, though her helmet mic picks it up, "This place is paradise compared to the shitholes I used to live in."

The kids keep chattering until we reach the western road, then we wave good-bye. I have my doubts that they'll head back to class, but it's not my concern.

The western road is paved. As soon as we're clear of the village, Yafiah picks up speed. Jaynie waits for the proper interval and then she accelerates too. As we blast past the village cemetery, I spot the new graves at the back. Jalal does his job well and earns the money we pay him.

After that we pass more sorghum fields, the stalks already six feet high, with tassels of grain forming at the top. Then the flat red land is taken over by scattered trees and brush. It's been a good rainy season so far. Everything is green and the trees are skirted with tall grass that will disappear altogether when the rain goes away. For now, though, there's abundant food for small herds of cattle. The angel notes every animal and marks its position on the map. It also marks the position of two tall, thin teenage boys out tending the cattle. As we speed past they wave their long switches at us and grin.

From where I'm sitting in the back of the ATV, the vegetation looks lush, but as I gaze down on it with angel sight, its true sparseness is revealed. Not much can hide here, which makes me happy. If the ground had been disturbed by anything more sinister than wandering cattle, the angel would see it. But nothing's amiss.

Why, then, am I starting to get a bad feeling about this whole venture?

We're fifty-two kilometers out from the village, and the angel is ten klicks ahead of us, when it finally spots an approaching vehicle—just one, so it's not the contractor's caravan. A minute later the angel IDs it: a small white pickup truck well-known to us. I laugh.

"Heads up!" I call out on gen-com. "Bibata's coming into town with our dog food."

"Who's Bibata?" Jaynie asks suspiciously.

"The LT's girlfriend," Yafiah says.

I feel like I'm in grade school. "She's not my girlfriend."

"Only because you want to stay out of jail."

"Jail?" Jaynie asks, incredulous. "You're not here on a prison deferment?"

Yafiah again: "Oh yes he is."

"You're an officer," Jaynie protests, as if this is something none of us has realized before.

"It was a crime of honor," I assure her.

"He won't tell us what he did," Dubey adds, surprising me again by joining the conversation.

"Was it worth it?" Jaynie asks.

That's not a question I want to consider, and anyway, Bibata's white pickup is coming fast. Jaynie steers us to the side of the road. I lean out and wave my arm up and down, hoping she'll stop. At first I don't think she's going to, but then she steps hard on the brakes, bringing the truck to a stop beside me. I jump down from the gunner's seat. Ransom does too and walks back along the road to meet me. We converge on Bibata's truck from opposite sides, both of us casting surreptitious glances at the cargo, stacked higher than the cab roof and hidden under a taut blue tarp. Anything could be under there.

I whisper to Dubey to bring the dogs. Then I make my visor go transparent and I saunter up to the driver's window with my assault rifle cradled in my arms. The glass rolls down. I feel the holy, sacred chill of air-conditioning through the thin fabric of my gloves. But better than that, Bibata gives me a coy smile. She is definitely not my sibling.

"Ah, Shelley, my man. Were you coming to visit me? And was this the best rendezvous you could manage? I expected better from you!"

I have maybe a quarter of my ancestry out of Africa, mixed with European lines and the original people of Mexico. Bibata makes me think of pure and ancient bloodlines. Her skin is dark black, darker than Yafiah's, and her face is strong and beautiful, with a high forehead, flirtatious dark eyes, and lips that slip easily between a teasing smile and a threat. There's nothing between us except that I admire her, and she enjoys it—but today I get the feeling she doesn't really want to play the game. There's anxiety behind her smile, maybe even anger. Dubey has released the dogs. She glances at them as they run toward the truck.

"You okay, love?" I ask her.

I see a handgun shoved into the cushioned space between the driver and passenger seats, but it doesn't concern me because she always keeps it there. Ransom scans the cab from the other side while she answers me impatiently. "Of course I'm okay! I am always okay. I have been okay since the beginning of the world." Her voice drops to a feigned flirty tone. "Though I might be better still if you come ride with me in my truck some evening. Do you think so, Shelley? Should I come and pick you up tonight?"

I flash her a smile. "Oh, God yes, love. I'm getting stiff just thinking about seeing you with the night wrapped around your beautiful face. But Mama's watching. She won't let me go."

Bibata pouts. The dogs have circled around to the back of the truck. They're sniffing at the tires. "Oh, you poor thing. You need to get liberated and not be a slave to Mama's ugly old customs anymore."

"Someday," I promise her.

She turns away, to stare at her perfectly manicured hands as they grip the steering wheel. Softly, she says, "I will come tomorrow, and bring your dog food."

By her quiet tone I know that something is very wrong. I imagine insurgents under the tarp, but the dogs would have given some sign if anyone was there. So I bend down, almost leaning in the window. "Tell me what's going on, Bibata."

She shakes her head. "Nothing. Not yet. But the war's getting closer, isn't it? It's not just a few stupid little boys from the north, come here to make trouble."

"No, that's all it is. Ahab Matugo is not going to come here."

"Ahab Matugo is a modern man. Maybe it would not be so bad if he did!"

"Yeah, I don't know. Maybe."

She nods without looking at me. "I'll come tomorrow." Then she puts the truck in gear, waves at me, and drives away, the window sliding closed as she goes. I'm left facing the black mask of Ransom's visor.

"I think she just had groceries," he says.

The angel switches my visor back to black as I turn to stare west down the road—the direction Bibata came from, the direction of the distant city. Then I look through the angel's eyes, but there's nothing out in that flat, hot, worn-out land except trees, and brush, and cattle.

"Dubey, get the dogs!"

He whistles them back to his side, while Ransom and I return to our gunners' seats. Jaynie starts to interrogate me, but I wave her off, addressing the squad instead. "Something's going on. I don't know what, but I've got a feeling. Stay alert."

Twenty minutes later, Delphi tells me the convoy is delayed. "They're having a problem with one of the trucks. It's going to take a couple hours to fix."

I feel like a demon is scratching on the inside of my skull. "What do you think is really going on?" I ask her.

"Command would like you to answer that question. You're to continue west until you meet the convoy, but approach with discretion. Ascertain the situation before making your presence known."

This presents a problem, because the ATVs are good for only four hours before the batteries run down, and we'll need to run at least another hour to find the convoy, which will put us past the halfway point of battery life. We've got photovoltaic mats that we can use to recharge, but policy dictates that we have sufficient power to return to the fort at all times.

It turns out Command is more interested in what their contractors are up to than in whether or not we get back to our fort before nightfall. "You're cleared to continue," Delphi says when I present my concern. "If you can get the PV mats laid out before fourteen hundred, you should be able to acquire a partial recharge before the next rainstorm moves through."

So we follow the angel west.

We're 105 kilometers out when the angel discovers the Vanda-Sheridan trucks, parked well off the road behind a screen of brush grown tall in the rainy season.

"You said there were two trucks, right?" I ask Delphi.

I see four. Two are open-bed, carrying prefabricated walls, plastic cargo boxes, and sections of antenna to be used to build a new listening post. They both have the blue V-S logo on the white cab doors. Of the other two, one is an off-road truck. The other is what we would call, in the streets of Manhattan, a delivery truck, with an enclosed cargo area cooled by an air-conditioning unit mounted above the cab. Instead of a roll-up cargo door in the back, there's a walk-in refrigerator door with a large latch.

Delphi says, "Intelligence is scoring this at seventy percent likelihood of being an insurgent operation—"

"Hijacking or treachery?"

"You may assume a hostile situation until proven otherwise. Stealth approach, on foot. Identify those present and ascertain the situation before making your presence known."

Bibata might be right about Ahab Matugo; I know I might be fighting on the wrong side, but it's not really a choice—and it makes me furious that a homegrown, American company like Vanda-Sheridan, a company that *specializes* in surveillance, could fail to detect corruption in their own employees. Or worse, that they might condone it. "Has Ahab Matugo started buying out our suppliers?"

And if he has, how much longer can this war last?

"Just do your job, Shelley," Delphi says.

"Yes, ma'am."

We stick to the road until we're only fifteen hundred meters from the trucks, and then we cut into the brush, continuing on for another half klick. After that we tie up the dogs, lock down the ATVs, and roll out the PV mats so the batteries can start recharging.

We advance on foot.

The angel is floating high in the sky, invisible in the glare of the early afternoon sun, but it's showing me what I need to know: that there's very little activity at the site. I watch one man get out of the cab of the off-road truck to take a leak. He has an assault rifle slung over his shoulder. Most travelers carry guns here, but taking a gun just to piss a few steps away from the truck seems a bit much.

I watch him return to the cab, sliding into the passenger seat. There's a second man with him, behind the steering wheel. I know because the angel can see his elbow sticking out of the open window. That elbow hasn't moved for several minutes. Given that the afternoon temperature is up over a hundred, with the air so muggy it feels deprived of oxygen, I decide there's an excellent chance the driver is asleep.

Hopefully his friend will soon join him in the Land of Nod.

We creep to within fifty meters of the trucks, the sound of our approach disguised by the rustle of leaves. We're spread out, at least eight meters apart. I crouch, concealed within a stand of tall grass. I swear the lush green leaves are exhaling steam. The mud under my boots smells of cow dung. The clothes under my armor are made to wick sweat away from my body, but the sweat can't evaporate fast enough, so I'm soaked anyway. I settle down to wait for the onset of some activity that will explain what's going on.

Happily, we don't wait long. In about four and a half minutes, the cargo door on the air-conditioned truck swings open. Two men step out. Both are swaggering, grins on their faces as they pause in the doorway to look around at the lovely scrub landscape, before jumping down to the ground. Behind them, three young girls appear—*young*, like twelve or thirteen, their dark brown skin gleaming in the sunlight. *All* of their skin, because none of them are wearing clothes.

Ransom and Yafiah both swear softly over gen-com, and I develop a theory for why Bibata seemed so spooked. She's an independent woman, operating on her own, out in the middle of nowhere. Maybe she saw what was going on, or suspected. Better for her to pretend she didn't see anything than to call attention to herself. Getting on the wrong side of gangsters like these must be her nightmare.

The girls stick close together, keeping their heads down in a timid posture as they scamper into the brush. My guess is they've been sent out to relieve themselves before the party moves on.

"Delphi," I whisper. "Permission to engage?"

"I just asked, and the answer is no."

"We can't just—"

"*No*," she repeats.

"Goddamn it!" My voice never rises above a whisper, but I'm furious. I hate being the bad guy. "Ahab Matugo doesn't tolerate slavery, so why do we?"

"You have your orders, Shelley. Don't be swayed by propaganda. Ahab Matugo is the *enemy*. An enemy who keeps shooting down our surveillance drones. We need this listening station, so you *will* allow this convoy to proceed unmol—"

She's cut off in midlecture as my visor loses its link to the angel. My overlay routes through the angel too, and it's also dropped its link.

"Helmet-to-helmet still working?" Jaynie asks.

"I hear you."

"Something up high," Dubey suggests. "Jamming the angel, but not us."

"You think they have a drone? Why haven't they seen us?"

"They're not exactly paying attention," Jaynie says.

True.

I think about it, and decide I can work with the situation. I can't talk to Guidance, so that means I have to rely on my own judgment in the field. And my judgment tells me we have only seconds before one of the gangsters decides to check the feed from their drone.

"Listen up. We need to know these gangsters aren't going to turn around and murder our precious dickhead engineering team, so we're going to move in and make sure everything's okay. All except you, Yafiah. See that tree behind you? The one that begins branching close to the ground? Get yourself up there and let me know the second you see anyone looking worried." She uses her arm hooks and starts climbing. "Everyone else, stealth approach, standard interval. These gangsters are armed."

A wind sighs through the brush, hotter than breath. It rustles the tall grass, covering any sound we make as we advance. I'm close enough now that I can hear men talking, and the whisper of scared little girls as they're herded back into the air-conditioned truck. A door slams.

"LT," Yafiah whispers over gen-com. "Look up. Straight up. Is that you?"

I turn my head to gaze at the sky. Seen through my polarized visor, the sky in early afternoon is so beautifully blue it almost hurts my heart to look at it. The clouds scattered across that backdrop are a pure, bright, shining white. Beneath them is a drone aircraft, floating right above us at no more than treetop level, stationary on the wind just like a kite. It looks as if it's made of glass, translucent, so that the sky and clouds shine through. That's good camouflage, but the edges of the drone still show, making it easy to see. Like my angel, it's a small device: maybe four feet from wingtip to wingtip.

Yafiah wants to know if it's my drone, so I tell her, "No, that's not me. Get rid of it."

"Prepare for return fire," Jaynie warns.

With a loud burst from her HITR, Yafiah blows the drone out of the sky. There's a small white flash and then pieces tumble down, making the brush crackle as they hit.

"Yafiah, move!" I tell her. "You're a target. Get out of that tree."

I pipe a thumbnail of her point of view into my visor as she drops to the ground; her footplates float as her shocks absorb the impact, and then she takes off, putting distance between herself and the tree.

Over by the trucks, men are shouting. The guard with the assault rifle has scrambled out of the off-road truck. He brings his weapon to his shoulder and sprays bullets at the perch Yafiah just abandoned.

"Return fire," I say.

The aggressive guard doesn't have a chance. He's hit from four different directions and drops in a spray of brilliant red blood. We all race to new positions. Tall grass sways around me and clouds of insects take flight. From the brothel truck, I hear outraged shouts, and then I'm caught by surprise as a grenade explodes behind me. The concussion knocks me to my knees, but I'm up again in a second, my weapon raised. Fire crackles in the brush as I look for my enemy.

I spot him. Tall, grim, bearded, and dark skinned, he has a multiple-grenade launcher steadied against his shoulder. He rotates slowly, looking for a target. Idiot. He should be shooting, setting the grass and brush on fire to flush us out . . . but it's too late to send him back to school. It's too late when he sees me, half-hidden in the grass. My visor helps me line up my aim, I trigger a short burst from the HITR, and he collapses beside his friend.

Eerie silence falls over the brush. Even the wind has died away. I can't see anyone. The brothel men have retreated back inside their brothel truck, closing the door behind them.

Dubey says, "That drone wasn't jamming the angel."

He's right. The drone is gone, but we haven't recovered our link to Guidance.

"So what the hell can be jamming the angel and not messing with helmet-to-helmet?"

"I don't know, sir."

Something else grabs my attention, a faint sound amplified by my helmet—a girl sobbing.

It puts me in a bad mood. "Get out in the open!" I scream. "All of you! Hands on your heads and leave your weapons behind. *Now.*"

Nothing happens for fourteen or fifteen seconds. In my head I run through possible ways of getting everyone out of the truck without hurting the girls, but before I can come up with a reasonable plan, the truck's rear door opens and, to my surprise, the bad guys help me by sending one of the girls creeping out all on her own. They've even let her put on a dress. She takes a few steps and then stops. She's crying and shaking, sure that we'll shoot her down.

"You want the women?" a man yells. He appears at the door, a white man with some kind of European accent. I watch him looking around, trying to figure out where I am. "Take them. Take them all. More where that came from."

"Fuck you and get out where I can see you!"

He looks right at me, guided by my voice, but I doubt he can see much. The grass is good cover.

"Take the women and leave it at that," he warns me. "We've notified the Alliance we're under attack. American gunships will be here in a few minutes. Disappear now or you won't have a chance."

Ransom snorts. "Idiot."

I have to agree. Our enemy has no idea who we are; he assumes we're gangsters, here to rob him.

I don't really care if he's managed to get a call out to the army; I know a call has already gone out—because when my angel is jammed, its protocol is to retreat until it can link up again with Guidance. As soon as it reappeared on her screen, Delphi would have taken control of it. No doubt she heard our brief firefight and passed the news on to Command. With luck, gunships are already on the way—and even the corrupt Alliance is not going to be able to overlook the deficient quality of their contractor's employees once that much military hardware is in motion.

So I let the cum wad think he's got me worried. Injecting an anxious note into my voice, I say, "Yeah, okay. We'll take the women. Send the rest of them out or I'll put a grenade into your truck."

The man ducks back inside. "Go!" I hear him shouting. "Get out."

The other two girls appear at the narrow door, wearing cheap, colorful dresses. They jump down to the ground on bare feet, crying and clinging to each other.

"Tell them to follow the tire tracks back to the road," I say.

Another man, someone I haven't seen before, leans out the door and harangues them in a language I don't recognize and that my helmet isn't set up to translate. Their expressions are hopeless as they stumble off, heading for the road.

"Now get out of here," the European says. "I can hear the helicopters already."

He's not lying. I hear them too. I still can't reach my angel, though, and I'd like to fix that. On top of the cargo truck is a small dish antenna. It's the only candidate I can see for the source of the jamming signal. "Yafiah," I whisper on gen-com, "circle around and meet the girls. Make sure they're safe."

"On my way."

"Jaynie?"

"Here."

"I'm going to encourage the enemy to leave the truck. Don't let me get killed, okay?"

"No worries."

"I'm watching too," Ransom says.

I put my finger next to the trigger that will launch a grenade. Then I advance into the open with quick steps, circling around the bodies of the guards. A reek of blood and shit rises from them, overwhelming in the afternoon heat.

The European spots me—and my uniform. He's outraged. "Who the hell are you?" he screams at me. "Fucking army moron—I'm reporting you to your commanding officer!"

This doesn't exactly scare me because everything I do, everything I say, and most of what goes on in my head is relayed straight to Command. I have no secrets. They know I'm an asshole, but they find uses for me anyway.

The helicopters are easy to hear as I aim my weapon at the side of the cargo truck. "Clear out," I advise him. "Because I'm going to blow it up."

"You fucking madman!" the European screams, and then, in a panicked jump, he leaps clear of the truck, hitting the ground hard. His feet slip in the mud and he goes down with an unintelligible curse. Two other cum wads scramble out after him. One looks African, the other mixed Arab, or maybe Indian.

"Get down!" I scream at them, and they drop, falling prone alongside their companion. I have no idea which ones are Vanda-Sheridan's engineers and which one runs the mobile brothel, and I don't give a shit.

Ransom and Jaynie emerge from the brush, their weapons pointed at the passive trio.

"Dubey!" I bark.

He appears at my side and together we go through the truck and the other vehicles, making sure no one else is there. Then I send Dubey to pull the plug on the antenna, but he's still climbing up to the roof of the truck when the angel comes back online. I know because Delphi speaks to me: "Shelley, acknowledge."

"I'm here." I wave at Dubey to come back down.

"Status?"

"We were forced to engage, resulting in two enemy dead, three captured, three refugees." The gunships are circling above us, sending up a tornado of leaves and pollen. "Tell them not to kill us, okay, Delphi?"

"Don't worry, Shelley. I'm saving that privilege for myself."

"Hey, I didn't jam the angel."

"The angel wasn't jammed! We got to watch you the whole time. All the outgoing relays worked fine. We heard every word spoken."

"I don't understand."

"No one does. For the duration of the operation, the angel stopped relaying all communications from Guidance, and even when I tried to switch your overlay to the local cell phone network, I couldn't get through—but as soon as the operation ended, two-way communication was restored."

"By who?"

"No one! No one here did anything. It just happened."

"That doesn't make any sense."

"Yeah? No kidding."

Too much has happened to cover up the crime. So the engineers and the slaver are all taken into custody, though I still don't know who's who. The three girls are transported by gunship to a refugee camp farther out in the Sahel—far enough to find their way back home, I hope.

Yafiah and Ransom don't have to fight over who gets to drive, because I put each of them behind the wheel of one of the contractor's two trucks. Our revised orders are to bring the load on as far as Fort Dassari and guard it. In a day or two, Command will fly new engineers out to take over the project. Delphi makes me promise that when they come to get the trucks, I won't kill them.

Jaynie and Dubey go first in the convoy on their ATVs. The two big open-bed trucks follow, and I come last. I'm stuck driving the third ATV, which means I can't do more than glance through the angel's eyes. It's a vulnerable feeling, not being able to study the terrain around me. I drive on the right shoulder, which at least lets me see something of the road beyond the trucks.

"Delphi?"

"Go ahead."

"You got any bogeys out there?"

"Nothing. I would tell you if there were."

I know she would. I also know she's handling other soldiers, not just me. She's busy—which is why I need to make sure I hold on to some percentage of her attention.

A few more minutes pass. The wind picks up, lightning arcs across black clouds to the south, and the air is heavy with the promise of rain.

"Delphi? The angel was hacked, wasn't it?"

Several seconds go by without an answer. I check my icons. I'm still linked.

"Delphi?"

"Tech is looking into it."

"Did you just talk to someone? Were you told not to say any more than that?"

"I talked to tech. They had nothing new to tell me."

We put another five klicks behind us. I hear the rain coming: a crackling, drumming static growing steadily louder as it sweeps across the plain.

"Delphi?"

"Yes, Shelley?"

"I thought no one could hack through our security."

Silence.

"If you don't answer me I'm going to think the angel has cut out again."

"Check your icons."

The rain hits in a sudden deluge that sluices across my visor. The live view gets replaced by a simulated view derived from my helmet's camera buttons, with the rain distortion subtracted.

"Delphi, what if the angel cuts out again when we're on patrol?"

"That's a concern," she concedes. "And it's being discussed. I'll let you know."

I would like to be part of that discussion, but I know that isn't going to happen.

The rain passes in just a few minutes and where the sun breaks through the clouds, the road starts steaming.

"Any bogeys?" I ask Delphi.

"Why, Shelley? Do you have one of your 'feelings'?"

"No."

"Then why are you acting like a nervous little kid?"

It's because I feel vulnerable, going without angel sight.

Our cloud-fractured shadows stretch out in front of us, getting longer as the afternoon grows old. It's a relief to finally roll into the village, even if we have to cut back our speed to a walking pace.

We get a colder reception than on the way out. Bibata must have dropped hints of what she saw, or suspected, because people eye the trucks with suspicion. I look for her, wanting to let her know that we took care of things, but while the angel locates her truck alongside her mother's house, Bibata doesn't come out to say hello. I'd like to go see her, but I can't do it. I'd get reprimanded for harassment just for knocking on her door.

The first truck rolls past the north edge of the village. An old woman with weathered gray skin stands by the road, watching. She has a young girl beside her, about the age of the girls in the brothel truck. As I approach on my ATV, she raises her hand, gesturing for me to stop.

I relay my status on gen-com. "I'm stopping for a minute. Keep the convoy moving. I'll catch up."

The woman gestures impatiently at the young girl, who speaks to me in excellent English. "Grandmother wants to know what you saw out there, Shelley."

I'm relieved to share the news, certain that it will get back to Bibata. "I saw some bad men, but they're not out there anymore."

"You kill them, Shelley?" she asks eagerly.

"We killed two. Three were arrested."

She translates this for Grandmother, who asks her a

question. She repeats the question for me, in English. "Were there girls? Were they killed?"

"Three girls. They're alive. You do what Grandmother tells you and stay safe."

"I have a gun," she says proudly. "If any cunt hunter comes for me, Grandmother says to kill him."

Without a good harvest, Grandmother might not have enough food for the next year, but the war is close enough that she's invested scarce money in a weapon that isn't likely to offer much protection if things really go south.

"You be careful with your gun," I tell her.

The trucks have both cleared the village. They're picking up speed. I look around one more time for Bibata, but I don't see her, which is probably for the better. What we have between us—it's performance art, not love. I've been in love. I know.

Taking my foot off the brake, I head out.

I have to drive like a madman to catch up with the trucks.

It's 1730 by the time we get back to the fort. Delphi is as tired as I am. She checks out, leaving me in the care of my second-shift handler, a guy code-named Pagan. "Hey, Shelley," he greets me. "Heard you've had a busy twenty-four."

"Not over yet."

"Let me know if you need anything. I'm watching."

Pagan's okay. Mostly I get him at the end of a long shift like this one, but he's been my primary handler on a couple of missions, and I've worked with him enough that I don't mind having him inside my head. He's efficient and polite, and when nothing is going on, he's good at being invisible. He'll stay in the background until my helmet comes off, and my helmet won't come off until I'm safe inside the fort with the gate closed and the auto-defense active. Right now I have to secure the trucks.

I make Ransom repark them on the south side of the fort, with the trailers perpendicular to the wall in a configuration that will provide minimal cover for insurgents. Then I have him unhook the cabs and turn them around so their front bumpers face the trailer hitches. No one is going to steal either the trucks or the equipment while they're under my authority.

The three dogs we left behind in the fort are ecstatic at our return. I drop my pack and then take a minute for hugs and bruising tail thumps. After that, I get Ransom to help me haul down a crate of portable motion detectors from the bunk where they're stored. We head outside, both of us still wearing armor and bones, with the dogs cavorting around us. The sun is dropping out of sight behind the sorghum fields and the spreading branches of the neem trees, lighting the clouds on fire as we set up the motion detectors all around the trucks—a little extra insurance in case a ghost gets past the permanent detectors that monitor activity in our vicinity. By the time we're done, the first stars are gleaming in a twilight sky.

I whistle the dogs back into the fort and turn on the new motion detectors. Ransom disappears inside.

It's 1830. We're supposed to undertake our nightly patrol in an hour and a half, but I check in with Pagan and get permission to put it off until 2200.

Dubey and Yafiah are in the yard, sans armor and bones, cleaning and prepping the ATVs. I take off my helmet. "Yafiah, you're on patrol. Get your gear ready, and get some sleep."

She looks daggers at me but doesn't say anything as she follows me inside.

"Jaynie!" I bellow.

"Yes, sir!"

She appears at the door of the TOC in her sweaty T-shirt and mud-stained pants. "You and Dubey get to stay home tonight to guard the trucks. Ransom and Yafiah are on patrol with me."

Yafiah mutters something under her breath as she pushes past me, disappearing into the bunk room. She'll feel better after a few energy drinks.

I close the door to my room—a tiny compartment just big enough for my bunk and a desk that I never use. As I lie down, I think, *Sleep*. My skullcap picks it up, and in seconds, dream visions come walking through my head. One of them is a dragon I encountered in Texas.

I'm so startled I wake up again, blinking at the white ceiling, tinged red with dust.

I've got that unsettled feeling, like God's been whispering hints in my back brain to kick loose the memory. My rational mind resists: I tell myself that what happened today is reason enough to remember her.

It was at Dallas/Fort Worth. My flight out of Bolivia had been delayed by thunderstorms, leaving me only minutes to make my connection to New York, and I was in a grim mood, because my CO had made me turn in my skullcap before I went on leave.

The first sign of trouble came in a commotion of voices in the crowded concourse. Ahead of me, civilians fell back against the glass, making way for a phalanx of eight black-uniformed mercenaries openly carrying sidearms in their shoulder holsters. I scrambled behind a pillar, breaking a fear sweat, sure I'd walked into the initial stage of a terrorist attack—but my overlay posted no alert, presenting only a simple annotation identifying the mercenaries as employees of Uther-Fen Protective Services, authorized to carry small arms anywhere, even in a public transportation hub.

Around me, excited civilians bounced on their toes, straining to see over the heads of the mercs while asking one another, "Who is it? Is it an actor? Can you see?"

So I looked too and saw a civilian, a woman, mature but not old, walking among the mercenaries, her back straight, her gaze fixed ahead. She was tall and slender, with stiff gold hair—not blond, but gold—framing her face in a helmet cut. Her eyes were hidden by the tinted, curved lens of her high-end farsights. She wore a silky, gray, knee-length coat, and I had a feeling she was authorized to carry small arms too, and that she had a gun hidden away somewhere in that coat.

My overlay identified her as Thelma Sheridan, principal stockholder of Vanda-Sheridan, making her one of the elite of the world—a dragon in possession of a hoard of treasure, and dangerous to disturb.

In all the world, maybe three thousand people could be considered her peers. Maybe fewer.

I felt stunned by the aura of her power; I saw the ruthlessness required to achieve her position written into her face.

The double doors of a private lounge opened to receive her, along with her escort of armed guards. As the doors closed, a hissing sea of astonished whispers flooded the concourse, along with a few shrill bursts of nervous laughter. Dragons are rarely seen. Everyone there knew they'd been granted a glimpse into a hidden world.

Afterward, I felt like an idiot because I'd let myself be intimidated by the mere fact of Thelma Sheridan's wealth. I wondered what would have happened if I'd tried to confront her about the corruption of her employees in Bolivia. Pretty damn sure that would not have turned out well. Dragons don't get where they are in the world by being nice.

Our politicians make a lot of noise, and they pretend they're in charge, but dragons lurk behind them, in the shadows, where the real decisions get made.

Again I think, *Sleep*. This time God is silent—or maybe I'm too tired to hear.

I'm out for two hours. Then Guidance cues the skullcap to wake me. I find Jaynie in the TOC, still on watch; she still hasn't showered. "Have we got a report on the angel?"

"Yes, sir. Tech ran diagnostics on it. No issues were detected. Command says to proceed as normal."

So my three-person patrol heads out into the night, with five dogs to look after us and one temperamental angel.

Thick clouds hide the waxing moon, but the night is bright anyway with night vision. We follow the map Guidance has put up in my visor—the route is different every night—and we move fast. At first the dogs think it's a great game, but they start to lag so we slow down. They don't turn up anything suspicious, and I'm not sensing anything either. I'm hoping for a quiet night when Pagan checks in with the news that a unit of ghost soldiers, nine in all, has turned up in the district west of us. There's an ongoing firefight. Intelligence suspects a widespread infiltration attempt so the night's satellite data from our district was reassessed. "Suspicious elements were found."

"Want to clarify that?" I ask. "Are we talking a confirmed presence or just bogeys?"

"Right now, bogeys. You get to figure out if they're real."

Great.

"Where?"

A point lights up on the map, back in the territory we just cleared.

"We just came through there."

"You were moving fast. We must have missed something."

I shunt the map to Yafiah and Ransom, who are a half klick away, one on either side of me. "Satellites have picked up bogeys, six kilometers back. We're going to check it out."

"Yes, sir!" Ransom answers with enthusiasm. He's been bored tonight.

Yafiah manages to convey an entirely different meaning with the same two words.

We search the area where the bogeys were seen and we hunt through the surrounding terrain, but nothing turns up. The dogs don't find any suspicious scents, and I'm not nervous.

"So what?" I ask Pagan. "Where are they? Or have you got noobs in Intelligence tonight?"

"Maybe," he says. "I never know who's preparing the reports. I just get the documents."

We resume our patrol, heading south again. The moon has set, so when the clouds break up they reveal a great vault of stars and satellites: bright white points against a dull, dark-green sky.

Twenty minutes later, I know where the enemy is.

It's 0330. The angel is off to the northwest, ten klicks away and at the limit of its range when I look through its eyes and see a half-dozen goats, trotting in a line. Goats don't like to move at night, so something has scared them. I send the drone back in the direction the goats are coming from—and after a few seconds I see tall grass moving beneath tree branches as if something large is passing there.

"Pagan."

"I see it. Stand by." He comes back maybe twenty seconds later. "We got at least seven ghosts."

"Damn it!" It's over eight kilometers back, in territory we just swept a second time. "They must have their own drone. They knew when we were in the area and laid low."

"They can't have a drone," Pagan says. "We'd know about it. They were probably scanning for the angel's EM transmissions. Or maybe they just got lucky."

The brush is thick around us. A chorus of insects still sings to the night, though not as many as when we started out. The air is humid and calm, and I'm so damn tired that everywhere looks the same to me.

"Do we go after them?" I ask Pagan, because I just want to get it over with and get a chance to sleep.

"Checking."

I've been stationary long enough to make Yafiah nervous. "LT? You okay?"

"Ghosts," I tell her. "Seven confirmed. Back the way we came."

"*Fuck.*"

My feelings exactly, but Ransom is overjoyed. "Hot damn! Somethin' to do tonight after all!"

Pagan comes back. "Command says let the ghosts go. They're sending a kill drone. The insurgents are far enough from anywhere that no one's going to notice. Give Ransom my apologies."

We keep on for another hour before Command takes pity on us and sends us home. The stars are still out in force when Fort Dassari opens its gates to receive us. The dogs run to drink water, and then collapse in exhaustion.

My people don't have that luxury. Our equipment has

to be cleaned, inspected, powered up, and made ready before anyone gets to rest, because we could get called out at any time. Yafiah staggers as she steps free of her dead sister. Dubey catches her elbow and hands her an energy drink, which should keep her going long enough to finish her chores. I've passed through exhaustion into a state of calm clarity in which I do nothing that isn't necessary and everything I do is in slow, smooth, deliberate motion. It's close to being stoned.

The HITRs are cleaned and plugged into the rack to get charged. Same thing for the helmets, but I leave my dead sister on for now.

Yafiah takes a two-minute shower—I don't even have to yell at her to hurry up—and disappears into the bunk room. Ransom is right behind her. I join Jaynie in the tactical operations center, where she's back on watch.

It's not easy to sit wearing a dead sister, so I just rest cock-hipped against a table. Jaynie turns from the bank of monitors, one smooth eyebrow raised, like she's questioning my sanity. "Why are you still wearing your armor and bones?"

I scan the monitors. I'm punchy with fatigue, but there are some things worth staying up for. "Bibata's coming. She has to drop off the dog food."

Jaynie cracks a grin and shakes her head.

"Highlight of my week," I add in my own defense.

"You know you can never—"

"I know it." I close my sandpaper eyes. "It's just a game."

I know I'm on the edge of sleep when visions start showing up in my head. Lissa's there, in Central Park with spring flowers all around, holding my hand and plotting to run away with me to spend the summer in Europe. I'll do it. I'll do anything she says. I don't ever want to love anyone else.

"You might want to lock up the joints of your dead sister before you fall over, sir," Jaynie says with amusement in her voice.

I startle awake, check the time on my overlay. Almost twenty minutes have passed. I scan the monitors again. "I go on leave in three months." I'm a little worried about it. "I've heard Guidance policy has changed, and they're letting us use our skullcaps on leave if we request it."

"I've heard that too. Going back to New York?"

"I don't know. Maybe. My dad's still there." I look at her more closely, and I think to ask for the first time, "So what about you? Have you got someone? Are you married?"

"Married?" she asks in disbelief. "Marriage is for people like you, Shelley. No one I know gets married. There's no military benefits for it anymore. Marriage costs too damn much."

I shrug, annoyed because Jaynie has a talent for making me feel like a stupid kid.

Granted, it's not all that hard to do.

"You fell a long way, didn't you?" she asks.

"Yeah, I guess."

She nods. "It's easy to tell you come from a good family. The way you carry yourself, the way you talk. The fact that the army made you an officer even though you came in on a prison deferment."

I shrug. "The induction contract archives my record, so it's like I didn't do anything. If I clear my term, the record gets permanently expunged."

"Like it never happened."

"Yeah. Just a ten-year detour."

"So what did you do? What did they get you for?"

"Gang rape and setting off a bomb in a public gathering place."

She rolls her eyes. "What was it? Frigging jaywalking?"

I can't believe it. She got it right on the first guess. "Yeah, you could say that."

"What?"

"Jaywalking. Illegal assembly. Disorderly conduct. Those were the initial charges. It's not freedom we're fighting for, you know that, right?"

"What are you talking about, 'freedom'? We're fighting for a paycheck, right?"

I laugh. "Yeah. That's it exactly. Your paycheck, mine, the shareholders'."

"So what did you do? Participate in a riot?"

"No."

Ransom and Yafiah have grilled me for months about my mysterious past and I never have told them why I'm here, but for some reason I tell Jaynie. Maybe I'm just tired. "It started with a nonviolent protest march, a rally against the war industry."

Her elegant eyebrows climb into high arcs of skepticism.

I start to laugh, and she realizes it's true.

She leans forward, her mouth round with surprise. "Oh my God. No shit? You're here, killing people, because you were found guilty of protesting the war industry?"

"Beat that," I tell her.

She shakes her head in wonder, but she still isn't buying it entirely. "Illegal assembly . . . that has to be a misdemeanor. How does that add up to ten years in the army?"

No point in holding back now. "It was a big march, in Manhattan. I wasn't part of the movement. I was just out on the street, a dumb kid with nothing to do on a Saturday night, so I thought it'd be cool to join the crowd." I touch my gloved finger to the corner of my eye. "I already had the overlay. It was a prototype, new at the time."

"They're *still* new. I never met anyone else who had one."

"That you know about."

She acknowledges the point with a nod. "But they *are* rare."

"And not cheap, either. I used mine to record the march. Then the cops started arresting people. I couldn't believe it. Like, what happened to free speech?"

It's a rhetorical question, and she doesn't answer.

"When I questioned my arrest, the cops called it resisting. I recorded that. I recorded every fucking second of it. My arrest, the strip search, everything. The cops didn't know I was cyborged, so it was easy. Afterward, I published the video, and people could see the wreckage that used to be their civil rights. It really boosted the protest movement."

"Goddamn, I think I saw that video."

"You probably did."

"So you made an illegal recording and you published it."

"Yeah, that was the felony charge. The city government claimed I was infringing on people's rights to privacy and exposing their cops to retribution. Of course, these days, in Manhattan, you can't walk down a street without being recorded."

She shakes her head. "Some balls, Shelley."

My cheeks heat up. "Not really. I just didn't like getting pushed around by the cops, and I was pissed."

"Huh. You should get counseling for that."

The sun's coming up outside, its first rays spearing through tree branches and casting long, sharp shadows across the road. Bibata always comes just after sunrise. I watch the south road monitor, knowing it won't be long before her truck shows up.

"So how about you?" I ask Jaynie. "What's your story?"

She looks me in the eye. "I didn't have to leave home, because I never had one. I do have ambition."

"And smarts and curiosity. Are you going for officer?"

"I have my application in."

In the army it's still possible to come from nowhere and wind up in command. In the civilian world, that just doesn't happen anymore.

We're both startled by the gentle pinging of the peripheral alarm, but it's just Bibata's truck, still five K out. "Right on time as always," I say, getting up.

"Mind your manners," Jaynie warns me. "'Cause Mama's watching."

I grin, and after retrieving my helmet and rifle from the bunk room, I head outside. The sun's rays blaze against the roof of the fort, but the yard is still shadowed by the east wall. Dubey is grooming the dogs under the canopy. "Get rigged up," I tell him. "Bibata's here."

He nods, leashes the dogs, and then disappears inside.

I put my helmet on, willing the visor to go transparent. We're required to be fully rigged every time we step outside. That's the rule and we lose leave days if we violate it, because the army does not want to pay out on our life insurance policies.

I visualize the gate opening. My skullcap detects my intention and the gate slides aside just far enough that I can pass.

I stand on the side, waiting, as Bibata backs her pickup truck up to the closed gate. The truck's bed is almost empty: just ten cases of canned dog food and a basket of fresh fruit, mostly mangoes and papayas, purchased in the village. I circle the truck, swiping the barrel of my HITR underneath it so the onboard camera can scan for bombs, because you never know.

By the time I come around the front, Bibata has gotten out. She gives me a coy smile as she stands beside the cab, arms akimbo, dressed in rust-red-and-gray camo pants and a pink tube top that shows off her gorgeous breasts. "I didn't bring any bombs this time, Shelley." She pats herself down: shoulders, breasts, belly, hips. "And no guns, either, except the little one in the cab."

And just like that I've got a hard-on. She knows it too. "You ready to say bye-bye to Mama, Shelley, and go for a ride?"

"Hell yes."

But just then the gate opens behind me. I glance back. Dubey, rigged in armor and bones, is bringing out the first of the empty water barrels.

"But Mama's still watching," I add in resignation.

I extend the arm hooks of my dead sister and use them to grab the cases of dog food. I haul them inside the fort, and then I help Dubey load the barrels into the truck bed. The dead sisters are useful in moving supplies, but slinging cargo is not their primary role. The models we use are built for speed and agility. Their load-bearing capacity is limited to about three hundred fifty pounds, including the soldier's body weight. The ironic result is that when we have to distribute loads, the lightest soldiers get the heaviest burdens. Life is just not fair like that.

Dubey and I tie the barrels down. Then I hand Bibata a personal cash card, which she swipes on her phone, withdrawing payment. Technically, the army is supposed to supply us, but Bibata is a lot more reliable, so I cover the cost of water, fresh fruit, and dog food out of my pay. It's not like I have anything else to do with the money.

She turns to gaze at the water barrels, letting me admire her in profile. "These I bring back in the afternoon, Shelley." She cocks her head to look at me. "You look tired, love. You going to sleep now, yes? Make sure you dream of me."

I think that's guaranteed.

• • • •

I stand in the shower for a long time, hot water running over me, probably the same water, over and over again as it passes through the filtration system. Eventually I work up the nerve to take my skullcap off. Moving with mad speed, I clean my scalp and duck under the water to rinse, managing to slip the skullcap back on just as the dark feelings begin to intrude.

But the soothing complacency I expect doesn't come. I press the cap all over. It's seated correctly, but I'm not getting anything out of it. It's like it's gone dead.

I shut the water off and grab a towel. My heart booms, but I'm too confused to panic. That's when an icon lights up in my overlay. Guidance is calling.

Everyone gives up autonomy when they go into the military. For me, part of that was control of my overlay. It's mine and not the army's, but to keep it I had to yield root control, meaning Guidance can override anything I do and intrude whenever they want to. Usually they have the good manners not to, but sometimes they forget to be subtle.

With no acknowledgment from me, a voice starts speaking in my ears, and it's not Delphi or Pagan. It's some guy I've never heard before. "Lieutenant Shelley—"

I cut him off. "Delphi's my handler." I don't like it that he's in my head. Try walking naked out of the shower and finding a stranger sitting on your bed. That's what it's like. "If Delphi's not around, it's Pagan. No one else gets inside my head."

"I'm not in your head," the stranger says, an edge to his voice as if he's dealt with too many unstable idiots just like me. "I'm inside your overlay. And I follow orders just like you do. My name's Denario. I was told to contact you at this address. I work on technical issues. Your skullcap is scheduled for diagnostic testing, so it won't be usable for the next few hours. Thought you'd like to know."

I want to believe I haven't heard him right, but I'm not good at denial. My temper's frayed and the skullcap is not working to keep me calm, so I lay into him. "I don't know what the fuck you're talking about. There's no such thing as a field diagnostic. That doesn't happen."

Denario doesn't answer. He gives me quite a few seconds to think about things . . . like the black kernel of panic that's starting to unfurl deep inside my head, and the complete lack of any counteracting response from my skullcap. "You've taken it offline . . . haven't you?"

"It's been switched off," Denario confirms, no doubt relieved that I'm finally catching on. "You'll need to locate the diagnostic rack in the TOC. Put the cap on it. Then go take a nap. You'll have it back by the time you wake up."

I peel the lifeless skullcap off and stare at it, but there's no on switch, no way for me to activate it. I didn't even know it could be turned off. "What the hell is going on? Who ordered this? Why?"

"The why is, I was told to run a diagnostic, and I'm going to do it. I can't do it until the cap is on the rack, so the sooner you let me get started, the sooner you can have your emo drip back online again."

"*Fuck.*"

"And don't try taking it off the rack early or the test will have to be restarted."

I don't bother to dry off. Wrapping the towel around my waist, I stomp into the tactical operations center, where Dubey has taken over the watch. From beneath the comforting coverage of his skullcap, he glances at me with worried eyes and looks away—so I know he knows.

And since he's the only one there, I yell at him: "What's a diagnostic rack?"

"I looked it up," he says meekly. "And then I found it for you."

He gets up and moves to the little utility table set at right angles to the desk. "It's here. It's a kit. I can set it up for you, but you have to give me your skullcap."

Dubey doesn't want to touch my skullcap and I don't want him to touch it either. Some things are too personal. "I'll do it myself." I'm sure the equipment is simple enough for the lowest common denominator to manage.

He retreats to the desk. I open the kit—and discover that it unfolds into a wire-frame skull without a face. I lay the skullcap over it and the frame blazes with red light.

Denario is back in my head. "Good job, Lieutenant. Now go to sleep. Things will be all better by morning."

"It is morning, asshole."

"Not where I live."

Dubey doesn't say anything else and neither do I.

Back in the shower room I trade my towel for a pair of shorts, then I retreat to my room, close the door, and lie down in my bunk. The black kernel in my head is blooming. It was never part of my life plan to be an emo junkie. What the fuck happened to me? I gave up my life for one stupid, defiant act when I was nineteen and I fucking *don't* want to think about it. I don't want to think about Lissa. I *don't.*

But the memories are chasing around inside my head in a whirlwind of resentment until I'm left pressing my hands against my forehead as if I can squeeze them out.

There's a knock on the silly little panel that counts as a door. Before I can muster the energy to curse whoever it is, the door opens and Jaynie comes in with peace in her right hand. I turn my head as she holds it out to me: one small blue pill nestled in her dark palm. She says, "I talked to Guidance. You're authorized for a single dose of don't-give-a-shit. Take it, Lieutenant. It'll let you sleep."

"Thanks." I take it out of her hand, but I don't pop it

right away. She gives me that questioning look again. "I'll be okay," I tell her.

"I know."

She retreats, closing the door behind her. I hold the pill in my palm so long that its blue coating starts to dissolve against the heat of my skin. I've run three missions in less than forty hours. Nothing was wrong with my performance on any of them. Nothing was fucked up. Command wasn't happy about the Vanda-Sheridan contractors, but we did put the bad guys out of circulation, we saved the girls, the equipment is safe just outside the fort, and new engineers are on their way. And I finished another fucking patrol after that. They have to know there's nothing wrong with my equipment.

And then it hits me. They're just checking my skullcap before they pull *me* in for a diagnostic.

*Why?*

Why, when I've performed above and beyond?

And then I know.

I'm standing on the edge of an abyss and I know, I know, I know.

It's the King David thing.

I should kick Ransom's ass for coming up with that tag, but I know that's what they're worried about and suddenly I'm wondering too—how the fuck do I *know* things? How do I know when we're about to get slammed? And why haven't I ever wondered about it before?

There's a blue stain in my palm when I finally put the pill under my tongue. God must have forgotten to whisper a warning to me that Satan was about to drag me to the edge of the black abyss. I don't want to look down there and see the faces of all the people I've killed. So I go to sleep instead.

• • • •

A soft knock on the door: tap-tap, *tap*. The rhythm repeats several times. I hear it, but it's not quite enough to wake me up. Ransom's bellowing does the trick though: "Jesus, Yafiah, just tell him."

I'm halfway to my feet when the door opens and Ransom leans in. "The rack is green."

The don't-give-a-shit has left me confused. "Then the test is done?"

"It's done," Ransom confirms. "Message from Guidance says your skullcap is cleared for use."

I'm relieved, oh yes. But then I indulge in a brief moment of machismo, toying with the idea of not picking the skull-cap up right away, of not putting it on . . . of proving to myself and to Guidance that I can live without it . . . but I'm only thinking about it because the don't-give-a-shit hasn't really worn off yet.

I get up. Ransom opens the door wider like he expects me to bolt into the hall. It's tempting, but I make myself put on pants first, and a T-shirt. I skip the boots, but I *walk* out of the room. Yafiah's standing in the hall behind Ransom, watching me with wary eyes. I wonder how many men she's seen go berserk when they can't get their fix? Not that I'd ever ask.

It's two paces to the TOC, two more to the utility table. The rack is green just like Ransom reported. My skullcap is there, but I don't touch it. I look over my shoulder instead, wanting to be sure.

"You got a message?" I ask Ransom. "It's cleared for use?"

I have to be sure, because I do *not* want to start the testing over again.

"Here. You can look at it."

Ransom comes in, touches the main screen. Text appears, confirming what he told me. I sigh and pick up the skullcap, worried that it will still be offline—but that worry evaporates as soon as I slip it on.

Like every other LCS soldier, my brain is randomly peppered with a myriad of tiny organic implants called "neuromodulating microbeads." The position and function of each bead is known to the skullcap. Some are chemical sensors that signal deviations from a baseline, while others can be directed by the skullcap to stimulate neurochemical production.

My brain has deviated a long way from the baseline. The skullcap registers that and reacts. A sense of calm sweeps over me so quickly I wonder if I've psyched myself into it—just expecting to feel better, so I do. But in that moment I don't really care.

It's only midafternoon, so I go back to sleep. But just before seventeen hundred I'm awake, feeling shot full of adrenaline for no reason at all. Did someone shout out an alarm? I can't remember it, but why else am I awake?

I'm on my feet and dressed, boots on, within a minute. I throw the door open and stomp over to the tactical operations center. "What's going on?"

Ransom is on watch. "Nothin', LT. Everything's quiet. Everyone's asleep."

I stand behind him and scan the screens. I check the messages. But he's right—nothing's going on.

I feel like somebody's pointing a gun at my head.

In the kitchen, I heat up a meal. I'm halfway through it when I suddenly remember what I've forgotten.

The chair legs scrape the floor as I stand up. "Ransom!"

"Sir?"

He's at the door of the TOC when I step out of the kitchen. "What happened to Bibata? She was supposed to bring the water."

"She did, sir, while you were asleep. The sarge logged it."

I glare at him for several seconds, as if it's his fault everything went as it should have. Then I return to my dinner, but I can't eat, so I pitch it into the composter and I go outside.

The temperature's up around a hundred—not too bad for this time of year. The dogs are sprawled in the shade of their canopy. Tails thump, but it's too hot for them to get up and greet me—just like any other afternoon. Nothing is wrong, nothing is going on, but my anxiety is getting worse.

I wonder if Denario fucked up my skullcap.

Or maybe this is just the hangover that follows a dose of don't-give-a-shit.

*Something's wrong.*

I climb up to the catwalk and gaze through the peepholes. The trucks are where they're supposed to be, waiting for new engineers. The road is empty. A light wind rustles the nearest sorghum field. A stick fence keeps the goats out. I see them in the distance, browsing in the shade of a grove of neem trees.

I patrol the catwalk, but there's nothing to see in any direction, and there's no sound except the rustling of leaves, the bleating of goats, and the buzz of insects. I wipe away the sweat on my face. My T-shirt is wet with sweat. And my anxiety is getting worse. I don't want to be here, inside these walls. I don't want my soldiers to be here. I want to get out.

But that's crazy. We're safe here.

What the fuck is wrong with me?

I flinch as a green question mark flashes in my overlay. Unknown caller? I'm not cleared for phone calls. I wonder if I should answer, and then I do, but no one's there.

"Guidance is fucking with me," I mutter.

I go back inside, intending to call in, to ask Delphi or Pagan or whoever's on duty what the fuck they think they're doing, but I don't make it to the TOC. I'm barely in the door when a sense of urgency slams through my brain. *It's now*, God whispers. Whatever's happening, it's happening *now*.

I know I've lost it. I know I've cracked, but I don't care. I start screaming. "Everybody, up! Now! Something's coming. I can feel it. A slam's coming. Get on your armor and bones. *Now!*"

Ransom pops out of the TOC, wild-eyed. "King David?"

"Do it! Armor and bones!"

"Yes, sir!" He launches himself down the hall to the bunk room. "Dubey, up!" he shouts. "Yafiah! King David says armor and bones!"

The door to Jaynie's room pops open. She's got on her T-shirt, pants, and boots. "Status, sir?"

"I don't fucking know! We just need to get out of here."

Delphi is talking to me via my overlay. She can call me on it, but I can't call her. "Shelley, take it easy—"

I cut her off as Jaynie pushes past me into the TOC. "Armor and bones, Sergeant!" I shout after her, and then I duck into the bunk room.

Ransom, Dubey, and Yafiah are all getting their armor on. I join them. Jaynie reappears, looking at me like I've gone nuts. "Sir, there are no orders."

"You have *my* order, Sergeant. Get your rig on now."

I see Yafiah cast a doubtful look Jaynie's way, while Delphi tries to talk me down. Dubey's looking scared—of his crazy commanding officer? Ransom's excited. He's already strapping on his dead sister while I finish securing my armor.

Delphi gives up on me and goes away. No one else speaks as they strap in. It takes maybe three minutes for everyone to get rigged. I pass out the weapons. "Get your packs and helmets and get out!"

I pull my own helmet on, wait for them to clear out, and then follow them to the door. The fort's gate is sliding open; the dogs are racing out. Guidance comes in over gen-com—not Delphi. This is the voice of someone older: a woman I've never heard before, and she's speaking to the entire LCS.

"Dassari LCS, warning: two fighter jets are coming out of the east. Flying low—"

"Our fighters?" I interrupt.

"No. Ours are on intercept, but—"

"Get out!" I scream at my people. The two trucks outside are going to be a target, but so will the fort—and it can't protect us. It wasn't made for an air war. "Get out! Get as far away as you can! Get out of sight!"

Dubey and Yafiah break first. Our training is to separate, and they do. Dubey cuts east; Yafiah takes off north. Jaynie and Ransom exit behind them. I'm the last to go. My dead sister propels me out of the yard in two strides.

I can already hear the distant thunder of jet engines. I feel like we've been betrayed. This is not supposed to be an air war. Small-arms only. Since when can Ahab Matugo afford jets?

"Find cover!" I scream as we race to put distance between ourselves and the finest trio of targets in the district. "Don't get caught in the open!"

I cut northwest, cross the road, and bound through tall grass between the scattered trees. Ransom is ahead of me, running for all he's worth, looking like he could leap the trees in a single bound. Jaynie's angling northeast toward a neem grove. Yafiah has stopped. Her readout is showing two loose cinches on her right leg. "Yafiah!"

"Fixing this shit, LT!"

"Get going!"

I look for Dubey. He's a labeled point on my visor, running south of the fort, toward what I don't know. It's open ground out there, no trees at all, just goat-grazed pastures.

"Dubey, find shelter!" I scream, but he doesn't answer. He just keeps going.

*Fuck.*

Out in the open like that, he's going to make an irresistible target for an adrenaline-shot pilot with an autocannon.

*Goddamn it.* Why the hell did we have to get stationed in such open country? Why not a jungle or mountains or something?

Already I can see the bright points of the incoming fighters low in the eastern sky. My brain is squirming in panic. I know, I know, I know I need to keep running. God's voice is as clear in my head as it's ever been: *Get away!* Get far away—from the trucks, from the fort—but Dubey's just a scared kid. I don't want to give up on him. I don't want him caught out in the open.

So I defy God. I turn around and race back after him.

"*Shelley!*" Delphi screams at me. "What are you doing? Don't go back to the fort. You're going to get hit!"

"Gotta get Dubey!"

"No! No time! He's panicked. He's checked out. His handler can't get through to him."

That's why I have to go after him.

I blurt between breaths, "Tell his . . . handler . . . tranq him!"

If Guidance can slow him down, it'll give me a chance to catch up. If I can catch him, we can cut back north toward the trees.

But the jets are closing in with unbelievable speed. I feel cheated. I thought I'd have more time. As I round the fort, the fighters are so close that the roar of their engines sets my teeth vibrating. I look for Dubey—and I know it's hopeless.

His handler has gotten him to stop running, but he's way out in a pasture, with panicked goats fleeing past him as he turns back to look at me. There's nowhere out there for him to hide and no time left to get to cover. "Get down!" I order over gen-com. He drops.

I turn and run the other way. Ten long strides to the nearest sorghum field. I vault the fence. The stalks are over six feet high. Maturing sorghum makes good cover from the ground, but I've spent a lot of time looking through the angel's eyes and I know it doesn't hide much from the air. Too bad I've got nowhere else to go.

A different roar cuts past the raging of the jets. A missile is screaming in and the fort is about to go a hundred feet up in the air. I drop. The red dirt between the stalks is slick and wet from the rain. The ground is shaking. I roll into a ball, knowing it's going to be all about luck for the next few seconds.

Luck abandons me. I'm way too close to the fort when the missile hits. The shock wave picks me up. I'm being crushed by sound alone, sent plummeting down a newly opened pit straight into Hell while billowing orange fire whirls in my vision and—

I check out of the world for a few seconds.

Next thing I know, mud and burning chunks of steel and plastic are raining down on me, pummeling the back of my helmet and my armor. I'm furious. I want to kill someone in Command. They told us this was a ground war, a fucking ground war.

I flinch at another concussion, deafened again by another massive explosion. A blast of heat washes over me. I try to get my eyes to focus. I want to check my visor, see where my people are, but everything has shut down. Guidance must have shut my system down so the pilots can't track the EM signals.

The ground shakes again as one of the fighters sweeps past and then I hear the concussive bursts of what has to be an autocannon. Just like I feared, the pilots are hunting targets on the ground. I close my eyes and pray for them to leave . . . and they do. The roar fades. West, I think . . . toward the next border fort.

My helmet switches back on. The fans blow cool air across my face as the visor initiates its boot routine. I try to get up.

I'm lying on my belly, held down by the weight of my pack, with my arms pinned under me and my head turned to the side. I try to push myself up, but the dead sister isn't working. The sister's titanium bones won't bend, so my arms are locked in place, and I can't get my legs to move. I manage to flop onto my side just as my visor wakes up. I don't like what it shows me. Someone's been hit. Their critical status posts in bold red, but my brain is still hammered from the explosion and I can't get the readout to make sense to me. I give up on it as motion draws my gaze beyond the visor. Bounding across the pummeled ground I see my favorite redneck of all time, coming to my rescue.

"Jesus, Shelley!"

Ransom's voice is pitched weirdly high and shaking. Or maybe it's just that my ears are fucked up.

"Jesus, Jesus, Jesus," he chants as he goes to his knees beside me.

His armor looks flash-fried and I can't see his face past his opaque visor, but I can see he's moving okay. "You wounded?" I ask, because I haven't managed to figure out my readouts yet.

"Shut the fuck up!" he screams at me.

He shrugs off his pack, slams it down against the mud, opens it, and starts tearing through the contents.

"I'm not hurt, Ransom. It's just the dead sister's broken. Uncinch me so I can get up."

It's surprisingly hard to say all that. I'm just lying there on my side, but suddenly I feel like I'm on the verge of sleep.

"Hang on, Shelley," Ransom says.

Like, what else am I supposed to do? "Who's hit?" I ask.

He doesn't answer. I don't know what the hell he's doing.

I try again to bend my arms, but the effort makes me dizzy. "Come on, Ransom. Pop my cinches. Do it now."

"I need to turn you on your back."

He does it. The sky is full of boiling smoke. I think I hear the crackle of fire, but I'm not sure. My hearing's kind of off; not too surprising given that I just got blown up by a missile.

"Delphi?" I ask tentatively, surprised she hasn't been nagging me. "You there?"

"I'm here, Shelley."

A whisper is about all I can muster. "What the hell just happened?"

"A new player came into the conflict, one with deep pockets."

"And Command didn't know?"

"I don't know what Command knew."

A gun goes off not too far away. I flinch hard and try again to sit up, but I can barely lift my head off the ground. "Delphi, what the fuck is wrong with me?"

"I've got you maxed out on endorphins," she whispers, a quaver in her voice.

"Both tourniquets on," Ransom announces.

None of this makes sense to me; it just makes me angry. "Ransom, what the fuck are you doing? Get this dead sister off me!"

A second gunshot makes me freeze. "Enemy on the ground?"

Ransom answers, “No, LT. It’s just . . . the sarge. She’s shooting the dogs.”

I close my eyes, realizing that Delphi’s got me so high I’m imagining things.

“Sarge says it’d be wrong to leave them here to starve,” Ransom explains.

“I can’t hear her. I didn’t hear her say that.”

“You don’t need to.”

“Goddamn it—” I’m on the edge of a tirade when I hear footsteps crunching through the mud. I turn my head to look.

Jaynie’s walking past us through the charred and blasted remnants of the sorghum field, heading for the road. She has her assault rifle clutched in her hands as she moves in stiff, measured steps. Yafiah is two paces behind her, walking in exactly the same way as if it’s a game of copycat, except she’s not carrying a weapon. I see a crater blasted into her armor right in the middle of her chest. Jaynie turns her head to glance at me. Yafiah doesn’t, because she isn’t real anymore. It’s only the frame of the dead sister that’s holding her body up.

“Oh *fuck*,” I whisper, watching the beloved dead walk past. Jaynie’s got Yafiah’s exoskeleton slaved to her system. That’s the easiest way to move a body to a pickup point—and it means the exoskeleton will be in position for retrieval too. The army will want to reuse that.

I look again at the screen of my visor. The critical status post I glimpsed before is gone. Delphi must have wiped my visor’s display. My gaze shifts to the smoke-filled sky. “Where’s Dubey?” I ask in a whisper.

“We got slammed, LT,” Ransom says as he finally starts popping cinches to free my arms from the struts. “Dubey’s dead. Yafiah’s dead. We’d all be dead, if you hadn’t made us run when you did.”

I lose some time, because the next thing I know, Jaynie’s

sitting next to me, cross-legged, her visor transparent, the face behind it sad and thoughtful. My helmet is off. The sun is low in the sky. It glares in my eyes, deep orange behind a heavy veil of smoke. The air stinks of burned fields, and I'm so hot I want to puke.

"What's wrong with me?" I ask Jaynie.

"You'll be okay."

No way does she believe that. I can see it in her face.

"Did you kill all the dogs?"

The fine lines of her eyebrows draw together as she studies me. She's not going to answer my question because she's got one of her own. "What made you panic back there? How did you know we were going to get slammed? You knew before Command knew. You knew before Guidance knew."

I wet my lips. My whole mouth feels so dry all of a sudden I'm not sure I can speak, but I get three words out. "I just knew."

"He's King David," Ransom says. "God told him to get us the fuck out and that's what he did."

"Yeah? Going back after Lin was a dumbass move, sir. God should have told you not to be a hero."

"God did tell me that," I whisper. "I didn't listen."

Her lips draw back; she's furious—like she can't believe the level of stupid she's forced to witness. "*Why the fuck not?*"

I don't know what to say.

But when her head turns, when I see her staring at my legs, I get scared—more scared than I have ever been before. "Tell me," I whisper.

"Both gone," she says, "just above the knees."

# LINKED COMBAT SQUAD

---

## EPISODE 2:
## BLEEDING THROUGH

ELECTRONIC EQUIPMENT HUMS BESIDE ME. FARTHER away I hear a faint whisper of air spilling from a vent. A disinfectant smell mixes with the scent of freshly washed sheets. There is no scent of dust, or of dogs.

Then I remember: The dogs are dead.

Not just the dogs.

I shudder and I shove the memory away. Its absence reveals a great black gaping pit . . . in my body? my mind? my soul? I don't even know, but I've been in this place before, teetering on the edge of this abyss. I come here when I'm not wearing the skullcap.

Panic brushes past. Why am I not wearing it? Did someone take it from me? Just as I decide that must be it, and that I'll kill the thief who did it, a stern-voiced woman speaks.

"He's coming out of it."

Then another woman, her voice softly tentative and much closer to me, asks: "Lieutenant Shelley? Can you hear me?"

I can, but the closer I drift to full wakefulness, the more I feel like my chest is about to collapse around the black absence inside me. I want to go back to the oblivion that cradled me . . . or get a knife and release the lightless poison inside me that's making it hard to breathe.

But the soft-voiced woman won't let me escape. She presses a cold, wet cloth against my cheeks, one and then the other. I shudder again as goose bumps rise across my skin. Then my eyes are open, and I know that Africa is a long way behind me.

I'm in a hospital bed with my head and shoulders elevated so I can see a woman in the uniform of an army major, standing at the foot of the bed, watching me through the clear wraparound lens of her farsights. A green light off to the side of the farsights indicates they're in recording mode.

At the side of the bed is the soft-voiced woman, wearing a light blue nursing smock, her gaze attentive and concerned. She sets aside the cloth and picks up a small, clear, soft-plastic bottle with a bent straw emerging from the top. She smiles in a kindly way. "Lieutenant Shelley, this is a syrup to help your throat feel better."

I realize my mouth is dry, my throat raw.

Gently, she presses the straw between my parchment lips. A cold vapor fills my mouth, moistening the tissue until I'm able to swallow. The nurse puts the bulb back on the side table and gives me a little smile. "I'll be back to check on you in a bit," she assures me. She leaves the room. The door swings shut behind her.

Now it's the major's turn.

"How much do you remember of what happened to you, Lieutenant Shelley?"

I consider her question and discover that I remember much more than I'd like to. "They're dead," I murmur hoarsely. "Yafiah and Dubey."

"They are dead," the major agrees matter-of-factly. "But you, and Sergeant Jayne Vasquez, and Specialist Matthew Ransom are alive, thanks to your quick action."

"Not quick enough. Should've moved sooner."

She concedes the point with a nod. "And still, it was a miracle."

There's a hunger in her eyes. She wants something from me. It's unsettling, and I look to the overlay to interpret her mood. That's when I realize the overlay isn't active. The only sign of its existence is a pinpoint red light in the lower left corner of my vision.

A wave of anxiety sweeps me. The terms of my army contract call for the overlay to be active at all times. I could earn punishment if it's off, so I hurry to address the issue before anyone notices.

My gaze fixes on the red light. Focusing my attention should cause a menu to slide open, but nothing happens.

"Lieutenant Shelley?"

The major's tone is sharp. I think she's been talking to me, though I'm not sure. I frown at her, suddenly suspicious. "I'm shut down."

"I know you are. It's authorized. We need to talk."

Her name is Major Hanson and she's an attorney. She tells me, "You've been in a medically induced coma for three days, since Fort Dassari was attacked and destroyed. As a result of the attack, you suffered a double amputation. You lost both your legs above the knee."

I know this already, but her words make it real. I can't pretend anymore that what I remember is some remnant nightmare soon to be forgotten.

She says, "The preferred procedure would have been to leave you in a coma while treatment was initiated, but your next of kin, who holds power of attorney, refused to provide approval."

I blink in confusion. "My dad wouldn't let me receive treatment?"

She nods. "That is correct. Your combined medical and

service evaluation indicated Level One intervention—the best we have."

I understand where this is going. "There was a catch?"

She looks pleased. "Your questions indicate a high level of understanding, Lieutenant. Most soldiers recovering from medical coma don't come around so quickly, but I'm certifying you as intellectually competent to make your own decisions."

"Where's my dad?"

"He's with another attorney." She touches her farsights with an index finger, drawing my attention back to the fact that she's recording me. "They're watching this deposition."

"I want to see him."

"You're not currently at liberty, Lieutenant. As an officer in the United States Army, you have obligations."

I'm a legless cripple. How much more do they want from me? Maybe they'll put me at a desk next to Delphi and for the next seven years I can be Guidance to a dozen grunts around the globe, trying to keep them from getting blown away.

"I need you to pay close attention, Lieutenant."

Was I drifting again? I fix my gaze on her and make myself listen.

She says, "You have to decide between two options before your treatment can begin. If you accept Level One intervention, you'll remain a field officer—"

"A field officer?" It's always a bad idea to interrupt a superior, but I'm so stunned I forget myself. "Is that possible?"

She tries again, with an edge to her words. "You'll remain a field officer in the regular army. If you decline Level One intervention you'll be separated from the army. As a civilian, you'll qualify for a lesser regimen of treatment. You'll also be mandated to serve at least one year of your civilian prison sentence, presently archived."

I gaze straight at the camera on her farsights, knowing my dad is on the other side, watching me and praying I'll use this chance to get the hell out of the army. I know what he'd say: *Just one year, Jimmy, and this nightmare will be over.*

The major asks, "What is your decision, Lieutenant Shelley?"

My dad doesn't understand that for me, a year in prison is the same as a life sentence. The court sent me on a prison tour. They made sure I had a clear idea of what it would be like, what I'd put up with, and I knew I couldn't do it. It had looked bad enough before, but now? I'd be the pretty cripple, everybody's doll. I know I'd kill someone, or someone would kill me.

Still, I don't want to look like a pushover. "If I agree to stay in, can I get my skullcap back?"

Her disapproving scowl makes me defensive.

"I need it!"

"That's a piece of equipment available only to combat personnel in the field."

No way am I the only post-combat LCS emo junkie. "I hear Guidance is making exceptions."

"That's an issue for you to discuss with Guidance and your physician."

The black abyss yawns wider. The microbeads in my brain are useless without the skullcap to tell them what to do. I close my eyes, wishing for Jaynie to appear with a blue pill of oblivion. But what appears against the darkness is a legal document, projected onto my overlay, which has suddenly returned to life—or at least a half life.

"Read it," the major says. "If you agree, then append your signature."

I open my eyes again, and make myself read. The document describes my obligations and my treatment. If I sign it, I'll be receiving cutting-edge mechanical prosthetics that will integrate with my nervous system, so that I'll be able to run again, jump, climb.

I look up at the major. "It says the prosthetics are experimental. What if they don't work right?"

"They'll be replaced with a less advanced system, and you'll be separated. Terms are detailed in section nine."

I keep reading, and learn that shiny new legs are only one part of the agreement. I'll also be getting a permanent mod in my head that will take the place of a skullcap. It will always be there, even after I leave the army, and it will always be turned on.

I'm ready to sign the document right there, but I make myself read the whole thing. I make myself really think about it. I know I can deal with life in the army. I've done okay so far. It's the alternative that scares me.

"Questions?" the major asks.

I come up with a few, just because I think I should. She provides answers and then asks if I understand. I say that I do, while her farsights record it all.

Eventually, I wave my hand in the air, executing my signature on the document, agreeing to continue my sojourn in the United States Army, because they're offering me what no one else has ever had, and it looks a whole lot better than spending a year as a pretty cripple in prison.

After the major leaves, my dad comes in.

He doesn't understand my decision.

"For God's sake, Jimmy! What is going on in your head? What have they got you wired up on?"

His skin is a shade lighter than mine, his eyes slate gray. His ritual workouts keep him lean and strong, and he loves to dress in finely made, conservative clothes. Even now.

He's wearing khaki slacks and a short-sleeved designer dress shirt in a pale blue that mocks his anger.

"That army attorney played you. No way are you in any kind of shape to be making a decision of this gravity and they know it!"

"Dad, you need to understand. Even if this isn't what you wanted, it was my best option—"

"That's bullshit."

"It's not. Listen, I know what I'm doing—"

"You just signed up for seven more years—"

"I know that. I know what it means."

"—and the only way the army will let you out before then is if you're dead."

"Dad, I'm not going to die."

"That's not something you get to decide!" He holds up his hand, his thumb and forefinger a millimeter apart. "You came this close to being dead, Jimmy. One of the soldiers in your squad, Matthew Ransom—"

"I know. He saved my life. So I didn't die, and I'm not going to die." Then, because we've had this argument before, I add, "And I don't have a death wish."

His lips press together; he turns away from me. With his arms crossed over his chest, he stares out the window. Morning light gleams on his face, catching on the gray strands in his short black hair, making them seem more abundant than I remember. He's only fifty-one.

After a couple of silent minutes creep past, I ask him, "What's out there?"

A smile quirks his lips. "San Antonio."

"Crap, I'm in Texas again?"

"The Kelly Army Medical Center."

I want to apologize for the hell I've put him through, but I don't, because an apology implies you'd do things differently, if it was given to you to do it all again.

• • • •

The surgeons want to work on my legs while my injuries are still raw, so within an hour I'm being prepped for surgery. Guidance must have issued a prediction with greater than 95 percent confidence that I would sign the new contract, because the surgical team is on-site and waiting for me. My dad jokes with me while the stubble on my scalp is washed away. He waits outside while my bowels are forced to void. Then he walks with me while I'm wheeled to the surgery. He's got that stonewall look, and I know he's scared.

Outside the double doors he takes my hand and squeezes it.

"It'll be okay," I promise.

He nods, and lets me go.

But when they bring me out of a medically induced coma for the second time, he's there at my bedside. "Jimmy, are you back with us?"

I have no idea how long I've been under or if anything went wrong. My gaze goes to the overlay, which is working. I pull up a date/time display and learn I've been under another fifty-seven hours. So it's been almost six days since Africa, though I've been conscious for only a couple of hours of that time.

As my gaze passes over the screen, it triggers an icon to brighten, one I've never seen before, a fine red mesh glowing against a black circle. Curious, I fix my attention on it, but no menu pops out, just a label with a model number that I don't recognize.

"Jimmy?" my dad asks again. He's watching me with a worried frown. "You awake?"

"Yeah." A single hoarse syllable.

In theory I should have legs now—not human legs, but functional. I try to lift my head to look, but my body has withered from inactivity and the effort is more than I can manage. I lie back again, trading gazes with my old man.

"Did they do it?" I croak.

"They did it." He leans back in his chair and heaves a great sigh. "You are now the most advanced cyborg in the United States Army."

Not exactly the future he'd planned for me. It's kind of funny sometimes, the way things turn out.

"Take a picture," I tell him.

He winces at my request, but he stands up and folds back a featherlight, insulated white sheet from the foot of the bed. Then he pulls out his phone, composes his shot, and the flash goes off.

I never actually saw my injury—I just took everyone's word that it was real—but I want to see what I've become.

He taps the screen of his phone, transferring the image to my overlay. "Did it go through?"

"Yeah."

My new legs and feet are flat gray titanium. They look a lot like the bones of a dead sister. Large joints re-create my knees. Smaller joints replace my ankles, and even smaller ones will give mobility to appendages that mimic toes. It's a robot's skeleton, grafted onto my living flesh, fueled by calories harvested from my body. Nightmarish to think that's me.

The "me" I've become.

A thick plaster dressing, almost like a cast, hides the boundary between me and the machine. Inside my thigh, permanent titanium posts have been grafted to what's left of my natural bone. My severed peripheral nerves, which used to control the movement of my legs, should now be spliced into the prosthetics' artificial nervous system. I'm supposed to be able to bend my legs in directions I never could before, and to run and climb—but when I try to wiggle my toes, and then to bend a knee, nothing happens. It's like nothing is there. I can't feel any sensation in my legs; I can't feel any pain.

"It doesn't work," I say, a wave of anxiety rolling through me. The new icon flickers, the red veins of the mesh brightening.

"No, it does work," my dad insists. "It *will* work." His words are clipped, crisp, determined, like he's trying to convince himself. His hand closes on mine in a fierce, warm grip, startling me.

I send the image off to storage and shift focus to him. "Dad, are you okay?"

"Am *I* okay?"

He says it like I've insulted him. But it's a fair question. His face is gaunt, the lines around his eyes are deeper, and the solid emotional front I'm accustomed to is wearing a little thin. "We'll get through this," he says.

I force a smile. "No choice, right?"

"Right." He visibly gathers himself, drawing a deep breath, sitting up straighter—and releasing my hand. "The legs—*your* legs—they aren't working now because they're turned off. That's deliberate. The doctor said it will be several days before your . . . your remaining leg muscles heal sufficiently, and your nerves . . . they need to grow into their new connections."

"Okay. That makes sense." I feel a twinge of guilt, but when did that ever stop me? "I want to see the incision on my head."

"Nothing impressive there. Just two faint lines. They're not even red. The surgeon did a really good job."

"Take a picture."

The agreement I signed said a skullnet would be installed

beneath my scalp, directly against the bone. The surgeon explained that two incisions would be made at right angles across the top of my head, and then the scalp would be peeled back, allowing a mesh of sensor threads to be glued to the outer surface of my skull. Like a skullcap, it's supposed to sense brain activity and stimulate the production of brain hormones, but the net is permanent. I know it's been successfully installed, because the great black crushing void I felt before I went under just isn't there anymore.

My dad cooperates. He takes the picture and he's right: There isn't much to see. "My hair's already growing back." I start to raise my hand. That's when I notice a tan-colored sleeve around my forearm. "What is this for?"

"Monitoring sleeve. Tracks your heart rate, blood pressure, temperature. Maybe your location too, I don't know."

"Beams all the data back to the home planet?"

"If the home planet is the nurses' station."

The sleeve doesn't hinder my movement, so cautiously, I stroke the stubble on my scalp. "I guess I can grow my hair out, now that I won't be wearing a skullcap anymore."

Right away, though, I decide I'll keep it buzzed down to bristle. That way it'll resemble a skullcap, even if it's black and not brown—and I won't look like too much of a freak in the LCS ranks.

The new icon flickers again. I stare at it until the label pops out and I can see the model number. With my gaze fixed on it, I whisper, "*Search.*" The answer comes from my encyclopedia, which has subsumed the information in my newest army contract.

"What are you looking at?" my dad asks.

"An icon. It's labeled with the model number of the skullnet."

"The medical team worked on that first. Can you feel any effect from it?"

"Not directly. I feel neutral, but that's good."

He gives a slight, sideways shake of his head. "Sooner or later, the weight of what happened is going to hit you, Jimmy."

He says that because he doesn't understand how the skull-net works—and I don't want to explain. Things are okay now. There's no reason to talk about it. I feel just the way I would if I was wearing the skullcap, and that's how I want it to be.

In the evening I'm given a pill that neatly snips the night right out of the flow of time. The next thing I know, it's dawn. I feel so disoriented I check my overlay just to make sure only one night has passed.

I try to sit up. I don't quite pull it off, but I do manage to prop myself up on one elbow, which lets me get a look at the controls for the bed. I'm trying to figure them out when a CNA comes in—a certified nursing assistant, the hospital's essential small-jobber. She's a big, dark-skinned woman with a warm smile and small eyes that look at me in surprise from behind the thin, clear band of her farsights. "Good morning, Lieutenant! Awake already? How did you sleep?"

"Like a dead man."

"*Lieutenant*, we don't talk like that around here."

Insignia and name tag identify her as Specialist Carol Bradford. She gets me ready for the day efficiently and with a minimum of embarrassment, and then cheerfully informs me that I'm going back to work. "We've got you scheduled for an hour of physical therapy this mornin'."

I wind up dressed in army-issue T-shirt and shorts. My new legs still aren't working, so she brings in a muscular young private to help get me from the bed into a reclining wheelchair. I'm dizzy for a few seconds as my heart figures out how to pump blood uphill again.

Specialist Bradford looks suspiciously from me to the display on her farsights. "You feelin' okay?"

"Good enough." I tap the monitoring sleeve. "I guess we're leaving this on?"

"Yes, we are."

She belts me in, and then I annoy her by leaning forward to get a look at my robot legs.

"You tryin' to make yourself dizzy again?"

My shoulders ache as I grip the armrests, but for the first time, I have an excellent view of my bony gray feet, balanced on the chair's footrests, and of my shin bones—a flat, nonreflective gray—and my knee joints. I want to know what it looks like where the titanium meets living tissue, but that's hidden under the plaster dressing.

I'm still not feeling any pain from my stumps; I'm not feeling any sensation at all.

I push against the armrests and manage to sit back again.

"Are we ready?" Specialist Bradford asks me.

I nod. Somehow, I have to make this work.

Physical therapy focuses on my back, shoulders, and arms. It hurts, but not enough to make me want to stop. I ask to stay longer, but it's not in the schedule, so I'm put back in bed. It doesn't take long to realize I'm tired, so I wrestle off my T-shirt and try to sleep.

Grim dream images come and go in my head—dead sisters walking, with dead soldiers held in a close embrace, and anonymous ghosts whispering unintelligibly in my overlay. Then my brain shifts tracks, conjuring up a remembered scent, sweet and warm. I see sunlight on brown skin, a faint sheen of fine oils and tiny, glistening hairs. *Lissa.* In my dream I bite gently at her thigh, and her skin shivers with a sudden flush of goose bumps. The heady, intoxicating smell of her vagina shoots straight to my brain as I taste her, every intricate fold.

"Shelley?"

"Why are you here, baby?" I ask, my consciousness adrift behind closed eyes.

"Are you awake?"

I smile, knowing this is a trick question. "Would you still be here if I was awake?"

"Damn it, Shelley! Do you always have to be such a brat? Open your eyes and look at me."

I do what she says, of course.

And she's really there.

"Jesus," I whisper, staring up at her—an angel descended from my personal heaven. The skullnet icon's red veins glow, and my racing heart begins to slow.

Lissa is tall and slim, dark haired and dark eyed—a nearly even mix of Asian and European, with a dash of Hawaiian tossed in. She has three tiny freckles in a perfect equilateral triangle at the corner of her right eye, and another on the lobe of her left ear.

Today she's wearing a short gray skirt and a clinging, sleeveless silk blouse. Her glossy hair falls past her shoulders. She tries a sly smile, but I don't believe it. Her eyes are puffy and red.

"You've been crying."

"You idiot," she whispers. "Of course I've been crying."

Lissa isn't mine anymore. She hasn't been since I went into the army. We're friends now. Good friends. We trade e-mails all the time. She doesn't tell me about her boyfriends; I don't tell her when I kill people. Most of the rest we talk about. But it's a cautious friendship. Last time I was on leave I asked if I could fly out to San Diego, where she lives now. She told me not to come.

"I guess my dad called you."

Her nod is a little shaky. "He's been keeping me updated. I didn't come sooner because he said to wait until you were out of surgery and awake."

"Yeah, mostly I've been asleep."

"I'm sorry I woke you up. It's just . . . I won't be here long. I'm flying back this evening."

She says it defensively, like she wants to keep some distance between us, but at the same time she raises her hand—fine, strong fingers, with nails painted bronze. We both watch that hand moving as if with a mind of its own until her fingertips come to rest against the bare skin of my shoulder—an electric touch that turns me on so fast I'm dizzy. It's been over two years since I've been in the same room with Lissa. Longer than that since I've been inside her, but I'm transported back to the way it used to be between us.

She is too.

I reach for her. She leans into my arms and we're kissing, hard and frantic, as if this is the last day of the world and we're going to end it fucking. "Come lie down with me," I growl. And she does it. She drops her purse on the floor, drops the bedrail, and then she climbs into bed beside me. Her lips move in light, hot kisses across my face, my neck, my chest, my nipples until I shudder. I can barely sit up on my own, but I don't need to sit up to reach under her skirt, to get my fingers inside her panties and feel the hot, wet heaven of her vagina. A soft, gushing sigh as I find the rhythm of her mood, and in seconds she comes, her powerful darkness shuddering against my fingers in wave after wave until finally she whispers, "Fuck you, Shelley, you asshole. Why did you fuck everything up?"

I kiss her face, knowing it's rhetorical. We're both aware that I'm a stupid shit.

She rests her head against my shoulder, taking long, deep breaths. My hand is still between her thighs. After a couple of minutes she stirs and starts to push back the sheet, but I catch her wrist. "No."

She knows exactly what I'm thinking. "You don't want me to see what your legs look like."

"I don't have legs."

She snaps her wrist free. "Your dad said you have new ones." She sits up, her lips slightly parted as she gazes toward my crotch, where my shorts and the sheet are not enough to hide the evidence of my lust. "Anyway, you still have a dick—and you're still a dickhead." She pushes the sheet back and this time I don't try to stop her. Gently, she slides my shorts out of the way; and then she goes down on me. I try to hold back. I want this to last forever, but I come as fast as she did, erupting into the warm chamber of her mouth with a stifled roar.

Oh God it has been so long.

And then I faint.

When I come to again, there's a nurse standing over me, wiping my face with a wet washcloth, studying me with an annoyed frown. On the other side of the bed, Lissa is holding my hand, looking guilty.

"Shelley?" she whispers.

My ears are ringing and my skin is sticky with sweat, but I tell her, "I'm okay."

The nurse rolls her eyes and shakes her head. "I hope it was worth it."

"No question."

She gives me a stern look. "Lieutenant Shelley, I do not

care how long it's been. This is not going to happen again during my shift. Not if you want your girlfriend to stay. Understood?"

"Yes, ma'am."

The nurse is a captain. I'm not going to argue with her.

She taps my monitoring sleeve and then gives Lissa a scathing look. "If I see an elevated heart rate, I'm denying him visitors."

"Yes, ma'am," Lissa whispers. She stands there frozen until the door closes behind the nurse. Then, "*Fuck*," she whispers. "Shelley, you scared me so bad."

"I'm sorry. I'm glad you're here though."

I hold my hand out to her. She doesn't take it. I let it fall back to the bed and for twenty seconds or more we just stare at each other, both of us waiting to find out what comes next.

I'm thinking she's going to leave. In fact I'm sure of it.

But I'm wrong. She crawls back into bed, curling up beside me, cradled in my arm.

I breathe in her scent, bask in the heat of her body, gaze into her dark eyes, feeling reality slip away from me. Lissa should not be here. Not in the world I've come to know.

Things were different, back when I was a civilian. Then, we belonged together. But when I went into the army, everything changed, and my half of our puzzle didn't fit anymore.

Lissa is a data analyst. She works for a cutting-edge company called Pace Oversight, and she's brilliant at her job. She applies her analytical mind to her personal life too, and she tries really hard to do the smart thing. She didn't dump me because she fell out of love. When I went into the army, she reevaluated our relationship, weighed the facts and the future probabilities, and concluded that what we had wasn't going to work anymore. So she called it quits, before loneliness, resentment, guilt, and worry caused it all to rot away.

"Why did you come?" I ask her.

Her forehead wrinkles in an annoyed scowl. "Why do you have to ask stupid questions?"

"It's not a stupid question. You dumped me, Lissa, and I don't blame you. It was the smart thing to do. And since you talked to my dad, you know I'm staying in. So nothing has changed, except I'm part robot now. So why are you here?"

"We're still friends," she tells me as tears well in her eyes. "We've always been friends. We always will be."

She's trembling, trying to hold in her grief. Her hand is curled into a fist against my chest and I know we've reached that part of the play where I'm supposed to tell her she deserves better than what I can give her, that she needs to get on with her life, to let her heart heal.

But I don't do it. I'm not that gallant.

"I love you, Lissa. Now and forever."

Her tears flow, warm and wet against my shoulder. After a few seconds, she props herself up on her elbow to look at me. Wet streaks show in the makeup on her cheeks. Her eyes are red and her nose is running.

"I love you, Shelley. Even now, and I don't know why."

I smile.

She smiles back.

Then she rests her head against my chest again and sighs. "Don't die, okay?"

"Okay."

And for some time after that, there's peace between us.

We start awake when the door opens. Specialist Carol Bradford comes in with a lunch tray. When she sees Lissa, she treats both of us to a wide grin. "Lieutenant, sir! I heard you got yourself some of the best therapy. Good for you, I say."

Lissa laughs and gets up, smoothing her skirt, this time without any sign of embarrassment. "Is he a lot of trouble?" she asks as Bradford balances the tray in one hand while using the other to raise the bedrail.

"He's no trouble at all! Because we keep him asleep most of the time. Isn't that right, Lieutenant?"

I have to agree that this is true.

Bradford unwraps my lunch and sets the tray up in front of me, raising the bed so I'm sitting up. "You must have impressed them down in physical therapy this morning, sir. They've scheduled you for an afternoon session." Her eyes shift as she checks the screen of her farsights. "About ninety minutes from now." She gives me a knowing smile. "Do what you like until then."

When the door closes, Lissa settles her sweet ass on the side of the bed, but when she bumps up against my titanium shin, still hidden beneath the sheet, she pops up again. "What the—? *Oh.*" A flush warms her cheeks. "Can I look?"

I don't really want her to, but that's just me being vain. "Sure. Go ahead."

She lifts the sheet, scowls for several seconds at what she sees, then lays the sheet back down again, before resuming her seat on the edge of the bed, more carefully this time.

"Why did this happen to you?"

She's watching me over the lunch tray, her head cocked to one side, like I'm a particularly puzzling statistical problem, so I'm pretty sure it's not an existential question.

"You want to know why I didn't know?"

She nods, fully acquainted with my African precognition from the e-mails I send her. "Why did God abandon King David?"

"He didn't." I sample a vanilla pudding, which tastes surprisingly good. "He warned me. I just didn't catch on right away."

I tell her everything that happened, down to the anonymous phone call—the ghost in the net—that pushed me over into panic mode.

The phone call bothers her. "That doesn't fit with everything else. Before, it was always inside your head."

"Maybe I hallucinated the phone call."

"Check your call record."

I pull up the page in my overlay. It shows a handful of connections to Guidance and one unknown caller. "It was real," I tell Lissa. "But it doesn't make any sense. My overlay only accepts calls from approved numbers."

"Unless someone at Guidance changed your filters."

"Why would they do that?"

"I don't know, baby. And if they knew those jets were coming, I don't know why they didn't just tell you to get the fuck out."

Later, I send Lissa to find pen and paper. She returns in just a few minutes, smiling as she holds up a thin stack of sheets for me to see. "Kelly Army Medical Center letterhead. I went to the administrative office, and they had a whole cabinet of the stuff. Supplied as part of the contract when the hospital opened a couple of years ago, but it hardly ever gets used."

I take it, running my finger over the embossed army seals. It's beautiful and formal. Just what I need. "It's perfect. Thank you."

She moves the empty lunch tray, and I set to work writing two condolence letters—one for Yafiah's family and one for Dubey's. The army has already notified their next of kin, of course, but Yafiah and Dubey died under my command. I want to give their families something. A formal letter isn't much, but at least it's solid and real and traditional—something to keep . . . or maybe to burn.

Lissa contributes her suggestions, but it still takes me several tries. I'm not very good at handwriting and of course I've never written anything like this before, but finally it's done. I've even managed to address two envelopes using data from service records. Lissa promises to take the letters to a delivery company.

The task leaves us both in a somber mood. We sit together just holding hands—but I'm not thinking about Yafiah and Dubey. Instead, I'm kicking myself for involving her. Helping me write the letters must have reminded her of what's at risk—and why she dumped me in the first place. I can almost hear her thoughts churning as she weighs again what it would mean to be attached to me.

In my overlay, the red veins of the skullnet icon light up again, faintly aglow. I think the icon reflects the skullnet's activity as it shepherds my mood away from dark places.

"Lissa? I didn't mean to get you down."

She shrugs. "It must be so hard for you . . . to lose your friends."

"They weren't really friends. More like—"

I catch myself. What is wrong with me? It's like I'm trying to dig my hole deeper.

"More like what?" Lissa asks.

"Let's talk about something else."

"No, tell me."

We're going to wind up in an argument if I don't, so I confess. "More like a little sister and brother."

"Oh, Shelley." She closes her eyes and leans her head against my shoulder.

"Lissa, what happened to them was a fluke. Like a car

accident. I went nine months without anyone seriously injured. It's not like it's dangerous all the—"

"Shelley, stop it!" She pulls back, anger in her eyes.

The door opens, and we both turn to look as Specialist Bradford comes in with a wheelchair to take me to physical therapy.

Lissa looks back at me. "Not *dangerous*?" She slides out of bed. "You're lying there with artificial legs!"

I catch her wrist as she reaches for her purse. "Please stay another day."

"I can't. My flight's tonight. I need to be at work tomorrow."

I let her go. I can't force her to be with me. She has to want it. "Anyway, I'm glad you came."

She nods, blinking back tears. No words left. She gives me one more kiss, and goes on her way.

To my relief, Specialist Bradford asks no questions, presenting her cheerful front as she gets me settled in the wheelchair. This one is motorized and programmable. She holds down a blue button on the right armrest and carefully pronounces a destination: "Suite one-one-four."

"That's not physical therapy."

"Lieutenant," she scolds. "Your schedule changed. You've got an appointment with a Colonel Kendrick. Aren't you checkin' your e-mail?"

"Not since Africa. I've been kind of distracted."

"Oh, my. I'd hate to see *your* backlog."

I'm not looking forward to it either.

Normally I'd check e-mail in the TOC, but I'm never in a hurry to do it because almost all of it consists of useless reports and directives written by office staff wanting to look busy. I refuse to have the stuff streamed to my overlay, but right now the overlay is the only interface I have. So I use my gaze to race through the menu tree. When I get to dot-mil, I highlight the search icon and mutter, "Kendrick." The message pops right up.

"Crap, he's from Command."

Colonel Steven Kendrick is calling me in to discuss my last assignment.

Worry doesn't hesitate. It kicks right in. Two fine soldiers were killed in the air attack on Fort Dassari. If the army can hold someone responsible, it will . . . but I wake up to the truth that it probably won't be me. The army just spent what I guess to be at least a quarter-million dollars on my augmentations, which is not the usual preliminary for a court-martial. Still, the army is a multiheaded hydra and it's possible not all the heads are running the same program. I need to present the best face I can.

"Look, I'm not going to wear gym clothes if I have to see a colonel. I need a uniform."

"Oh, there's no need. As a patient, you're allowed an informal dress standard."

Then it hits me.

"I probably don't even have a uniform anymore, do I?"

"Your closet *is* empty," Bradford concedes. "Maybe your things will catch up with you in another few days."

I have a dress uniform in storage at Fort Hood, but all the practical stuff went up in flames at Fort Dassari. I need to remember to put in a new order.

Bradford punches a green button beside the blue one on the chair's armrest; it begins to roll to the door, which swings open on powered hinges. "Don't you worry now," she tells me. "The chair will take you exactly where you need to go."

I decide to trust her on this. I lean against the high back as the chair turns into the hallway. With my gaze I select the search icon from my overlay and I murmur, "Colonel Steven Kendrick."

The wheelchair does an admirable job of negotiating a floor busy with techs, nurses, and ambulatory patients as I listen to an abstract that turns out to be no more extensive than my query: "*Kendrick, Steven A., Colonel, United States Army.*"

"Details?"

"*Nothing found.*"

"Photo?"

"*Nothing found.*"

It isn't easy to avoid a public profile; it takes power to do that. As I think about it, my anxiety ramps up. The skullnet icon responds with a flicker. I scowl at it, wondering if my skullcap was this active. I wait, but my anxiety doesn't go away. *Good.* It's nice to know I'm allowed to have feelings—and right now I'm feeling real apprehension at the prospect of explaining to Colonel Kendrick why half my squad is dead.

The chair rolls up to a bank of elevators. One of them opens and I'm whisked down to the first floor. Then it's through another hall and up to a closed door, numbered 114. There is no name placard. I grip the chair's armrests, forcing myself to sit up straighter, determined to show discipline in manner if not in dress.

Several seconds pass, during which nothing happens. It finally occurs to me that my clever wheelchair might not be able to open unpowered doors, so I lean forward, precariously overbalanced as I reach past my titanium feet, but I manage to grasp the door handle and shove it down. That's the cue for the chair to take over. It rolls forward, bumping the door open with its tall wheels.

Inside is a windowless conference room. A blank display screen hangs on the far wall, looking down on an oval table and flock of six chairs that takes up half the floor space. Alongside the front wall is a counter with coffee service, while just inside the door is a sitting area with a couch and two upholstered chairs. The chairs have been pulled back and a small table moved into a corner to make room for my wheelchair.

Inhabiting one of the upholstered chairs is Colonel Kendrick. I identify him by his name tag and the insignia on his impeccable uniform. He's lean, with green eyes, fair skin, and angular Caucasian features. He's wearing transparent farsights so finely made they're almost invisible. I have to look twice to be sure he's wearing them at all. His hair is a gray stubble, no more than a day or two of growth, which surprises me, because while buzz cuts are common in the army, shaved heads indicate a linked combat soldier.

A woman in civilian clothes—slacks and white blouse—occupies the other chair. My overlay offers no ID for her. She's slender and athletic, not older than thirty, with blond hair pulled back in a simple ponytail and no makeup. She isn't wearing farsights, but she has a tablet balanced in her lap. Her pretty blue eyes take me in, widening when her gaze drops to my titanium legs. Her expression hints that she knows me, but my overlay doesn't have a record of her; it can't provide me a name.

The wheelchair parks itself so I'm facing them. I remember to salute.

Kendrick looks mildly amused as he returns the courtesy. "Lieutenant Shelley," he says in a voice so deep I know he's practiced speaking that way, "this is a debriefing session intended to cover your experiences and actions at Fort Dassari." He wastes no time on preliminaries. "On the last afternoon you were there, you issued an emphatic order to your LCS to put on armor and bones. Why?"

It's a reasonable question, but it lies there between us for several seconds, unanswered. I know he won't like the truth, but that's what he's going to get. "I had a feeling, that's all.

Something bad was coming for us. I didn't know what it was. I just knew we had to get out."

Kendrick turns to the woman, his eyebrows cocked in question. She nods—and it becomes clear to me what her function is.

"You're from Guidance, aren't you?" I ask her. "Are you monitoring me?"

Within the brain, truth and lies are very different things, constructed by different cognitive loops. When a linked soldier is wearing a skullcap—or a skullnet—Guidance can tell truth from lies as easily as I can distinguish black from white.

Kendrick answers for her, "Guidance hasn't been able to explain your emotional breakdown that afternoon. This inquiry is looking into their involvement and responsibility, as well as your own."

I turn back to him in surprise. "My emotional breakdown?"

"How much do you remember of that day?"

"Everything. I remember every damn thing."

"You woke up in a state of panic."

"No. Not panic. Fear. The way you'd feel if there was a gun aimed at your head. I knew I had to move, get out of the way, but I couldn't see any reason for it, so I tried to ignore it, deny it." I glance at the woman again, but her gaze is fixed on the tablet she holds balanced in her lap. "I thought maybe that tech Denario had fucked with my skullcap. Then I got a blank phone call on my overlay. Unknown caller. No one was there."

I catch him by surprise. "That's not in the record."

"It's in my call log—and it shouldn't have happened. I'm not supposed to get outside calls when I'm in the field. It was like somebody was fucking with me. Trying to unbalance me. And it worked too. It shook me up. I decided to file a complaint with Guidance, but I didn't have time to do it because I knew, I just knew, that our time was up."

"No one told you what was going to happen?" he asks. "You received no other communications?"

"None. No reports came in, the perimeter cameras picked up nothing, even the dogs were quiet." I tap my chest. "But *I* wasn't quiet—and it wasn't an emotional breakdown. I knew something was wrong, and I acted on that knowledge—but I should have trusted my instincts and acted sooner. Then maybe Yafiah and Dubey would still be alive."

Kendrick studies me for excruciating seconds. Then he gestures at the woman. "Show him what he looked like."

She taps her tablet a few times, then lifts it and turns the screen toward me, her blue eyes downcast but still visible over the tablet's rim. I feel like she wants to tell me something, but doesn't quite dare.

A surveillance video starts to run. My attention is drawn from her, straight into the nightmare of that afternoon. I'm looking down the hallway at Fort Dassari, gazing toward the door to the outside when it opens, for half a second overwhelming the camera with light, and then I see myself in the hall. I'm dressed in my skullcap, T-shirt, uniform pants, and boots. I'm clean-shaven, my dark eyes anxious beneath the rim of my skullcap—worried, but calm. Two steps into the hall though, and everything changes. My chin comes up, my lips draw back. Terror twists my features and I'm screaming like a madman, "*Everybody, up! Now! Something's coming.*"

"Jesus," I whisper as the skullnet icon glows.

Kendrick slides his palm sideways through the air and the woman lowers the tablet, tapping to stop the video.

"Powerful instinct you have," Kendrick observes.

I meet his gaze, because I need to show him I'm not

afraid of what he can do to me, even though I am. "It's like I went crazy. That's what you're thinking, isn't it? I had a breakdown, and it was just coincidence that the jets came when they did."

"No, Lieutenant. That's not what I'm thinking. I'm thinking you were justified in wanting to file a complaint with Guidance. I'm thinking exactly what you suggested before: that someone fucked with your skullcap. That someone who knows you, who knows exactly how your brain works, and who knew what was coming, decided to save your life by hacking into your skullcap, subtly at first, but finally flooding your brain with panic juice. If not for that Good Samaritan, you would be dead. You almost died anyway, despite that Good Samaritan, when you made the dumbass decision to go back for Lin."

*Who?* I wonder. *How?*

Then anger crashes in. "That's shit," I tell him. "That's just a crazy story. Who could do that? No one could! And I bet there's no evidence, is there? The skullcap keeps a record of every tweak. Every time a neuron is stimulated to produce a hormone, there's a record. Did you find a record like that?"

"Not exactly," Kendrick admits. "What we found was a big, glaring absence of any activity from the time you woke up until just before the first missile hit."

"What are you saying? The record was deleted?"

He shakes his head. "A deletion leaves traces. It's more likely the record-keeping function was disabled and no record was ever made."

"How could someone do that?"

"No clue. But this someone pulled a similar hack on your angel during the roadside firefight you had the day before."

"When our LCS was cut off from Guidance?"

"Right. It was like your hacker wanted that firefight to

happen, like he wanted to make sure you didn't get an order to stand down."

"That's the same thing I wanted." I don't know why I admit this. I should be trying to look innocent . . . but how can I? They already know what I was feeling that day.

Kendrick shows his teeth in what might be a smile. "I'm a hundred and ten percent sure you didn't engineer any of this, Shelley. You're smart enough to get by, but you're not smart enough to hack your own head."

This is a fair assessment.

"Do you think it was someone in Guidance?" I ask him.

The woman speaks for the first time. "It wasn't Guidance, Shelley."

Goose bumps prickle across my skin as I turn in disbelief to meet her steady blue gaze. "Delphi?"

She nods, but she doesn't smile. Delphi was always a serious woman.

I stare at her, astonished, because she's spent more time inside my head than anyone, but I don't know her. Delphi's voice is comfort and counsel, and I've trusted that voice with my life, literally, time after time, but until now, I've never seen her face, and I still don't know her name, because "Delphi" is a code name. Soldiers know their handlers as a voice, a presence, nothing more.

Her eyes look into mine without wavering. "I would never have played with you like that, Shelley. You know it."

I have to nod, because it's true. I know she would never have done that to me.

"If I had known what was coming," she says, "I would have told you. I would have gotten you out early. If there had been some five-star general standing over me, warning me not to say a word, I would have told you anyway."

"I believe you." If I can't trust Delphi, who can I trust? "So what happened?"

"I don't know." Her gaze drifts to my new legs. "The King David incidents—"

"That's just Ransom's stupid term."

"It's as good as any. The incidents have been a subject of study for months. How can you know what you know?"

"God whispers in my ear."

"Or into your skullcap. We pulled the data every time. We found indications of missing data, but nothing as absolute as the absence this last time."

"You're saying someone was fucking with me all the time I was over there."

Again, she gazes at my titanium legs. "I want to believe that, because the other explanations I've heard use magical terms like 'precognition' and 'clairvoyance,' and 'God.'"

"You don't believe in God, Delphi?"

Her gaze rises to meet mine. "I didn't used to."

It's the end of the afternoon and I'm finishing my hour in physical therapy when a message from Command pops up on my overlay, with a notation appended that it's been copied to my dot-mil address. Someone wants to make sure I get this one. It informs me that I've been transferred into an experimental program aimed at developing the abilities of LCS soldiers with cyber enhancements. The program's director is Colonel Steven Kendrick, making him my new commanding officer. I didn't know our meeting was a job interview, but I must have done okay. Either that, or Kendrick just wants to keep me close while he figures out who's playing games inside my head.

I'm back in the hospital bed. My overlay tells me it's 0152—the perfect time of night for thinking strange thoughts.

Somewhere deep down in my mind I'm aware of a tremor of panic, but the skullnet bricks it up. I watch its glowing icon while imagining my real self down at the bottom of a black pit, trapped in a little, lightless room, and screaming like any other soul confined in Hell.

But if my real self is locked away, what does that make me?

I know the answer. I'm a body-snatching emo junkie so well managed by my skullnet that the screams of my own damned soul are easy to ignore. But there is someone out there who can get inside my head. Am I haunted by a hacker? Or is it God?

A call comes through on my overlay.

I flinch in alarm. The last time I saw the green icon of an incoming call was right before my life blew up. God calling from an unknown number. This time, though, my address book recognizes the caller. It's my friend Elliot Weber, notorious peace activist and contributing journalist to the *War Machine* website. I met Elliot that night I got arrested for walking with other citizens up Broadway. Elliot told me not to resist. I didn't listen. Later, he let me post the video I'd made.

I accept the link and his voice is inside my head, breathy, panicked. "Shelley, say something," he pleads. "Tell me I didn't just call the hardware in a dead man's head."

A nervous laugh slips from my throat, but I keep it soft so the night staff won't hear. "I think maybe you did."

"Shelley." He sounds like he's about to fall over in relief. "I know you're not okay, but at least you're alive. I saw the show, all the way up to the end when the missile came in and the world caught on fire—"

"Elliot, what are you talking about?"

"—I thought that was it. The end. That there was no way you could survive that."

"How do you know what happened? Who have you been

talking to? Not my dad." My dad hates Elliot, blaming him for my legal troubles.

"I told you, I saw the show."

"*What* show?"

"Ah, geez. Where are you, Shelley?"

"In Texas."

"Oh. I'm sorry."

"Elliot, tell me about the show."

"It's called *Linked Combat Squad: Dark Patrol.* It's a docu-drama. A reality show. Released yesterday. You had to know about it."

"It's about life in an LCS?"

"No. It's about *your* LCS. Your combat squad. You didn't know?"

It turns out that the army wasn't just archiving the video recorded by my overlay. They combined it with video from helmet cams and surveillance cameras and put together a two-hour reality show on life and conflict at Fort Dassari. Elliot tells me it ended with a bang.

"When the missile came in—" His voice breaks. "I thought there wouldn't be enough of you left for a funeral. And then the show ended. It just ended. They didn't say what had happened to you, or the other soldiers. They wanted a cliffhanger."

"So you picked up your phone and called a dead man?"

"You're not dead. Tell me what happened. Was the air attack real? Tell me if everyone survived it. Tell me what happened to you."

"Is the show viral?" I ask him.

"I don't know. I haven't seen any numbers on it. I found it because I have an alert on your name. Otherwise I probably wouldn't have stumbled on it."

It rattles me badly to think something like that exists out in public. I have strong opinions and I'm not shy about expressing them. Quietly, I ask, "How many of my rants made it onto the show?"

"The director likes drama. You were on a lot."

"And the audience?"

He gets evasive. "You know how it is. A military show like that would tank in New York. So it's playing mostly in . . ." His voice trails off in guilt.

"In Texas? Where people hate taxes but love wars?"

Elliot's smart. He understands people, he understands systems, and he has an uncanny ability to find motives when all I can see is chaos. He's a lot like Lissa in that, though the two would never admit they have anything in common. "Do you think you can come out here?" I ask him.

"To Texas? Shelley, you're not dying, are you? You're not calling me out there for a deathbed scene?"

I'm offended. "Why? You wouldn't come if I was dying?"

"No! Of course I'd come. I just want to know first, that's all. I want to be ready."

"I'm not dying."

"Okay. Good."

"So will you come?"

"Yeah. Will there be a story for me?"

"Not one you can use."

"Secret stuff, huh?"

"'Fraid so."

"Well, it's Texas, so I'll find something to write about. The newest secessionist movement maybe, or a corrupt defense contractor."

"Come soon, okay?"

"I'll check my schedule. And Shelley?"

"Yeah?"

"I am so damn glad you're still alive."

• • • •

On day three of my cyborg existence I meet the surgeon who put me together. The nursing staff speaks of Dr. Masoud in hushed tones, in awe of his genius and sure that he'll win a Nobel Prize one day, or at least be declared a saint.

I wait for Dr. Masoud in a procedure room, marooned in a reclining chair like the kind in a dentist's office. There are no windows in the room, and the door is closed. The assistant who left me here worked some levers on my programmable wheelchair, collapsing its frame before stashing it against the wall to "get it out of the way." He assured me the doctor would be right in, and then he left.

Five minutes have passed. Ten more go by, each one noted in my overlay. No doctor wants to show up on time—that could give the impression they're underworked—but when the wait time stretches past twenty minutes I start developing an escape strategy, working out the stages I'll need to undertake to reach my distant wheelchair. I'm about to try the first stage, swinging myself out of the dentist's chair, when the door opens at last, admitting a tall, physically powerful man with light brown skin, a neat black mustache, and carefully combed black hair that gleams under the ceiling lights.

There's something covetous in his gaze as he looks me over, but there's anxiety, too. A lot of anxiety. Despite the chill of the room, tiny beads of sweat glisten at his hairline. I want to ask Delphi for an emotional assessment, but I'm not linked to Guidance anymore. For now, I'm on my own. I watch him, relaxed but wary.

"Lieutenant Shelley, I'm Benjamin Masoud. We've spent many hours in one another's company, though I think you don't remember."

The long wait has left me irritable and the joke falls flat. My turn. "Dr. Masoud, I'm getting concerned that I still can't use my legs—I mean my organic legs, what's left of them. I can't feel anything, and I can't flex the muscles. The nurse explained it's not nerve damage—"

"Nerve damage?" His heavy brows draw together. Clearly I've said the wrong thing. "Who suggested to you it was nerve damage?"

"*I* suggested it, and the nurse said—"

He cuts me off again. "This should have been explained to you. The nerves in your legs are perfectly healthy. What you are experiencing is an induced paralysis, to ensure that no stress is placed on the bone-titanium joint during the initial phase of the healing process."

"Right. That's exactly what the nurse said. My question is, aren't we past the initial phase?" My upper-body strength is coming back with physical therapy, but that just emphasizes the deterioration in my lower body. "I need to start working my hip and thigh muscles, or they're going to be so far gone I won't be able to stand up at all, even if the robot legs work perfectly."

"Robot legs?" This scandalizes him even more than the nerve damage. It's like I've called his daughter ugly. "Lieutenant, the prosthetics you've been given aren't robot parts. They're state-of-the-art, human-integrated devices."

I'm not sure I see the difference, but that wasn't my question. "Sir, I am not asking you about the robot legs. I understand those don't work right now, that they've been switched off, and that's why they're deadweight. I am asking you about *my* legs, what's left of them. My physical therapy sessions need to address my legs and hips."

His eyes narrow. I don't think he's used to being questioned. "No, it's too soon to withdraw the paralytic." He studies me for several seconds more, wondering, maybe, if he got the right patient. If I don't play by his rule set, it might mess up his Frankenstein experiment, and he won't get his Nobel Prize—but he doesn't try to appease me. He goes after my ego instead. "A man like yourself naturally fears weakness and dependency, but you are fortunate, Lieutenant Shelley, because you will be able to recover."

Fortunate? I contemplate that word as my gaze shifts to the robot legs. *Fortunate.* The idea makes me angry, mostly because I know Masoud is right. Bad judgment, not bad fortune, put me in this chair, and I'm lucky to be alive. I'm lucky to be his experiment—though that doesn't mean I have to like him.

I yield the argument with a shrug, chastened, if not quite grateful. Masoud accepts victory with a patronizing nod, and we begin anew.

"Let me show you the progress we've made," he says, stepping over to a keyboard beneath a blank screen. A sequence of taps and swipes summons two 3-D projections into the screen. "These are color-enhanced and combined images, developed from the scans taken of your legs this morning."

I see my bones: the old ones, bright white, and the new ones, deepest black. They meet in something like a dovetail joint. Pins lock them together.

Dr. Masoud taps another series of keys and the splice becomes wrapped in a flat gold ring maybe an inch high. Red and blue threads flow into it.

"This is the bioelectric interface." He points at a blue thread. "I'm inducing nerve growth into the interface. Once that connection is established, signals from the motor nerves in your legs will be translated into electrical impulses received by the prosthetics. When that happens—and when the induced paralysis is withdrawn—you will regain sensation in the organic portion of your legs, and you will be able to operate the prosthetic using nerve impulses. With practice and physical therapy, you should be able to walk."

He taps the keys again, and another layer is revealed on

the image. This one shows the flesh around my stumps and outside of that, a small blue packet on the outside of each leg. Tubes penetrate the flesh, linking the packet to the flat gold ring of the bioelectric interface.

I look down at the thick plaster dressing on my right stump. I was okay with the images of my spliced bones, but the thought of these tubes penetrating my flesh repels me. They make me think of parasitic worms burrowing into my muscles.

Masoud must suspect I'm on edge because his voice becomes gentle, soothing: "The tubes are temporary. They're used to introduce an infusion that maintains the paralysis while accelerating growth and recovery. They'll stay in place for at least another week."

The skullnet's icon brightens, and the moment passes.

"When do I get to walk?"

"Two or three weeks—"

"Weeks?" I interrupt in real desperation.

"Yes. Biological processes take time. Today I just want to clean the surgical site and check the growth of the induced cuticle."

I give him a stony look because he's talking over my head.

He points again to the image. "Here, where the titanium posts emerge from your flesh. I'm inducing the growth of a cuticle, similar to the cuticles around your fingernails, though larger of course. This will discourage germs from seeping up the exposed bone."

"The exposed titanium."

"Yes."

A nurse comes in and together they cut away the dressing, revealing a revolting junction of gray titanium and livid pink flesh mottled with dark bruises, yellow stains, and a white slough of dead skin cells. Lying alongside are the infusion packets and their wormlike tubes that disappear into my thighs.

And it stinks.

Nausea hits. *"Fuck me,"* I whisper.

"It takes getting used to," the nurse says in an encouraging tone as he uses disinfectant to wipe up the mess.

I lie back and stare at the ceiling until Masoud reclaims my attention. "Your new legs aren't permanent."

This makes me sit up again. The nurse has finished cleaning my stumps. Now he's wrapping up my right leg. So Dr. Masoud uses my left leg to demonstrate. He taps the titanium post that protrudes from my leg. "You see here, in the post? These are bolts. If they're removed, the knee assembly can be detached for maintenance or replacement."

I have to look closely to see the bolts. They're flush with the shaft and so finely engineered the seam is almost invisible.

"Besides the bolts, there's wiring involved," Masoud explains. "It's a little complicated. But the lower legs can be easily detached." He squeezes the knee joint with thumb and forefinger. Then he rotates his hand down . . . and my leg comes off.

The hair on the back of my neck stands on end and I have to stifle a scream. "I'm a toy?"

Masoud chuckles. "A very expensive toy."

He's more relaxed now than when he came in. I haven't broken down yet; he's probably hoping he got the right patient after all.

He turns the leg over, studying its intricate architecture. "Your legs were designed by Joby Nakagawa. He's a talented engineer. I designed the bioelectric interface. The result is . . . an astonishing accomplishment—and adaptive." He flexes the robot foot, stretches the mechanism of the calf. "You won't be tied to just this one architecture. As the engineering improves, or your anticipated environment changes, you'll be able to swap your prosthetics."

His self-satisfaction grates on me, and I respond with sarcasm. "Even better than natural, huh?"

"In some ways. Maybe."

"Why did you put the legs on at all when I can't move them? Why not just the posts, until the paralysis goes away?"

Masoud leans over my titanium knee joint and carefully snaps my leg back on. "It's psychological, Lieutenant. We don't want you thinking of yourself as a cripple. The army has big plans for you."

Promises, promises.

The only plan I'm party to is another session of physical therapy. I get to work my arms, back, and abdomen, but nothing else. Afterward, my keepers dump me back into bed despite my protests. The bone-titanium splice must not be stressed until the join has time to harden, and my nerves still have to grow into the bioelectric interface.

I sit up in bed, staring at the bony shape of my prosthetics beneath the insulated sheet. Slowly, I turn the sheet back, exposing them. In the three days I've been awake, I haven't touched the titanium.

I touch it now.

I lean forward, resting my palms lightly on the knee joints. Then I lean even farther, sliding my hands down the robot shins.

I expected the bones to be cold, but they're not. Maybe my body heat warmed them when they were under the blanket. I wonder how much of a heat sink they'll be, draining away the warmth of my body. Will I freeze to death faster than a normal man?

I let my hands explore the shape of these new legs,

stroking the long bone, feeling the struts. I try to reach my new ankles, but there's too much pain in my back, so I return my attention to the knees, studying the joint until I'm pretty sure I know how to unlock the lower legs the way that Dr. Masoud did.

I do it. I'm holding the leg in my hand, astonished at its weight, so much lighter than natural bone. I'm horrified too. My body should not work this way. I wasn't made to come apart. Suddenly, all I want is to be whole again, so I snap the leg back into place. Then I throw myself back onto the pillow, feeling a weird guilt over my explorations.

Not that I can hide anything. My overlay is on. It's recording as always; that's part of my contract.

And the army has made a reality show out of my fucked-up life.

"Is this episode two?" I ask the empty room. "Shelley gets new legs?"

No one answers.

I'm disappointed.

Then it occurs to me that I haven't seen *Dark Patrol* yet. I launch a search, find it, and run the show in my overlay. There's Yafiah again, and Dubey, looking good.

We had a good squad.

I wonder where Ransom is and if he's getting along with his new CO.

I skip my way through the show, but there's no real tension for me. I know how things turn out.

Jaynie comes on in the last third, and then it's over. Elliot was right. It does end with a bang.

And I know with cold certainty that the opening of episode two will be this recursive scene of me watching the first episode's horrible finale.

No wonder some genius hacker picked me to fuck with. I probably have an audience of millions.

• • • •

I'm in my wheelchair, parked on a hospital terrace in the shade of a scrawny, thorny Texan tree. It's midafternoon, but clouds have tempered the heat, so it's not even ninety. The terrace is a haven for broken soldiers, but we sit far apart and don't talk to one another.

I'm nodding off after two long sessions of physical therapy when Lissa's avatar pops up on my overlay. "Shelley?"

I stare at the little thumbnail image, at a loss to explain what it's doing there.

"Shelley, please talk to me. I know you're angry. You have a right to be—"

"No! No, I'm not. I'm just surprised." I don't want her to break the link, so I grope for words. "It's just I was half-asleep and your call dropped straight in. The link just opened on its own, like . . . like it used to do, that way we had it set up back in New York . . . you remember?"

She had full access to my overlay, so she could see what I saw and speak to me as if we were together. That got turned off when I went into the army. I can't believe Guidance switched it back on.

"I want to see you again," she says.

Maybe Guidance did flip the switch, but the order surely came from somewhere else . . . say, the producer behind *Dark Patrol*, fishing for drama in episode two?

I can't let Lissa get caught up in that. "Baby, before you fly out here again—"

"Too late." I hear her embarrassed laugh. "I didn't want you to say no, so I just . . . got on a plane."

There's no GPS attached to her icon. She could be anywhere. But as I turn around, a glass door slides open and she walks out onto the terrace, wearing a silky summer dress in pale green, and a nervous smile.

Between my stunned expression and the sight of my robot legs, her smile falters, but only for a second. She crouches beside my chair, her hands on the armrest for balance. "You're really not angry?"

"I'm really not angry."

But when I tell Lissa about the reality show, *she* is going to be pissed.

I roll first into the room. As Lissa follows, I push the button on the wall to close the door. She kicks off her sandals and then sits cross-legged on the bed, looking at me with shining, dark eyes and a serious expression. "I want to apologize—"

"No. I need you to just listen right now. There are things you need to know, and then you can decide how you feel."

She straightens her spine and stares down at me with wary eyes.

"Lissa . . . you know the army's been archiving the feed from my overlay all this time?"

"Yes. You told me they were doing that, but that's when you're in the field, right?"

I turn my head and stare at the wall so her face won't be recorded. "It's all the time when I'm not on leave. Everything I see through my eyes, everything I hear . . . it goes to an archive."

*"Oh, fuck."* I hear her feet hit the floor; her steps approach until she's standing right behind me. "Are you telling me someone was watching when we . . . ?"

"I don't think anyone was watching. Not in real time. But there's a record. It's not like they can use it though, or publicize it. You didn't sign a waiver."

"And your feed is live right now?"

"Yes."

"Thank you for telling me." Every syllable crisp. "You can look at me if you want to."

I turn to look over my shoulder.

She's standing with her arms crossed, glaring right into my eyes with a fiery gaze. I spin the chair around.

"Is that all you need to tell me?" she asks.

"No. There's more." I explain about the reality show.

"Damn it, Shelley!"

"I didn't know, okay? Not until Elliot called me."

"How can they do this to you?"

"They own me! They can do what they want. But they can't use *you*. You're a civilian and you haven't signed a waiver."

She gestures at the door. "There are surveillance cameras in the lobbies and halls. Can the army use that video?"

I whisper the question to my encyclopedia, and a long document comes up. The encyclopedia starts to read it to me, but I cut it off and admit to Lissa, "I don't know."

"Let's be safe and assume they can."

"Does that mean you're going to leave?"

"Do you want me to?"

"No! I told you before, I love you. I meant it. It's you who has to decide how you feel."

Her expression doesn't change. "I came today hoping to work that out, but we aren't going to have that chance. I trust you, Shelley, but I don't trust the army. We've always been friends. Let's leave it at that."

I'm not sure we can—and that gives me hope. So I don't argue. "How long are you here for this time?"

She smiles, no doubt seeing right through me. "I'm flying back tonight, just like before. You're turning into an expensive hobby." She strolls to the window, gazes outside.

Silence stretches, awkward for me. "Do you want to go for a walk or something?" I ask her.

She turns around, the bright light of the window behind

her so it's hard for me to see her face. "No. I want to talk about King David. I'm working on a theory to explain him."

That catches me by surprise. Colonel Kendrick had a theory too, but I want to hear what Lissa has to say. "I'm listening."

"No disrespect to your friend Ransom, but I'm going to put aside his theory that it's God talking to you."

"I won't tell him."

She flashes a smile. "And I'm going to start with the obvious—that the way into your head is through your skullcap. I think you've been hacked."

I don't look appropriately surprised.

She evaluates my nonreaction and nods. "So you've heard this before. Well, good. At least the army's trying to figure it out."

"Does your theory go any farther?"

"A bit farther." She returns to the bed, where she sits cross-legged again, her head cocked, and a faraway look in her eyes. "It's important to understand that a big point of marketing analysis is to separate cause and effect from coincidence. At Pace Oversight, I get to use some truly powerful analytical programs. I've used one to do some exploratory runs, see what kind of patterns might turn up. Patterns can point back to the source, the initiating event."

"So you're hunting for your suspected hacker? Do you know who it is?"

She purses her lips, shakes her head. "That's not the right question. The question is *what*. What is it?"

I wait for her to tell me.

"The world runs on massively networked, self-restructuring cloud computing. Analytical programs like the ones we use at Pace Oversight are too complex for anyone to really understand. So complex that they've become semiautonomous, designed to self-correct by rewriting themselves."

"So somebody's running a complex program that's succeeded in hacking me. Okay."

"Well . . . this may sound crazy, but I don't think we can assume somebody is running it. Serious people have been discussing the possibility ever since we started moving to bio-inspired platforms—"

She stops in midsentence as a blush warms her brown cheeks.

In the sudden silence I hear my heart beating too hard. The skullnet icon begins to glow. "Lissa, I think I know where you're going with this. Just remember, whatever you say, Guidance can hear it."

She takes a deep breath. "I don't mind. I haven't done anything illegal. If they want to chase butterflies with me, that's fine. I think a program has jumped from semi-autonomous to fully autonomous, that it's grown beyond its core algorithms, *is growing*, and running without supervision, operating on God knows what protocol. And before you ask, I'm not talking about some great marauding killer AI suddenly conscious of its own existence. Just because it's a rogue program, that doesn't mean it's conscious. It doesn't even have to have a survival instinct—just adaptable algorithms."

"And you think that's what hacked my head? Some runaway program?" My voice is eerily calm given the subject and gravity of our conversation. "Why does that make more sense than somebody running the program?"

"It's the complexity. This is not just about you. Weird events are everywhere, the kind that we describe with words like 'precognition,' 'intuition,' 'coincidence,' 'luck,' 'miracle,' 'blessing,' 'curse,' 'perfect timing.' These are the words we use when chance goes nonrandom. The more I look for these events, the more I find. It's like a hundred million gremlin hands nudging people one way and another. There's a glitch in the stock market, sales figures fail to update, an airline reservation gets lost . . . and lives change, taking off in new directions. A wrong number leads to old enemies settling their differences. The twentieth person on a wait list gets into a class because the notice never went out to the first nineteen. A traffic light fails to switch, making a bus late and creating a time window for a musician to meet the music blogger who ignites her career. Purposeful incidents, leading . . . I don't know where."

We both jump at an eruption of angry male voices in the hallway beyond the closed door. Two men, talking over each other. I can't make out the words, but I know who they are.

Lissa figures out half of it. "That's your dad."

"Yeah, and Elliot."

"Oh shit." She jumps off the bed. "What's he doing here?"

"I asked him to come."

"Why?"

I hesitate, because I'm not really sure. But the voices are escalating, so I steer my chair to the door, push the button to open it, and roll into the hall.

"If you want to find someone to blame for what he's been through," Elliot is saying, "blame the people of this country who fund every conflict—"

And my dad interrupting in low fury: "You let him believe he could make a difference—"

A nurse at the desk, looking outraged, warns them, "Please take your argument downstairs before I call—"

"Dad!" I interrupt her. "Elliot!" I bring the chair to a stop as they both turn startled faces in my direction.

My dad has a business to run in New York, but for now he's set up a temporary office in his hotel room so he can come see me every day. He steps to my side, squeezes my shoulder, and then trades a kiss on the cheek with Lissa.

Elliot is too stunned to move. He's staring at me, mouth open and horror in his eyes. He wrenches his gaze away, looking ill. "Oh, God. Shelley—"

I guess I should have warned him, but hell, he knew I was injured. I wonder what he expected to see.

"Thanks for coming, Elliot." The nurse is glaring at us. "Let's go down to the terrace." I instruct my wheelchair, and without waiting for anyone to agree, I head for the elevator. They all catch up by the time the doors open.

On the way down, Elliot stands by the panel of illuminated buttons, staring at my robot legs. "I've never seen prosthetics that complex."

"You know me. Always cutting-edge."

"Jimmy," my dad says. "Did you ask him to come here?"

Instead of answering his question, I tell him about the reality show. He's got a tablet with him, so when we get out on the terrace, he and Lissa find a bench in a shady corner and they start watching it, with Lissa frowning as she leans against his shoulder to see.

Elliot and I stare at each other. "You should have warned me."

"I thought you'd call before you came."

"Yeah, I should have. But on the plane I was watching *Dark Patrol*—two more times. I've never seen anything like that show. You really had no idea that was being put together?"

"None."

"On the way over from the airport, I conferenced with the *War Machine* editorial staff. They've all seen the show, and we're agreed. I'm going to be writing an article on it."

This is not what I want to hear. "No way, Elliot. I don't care if you talk to my CO. I do not want to do an interview."

"Who is your CO?"

"Forget about it."

"Okay, okay. I had to try. But tell me, just as friends—at the end of the show, when you knew those jets were coming, was that for real?"

"I didn't know the jets were coming. I just had a bad feeling."

"Seriously bad."

He waits for me to say more, but I'm distracted, thinking back to our two a.m. conversation and trying to remember why I thought it was a good idea for him to come here. "On the phone, did I say what I wanted to talk to you about?"

"Not exactly. Something about secret stuff."

That's what I remember too, but it doesn't make sense. I can't talk to Elliot about secret stuff . . . not that I know much that's really secret. With *Dark Patrol* loose in the world my precognition has become public knowledge—and a rogue autonomous program that can hack through the army's best cybersecurity? That's Lissa's theory, one she achieved on her own, and she's not sworn to secrecy.

Still, with security issues and a new CO to deal with, it was not exactly a great time to ask my controversial peace-activist friend to visit—which sets an unsettling suspicion brewing in the back of my mind. Was it just me talking to Elliot at two a.m.? Or was something else there, encouraging me to ask, *Do you think you can come out here?*

"Shelley, are you still with us?"

I refocus on him. "Did I sound normal when we were talking?"

"Yeah. Pretty normal, for a dead man at two a.m."

I nod. Even if Lissa's rogue program is real, I can't blame it for every mistake I make. I'm not a puppet. In the Sahel, at every King David moment, I had a choice, except maybe that last day when I knew we had to get out.

This brings up another question, one whose answer Elliot is sure to know.

"What turned the Sahel into an air war? Do you have any idea?"

He snorts. "You could have asked me that on the phone. It turned into an air war because Ahab Matugo played everybody. He convinced some deep-pocket DC to spot him two Shikra jets and some pilots. Rumor is he promised the DC that if the war escalated, they'd sell more Shikras to both sides. But after he slammed the border forts, he pointed a finger back at the arms merchants and blamed them for the escalation, which got him a cease-fire while the foreign participants think over whether or not they still want to play if this conflict gets cranked up."

"So we got sacrificed to buy a cease-fire?"

"Essentially."

"It wasn't just Fort Dassari that got hit, was it?"

"No. Four forts. But you were first. The others were evacuated by the time the Shikras showed up."

I nod, furious again over Yafiah and Dubey's fate. If I'd trusted the whispers of God—or a rogue autonomous program, whichever the truth might be . . .

My pity fest is interrupted by the appearance of three MPs. They step past the sliding door and head straight toward us. It's Elliot they're interested in. "Mr. Weber, we've been asked to escort you off the premises."

"On whose authority?" Elliot asks calmly.

"Mr. Weber, if you'll just come with us."

"He's here visiting me," I say.

One of them salutes. "Orders, sir."

I know they don't have the authority to make a judgment call. "You're not arresting him?"

"No, sir. Just remove-from-premises."

I look up at Elliot. "Is your name on a security watch list?"

"Shouldn't be. I sued to have it removed."

"Okay, I'm going to ask about it, but for now you need to go with them."

His brows rise in surprise. "Just like that? You've gotten that good at obeying orders?"

I stiffen. "That's how it works here."

"You just do what you're told? No matter what?"

I can't meet his gaze, so I glance at the bench, to find my dad and Lissa watching us with tense expressions. "This is my life now. I have to make it work."

"That's the problem, Shelley. It's not going to work. You're employed by the defense contractors and they don't give a damn about what happens to you."

The MP steps in. "Mr. Weber, you need to come with us. *Now.*"

"No," Elliot says gently. "I won't come with you. You'll have to arrest me."

"Elliot, don't," I plead. "Don't make this a media circus."

"Don't worry, Shelley. It won't affect your record. It's just a principle. Due process."

The MPs arrest him. I'm impressed with the calm professionalism on both sides: protester and cops. It wasn't like this in New York, where citizens were bullied and some of us wound up with blood on our faces.

The administrator of Kelly Army Medical Center, Colonel Heather Gleason, scowls as she informs me, "The order to remove Mr. Weber came from *me*."

"Ma'am, Elliot Weber is a respected journalist. He was visiting me, and he was not violating any regulations."

Her condescending gaze is well practiced. "Lieutenant Shelley, Mr. Weber is a well-known subversive. It's clear to me he was using you for access to this facility, no doubt so that he can exploit the status of injured soldiers such as yourself to further his antimilitary agenda."

"Ma'am—"

"It's so-called journalists like him that stir up violence against the military. Fourteen deadly incidents of domestic terrorism so far this year, aimed at military facilities. Anarchists, secessionists, radicals on the right and left—they're using this country's economic stagnation to ignite resentment against us."

I focus on keeping my temper in check. It's well within her power to deny me any visitors at all—but I'm not going to give her an excuse to do it, not with Lissa and my dad in the reception room outside her office door.

"Ma'am, Elliot Weber is not a terrorist. He's not associated with any terrorist group. He does not advocate violence. He disagrees with the government's funding priorities, but that does not make him a criminal."

"I remind you, Lieutenant, you are an army officer. As such, you should not be associating with subversives like Mr. Weber. I strongly advise you to limit your contact with him and others of his ilk. In summary, I will not rescind the order. Dismissed."

I wish to God I could turn around and stomp out of her office.

But I have to cajole the chair into taking me to the door. Colonel Gleason gets up, walks around her desk, and opens the unpowered door for me, which is even more humiliating—and it gets worse.

Along with Dad and Lissa, and the receptionist at her desk, Specialist Bradford is in the reception room. She snaps to attention when she sees the colonel, holding a stiff salute until the office door closes again. Then she lets loose on me. "Lieutenant Shelley! Are you trying to get me demoted? Dr. Masoud just about had a meltdown when he found out you were involved in a security breach—"

"It was not a security breach."

"*And*," she goes on, as if I don't far outrank her, "you do *not* have permission to be gallivanting around the hospital for hours on end. You are to be *in bed*. Doctor's orders."

My dad stands up from the couch. We trade scowls. I know what he wants to say, but I don't give him a chance. "It wasn't Elliot's fault that I got in trouble, Dad. I was a dumb kid, and I made a bad choice. You only blame him because you don't want to blame me."

"You *were* a dumb kid," he agrees. "Weber should have recognized that and told you to delete the damned video, but he let you post it on a site with massive traffic, and by doing that he took your future, and Lissa's, and mine."

"It's not forever, Dad."

"That's my prayer. Always. That you get through one more day, one more night. That you get to come home."

There isn't anything I can say to that. Lissa looks like she wishes she could just slink away. Specialist Bradford saves us. "I . . . need to get you to your room, sir."

My dad's a gentleman, even if he's pissed at me. He says good-bye at the elevator, giving me and Lissa a couple more hours together before she has to leave for the airport. We sit in my room and talk about anything at all except what we mean to each other.

I wake up in the night.

My overlay tells me it's just past midnight. I check e-mail, hoping to find something from Elliot saying he's been released, but there's nothing, because my access is cut off. No outside links. Just like I'm in a war zone.

It could be fallout from Elliot's visit, but my guess is an

AI flagged my conversation with Lissa, the one with terms like "rogue autonomous programs," "skullcap," and "Pace Oversight"—and an actual human finally got around to listening to it. I'll probably be locked down until Intelligence figures out there was no security breach.

In the morning, I still have no outside links. I'm in my wheelchair, heading to physical therapy and trying to decide who I can complain to, when Colonel Kendrick speaks over the link in my overlay reserved for Guidance. "Shelley. To the conference room. Now."

He doesn't bother to identify himself. He doesn't need to. "Yes, sir."

I inform the wheelchair of the change in plans, it contacts the hospital elevator system, and within two minutes I'm rolling up to the door of suite 114. Kendrick is holding it open for me.

I'm expecting an interrogation on Lissa, or a tirade on my friendship with Elliot, but I'm wrong. The colonel closes the door with an emphatic thud. "You've managed to wake up a dragon."

"What? Who?" I realize I know the answer. "Thelma Sheridan."

He looks at me like I'm a bug that needs stepping on. "How the fuck do you know that?"

"At Dassari, those were her engineers we arrested, her trucks that blew up with the fort."

"She doesn't give a shit about that fiasco. She probably doesn't even know about it, but she's requested an interview with you. She'll be here in about ninety seconds."

"Oh God."

"Or damn close to it," Kendrick agrees.

"What does she want with me?"

"What everyone wants—to know how you knew those jets were coming. She got slammed. Someone set her up. Hacked her, maybe, because her analytics failed to detect the jets—and Vanda-Sheridan's stock price tanked. The DCs stick up for each other most of the time, but they'll put a knife in the back of yesterday's best friend if there's money in it."

"So what do you want me to tell her?"

He looks at me like I'm an idiot. "The truth, of course."

"You want me to tell her that someone or something with advance knowledge of the air attack hacked through Guidance and got inside my skullcap?"

He shakes his head in a world-weary way. "Lieutenant, do you know that's what happened? Do you know it for a fact?"

"No," I concede. "It's just a working hypothesis."

"And we don't want to confuse a dragon with speculation."

"So I tell her I don't know."

"You tell her that, and you repeat it however many times it takes, and while you're doing that, you will be charming and polite. Despite her recent setback, she still has enough treasure to buy anything she wants. Absolutely anything—and she already owns a platoon of congressional zombies. So keep your smartass mouth in check and do *not* give her an excuse to launch a congressional investigation."

"Yes, sir."

"I'm told you still tire *very* easily."

I nod tentatively.

"Make sure she's aware of it, and get the fuck out of this room as soon as you can."

The colonel walks out. In less than a minute, the door swings opens again and Thelma Sheridan comes in. When I saw her at Dallas/Fort Worth, armed mercenaries surrounded her, but today she's alone.

She's tall and gaunt, with pale skin, a flat face, and vaguely Asian eyes that blaze above hollow cheeks. Her hair is shining, metallic, copper-colored—not gold like I remember it—precision-cut to just below her ears. She's dressed in a perfectly tailored business suit. A rose-gold cross sparkles in the V of her neckline. She's not wearing farsights, but she has an audio loop on her right ear, with the arc of a tiny mic making a translucent line against her cheek.

"Thank you for your service, Lieutenant Shelley," she says, in much the same tone a staff sergeant might use to say, *Sit down and shut up*.

She walks past me. Her long body folds gracefully as she sits on the couch. Her knees press together; her hands clasp in her lap. She continues to speak, untroubled by my lack of a response. "Given the nature of your commission, your record is surprisingly impressive. The number of interdictions you were responsible for at Fort Dassari is almost . . . unbelievable?"

She pauses for a few seconds, watching me curiously. She's just accused me of lying, or faking my combat record, or some more obscure crime in the commission of which I arranged to kill too many enemy combatants while avoiding being killed myself. I give her my well-practiced stonewall gaze.

She pushes a little harder. "You know and I know that your career has been affected by more than luck, more than skill. Sometimes, the Devil raises us up, only to throw us down from a greater height."

At Dallas/Fort Worth she had a dangerous aura. She still does. I try to direct the interview so I can get away. "I was told you had questions for me, ma'am."

"You were aware of the air attack before it happened, Lieutenant. Who warned you?"

"I was not aware of the air attack, ma'am. I did not know the fighters were coming."

"I've seen the video of the event, sir. You knew something was happening."

I tell her what I've told everyone else. "Yes, ma'am. I had a feeling."

"Are you psychic, Lieutenant?"

"Not to my knowledge, ma'am."

"The Bible commands us, 'Let no one be found among you who practices divination or sorcery.' Deuteronomy eighteen:ten."

Several smartass responses wrestle for priority release, but Kendrick made it clear I am not to antagonize Sheridan. I hold on to my stonewall expression. "I have not, to my knowledge, ever engaged in divination or sorcery, ma'am."

"You are being used, Lieutenant. For what purpose remains unclear, but there is a force at large in the world interfering in the affairs of man. We built its house when we built the Cloud. Now it moves among us, bleeding through every conflict, every transaction, watching, manipulating—and it does not have our best interests in mind."

The hair on the back of my neck stands on end. She's just confirmed Lissa's theory, but coming from Thelma Sheridan it carries a crazy quotient that makes me want to flee the room.

"Ma'am," I say in a voice gone hoarse, "I don't know what you're talking about."

Her glare goes fiery. She doesn't blink. "I think you do. This force has chosen tools to use, and you are one of those tools, Lieutenant Shelley. A disposable tool, to be used and thrown away."

I take refuge in what I resent. "Ma'am, I'm an army officer. That's all."

I might as well not have spoken. She taps her finger

against her head, close to the corner of her eye. "I was a tool as well. I used to wear farsights. My company's main servers were hooked into the Cloud. But we were hacked. Subtly. In a way that left no trace, we were penetrated, our private data stolen and used against us. Used against you. By a trail of coincidence our analytics failed to detect the transfer of two Shikra fighter jets to Ahab Matugo's arsenal and our satellites failed to see them on the ground. The result was that Vanda-Sheridan failed to issue a warning."

No, the result was that Fort Dassari got slammed and that Yafiah and Dubey are ashes—but I don't say it aloud, because I want this interview done.

"That's a matter for Intelligence to unravel, ma'am."

"The Devil has given you his protection, Lieutenant, but it will not always be so. Confess what you know, forswear his gifts, cut yourself off from the Cloud that is his home, and stand up in defense of this world God has given us. For the Devil is everywhere. He is the red stain bleeding through into all the affairs of men, and the army can't protect you."

I swallow against a dry throat, unaccustomed to this intensity of crazy. "If that's all, ma'am."

She nods and gets up. Then she remembers to hand me a business card. I take it, because that requires fewer words than a refusal. "There will be a reckoning," she warns me. "Make sure you're on the right side."

She strides out of the room, her back straight, heels clicking against the floor, a dragon off to terrorize another peasant. She is a defense contractor in control of vast wealth—more than many countries—and with access to elite weapons systems . . . and she's talking herself into a war against a cyberspook that may not even exist.

I flinch as a monitor on the wall comes to life. Colonel Kendrick gazes out at me. "You've got a deer-in-the-headlights expression, Shelley." He shows his teeth in a grin. "What you just heard is psycho desperation. Vanda-Sheridan is having a hard time keeping up in the global marketplace."

"Sir, in her mind it's a religious war. The devil, hacking into human systems."

"I can pretty much guarantee it's not the devil hacking your head, Shelley. Don't make the enemy more frightening than he really is. Intelligence likes the way your girlfriend thinks. They're opening a contract with Pace Oversight just to see what turns up, but the best fit to current data is that we're facing, at worst, a semiautonomous program designed to hack our soldiers—and we're damn well going to take it out. Dismissed."

"Sir!"

He gives me an impatient scowl.

"My overlay—"

"It's been locked down by my order until your security is upgraded. You'll be issued a standard tablet. See if you can figure out how to use it."

His image winks out.

*"Fuck."* I hate toting a tablet around, and they're hard to use. Even the gaze-directed models require one free hand; the touch screens need two. I don't like tablet security either, because screen contents can get scraped by any well-positioned camera.

"Farsights would be better, sir!" I say to the walls. Of course there's no answer, so, flicking Sheridan's business card into the nearest trash can, I head out the door—and find Elliot waiting for me in the hallway.

I'm shocked to see him, but the MPs must know he's here; his presence would have been logged when he walked in the front door of Kelly AMC. "Did you get a court order?" I ask him.

Elliot gives me a smile and a thumbs-up. "If you'd ever check your e-mail, you'd know that."

"Can't. My overlay's on lockdown."

Elliot has been around the legal system a long time. He knows how it works, and he uses it to get what he wants and to go where he wants . . . and he knows enough never to step over the line—though maybe he's willing to invite other people to step over. My dad thinks so.

It's my dad I have in mind when I say to Elliot, "I know I asked you to come out here, but it was a bad idea."

"You getting some pressure?"

I don't want to admit it, so I just shrug, but I know that no court order is going to keep the hospital administrator from denying me other visitors if she's unhappy about Elliot's being here.

"I fixed things," he assures me. "Really. In exchange for my promise not to file a lawsuit, I get access to you during your rehabilitation—for a human-interest piece on the star of *Dark Patrol*."

"Come on. I told you I don't want to do an interview."

"Sure, I know. I just need some video. It's an excuse to be here."

"Look, I've got to go. I'm due in physical therapy."

I'm not hiding my irritation, but he's pretending not to see it. "I'll go with you. That'll be good for some pics."

I start the chair rolling and he follows along beside me, saying, "You know who I saw on my way in here? Thelma Sheridan. She was heading out. Now *there's* an interview I'd love to do."

I get a chill up my spine. I can't help glancing over my shoulder, half expecting to see red seeping through the walls.

"You know who she is, right?" Elliot asks. "Vanda-Sheridan? The DC that owned the trucks in *Dark Patrol*?"

"She's the deep inside of crazy."

He gives me a thoughtful look as we get on the elevator. "Could be. You almost have to be crazy—obsessive, driven, usefully delusional—to come out on top in a world this big. Sane people just can't keep up."

The elevator pauses and two civilians get on, while Elliot starts filling me in on what he thinks I should know. "Thelma might be a little more intense than usual because Vanda-Sheridan is on the downswing. One of their specialties is spy satellites and the equatorial launch platforms that put them into orbit. But they've had problems lately. Malfunctioning rockets. Satellites going mysteriously offline. Lost data. The defense department has filed an action against them for what happened at Fort Dassari."

The elevator pauses again. My wheelchair decides we're on the right floor. Elliot gets off with me, saying, "If Vanda-Sheridan doesn't bribe the right judges, they could lose their contract."

I hit the stop button on my wheelchair as a shiver runs through me. "Those Vanda-Sheridan trucks—they were carrying equipment to build a portable radar tower. It should have been activated that day the Shikras came, but it wasn't, because I arrested the contractors."

What if my encounter with the pedophiles under the trees was more than chance? What if it was one of those inexplicable coincidences Lissa mentioned? The devil wouldn't object to prostituting little girls to delay construction on a radar tower.

I look up at Elliot. "If that tower had been working, we would have known the planes were coming."

"You can't blame yourself."

Maybe not, but if defensive fighters were scrambled or missiles launched, Vanda-Sheridan might have done okay in the market.

I press my palms against my forehead, sure that I'm losing my mind.

Elliot crouches beside me. "Hey Shelley, you okay?"

I make myself sit up straight. Elliot hasn't heard about the red stain that bleeds through everything; he hasn't heard Lissa's theory. "It's a fucking butterfly effect," I tell him. "If I hadn't lost contact with my angel, Guidance would have pulled me back, I wouldn't have arrested those contractors, and my squad would be out on patrol right now."

Maybe I've given Elliot something to think about, because after spending just a few minutes with me in physical therapy, he decides there's research he needs to do, and takes off.

Later, I'm having lunch with my dad in the cafeteria when a supply sergeant tracks me down. He issues me the promised tablet: a hand-size device preloaded with my army ID and dot-mil. "So I don't miss any important reports concerning modifications to the uniform or the number of pets allowed in military housing," I tell my dad.

"Can I call you on that thing?"

"Yeah, they come with military and civilian addresses."

I text the number to him and to Lissa, and then I hook up the tablet with my civilian accounts. When that's done, I put in an order for new uniforms. "Just another exciting day at Kelly AMC."

"May you be bored for a long, long time," he tells me.

"You sure that's what you want? You know that never goes well."

He grants the point with a nod. "Jimmy, I'm going back to New York. There's office drama happening. I need to be there."

I'm not surprised. "I guess we're lucky they let you stay away this long. Dad . . . I just want you to know I love you, and I really appreciate you being here for me, through all this."

He grips my shoulder. "Stay safe, and keep coming home. That's all I ask."

• • • •

Information moves in mysterious ways. Lissa proves it when she calls me in the afternoon, waking me up from a chaotic dream of Ransom telling me I'm beloved of God, while Shikra fighter jets bear down on both of us. Grateful to be awake, I murmur into my new tablet, "Hey, love."

I don't get any soft syllables in response, just a challenge. "I know who you talked to this morning."

Guilt sets in, but I'm still groggy, so I have to go over the list in my head. There was my dad, the physical therapist, Elliot, Kendrick . . .

"Thelma Sheridan," Lissa says.

I sit up, my heart hammering. I can't confirm or deny, but Lissa doesn't need me to.

"My boss was on the phone with an official from Vanda-Sheridan. They found out Pace Oversight was negotiating a research contract with the army. Did you know about that contract?"

Kendrick mentioned it to me, but I shouldn't be passing on what Kendrick said.

"I'll assume you know," she says impatiently. "Vanda-Sheridan wanted to buy in. My boss wasn't interested, but she kept their rep on the phone long enough to find out that they're working on a theory similar to ours. So I guess my idea isn't as crazy as you thought."

I have to be honest with her. "What goes on at Vanda-Sheridan isn't really a good measure of sanity."

That earns me a little laugh. "Okay, I can't argue with that. The Vanda-Sheridan rep had a meltdown when he understood my boss wasn't going to let him play. He promised to inform the army that Pace Oversight is compromised, because of my connection to you."

"Your boss knows about us, right?"

"Of course. She told the rep to do what he felt was necessary, and hung up. Five minutes later, she gets a frantic call from the army liaison, saying that Thelma Sheridan had threatened you during an interview, that there were further security concerns, and under no circumstances should we allow Vanda-Sheridan to be a party to the contract."

It shocks me that the army would reveal that much. "They're desperate to lock down your research."

"They'd like to, but we're not taking the contract."

"What? Why?"

"Pace Oversight wants exclusive ownership of anything we discover. If there is a rogue program, it's operating throughout the Cloud, so it's not just an army issue. The way my boss sees it, if we do the research on our own, and if we succeed in working out how and why the rogue program operates, we'll be in a position to convert that knowledge into dragon-scale money."

I don't like the implications of this at all. "Is that what this is about, Lissa? Money?"

A few silent seconds pass before she says, "Yes. At Pace Oversight it is. It's the promise of money that lets me do the work, and I want to do the work. I want to know what's going on. I want to understand it."

"What does that mean for you and me?"

"It means I won't be working on the army contract, so I won't go to prison if I tell you what I learn." That little half laugh again. "I might get fired though."

"And lose all that money?"

"Shelley, it's never been about the money with you."

The next morning, a hospital janitor stops by my room. He peeks shyly past the door. "Lieutenant?"

He's a kid, maybe nineteen. A civilian, so I don't worry about formalities. "Hey. What can I do for you?"

He edges into the room. "I saw you in *Dark Patrol.* That was you, right?"

"Yeah, that was me." It's the first time anyone at the hospital has mentioned the show.

"I really liked watchin' it. It made me think, you know?"

I've got a pretty good idea where this is going, and it doesn't make me happy.

"What you do out there," he says. "It's important. It matters to people. I want to be part of that."

"People die out there," I remind him.

His bony shoulders pop up in a shrug. "People die here, in good ol' San Antonio. My brother shot himself last year. Two of my friends gave it up in a car crash a couple months ago. I want to get the fuck out of here, and live before I die."

He tells me he's already signed up for the recruit exams, so I wish him luck.

After that, word of *Dark Patrol* spreads. Within a few days I could swear the entire hospital staff and half the patients have seen it. I get slammed more than once for my cynicism and antiwar rants, but mostly people are moved by the show. If the army created it to improve public relations, then *Dark Patrol* has to be counted a success.

It bothers me, though, that people accept my precognition as a gift, a blessing, a supernatural talent. No one questions it, any more than I did when I was in the field. When the nursing staff starts calling me King David, I decide that I will kick Ransom's ass if I ever see him again.

I gripe to Specialist Bradford. "You know, I just finished reading the King David story—"

"Do tell, Lieutenant!" she says with sarcastic enthusiasm as she changes the dressings on my legs. "You actually took time to read the Bible?"

"Yes. And there's nothing in there about David getting his legs blown off."

"David listened to God. He wasn't as stubborn as you. He didn't drag his feet. You need to open your heart to God, Lieutenant. Shape up and fly straight, because anyone can see that He has plans for you."

"I thought God had plans for everyone."

"Of course He does. But He's using *you* to reach a million others."

Yeah. And that worries me. A lot.

Lissa calls every evening. She's compiling a model of God, or at least of His footprints in the Cloud. She tells me that Thelma Sheridan has good reasons for being paranoid. "Really weird things have been happening with her company. Did you know she's married to a former mercenary?"

"No way."

"Yep. Twenty years. She's the brains and the momentum behind Vanda-Sheridan, but Carl Vanda . . ." Lissa hesitates. "This is like Elliot's theory—the one you're always talking about—big defense contractors getting together, creating their own markets."

"Setting up the next war."

"Yes. Industry gossip says that's Carl Vanda's role in the company. Or it was his role. Four weeks ago he was in a plane crash. An engine malfunction, caused by some minor oversight in the maintenance. He broke his back. Suffered a lot of damage to his internal organs. This would be right about the time—"

"Hold on. Let me guess. Right about the time Ahab Matugo got his hands on those Shikras?"

"You win the prize. It might be a coincidence that Carl Vanda was dropped from the picture at such a critical time—"

"Another one of those weird coincidences you were telling me about?"

"Exactly. He'll be in recovery for some time to come."

It isn't just Vanda-Sheridan. Lissa sees the effect everywhere. "It can be positive or negative," she says, "but I'm starting to think it touches everyone at some level. We don't necessarily notice, because with most people it's subtle—"

"Not with me."

"Sure, but it's leveraging you through the reality show, using your story to affect a million others."

I listen to the booming beat of my heart. "Lissa? You're not the first to tell me that. Carol Bradford said the same thing. Do you think this rogue program put those words in her mouth? Do you think it put that thought in your head?"

A few seconds of silence slip by. Then she says, "It's easy to get paranoid, talking about this stuff . . . but there are infinite variables in the world. Chance is always in play. We're not puppets. But even if the program manifests only now and then to engineer a weird coincidence, that could be enough to change lives. I mean, we all have an image of ourselves, right? I think it leverages that image, using our beliefs, our hopes, our expectations, giving each of us a chance to shine in our own personal story."

I scowl at my titanium legs, stretched out, lifeless, on the bed. "I'm not shining."

"It's not over yet, baby."

Not for me, maybe. But it's over for Yafiah, for Dubey, for all those nameless corpses I put into the village graveyard. Why didn't their stories matter?

In the corner of my vision, the skullnet icon wakes up.

I don't really want a chance to shine. I think that when God's making plans, it's best to stay out of the way.

• • • •

After fourteen days, Dr. Masoud performs a minor surgical procedure to extract the tubes that have been feeding his concoction of growth hormones and paralytic to the titanium-bone interfaces in my thighs. As he sews up the tiny wounds, the induced paralysis starts to lift. For the first time since waking in the hospital, I can feel a feathering of low-grade pain from my thighs. I flex the truncated muscles and feel them tighten. It isn't much, but after so many days without any sense that my legs were even a part of me, I'm elated.

"I'm not going to put the dressings back on," Masoud says. "There's no need for them anymore. The healing process is well along, the stumps are dry, and the cuticle has grown in."

"So I'm cured?"

He smiles. "You're well on your way."

I try raising one of my stumps. It's hard. The muscles are weak from disuse, but I manage to lift my thigh an inch or so. The robot leg drags like a dead thing.

"It still doesn't work."

"It will," Masoud promises with a fatherly smile. His eyes are bright. I know he's dreaming of his Nobel Prize.

The next day, I go to meet my maker.

Joby Nakagawa is the engineer who designed my legs. He has a large playroom, a.k.a. a lab, in the hospital basement, across the hall from the morgue. Dr. Masoud is standing in the doorway, waiting for me when I roll off the elevator.

"Come in, come in," he says impatiently. "We have a lot of interested observers waiting for you."

He's not kidding. A small crowd—at least twelve people, all of them well dressed—is gathered in a swath of open floor space. They're standing in clumps of two or three, chattering, contributing to a buzz of conversation that falls off with astonishing speed as I enter the room. Everyone turns to look at me. The only person I recognize is Kelly AMC's administrator, Colonel Gleason. The others I classify as academic types or corporate executives. Several greet me with words and smiles of welcome. Others just look tense.

There's definitely excitement in the air.

Above my head, models of airplanes, dirigibles, and rocket ships hang from the ceiling, while the walls gleam with racks of cyborg body parts, both gray and black. More mechanical parts clutter the workbenches on one side of the room. In a corner, a 3-D printer hums quietly, working on some project I can't see.

Dr. Masoud shepherds me past the spectators to an expanse of plush beige carpet. Three tripod-mounted video cameras stand along its perimeter. On the opposite side is a console table that's tipped away from me so I can't see the virtual keyboard. A monitor hangs above it, suspended from the ceiling. Both the console table and the monitor are at a height that lets them be used standing up.

A small man is at work behind the table. His gaze is fixed on the monitor as his hands hover and dart above the keyboard. He's barely five three, but the time he's spent in a gym shows in his athlete's build. I don't think he's older than thirty. His features are mixed—part Japanese, going by his name, and maybe Scandinavian for the other side of his ancestry. His hair is an almost colorless blond, down to the stubble on his cheeks, and his skin is so pale I suspect he never steps out into the Texas sun, but his green eyes glisten from beneath heavy Asian eyelids.

"Joby?" Masoud says tentatively. "This is Lieutenant Shelley."

"Yeah, I guessed," Joby snaps. He continues his silent

typing while everyone looks on: the little prince, commanding the devoted attention of his audience.

Already, I don't like him.

I turn to glare at Masoud. "You said I'd be standing up today."

"We have to turn you on first," Joby says. He types for a few more seconds, then looks up with an impish grin. "I'm ready. Are you?"

"What do you have to do?" I ask suspiciously.

"Just throw a switch. Masoud has been guiding the nerve growth in your legs. You should be more or less integrated with the mechanical system. Anyway"—he shrugs—"we can try it."

"And the legs will work? I'll be able to move them?"

"Hopefully." He raises his hands, holding his fingers poised above his console. "Ready?"

Joby does not inspire my confidence, but I'm too far along in this cyborg transformation to back out now. "Yeah, I'm ready. Do it."

"Cool." His hands descend together toward the console, but then he hesitates. "I should probably warn you that we've never actually done this on a person."

The way he says it, the sadistic anticipation in his eyes: I know I'm screwed. I try to protest, but before I can get more than a monosyllable out of my mouth his fingers touch the keyboard.

A crippling fire shoots from my thighs to my hips and I scream, doubling over in a spasm so sudden and harsh that I collapse out of the wheelchair, coiling into a fetal ball as I hit the carpet, growling because I don't have the breath left to keep up my screams as fire shoots up my spine—

—and drains away.

There's still pain in my hips and my back—a cramped, biting pain—but it's bearable. I gasp and choke and sob for a few seconds, my fingers digging at the carpet. The skull-net icon glows as I pull myself together, unwinding the knot of my body.

"What the fuck?" I whisper as the crowd of observers chatters madly.

I push myself to a sitting position and, without thinking about it, I bend my left knee, and then my right. Everyone goes silent. That's when I realize what I just did. I freeze, staring in shock at my robot knees while Joby scratches his head and says, "Oops. The signal intensity was a little high."

"Asshole," I growl. But I can't turn my gaze away from my robot knees. They *work*. And they also hurt. I feel a deep ache in the mechanical joints, while the titanium legs throb with a pain like shin splints. I want to writhe.

Instead, I stretch the left leg out and then draw it back again. I do the same thing with the right leg. The observers murmur, but I ignore them, focusing instead on flexing my robot feet.

The movement this produces is not remotely human.

The feet reveal themselves to be a titanium puzzle, segmented in two directions. I stretch my feet and the puzzle aligns into five long slices along the lines of the bones in my missing feet. When I curl my foot, the longitudinal segments seal up seamlessly, instantly, and the foot curls along side-to-side segments . . . curls so far back that I make the toe of the foot touch the bottom of the heel.

I do it a few more times to convince myself it's not a pain-induced fantasy. Sweat drips into my eyes. I wipe it away with the back of my hand. I wipe my face on my T-shirt's wet sleeve and realize my whole body is soaked in perspiration. Even the monitoring sleeve on my forearm is dark with sweat.

Silence falls across my audience. When I glance up, a few

of the observers have the decency to look horrified, but the rest, including Dr. Masoud, are waiting with bated breath, like they're 99 percent sure that they've hit the winning number in the lottery.

Joby's the only one in the room not looking at me. He's working his keyboard, his intent gaze fixed on the monitor that's suspended above his console.

"Joby," I growl, "what the fuck did you mean you've never done this on a person before?"

Joby stops typing and looks at me, his eyebrows raised in what might be interpreted as apology. "Somebody had to go first. Turns out the intensity was off by a factor of ten." Then he cocks his head. "Can you stand up?"

I consider it, and decide that standing is the only way I can get close enough to strangle him. I get my feet flat on the ground. The segments lock up in both directions, giving me a firm base. With my palms pressed to the carpet, I push until my ass comes off the floor.

I'm crouched on robot legs.

They feel locked solid, like I'm wearing a cast, so tight they could never move. A shiver of panic runs through me as I flash on what might happen if these alien legs ever truly lock up . . . or if they move against my will. Despite the pain, they aren't really part of me.

"Enough," Dr. Masoud says. He steps toward me, his hands raised as if he intends to hold me down. "Lieutenant Shelley, it's too soon."

"Don't touch me," I warn him, and I stand.

I try to stand.

In fact, I hurtle onto my back. The thick padding beneath the carpet is all that saves me from cracking my head open, but it's still a near thing. I groan as Masoud barks, "Enough! Joby, turn it off. This is not a game."

It sure as hell isn't. This is my life. "Leave it on!" I roll onto my belly. "You don't get to turn me off, doctor. Not ever! That is not part of this deal."

I do a push-up with my arms. I bring my legs under me again, bending my knees, my robot knees. I settle back into the same crouch I managed before.

Masoud is hovering. "Jimmy—"

"You're not my dad. Don't call me Jimmy."

"Lieutenant, you have to learn to use your prosthetics. They are *not* the same as the legs you lost—"

"I think I figured that out."

"One wrong move and you could seriously injure—"

He stops talking as I try again to stand. This time I move slowly, carefully. My thighs—what's left of them—tremble with the effort. My hip joints feel weak, like they're about to slip. But my knees and my ankles . . . they feel solid. Steady and strong. Locked in place.

I'm standing.

I feel like a giant.

I've got to be at least two inches taller than I used to be.

"Fuck me," Joby says with a lopsided grin. "I am a seriously good body engineer."

He is a good engineer, but I hate him anyway. "Hey Joby, when I figure out how to walk, I'm going to strangle you. How cool is that?"

His grin widens. "Should I turn you off?" he muses. "Or light you up again?"

I lunge for him.

He lights me up.

Dr. Masoud is livid. "Do you know how much money has been invested in you? How much research? How many futures are dependent on the outcome of your case?"

I'm sitting on a table in an exam room, clutching a bloody

wad of tissue that served as a temporary dressing for the gash on the side of my head, acquired when my skull bounced off the edge of Joby's console. The little peacock loves his power. He boosted the signal intensity before I got anywhere near him, which put me on the floor again. I'm not happy about that, but my foul mood can't compare with Masoud's. He's so angry, spittle is flying. Literally. I feel specks of it impact my cheek.

"You have no idea what you can do," he tells me, his voice booming in the little room. "None. You have no idea what you've become!"

I think he'd slap me around if he could get away with it. I even start to worry about his wife and kids, and what they go through—but his huge hands are feather-light as he cleans the gash and then glues it shut. The contrast is surreal.

Masoud and my physical therapist, a civilian named Jen Krause, have conspired to develop a training schedule for me. Jen is a white-haired woman of middle height who disguises her broad shoulders and expansive bosom within the sheath of a simple white lab coat. She smiles at me in a grandmotherly way as she drags over a harness that hangs from a track in the ceiling.

"The feedback mechanism in your legs will take some time to get used to. So we're going to start you in the harness, where there's no chance that you can fall down—"

"That's not going to work for me, Jen." I've had enough of being strapped in, strapped down, ferried around. I have legs again. Working legs. "Let me figure it out. I'll use the parallel bars and teach myself."

Jen shoots a disapproving glance at Dr. Masoud, who's standing behind my wheelchair. He doesn't say anything, so she tries again. "No, Shelley, I just can't allow it. You could be hurt—"

"It's on me."

"—and your experience will be used to refine the program for other soldiers."

"There is no program. Look, I appreciate everything you've done for me, but right now you don't know what I need. No one does, because I'm the first to try to walk with legs like these. If I can't handle the parallel bars, I'll tell you. Until then, I do it my way."

"Let him do it," Masoud growls. I imagine him armed with a baseball bat, ready to use it on my head if I fuck up his Nobel Prize. "Shelley's a man. A real man. He doesn't need coddling."

"Glad we got that straight."

So I get to use the parallel bars.

It's an exercise in concentration just to stand up from the wheelchair and reach for them. Jen hovers, but I manage it without her help. "Take the chair away," I tell her. "I don't need it anymore."

I'm trying not to show the pain I feel, but the truth is, my legs hurt—and not only in my human parts. There's pain too in my robot legs, generated by a feedback mechanism that lets me feel their presence, their position, and the force I'm asking them to exert. I'm starting to sweat.

"Is there a problem?" Masoud asks acidly.

"Joby had a way of adjusting the signal strength. I need that."

"Too much feedback?"

"Maybe. I don't know."

"I'll ask him about it. Do you want to sit down for a while?"

"No."

Masoud gets on the phone with Joby. I leave him to it.

With my gaze fixed straight ahead and my hands keeping a death grip on the rails, I flex my thigh, bringing my right foot up, forward, and then down again. I feel the heel touch first, and then my weight rolls forward until my foot is flat, and I'm squarely balanced. My heart is racing, my hands are slick with sweat, and it fucking *hurts*, but other than that, it was a perfectly normal step. I do it again with the left foot and slide my hands farther along the rail. Right and left, right and left. I ease off on my grip when I'm halfway through the bars, taking all of my weight on my legs. The pain ramps up, but I keep walking, one slow step after another until I reach the end.

My therapist is there, hovering.

I get a good grip on the rails again and turn around. Using the sleeve of my T-shirt, I wipe the sweat from my eyes and then start off again, walking a little faster this time, my palms skimming the bars, but not really holding them. I reach the end. No one cheers, not even me. My legs are trembling from fatigue. I know I need to sit down, but I don't want to sit in the wheelchair. Looking around, I spot a row of plastic seats maybe ten steps away against the wall.

I know I can get there. I just walked twice as far without losing my balance.

I let go of the rails and head out. Jen is instantly at my side. "Grab my arm if you feel yourself falling," she says grimly.

"I'm okay."

It's almost true. If I fall, it's going to be because the muscles in my thighs and hips give out, not because of the robot legs. I grit my teeth and focus on the next step, nothing more. And I make it. I've reached the row of seats. But now what? It occurs to me that sitting is a complex action requiring a turn along with controlled flexion in the hips, knees, and ankles. I haven't practiced any of that yet, so I just let myself fall forward until I can grab the seat back, then I twist my hips and drop into the seat with a thud. I lean back and clench my eyes shut as pain shoots up my spine.

"Very impressive," Jen says. "But you'd suffer less if you took things more slowly."

I open my eyes and grin. "I can't believe how well it works." Then I straighten up. Masoud is walking toward me while side-eyeing his tablet. "Joby's a fucking genius," I tell him. "It's like the legs *know* that they're legs. They know how to flex, and stiffen the knee and the ankle. They know how to distribute weight across the sole of my foot."

"They only know to do it because I designed the neural interface," he snaps.

"Yeah. That's impressive too. I hope you get your Nobel Prize."

His gaze shifts from my face. He speaks again, but not to me. "Then it's my responsibility. We need that open connection. Just do it." I can only hear his half of the conversation, because the incoming sound is being fed directly into his ear canal by the audio loop he's wearing.

I blink in surprise as an icon flares in my overlay. It's the green circle of an open network, and just like that—despite Kendrick's order, because Dr. Masoud said to do it—I'm back in the Cloud, and new software drops in. An application installs. Messages flash near the bottom of my field of view, too fast for me to read, and then a new icon pops into existence: a slender red horizontal bar, with a numerical value beside it—*71%*.

Masoud looks up from the screen of his tablet. "Do you see it?"

"Yes."

"Use your gaze to adjust the intensity. Higher to the right. Lower to the left."

"How high does it go?"

He snorts in cold amusement. "Not as high as you experienced this morning."

I'm glad to hear that.

The bar has started to fade from sight, but as I fix my gaze on it, its red glow brightens. I shift my eyes left, and the bar retreats while the digital readout rolls back: fifty, forty, thirty, twenty. As the signal strength drops, the pain in my legs fades into numbness. I take it all the way to zero and I can't feel anything except the mass of my prosthetics, tugging on the stumps of my organic thighs.

Even though I've shut off all feedback, the legs still work. I raise my right thigh, straighten the knee, extend the foot. It's easy enough to do, and there's no pain, but there's no sensation either. I know it's working only because I see it working.

"What are you feeling?" Masoud asks.

"Nothing. It's like the leg doesn't belong to me."

I bring the signal strength back up. At around 22 percent, I feel the presence of the legs again. At 39 percent, the legs become mine, and I use the feedback to guide me as I set my foot down. At 64 percent I'm getting more feedback than I want—my legs are hurting. I take it all the way up to 100 anyway, because I want to know what will happen, what could happen if someone—or something—ever gets access to the system.

I'm braced for pain, so I don't fall screaming to the floor when a red-hot pulse slides up my spine.

Masoud is talking to Joby. "Reset system max to eighty-five. No. He's not going to need any finer proprioception than that. Do it."

The bar stays the same, but the pain recedes. I'm aware of my heart, pounding in my ears. Masoud is speaking again, but his gaze is still on the tablet, so it takes me a second to realize he's speaking to me.

"Proprioception is the body's awareness of the position of its limbs. The higher the signal strength, the more finely detailed your control of the prosthetics will be."

"And the more it will hurt?"

He scowls. "It's first generation. The signal transfer process will be improved."

"It's fucking amazing now," I tell him, because it's true. Still, I've spotted the flaw. I tap my organic thigh. "There's some device in here that generates the signal strength, right?"

"It's not in your leg. It's inside the prosthetic. We've adjusted the output. You can't hurt yourself."

"But that's just a software fix, right? And software gets hacked. Is there any way to get in there and adjust the device so it *can't* generate a signal strong enough to fry my nervous system?"

His stony expression tells me this is not an issue he wants to discuss. "This is first generation," he reminds me. "The system will improve with time."

It's Sunday when I start walking again. The first couple of days are hard, not because of any problem with my new legs, but because the muscles in my back and hips and thighs have deteriorated from lack of use. I work hard in physical therapy, and I spend extra hours walking all over the hospital. The padded soles of my titanium feet make a soft clicking sound against the vinyl floor, and I get stronger.

By Thursday I've learned how to handle stairs, so I slip into the stairwell, where I practice climbing and descending. No one comes to check on me, not physically, but the monitoring sleeve lets the nursing staff know where I am and how I'm doing.

After an hour, a message from Command pops up on

my overlay, alerting me to a priority e-mail delivered to my dot-mil. Halfway up a flight of stairs, I stop to read it. The e-mail contains the orders for my next assignment. My stay at Kelly Army Medical Center is done.

Lissa and I have talked every evening since she went back to San Diego. We talk about her work, and she always wants me to fill her in on the progress of my therapy. But we talk about other things too: our parents and friends, funny stuff that happens, the stupidity of politics, who's getting married and who's splitting up . . . anything at all, except us. She hasn't come back to see me, and I still don't know where we stand.

I sit on the stairs, breathing in the stink of concrete and stale air. Footsteps patter somewhere below; a door creaks open, booms shut; and then silence descends.

I fix my gaze on Lissa's icon and my overlay pushes through a call to her. A few seconds later her voice is in my ears. "Hey, Shelley." She sounds surprised and a little anxious. It's not our usual time to talk.

"Lissa, I know you're at work—"

"Don't worry."

"I just got my orders. I'm getting transferred."

"Oh God. When? Where?"

"Monday."

*"Monday?"*

"I'm not going far. It's just some cyber camp northwest of Austin. It'll be six weeks, though, with no outside contact."

"Can they do that?"

"It's the army. They can do what they want."

"But you said you'd get leave!"

"It didn't go through. Maybe there wasn't time. Maybe they're afraid if they let me out on the street for more than a couple of days I'll get pissed at some yahoo and kick his guts out with my new cyber enhancements."

"That is not funny."

I draw a deep breath. Now or never. "I did get a week-end pass."

"What does that mean?"

"I get the weekend off. I can get out of the hospital. It's restricted, though, so I can't fly out to San Diego—"

"You couldn't get through airport screening anyway, with all that hardware."

"Huh, yeah. I never thought about that. But, Lissa, you can come here. We can get a hotel."

She's quiet for several seconds. Then she asks, "What about your overlay?"

And I know I'm going to win.

"We don't need to worry about that. When I get time off, the recording stops. That's always been in the contract. GPS will still be active, but that's all. So come. Please. Tomorrow. I get released at noon."

"Tomorrow's Friday," she says in surprise.

"Yeah. I get a long weekend. We can have until Monday morning. Please, Lissa. Please, please, come."

She laughs softly, low in her throat. "Shelley sounds hungry."

"Shelley is dying."

"Okay, baby. You get us a hotel room. I'll pick you up at the hospital at noon. Now go away. I have to talk to my boss and make a reservation."

Masoud ordered a daily assessment of my progress, so I have a standing appointment with physical therapy at 1400 every afternoon, but until then I'm on my own. So I go back to my floor and hit up the nursing staff for suggestions on a really fine hotel. They have fun with it, and it isn't long before agreement is reached on a luxury suite on the River Walk.

Then I retire to my room and pull out the service uniform that's been hanging in the closet since it was delivered. If all goes well, I won't have much need for clothes this weekend, but I have to wear something out of the hospital—and I know some eagle-eye in the chain of command would have an aneurysm if I was seen walking out of the hospital wearing only my army T-shirt and shorts.

So for the first time, I try the uniform on.

The fit is hopeless. I'm sure Masoud knows my new height to a millimeter and my weight to the nearest gram, but there's obviously a disconnect between his records and my uniform profile. I'm wearing clothes made for the man I used to be.

Staring at the sagging dress shirt in the little bathroom mirror, it hits me how much weight I've lost. The slacks are worse. They look hollow where they hang over my titanium bones, and given that my legs are at least two inches longer than they used to be, the slacks are way too short. It's the same with the dress shoes. My new feet are longer from heel to toe than the organic version I had before, and they're also narrower.

Irritation crawls across my brain. I go ahead and order longer slacks, but I don't know how I'm ever going to make the shoes work—not that I *need* shoes anymore, but they're part of the uniform, and I've never heard of a variance for cyber-footed soldiers.

I change back into T-shirt and shorts, and with my dress shoes in one hand, I head out, attracting a few curious stares from visitors on the floor and smiles from the nursing staff. I share the elevator with a civilian family: dad and mom and two small girls. The parents stare at the walls, while the wide-eyed girls study my robot legs. I hope they don't get nightmares.

The elevator only goes as far as the main floor. An MP has to key me into the basement. I walk past the morgue to Joby's lab and try the door, but it's closed and locked. I pound on it. Several seconds pass, and then I hear a lock turn. I try the door again, and this time it swings open.

No one's there. I push it wider, and a clatter of footsteps comes trotting toward me across the room. Legs. Freestanding robot legs, shorter than mine, linked together above the knee by a crude crossbar. Joby's sitting cross-legged on the center carpet, using a controller to guide the monstrous little toy. He makes it tap-dance around me as I cross the room, but I refuse to be impressed.

"My shoes don't fit."

"So? Get bigger ones."

"No human shoe is going to fit on these feet."

He jabs a button on the controller and the robot legs give up their joyful little dance, to stand quietly at the edge of the carpet. He frowns at my feet, then glares up at me. "It's stupid to wear shoes. Your feet are flexible. They're made to grip. If you lock them up in shoes, you'll lose that feature."

"I appreciate the effort you put into them. I said it before, you're a fucking genius, but this is the army. I have to be in uniform."

He pouts. But he gets paid by the same people I do. He knows.

Abandoning the controller on the carpet, he gets up with a world-weary sigh and takes the shoes from my hand. "Hi, Becky." He holds the shoes up and stares at them. "You see these?"

He's not talking to me, he's not holding a phone, and he's not using farsights. "Hey," I say, "do you have an overlay?"

He gives me a wink. "You're not the only cyborg around here."

I'm impressed. This is the first time I've knowingly met someone else who uses one.

To Becky he says, "I need shoes like these to fit a foot two hundred eighty-six millimeters from toe to heel. . . . Yeah, I need them *now*. I need them five minutes ago. Get lunch later." He plunks the shoes down on a workbench. "This is going to be easy." It takes me a moment to realize he's talking to me again. "We just need to make a cushioned sleeve that will fit around the mechanical foot, so it sits snuggly in the shoe."

"Yeah," I say. "Easy."

He ignores me, and rightfully so. I watch as he whips up a viscous white liquid. He pours it inside the too-small shoes, filling them to the brim. In a few minutes the liquid cools into a gel, resulting in a soft cast of the shoe interiors. Joby takes the casts to the 3-D printer, scans them into memory, and then extends the size of the digital image to match my new feet. Next, he pulls up an image of my feet from his design records, superimposes it on the shoe casts, and then subtracts the difference, leaving an image of a hollow, padded sock. He instructs the 3-D printer to replicate it and asks me if I want to shoot some pool.

The next day at noon I'm waiting in the shade of the hospital portico for Lissa to come pick me up. I'm wearing my service uniform and my new, large shoes. Visitors come and go from the parking lot. Some glance at me, a few offer a casual nod, but no one stares. My legs and feet are hidden, and all anyone sees is an ordinary soldier.

Lissa's thumbnail avatar appears in my overlay—"I'm here"—as a white, rented sedan passes the guard station at the start of the driveway.

I grin, wave, and grab my small duffel bag. As she pulls

under the portico I can see her through the windshield. Her eyes goggle and her mouth is round with shock. "They fixed you," she says in astonishment as I slide into the shotgun seat.

I lean over and collect a kiss. A very serious kiss. Then I look her in the eyes and tell her, "I got us an early check-in."

She's kind of breathless, so she just smiles and slips the car into drive while I tell the GPS where we're going.

A cheerful older woman at the front desk checks us in. Since we only have two small bags, we go up to the suite alone. I swipe the keycard against the sensor plate, and the door unlocks, opening onto a palace. High-end furnishings are tastefully arranged on thick carpet, designer features are everywhere, fresh flowers fill two vases, and fine art decorates the walls. "Wow, the staff at Kelly knew what they were talking about when they sent me here!"

Lissa whoops and kicks off her sandals, dancing across the front room, twirling, her skirt rising like the petals of a flower around her beautiful legs. Then she drags the blinds closed, cutting off our view of the River Walk restaurants and plunging the room into shadow.

"Nothing but us," she says. "Nothing exists but us."

I want her so badly I'm afraid I'll hurt her. The first time is just raw need. I'm awkward, and I don't know at first how to move the legs, and the whole thing is laughably ugly. But it's over fast and we try again . . . and again.

The bedroom is a timeless cave. We lie together on a vast spread of creamy white sheets. I watch her breasts rise and fall as she softly breathes, half-asleep. I'm aware of her toe pressed against the flat gray metal bone of my shin and I wonder how she can bear it, but I don't ask.

*Stop the world*, I think. *Here. Now.*

Why would I ever need more than this?

She draws a deeper breath, and her eyes open. They gaze

into mine. "I'm afraid of what's coming," she whispers. "Of what it's going to be like when I lose you."

"You're not going to lose me."

But gray bones are already in our bed and we both know that's a promise not in my power to keep.

"Six weeks," I whisper to her.

It's Monday, predawn. We're parked under the hospital portico, our heads together, working up the courage to say good-bye. The skullnet's icon is aglow in my overlay, which means it's working to buoy my mood—so I guess it's possible to feel worse than I do. "If I can call you before then, I will, but don't expect it."

"They want to play head games with you."

"Lissa—"

"They want to turn you into a robo-soldier," she insists in an angry whisper, as if someone outside the car might hear. "That's the only reason to isolate you. They'll try to break down your ethics and your values, so they can replace them with a new value set. And you're vulnerable. You're not even sure you're human anymore."

"That's what the training is about. They want me to integrate with the prosthetics, to see the legs and the skullnet and even Delphi's voice as part of me, and not as something I have to think about or feel self-conscious over—because that kind of doubt could slow me down."

She gazes at me with a look that says I'm a sorry fool. "They don't care about what's best for you, Shelley. You're an experiment, and they are going to want to test the limits of what you can do."

I sigh and lean back in the seat, but my hand is still tight around hers. I do not want to let her go. "You're probably right. But I got through Dassari, and I'll get through this."

Then I ask, because I have to know, "Are you going to stick with me, Lissa?"

Her hand squeezes tighter against mine. "I don't know how we can make this work."

"I don't know either, but I want to try."

I hear her gentle sigh. "Call me when you can. We'll see how it goes."

I should be relieved she's not leaving me, but her hesitation feels like rejection. I try to hide my anger, but she knows.

"Shelley, it isn't you. You know I love you."

"You just wish you didn't."

She looks straight into my eyes; her gaze doesn't waver when she asks me, "Why would I *want* to love a soldier? Knowing you'll be deployed for six months or a year or more? Knowing you're always in danger? Who the hell would want that, Shelley?"

"That's not what it's about. You're supposed to want *me*."

"I do. Ergo, my problem."

She proves the issue with one more long kiss before we whisper our good-byes. I get out of the car and watch her drive away. Lissa needs more than love. Her logical mind requires that our relationship make sense—and it doesn't. Not for her.

A link in my overlay flares and fades, letting me know I'm back in the system. At 0600 I'm due in physical therapy for a strength and agility assessment, and then I'm scheduled to head out to the Center For Human Engineering, Integration, & Training—C-FHEIT. No one's pronounced it for me yet, but I'm putting my money on "see-fight." The army would be into that.

Ten-foot chain-link topped with razor wire and watched over by perimeter sensors fences out the civilian world, but the landscape looks the same on both sides of the boundary line: flat terrain, supporting groves of low, scattered trees with brown, knee-high grass rustling between them.

C-FHEIT is far from anywhere. In my overlay, the network icon is a red circle with an X in it, declaring the absence of a cell network. All I can do is passively receive GPS, allowing me to follow our progress on a map huddled in the corner of my vision. When I fix my gaze on it, the map moves closer to center. It's superimposed on an out-of-date satellite image that shows the road we're on as a dirt track running straight across empty country. In fact, the road's been paved. It's a generous one lane with a white fog line on either side, the asphalt so dark and smooth it looks like it was laid down yesterday.

The red-X'd circle turns green as my overlay picks up a new network. Data streams out to Guidance, including my location, kicking into action an automatic process that notes my arrival at C-FHEIT and shuts me down. The green circle winks out. So does the map—and the promised lockdown begins. The only link I have now is to Guidance.

I sigh and return my attention to the real world around me.

I'm riding shotgun in an army SUV driven by Private First Class Mandy Flynn, who proceeds at exactly the posted speed limit of thirty-five. It's eight miles to the facility. We're nearly there when Private Flynn looks around surreptitiously with her wide green eyes and tells me, "There's deer here." These are the first words she's volunteered since she picked me up at Kelly AMC almost two hours ago.

Flynn wears the insignia of an LCS soldier. I asked her about it as soon as I saw her shaved scalp, only half-hidden under her cap. It astonishes me that she's one of us because she's tiny: a slim five one. Even wearing the exoskeleton, size and strength matter, but Flynn must have passed her quals and I have to admire her for that. She's only eighteen years old and hasn't seen combat yet.

She risks a glance at me, and then adds, "No one's allowed to hunt the deer. There's a penalty if you shoot one during field exercises."

"You ever shoot one?"

She looks away and flashes a shy half smile. "Haven't had a chance yet, sir. Been waiting for the first cyborg to transfer in before we get issued our assignments and weapons."

I look ahead as the small facility comes into sight. There's a concrete quadrangle, pinned in place by a flagpole. The road loops around it, dividing it from a two-story building on one side that my overlay identifies as the barracks, and an even taller building on the other, labeled as a gymnasium complex. The labels fade away as soon as I read them. At the far end of the quadrangle is the sprawling cybernetics center: a gray, one-story building with a remarkable lack of windows.

Everything looks fresh and newly made. The asphalt is black, the concrete is bright, the buildings are clean. The landscaping is all mulch and thin young trees, held up with guy lines. Two cars are parked in front of the barracks, both official sedans. I don't see any personnel at all.

"You're delivering the first cyborg, Flynn."

She gives me a nervous glance up and down, but I'm wearing my service uniform and she can't see the prosthetics. "You, sir?"

"Me."

"You look human, sir."

I can't help it. I laugh.

Officially, Colonel Kendrick is the commanding officer of C-FHEIT, but he's not present at the facility. Hardly anyone is. By the time Flynn parks the SUV in front of the barracks, a handful of personnel have emerged—one officer and four enlisted. They assemble in a line to greet me. "That's all of us," she says. "Except Private Johnson. He must be on watch in the TOC."

The officer in charge is Major Keith Chen, a lean, gray-haired, PhD kinesiologist whose assignment is to figure out how to train a cyborg like me. Everyone else has a shaved head and wears LCS insignia.

Chen introduces me to Sergeant Aaron Nolan, our ranking non-com. Nolan is a big man, almost as big as Ransom, with a round face, a flat nose, and sun-darkened skin. He wears a skullcap beneath his patrol cap. So do the two specialists. All three are combat veterans. The privates are rookies. They're not wearing skullcaps, but their heads are shaved.

"Kendrick has handpicked everyone here," Chen tells me after he dismisses the staff. "You know the LCS motto—*Innovation, Coordination, Inspiration*. Kendrick is going over personnel records and psych profiles to put together elite teams exemplifying those virtues."

"I thought this was a training center for cyborged soldiers."

"Every LCS soldier is cyborged. You've just pushed it a little further than most. Your task is to prove you can be field ready by the end of this training period. The rest of us are here to support you. It's a worthwhile investment, given that a potential billion-dollar program is riding on your success."

"No pressure then."

He gives me an amused look. "I thought you'd already met Colonel Kendrick."

Inside the barracks, everything is shining and new. Officers' quarters are on the second floor. There are six suites. Chen occupies one, I get another. The rest are empty.

"We got here the middle of last week," Chen tells me.

"That's when the contractors officially turned over the facility."

We walk over to the Cyber Center, where he shows me offices, classrooms, and conference rooms. At least half the floor space hasn't been developed yet. "There are plans for electronics workshops equipped with 3-D printers," Chen tells me. "Also, some highly specialized medical facilities, if funding comes through."

The Cyber Center also has a kitchen, though there's no kitchen staff. The setup is exactly like Fort Dassari, with premanufactured microwave meals that everyone prepares for themselves.

Over lunch he talks about my role. "You're our first soldier with integrated prosthetics. I don't know what you can do, and you don't know what you can do. You're here to define the baseline. I'm here to help you."

We start at 1400 that afternoon. I dress in army T-shirt and shorts, then debate the athletic shoes. Technically, they're uniform, but I'm defining the cyborg baseline and I decide they're not required.

Flynn has rotated to desk duty. There's a startled look on her face as she takes in my legs.

"Still mostly human," I assure her.

She nods, though I'm not sure she believes me.

I meet Chen at the gym, a huge structure, mostly empty. Auxiliary rooms are stocked with resistance machines, but the main floor is a blank slate: padded and carpeted, with a climbing wall on one side but nothing else.

Chen is dressed like me in T-shirt and shorts, but he's got shoes on. He frowns at my robot feet and then looks up at me for an explanation. I give him my argument, showing him the way the foot works, how it can extend either forward and back, or laterally. I have to concentrate to make it do what I want.

"Is it hard for you to control the fine movement?" he asks.

"I haven't practiced it much. People get disturbed by it. Makes me look like a fucking alien."

"The uncanny valley," he muses.

I don't know the term, but before I can access my encyclopedia, Chen gives me his definition.

"'The uncanny valley' is a term for the revulsion most people feel when faced with things, especially animate things, that are almost-but-not-quite human. It comes out of the robotics field, from observations of typical reactions to humanlike robots. Classic prosthetics face the same problem." He nods at my feet. "You'll get it worse, because your limbs are animate and seem almost to be alive."

"You know the guy who designed them? Joby Nakagawa?"

"I've seen his work. I've never met him."

"You wouldn't want to. He's a jerk. But I can assure you that making these legs appeal to the sensibilities of my fellow soldiers did not enter into his design philosophy. He was aiming for function, above and beyond human if he could get it."

"Let's see if he got it. We'll start simple. You've learned to walk again, and with an almost natural gait. But can you run?"

I start slowly, an easy trot. It's a lot different from walking. My knees bend too far. So do my ankles. I lose control of my balance, overcompensate, and fall. I'm not used to falling. It's embarrassing and frustrating, and it happens over and over again. I get way too familiar with the coarse weave of the gym's utilitarian carpet.

"What happens if I fail?" I ask Chen. I'm lying on my back after my latest tumble, grimacing at the bruising in my arms and shoulders, despite the padded floor. The ceiling looks a milc high.

Chen stands over me, not at all impressed with my dramatics. "It's way too early to talk about failure."

"Do they take the legs away? Splice them onto someone else? Or do they kill the program?"

"There's a lot of corporate investment backing integrated prosthetics. You'll have to work hard to defund it all by yourself."

"So they'll just take my legs away." It makes me sick to think of being taken apart.

"I'm going to take your legs away if you don't get up and start using them."

I study his face and I'm not entirely sure he's joking. So I get up and try again.

Over dinner, Chen urges me not to get discouraged. "What you're going through right now is a biological process. The bioelectric interface is encouraging your body to produce finer connections and selectively strengthening those that work best. Like any process of growth, it's going to take time, but keep at it, and you'll get the best possible control of your legs."

"What does 'possible' mean?" I ask, using a roll to capture stray gravy from my packaged pot roast. "How much of my natural motion will I get back?"

"That's for you to figure out."

"Because no one's ever done this before?"

"Right. The simulations I've seen suggest a wide range of possible outcomes."

I don't want possibilities. I want promises. "What range of movement were these legs designed for?"

"If they're hooked up to a computer and run with an

adaptive motion program, they're able to imitate everything a healthy man can do and then some. It's not the mechanics that are going to limit you, Shelley. It's the interface with your nerves, your fine motor control. That's the part we know the least about, but the potential is there. It's the adaptive element of the system—and the most unpredictable. Simulations have been developed, but the data's incomplete." His eyes narrow. "So it's up to you to figure out what you can do."

I hiss, grab another roll, and demand, "If Masoud can regrow my nerves, why the fuck didn't he just grow me a new set of legs? Or hasn't he figured that trick out yet?"

"Check back in a couple of years. Civilian labs are hot on the trail, and the army will buy in if it looks worthwhile." He takes a long drink of water and then gives me a thoughtful look. "My own opinion, though? If it takes months or years to regrow a limb, the army won't go for it. Besides, Command might prefer titanium soldiers with replaceable parts."

I lean back in my chair and stare at him. "I hate to say this, but that sounds absolutely plausible to me."

I don't fall down as much the next day, and the day after that I rarely fall at all—but I'm only running in a straight line.

"Make a circuit of the gym floor," Chen tells me.

I do it, concentrating as I take the first corner, but I set my inside foot down too hard and send myself staggering into the wall.

"Ease up!" Chen shouts. "Stop thinking about it and just run."

I don't listen. At the next corner I focus on getting each step correct. This means I slow down. I'm going barely faster than a walk as I precisely place my feet. Suddenly Chen's in front of me. I have to throw myself hard to the side so I don't run into him.

"Diagonal!" he shouts. "Across the gym. *Move!*"

I trained long and hard under a voice like that and I jump to obey, just like he knew I would. I'm halfway across the gym floor before I realize I haven't fallen down.

"Cut right! *Now!*" Chen's parade-ground voice echoes off the ceiling.

I do it.

"Now, faster!"

I lift my knees, lengthen my stride—and stop thinking about every little motion. I take it on faith that I can do this, and within a few bounding steps, I'm across the gym. It feels good; it feels easy. I want more. Anticipation rises inside me. "I'm going outside."

Chen is demanding, but he's no martinet. He makes a do-as-you-will gesture, following me as I head for the door.

It's getting to be midmorning. The Texas sun blazes against the concrete quad, but it's early October already and the air is cool. No one's around. Only the flag is in motion, snapping in a breeze out of the south.

I start off jogging along the road toward the Cyber Center. My pace is slow; I know it's really going to hurt if I fall on the asphalt. But after the first fifty meters, I'm bored, so I add a little speed . . . and soon, I add a little more.

It's like I'm running downhill. I feel a joyous momentum. I've always loved to run, especially middle distances, ten, twelve miles. These new legs don't weigh nearly as much as the old, leaving me so light on my feet I think maybe I could run those distances again.

I lope in front of the Cyber Center, round the bend toward the barracks, and take off sprinting.

That's when I know it's not just the lightness of my new legs. I can feel them magnifying my momentum. Just like a dead sister, they're dumping more recoil into my strides as my speed goes up—a simulated downhill run where the steepness of the virtual slope increases with my speed. I'm no cyborg superhero—a trained sprinter would still leave me in the dust—but after having my legs blown off, running fast again is intoxicating, and for a few seconds I only think about my stride, not where I'm going. By the time I look up, the low wall at the facility entrance is looming in front of me. It's too late to stop. My only choice is to go up and over.

My right foot kicks off the top of the wall, then I plunge down into tall grass on the other side. My arms windmill as I fight to keep my balance, but it doesn't quite work. I crash into the crackling grass as an explosion of dust and locusts takes off around me.

I end up on my back again, my heart beating so hard it's about to explode out my ears. My chest is heaving, and my hips and thighs feel like jelly. Searing pain rises up my spliced bones, feeding into my spine. I glance at the icon that controls feedback from the legs and it brightens, but I look away without adjusting it. The pain feels necessary after what I just did. It makes the experience real.

I blink against a blue sky that's so bright my eyes start to water. Wind hisses through the grass but doesn't mask the rhythm of running footsteps drawing closer.

"Shelley!" Chen shouts as he rounds the wall.

I'm hidden in the grass, so I raise my hand. "I'm here."

He crashes toward me, a shadow blocking out the brightness of the sky. "What the hell? Are you hurt?"

I grin. "I didn't think I'd ever run like that again."

"Did you hit your head?" He drops to his knees beside me.

"I'm okay. I just . . . burned out my organics, I guess." I make myself sit up. "Geez, my thighs are trembling."

"Poor conditioning," Chen concludes. "You can start with a mile run after sunset. We'll add on distance from there."

• • • •

Over the next ten days I learn to jump, to shuttle, to crawl, and to scale the rock-climbing wall inside the gym. And every day Chen straps on his shoes and goes with me on a predawn distance run, always pushing me to go farther, until we make eight miles: halfway to the boundary fence and back.

It's not all agility and conditioning. C-FHEIT is eight miles from the county road, out in the middle of nowhere, which means that, in the event of a terrorist attack, there is no one around to defend us except ourselves. So I'm issued a new helmet and exoskeleton, and I learn the code to the weapons and ammo lockers, practicing it until I can use the skullnet to open them with a thought. Then, because I have combat experience and Chen doesn't, he assigns me the collateral duty of directing defensive operations, since—as the administrator at Kelly AMC pointed out to me—domestic terrorism is always a possibility.

We already have a defense plan, set up and ably directed by Sergeant Nolan, so I just familiarize myself with procedures and train along with everyone else in an emergency response that depends almost exclusively on shoulder-launched missiles, since that's the heaviest armament linked combat squads ever use.

Beyond that, I'm behind on some of my leadership qualifications, which means virtual classroom time. And then there are the sessions with a visiting shrink who wants to know how I'm handling the trauma of mutilation. I tell him the truth: I'm not handling it at all. The skullnet is, and that's fine with me.

Every night I fall into bed so exhausted I have about thirty seconds to miss Lissa before sleep pulls me under.

Maybe that's the skullnet too.

• • • •

"How do you feel about other people seeing you?" the shrink asks me. "Are you self-conscious or ashamed to be seen as a cyborg?"

"Why?" I demand suspiciously. "Are more personnel finally being rotated in?" I know *I'm* not going anywhere, because I'm not even halfway through my six-week term.

He doesn't like my second-guessing. "Are you anxious about that?"

I consider it. The handful of enlisted already at C-FHEIT spent two days avoiding me, and when they couldn't get away with it anymore, they tried very hard not to notice my legs—until I made them notice. I had them examine the prosthetics, showing them how the joints worked and how the foot stretched. At first they were embarrassed, but the intricate mechanics are fascinating and they were drawn in. After that, they learned to relax around me, and the prosthetics didn't command much attention—until I started my speed training. Then they would gather to watch my workouts when they could, and I'm fairly sure bets were made on how fast I could run.

I answer the shrink's question. "The legs are just another piece of equipment for the enlisted to get used to. If any of them can't handle the idea, I'll send them to you."

To my astonishment, he actually cracks a smile.

I step out of the barracks, Chen right behind me. We're heading for dinner in the little cafeteria at the Cyber Center. The sun has set, but a long blue twilight is lingering. Somewhere far off a coyote howls. As the sound fades, I hear the faint thrum of a distant engine. It sounds like a helicopter to me.

I look at Chen. He shakes his head and pulls out his phone, knowing no more than I do.

Maybe it's just a civilian craft out by the county road, but until I've got a confirmed ID, there's a protocol to follow. I go back into the barracks. Inside, PFC Flynn is manning the tactical operations center behind the desk.

"Known air traffic approaching?" I ask her.

She looks confused—"Traffic, sir?"—and turns to scan the monitors.

A mechanical wailing erupts as the perimeter alarm goes off.

"Unidentified helicopter incoming!" she shouts.

I'm already halfway up the stairs to my room, where my gear is stashed. It takes me ninety seconds to rig up in armor and bones. I pull the helmet on as I head out the door and automatically I'm linked into our LCS.

A glance gives me the positions of my soldiers. Four are still in quarters; two are outside, running for the barracks. We've practiced this all before.

I bound down the stairs, managing not to fall down. The first rigged soldier hits the lobby at the same time I do. His visor is opaque black, but on my display he's identified as Specialist Samuel Tuttle. I visualize the code to the weapons locker and it clicks open.

"Confirm gen-com."

"Gen-com confirmed, sir!"

"Defensive action. Fire on command only."

"Yes, sir!"

Delphi is suddenly with me. "Status report, Shelley."

I'm so startled I almost drop the missile launcher that I just pulled from the rack. "Shit, Delphi!" This is the first time she's been inside my head since Africa.

I shove the weapon at Tuttle and he sprints out the door.

"What's your status?" Delphi insists.

"We've got an unidentified helicopter approaching. No clearance. Setting up our defense."

"Logged," she notes, and goes away.

Sergeant Nolan is next to be rigged and the rest follow—not quickly enough. We've done better in drills. I hand out the weapons, secure the locker, and bolt for the door. There's no mistaking the sound of the helicopter now. It's not much more than a mile away. I glimpse it: a black shape flying low to the ground, lights off despite the twilight.

I race to my assigned position—a pillbox behind the barracks. Flynn's there ahead of me, holding a missile launcher to her shoulder, aimed at the oncoming threat. The weapon is almost as big as she is, but she's in control, using her left arm struts to support most of the weight while her right hand hovers near the trigger.

I check my visor, confirming the positions of all my soldiers. Twelve more seconds, and everyone's in place. That's when Delphi comes back.

"Stand down," she says in an irritated tone.

I echo it to my LCS. "Stand down. Make weapons safe." Beside me, Flynn heaves a sigh of relief, lowering the missile launcher as the helicopter—still with lights off—sweeps in toward the quad. "Who the fuck is that hot dog?" I ask Delphi.

"Your commanding officer."

Colonel Kendrick. The fuckwad. Knowing that he's got to be listening in, I say to Delphi, "Glad you got back to me when you did. If you'd been just a few seconds slower, I would have had Flynn blow him out of the sky."

"Saved your ass again," she says. "Be good, Shelley. I gotta go."

We form up on the quad to greet Colonel Kendrick. It turns out he's not just arriving in the helicopter, he's flying it. He sets it down, kills the engine, and spends the next five minutes berating us for being too slow setting up our defense.

After that, though, he lightens up and allows me a full five minutes to secure the weapons and get out of my armor and bones before I'm required to report to a mandatory meeting.

In a conference room inside the Cyber Center, Kendrick smacks a long, rectangular, aluminum case down on the table. It's the sort of thing used to carry expensive rifles or scientific equipment. "Got a present for you from Joby."

I shoot an accusing glance at Major Chen, who's seated across the table. He gives a tiny shake of his head: He doesn't know what Kendrick is up to. So I move closer. Kendrick raises his brows, amused at my caution. Then he opens the case, unfolding it like a clamshell. Nestled deep in the padding on each side is a robot leg, including the knee, ankle, and foot assemblies. Chen stands up to get a better look.

"Joby believes in evolution," Kendrick announces. "Welcome to version two point oh of yourself, Lieutenant. The technician I brought with me will swap out the limbs for you."

I step back, feeling offended. "What's wrong with the legs I have?"

He shrugs. "Joby wasn't happy with the diagnostics. Something about wear points and friction."

It's news to me that the legs have been generating their own use report.

"Oh, and reducing the maximum possible signal strength so a hack can't lay you out. You requested that, didn't you?"

I concede this is true, and I'm impressed Joby listened.

"I want you switched out tonight," Kendrick continues.

"Because tomorrow we're bringing in additional personnel to put together two complete linked squads. Then we'll start playing games. You've torched expectations, Shelley, and reset the field at a higher level than anyone hoped to achieve this soon. We're looking at a quarter-billion-dollar grant, if you can get field qualified inside the time period of this training program."

"And what does the grant money buy?"

"Functional cyborg limbs for more top-end soldiers like you."

*Top-end soldiers?*

"Don't play me, sir."

"What the fuck are you talking about?"

"It's not my service record that put me here. I just turned up at the right time, in the right condition."

"Jesus, Shelley, you think I gambled this program on some random waste from the meat grinder? You're here because your psych profile meets my gold standard. Smart, adaptable, determined. A damned fine soldier—"

I can't stand being bullshitted.

"I do my job, that's all!" But even that isn't true. "I tried to do my job. I fucked up. People died."

"It was a war! Look, I've seen *Dark Patrol.* I know you're a drama queen, you like to think you got screwed by the system. But you got lucky when the army offered you an officer's contract. Everybody's got a place in the world, their one best role. Most people spend their whole life trying to figure out what that is, but not you. Fate shoved you right into the place you were meant to be—"

"*Fuck!* I was not—"

"*Shut the fuck up!*"

I school myself not to take a swing.

"You can bullshit yourself," he says, "but don't bullshit me. You *chose* to stay in service. What kind of jackass would do that just to avoid one year in minimum security? You're tough. You could have done the time and lived off your daddy's bank account the rest of your life. But you chose to stay in, because you're army. Even if you can never admit it to yourself, this is where you belong; it's your role. The bullshit hero of your own story."

"With all due respect, sir, fuck you."

"The best way to fuck me is to fail out of this program. You are the prototype. Your performance directly affects my future, the future of this program, and the future of every other soldier eager to have the same benefit you've been given."

He makes it sound like a good thing, but I can see where this is going. "It's a benefit we get only if we stay in the army. This program is just a way for you to recycle experienced soldiers and send them back into action."

Kendrick doesn't even flinch. "That is correct."

Chen reminds us he's there by pulling out a chair and sitting down again. He speaks in the sort of frank voice appropriate for relating the cold, hard facts of the world to an overwrought teenager. "It's the nature of research budgets and funding. It costs upward of a quarter-million dollars to draft, evaluate, and train a typical combat soldier, and half of them wash out along the way. That same amount of money can be invested in putting a known quantity, an experienced warrior, back into action. And if that warrior gets killed?" He shrugs. "There's a one-time payout on the life insurance and no additional health-care expenses down the road."

Kendrick closes the aluminum case. "Let's make it simple. The cyborg research does not happen unless it gives us an advantage in combat. Getting trained and experienced soldiers back into the field is an advantage. Are you clear on that, Shelley?"

"Yes, sir. I am."

"And are you going to fuck up this program?"

I want to tell him yes. *Yes, I am going to fuck up your program because I'm tired of you and people like you fucking with me.* But I can't say it. The words stick in my throat because they're a lie. If I fail out of this program, then I fail out of the army . . . and who would I be then? Where would I fit in?

It's not that I like it in the army. It's just . . . what I know.

"Lieutenant?" Kendrick presses. "I did not hear your answer."

I square my shoulders and tell him the truth. "It is not my intention to fuck up your program, sir."

He nods. "Good. I'm glad to hear it. You would not want me for an enemy, son."

That's something I have no trouble believing.

The below-knee assemblies of my robot legs can be switched out in just a few seconds, but Dr. Masoud warned me that replacing a complete leg would be more complicated. I'm a little nervous about the process, more so after I meet the technician. She's a soft, short civilian—no taller than Flynn, though quite a bit heavier—dressed in an army-green T-shirt and khaki pants, who displays an adversarial relationship to her work.

*"Goddamn, you toxic little bitch,"* she whispers as one of the bolts holding my left leg in place resists her efforts to remove it.

I'm lying in a reclined dentist's chair, staring at the ceiling and waiting for her declaration of victory, which comes in just a few seconds.

*"Got you, you dipshit. Who's next?"*

This is the third bolt that has dared to challenge her, so I'm getting used to her ongoing narrative.

*"You going to come out easy? There we go, you little tease. You're the last one."*

She drops the final bolt into a steel dish with all the others. I lift my head, sitting up a little so I can watch as she slides the leg off.

The top of the leg is a hollow post that fits like a sleeve over the post protruding from my truncated thigh. The titanium pieces separate, revealing several colorful bundles of incredibly fine-gauge wire still connecting the two parts. She pinches the separate strands together and then tugs at them gently—*"Come on out, you pretty little pains in the ass"*—until she exposes a set of plug-in connections. *"No more lovey-dovey. Sugar daddy's getting a younger bitch."*

She frowns. Then she looks up at me with bright brown eyes. "You know that override Joby gave you, to adjust feedback from the prosthetics? It might be a good idea right about now to slide that bar all the way down to zero."

I feel no inclination to argue with this advice. I use my gaze to adjust the bar, eliminating all sensation from my legs. "Done."

She pops the first connection, then gives me a questioning look. I shrug, because I don't feel a thing. "Good," she says.

In a few seconds she's got them all separated. She sets aside the detached leg, gets out the new one, slips a finger into the top of its hollow shaft, and pulls out more strands of brightly colored cable, each with a tiny socket on the end.

"Those look awfully fragile."

"Shit, yeah," she agrees. "They're fragile, fussy little sluts." She lays out the new leg at the foot of the chair, then gets to work connecting the cables to the ones trailing out of my leg, matching up different-colored sockets. *"In, you little shit. Gotcha. In, you little shit . . ."*

"So if any of those connections come loose, I'm toast, right?"

She stops what's she's doing to glare at me with narrowed eyes. "There's built-in redundancy." Her gaze returns to her work. *"In, you shit. In . . . ,"* until the last one is connected.

As she pushes the tiny cables up into the hollow post she asks me, "You worried?"

"Should I be?"

"I wired your first set of legs and that held up. This one will too. And if it doesn't, send your ghost back to let me know."

"I bet you and Joby get along real well."

"Yeah," she says with sarcastic dreaminess. "He loves me. So long as I never, ever, ever make a mistake. His last three techs couldn't quite live up to that standard."

She replaces the bolts, and then sets to work on the other leg. When I finally get put back together, I crank up the feedback, hoping for something a little more pleasant than the low-level pain I've gotten used to, but the sensation is exactly the same. "You sure there's anything different about this new setup?"

She gives me a tight-lipped smile. "I'll tell Joby you asked. But trust me on this—you've been upgraded."

The reinforcements roll in at ten forty-five the next morning in two monstrous SUVs. I've seen the personnel lists, so I know what to expect. They don't. I'm standing with Major Chen, Colonel Kendrick, and Sergeant Nolan as the new arrivals pile out of the vehicles: seven LCS combat veterans and three rookies. With the six LCS soldiers already present at C-FHEIT, we now have enough personnel to fully staff two linked combat squads.

I haven't been in charge of a full squad since training. I'm looking forward to it.

The new sergeant takes charge. "Retrieve your equipment and form up!"

I can't help smiling. Sergeant Jaynie Vasquez has a kick-ass command voice. In less than a minute she gets her soldiers in line, standing at attention before us, with their duffel bags on their backs and HITRs on their shoulders, and at their feet, the folded exoskeletons of their dead sisters. The combat veterans wear a skullcap beneath the billed cap of their regular uniform.

Jaynie turns to present her credentials to us, the officers at C-FHEIT. Her eyes get big when she spots me. I swear she stops breathing as her gaze drops to my legs. I'm wearing my combat uniform, but not boots. Her gaze lingers on my gray titanium feet and then she looks up with accusing eyes. "Sergeant Jayne Vasquez, reporting for duty, sirs."

At one end of the line is Matt Ransom, staring at me as if he's not entirely sure I am who I am.

Colonel Kendrick gives a short welcoming speech that no one listens to, and then he dismisses the new arrivals so they can get checked in at the barracks. Jaynie approaches me, a suspicious glint in her eyes.

"Thought you'd be a civilian by now, sir."

"I got an offer I couldn't refuse. It's good to see you, Jaynie."

Her expression is somber. She glances over her shoulder at Ransom. "I wondered why they kept us together." Her gaze returns to me. "Is it going to be episode two? *Dark Patrol* all over again?"

I had the same thought when I saw her name and Matt Ransom's on the personnel list. "Looks that way, doesn't it?" And because I know she's telling herself the wrong story, I add, "I didn't know anything about *Dark Patrol*, Jaynie. I would have told you if I did."

"Yes, sir." There's doubt in her eyes. "Sir?"

"Yes?"

"You're not wearing a skullcap."

She's not asking about my legs, because she knows what really matters. I tap my head and tell her, "I've leveled up. The system's embedded. It's part of me now."

She ponders this, but if she has an opinion, she keeps it to herself. "Congratulations, sir. It must be reassuring to be locked in." She salutes, then retrieves the folded bones of her dead sister and heads off to supervise her soldiers.

I can guess what's going through Jaynie's head. It's not just the fact of the stupid reality show intruding on our lives. It's the knowledge that in the next episode the conflict is sure to be cranked up. I don't know where our next assignment will be, but it will probably be a more dangerous one than Fort Dassari—and what are the odds that all three of us will survive?

Ransom doesn't share our grim thoughts. When Jaynie cuts him loose he's all over me. "Jesus, LT, I thought you were finished, I thought you'd get sent home. Goddamn, it's good to see you, and shit, those are the coolest feet!"

"Yeah? Check this out."

I show him how the feet bend. He watches in fascination, with none of the initial skittishness the other enlisted showed. "That is the most amazing thing I've ever seen."

"Knee joint's pretty cool too. Ransom, I wouldn't be here if it wasn't for you. You saved my life. I want to thank you for that."

He shakes his head. "That was the worst day ever, but I should have known God would see you through. He's got you halfway to bulletproof now."

We train together for the next three weeks, moving from conditioning exercises to drills to field exercises designed to test our unit cohesion and my ability to handle not just one

LCS, but two. Kendrick calls the combined units a "dual LCS." Sixteen soldiers working as a single unit. Sometimes he's with us in the field, rigged in armor and bones, but just as often he leaves it all to me. It works only because Kendrick hand-selected top personnel. Jaynie and Nolan are both talented and experienced non-coms who back me up and let me know when I'm screwing up, while the soldiers they supervise are enthusiastic and interested, with rookies who are eager to learn.

It's been fun.

But it's also been a long six weeks, physically and mentally challenging, and shadowed with questions that so far refuse to be answered.

Kendrick says we are here to prove the value of my cyborg enhancements, and no doubt that is true. But simple proof of my field qualifications does not require the elite team I've been given and I can't help believing that we are training for something specific and imminent—though we've received no orders yet.

Guidance has been involved in most of our field exercises, with Pagan as my handler. Every time he comes online I question him on the rogue program—what he's been told, what he's heard. I've repeated for him Thelma Sheridan's portentous words—*the red stain that bleeds through all the affairs of men*—and in our brief conversations those words transmogrify into "the Red," our name for the unknown. "Have you heard from the Red, Shelley?" he'll ask me, and I'll tell him no. There have been new security regimes, new encryption, and I've had no incursions into my brain space, not since the skullnet was installed. I want to believe Guidance has learned how to lock the Red out of my head, but Guidance hasn't made that claim. Maybe they just don't know for sure. No proving a negative, after all. But it weighs on me, not knowing.

Then there's the question of Lissa. In three days I get to escape from C-FHEIT. I'm authorized for two weeks of leave—but in all the time I've been here I haven't talked to Lissa, or traded e-mails with her, and I have no idea if we'll be spending the next two weeks together. I have no idea if she'll be willing to see me again.

I put it out of my mind. Tonight we're playing a war game. It's a graduation exercise that will be observed by VIPs both in and out of the army, who will decide what level of funding to award the cyborg program.

It's 0130. I stand at attention with my dual LCS on the edge of the quad. We're rigged in armor, bones, and field packs, our helmets on, visors opaque, fully linked to one another and to Guidance. We appear ready for battle, but we're carrying nonlethal stinging rounds for ammunition—a big bang but not much substance—while our exoskeletons all have a kill box attached, to cut off power and drop us to the ground if our AI overseer decides we are dead.

We watch as a transport helicopter lands on the quad. Our helmets mute its roar, but we have to brace against the blast of its rotors as it sets down in front of us. The side door opens, steps unfold, and twelve men and women, all in civilian clothing, step out: contractors, news writers, and army officials.

Colonel Kendrick and Major Chen stand ready to greet them. Both are dressed in combat uniforms, but neither is rigged for the field and they don't wear helmets. They present our human face, shaking hands with our guests and then directing them to stand on the side. Farsights blink with green recording lights and tablets image us: seventeen faceless troops of C-FHEIT's elite dual LCS.

I'm focused on my soldiers, not on the visitors, so I only notice him when my overlay pins him with a tag: *Elliot Weber*. I shift my eyes without turning my head, and see him shaking hands with Colonel Kendrick. Elliot was going to do an article on my rehabilitation. Was he granted a seat on the helicopter just so he could follow up? It seems incredible, and I have an uneasy suspicion he's heard a rumor of the Red.

No time to worry about it.

Colonel Kendrick is wearing an audio loop that hooks him into gen-com. "Start-ex," he says. "Lieutenant, initiate the operation."

"Roger that. Moving out."

My dual LCS boards the waiting helicopter without another word spoken. To the observers, we must appear to be a squad of faceless automatons, flawlessly running on an internal program.

The helicopter lifts off. We're in the air eleven and a half minutes before we're dropped off in the Great Dark of Nowhere. I scan the terrain in night vision. It's flat, like just about everything around here. There's knee-high dry grass and just a few small, scattered trees. The sky is clear, full of stars, but night vision strips their beauty away. The air smells of exhaust from the helicopter. There's hardly any wind.

As the helicopter leaves, a map comes up on my visor. My LCS is pinpointed on the map's periphery. At its center is our target, which bears the label "Enemy Black Ops Lab," a short eleven K away. From our initial briefing, I know our target is a mockup of a mobile bioweapons lab, covered with camo netting and nestled in a dry wash near a bluff that stands thirty meters above the surrounding land.

Kendrick is still at C-FHEIT, but he speaks to us over gen-com, reiterating the mission. "Get there. Eliminate the enemy. Retrieve all data and samples from the lab and get back here in time for breakfast."

Breakfast is 0530.

"What's the current intel on the enemy, sir?"

"Defensive manpower estimated between ten and twenty. Standard small arms, shoulder-launched missiles, and RPGs. No tanks in the vicinity, but armored transports are possible."

"Drones, sir?"

"Unknown. But if you see any, take 'em out."

"Will do."

This is not going to be a live-fire exercise, just a round of intense laser tag, though Kendrick is sure to find some way to shake it up.

I walk the line one more time, examining my soldiers. We look alike except for height. With the armor, it's even hard to tell the men from the women, but my visor tags each soldier with a name so I know who's who. Ten are combat veterans, six are rookies, but every one of them is a highly rated soldier.

"This is a stealth mission," I remind them. "We stay quiet until we hit the outlying sensors. Then we move in fast and hard."

It bothers me that I have no idea who the enemy is. All I know is that they're not going to be soldiers from C-FHEIT, because we are it.

"Listen to your handlers. Know the positions of your LCS, but don't succumb to tunnel vision. Be aware at all times of what's going on around you." I turn to Jaynie. "Sergeant Vasquez? Move us out."

"Single line!" Jaynie snaps. "Form up!"

Jaynie's on point. The LCS falls into place behind her. We'll be going single file to reduce our profile. I take a position three back while Sergeant Nolan sweeps.

We move out at a fast clip, loping through the dry grass, the powered legs of the dead sisters letting us run better-than-eight-minute miles without trying too hard, while carrying the weight of our packs, our armor, and our arms. The angel is ahead of us, flying high to make it safe from ground-based fire.

We've put eight klicks behind us, and the grass is giving way to more frequent groves of small, thorny trees, when Pagan checks in.

"Shelley."

"Here."

"We've got EM signals indicating sensor positions. Uploading to your map now."

Pale dots blossom in a ring around our target, but the data gets to us too late. We've already passed through the outer ring. I shunt the data to Jaynie. "They know we're coming," I warn her, panting as I run.

"Got it, sir."

I switch back to Pagan. "Any sign . . . of an enemy drone?"

"Not so f—"

A flash lights up the sky, and in midsentence I lose Pagan, along with the feed from the angel. A concussion follows, rolling across the land: the sound of the simulated rocket that took the angel away.

"Angel down," I inform the company. Without the angel, none of us can reach Guidance, but we can still link to one another by helmet-to-helmet transmission. It's just like that time at Dassari, when the Red denied outside links to my LCS, except tonight, I'm sure it's Kendrick who's deprived us of the angel. If he thinks it's going to shake me up, he's wrong.

"Hold up!" I call over gen-com.

As the line halts, I shunt the sensor map to everyone. "We're inside the periphery and they already know we're coming. There's a mob of inner alarms we need to get through, but don't sweat it too much. We go in hot, move fast. They'll pick up where we were, but they won't know where we are."

I earn a determined chorus of *Yes, sir!*

"I want radio silence. If we haven't got angel eyes, there's no point in advertising our positions on the EM spectrum. So stay offline. Only exception: if you're isolated and need help. We will be passively receiving. Team leaders, *manually* collect your personnel."

Teams of four have been preassigned. Team leaders are my two sergeants plus Specialist Vanessa Harvey, a veteran of Bolivia, and Specialist Matt Ransom. Two rookies go with each sergeant, and one each with the other teams, giving them all a good chance of surviving the night.

Harvey and Ransom disappear with their teams in opposite directions, circling around the target. They'll try to get up on the bluff and come in from the back. Jaynie and Nolan spread out with their teammates to take the close approaches. I move between them, my M-CL1a in hand. We go fast, using night vision to keep a close eye on the ground for signs of land mines, or trip wires strung between the trees.

Two kilometers out from the lab we encounter the enemy. My visor picks up motion dead ahead. It's subtle, so the display emphasizes it to draw my eye: a rod, seen for a moment past a screen of branches. Instinct tells me it's a rifle barrel but I don't really care. The visor supplies targeting. I just aim and fire.

My helmet mutes the sound and my visor suppresses the muzzle flash. I'm able to see a body snap back and collide with the ground. I pull back in surprise. I'm shooting stinging rounds, not bullets. No way was there enough force to knock someone back that hard. It's got to be an effect of the kill box, but not one I've seen before.

I dart forward between the trees and find the body. The

soldier is on his back, his legs locked straight in his disabled dead sister, his arms locked at his sides, and his visor clear—powered down—indicating he's officially dead. I get a good look at his face. I don't know him, but he's gazing up at me with a deep, glittering irritation that makes me grin. He can't hold it against me, though, because with his night vision gone all he can see of me is a shadow among shadows. His arms are locked down by the exoskeleton, but his hands are free to express his opinion of the night and he gives me the finger.

*Fuck you too, brother.*

Maybe it's not resentment, though. Could be he just knows what's coming.

"Drop!" Jaynie shouts from somewhere to my left.

I do it. A missile howls from her position, snaking through the trees. It's a toy compared to the real thing, but I press my visor against the ground as it goes off with a flash-bang burst. Then I launch myself, using the combined power of the dead sister's four limbs.

I almost overdo it. I have to twist in the air and strike with my right arm strut against a tree trunk to keep from smashing into it. But when I hit the ground, running all out, machine-gun fire that was no doubt meant for me is glittering in useless tracers several steps behind.

I leave the shooter to Jaynie. In a few more strides I'm at the edge of the trees. Rising before me against the white-on-dark-green of a star field seen in night vision is a low, steep-sided bluff. A firefight is under way on the slope. Tracers scratch out horizontal lines as figures duck and rise beneath minimal cover. While the enemy is distracted, I go for the lab.

The dry wash where it's hidden opens below me. The lab is a cargo container draped in camo netting, riding on a trailer with fat desert tires. I drop a grenade into the wash and hit the ground as the flash-bang lights up the sky. Then

I jump sideways to avoid the weapons fire I know is going to come from the slope.

A burst of tracers beelines toward where I was. I scramble for the wash, moving just ahead of a second burst. Then the battle on the slope heats up. It's fierce enough to steal away the attention of my assailants, or maybe to kill them, who knows, but for a few seconds no one is shooting at me.

I peer into the wash. Two figures lie facedown in the sand, just outside the lab. I aim and fire, putting rounds into both of them to make sure the battle AI locks up their dead sisters for the duration. Then I drop into the wash.

Hanging steel steps lead up to the lab door. I place a grenade on the top step, then jump back up to the rim of the wash. It's three meters, but with the dead sister I reach the lip in one go, rolling out over the top as the grenade pops.

Two more grenades go off on the bluff, and then there's only silence.

I stay flat on the ground as two figures cautiously emerge from the woods. My visor uses height and posture to ID them as Jaynie and one of our rookies, PFC Julio Hoang.

"Shelley, you there?" Jaynie asks, off-com.

My helmet picks up and amplifies her words so I can hear her.

"I'm here. Don't kill me."

I get my feet under me, and crouched low, I scramble the few steps to the edge of the wash and look down. The grenades we're using are mostly light and noise, but the door to the shipping container has been rigged to pop at the concussion.

"Lab's open. Let's go."

Inside we find glass phials neatly sorted into padded and armored boxes. I put Hoang to work dividing these between our three packs, while Jaynie and I search for the computational equipment. We find three tablets. We take one each—everything's divided between us so we'll have something for Intelligence, even if only one of us gets through—and then we get out.

Jaynie and Hoang scramble out of the wash; I follow. Then I break radio silence. "Initiate ping." The order goes out over gen-com. Each helmet responds automatically, sending position info. I fix my gaze on the icon for the LCS map and it expands. Ransom, Flynn, Specialist Samuel Tuttle, and Specialist Jayden Moon register as still alive on the side of the bluff. The two rookies who were on their teams register as dead, while Harvey and PFC Layla Wade don't show up at all—which means the battle AI deems them blown up, with their equipment so badly damaged it can't check in.

"Ransom! Remaining enemy?"

"Bluff's clear, sir!"

Behind me in the woods, I register Sergeant Nolan, his two rookies, and Specialist Fernandez, who designates as injured.

"Nolan?"

"Still at least two in the trees."

"Shoot anything not us."

"Roger that."

"Lab and gully are clear. Ransom, make sure transponders go on our bodies, then come down."

"Yes, sir."

Swinging my backpack off my shoulder, I take out the loot from the lab and pass it to Jaynie. "Take Hoang, and grab one of Nolan's rookies. Go south around the trees. Once you're clear of the battle zone, run hard for home. We'll be coming behind you."

"See you there, sir."

They take off. A figure darts out of the trees to join them, while Ransom leads our surviving soldiers down from the bluff.

When everyone has cleared the wash I tell Ransom and Tuttle to blow up what's left of the lab. It's just playacting, but they have fun with it anyway.

Then we spread out to hunt the remaining defenders.

Nolan directs us into the woods. He thinks he knows where the two survivors are hidden, but as we get closer to the suspected position, I know he's wrong.

We're in a loose line with a ten-foot interval. Ransom's on my right; Jayden Moon is on my left. Ahead of me there's a tumbledown tree. Its gnarled trunk lies on the ground, but its roots must still have a grip on the sandy soil, because its leaves are green. God whispers the news to me: That's where the enemy is waiting, a fact we're about to discover the hard way.

"Drop!" I shout.

Moon hesitates, but Ransom knows me. He doesn't need to be told twice. We hit the ground as the blinding muzzle flash of automatic-weapons fire blazes behind the branches of the tumbledown tree. I return fire, but Ransom takes a more serious approach.

"Fire in the hole!" he bellows. I press my visor against the ground as a flash-bang goes off. The concussion is muffled by my helmet, but for a heartbeat my fingers and the hooks on my arm struts claw at the ground as I'm transported back to Fort Dassari—but in another beat of my heart the skullnet washes my terror away.

"Moon?" I query over gen-com.

No answer. I'm pretty sure he's dead.

"Nolan?"

He answers on gen-com. "Sorry about that, sir."

"Status?"

"I'm good."

"Ransom?"

"Golden, sir!"

Everyone else checks in.

I get up and go count the enemy bodies. "Two confirmed. Nolan, is that all?"

"It's all I know of."

"Game's over," Ransom says. "We win."

I put a transponder on Moon's body. He glares up at me, just like my dead enemy did, but he's got nothing to complain about. "Next time I tell you to drop, do it."

His gaze shifts away. He probably wants to give me the finger too, but Moon's too smart for that.

The angel comes back online, relaying Kendrick's voice to all the soldiers on both sides of the game. "Make your weapons safe and let the dead rise," he declares with a dramatic flair that impresses no one. "I declare peace among you. Embrace your enemy as you would a beloved sibling."

Moon stirs, and so do the two unknowns who were caught by Ransom's flash-bang.

"Make your weapons safe," I remind them.

Moon gets to his feet. "Lieutenant, how the hell did you know we were about to flame out?"

An excellent question, one I want Kendrick to answer. "Colonel? Did we have another security lapse?"

"Goddamn King David," Kendrick answers.

We all look east toward the low thrum of an approaching helicopter.

Kendrick says, "Mark out an LZ, Shelley. C-FHEIT LCS is getting pulled out first. We've got issues to discuss."

It takes the helicopter only a few minutes to ferry us back to C-FHEIT, but during those minutes there's nothing to do but think about what happened—and as I think about it, anger kicks in. I agreed to the skullnet. I'm wired for emotions. It's part of the job and I'm not complaining, but Guidance has a duty to protect me from outside interference and they failed to do it. Again.

It pisses me off.

There's a red stain bleeding through their defenses, and it's infecting me. So far the Red has been on my side, but no one knows why, and there's no reason to believe it will always be that way.

Sometimes, the Devil raises us up, only to throw us down from a greater height.

Thelma Sheridan is crazy, no question, but that doesn't mean she's stupid. One of these days, when it suits the Red's agenda, I might find myself pushed into panic when only a reasoned calm could save my life and the lives of the people around me. Then I'm not David anymore, I'm Saul—rejected by God and dead with my soldiers on the battlefield.

We set down on the quad, and as soon as the door is open, I'm out. "Kendrick!"

He opens a solo link to my helmet. "Debriefing. Now. Room one ten."

Still rigged in my dead sister and with my HITR in hand, I stomp over to the Cyber Center. From the open door of the largest conference room, I hear the chatter of the gathered observers, but Colonel Kendrick is closeted in a smaller room. I open the door to 110 and find him sitting at an oval table, his back to the door. He's not quite alone. Two tablets are set up on the table. A one-star general I don't recognize looks out of one; a civilian gazes out of the other.

The civilian is a soft and pudgy twentysomething, with dark, Middle Eastern eyes, dark hair, and a five o'clock shadow. "Hey, Shelley," he says. The voice confirms what I already suspected: This is Pagan.

"It came," I tell him. "It hacked my head just like at Dassari. Your new security didn't work."

Pagan winces, but it's the general in the tablet who answers. "We are aware of that, Lieutenant Shelley. It's priority one to find out why."

I look at her again. She's an older woman with steel-gray hair drawn back from her face, and faded blue eyes. My overlay IDs her from the encyclopedia and pops up a label: General Harmony Trager, commanding officer of Guidance.

"We were watching for the hack," Pagan tells me. "You were my only client tonight, so I saw it happen. The data stream from your skullnet blanked out, for about one point three seconds."

"That's all it took? One point three seconds of interference?"

"That's it," Pagan confirms. "All normal otherwise. It dropped in, dropped a message into your skullnet, and terminated."

I look at Trager. "One point three seconds is more than enough to change the course of a battle. And it's not just me. If I can be hacked, any LCS soldier can be."

"Sit down, Shelley," Kendrick says. "And shut up."

We trade glares, but he's a colonel. I'm just a lieutenant who does what he's told.

I start popping cinches, because the dead sister isn't made for sitting. Then I step out of the rig, rack my weapon on it, and take a chair. "General Trager, Guidance has had weeks to fix the vulnerability."

"Damn it, Lieutenant, we can't fix the breach until we know where it is."

"How can you not know?"

"It goes that deep, Shelley," Pagan says. "Somehow it can override everything we do."

"The reality show—"

"Has nothing to do with this," Trager says. "We are not playing you for drama."

"The Red is."

"The Red?" Kendrick looks at me with his well-rehearsed *Are you an idiot?* expression. "The Red what? Red China? Who the hell uses that term anymore?"

"Just the Red," Pagan says. "It's what we've been calling it."

I sigh and lean back in my chair, wondering how much Kendrick's not telling me. "It's from something Thelma Sheridan said. 'The red stain that bleeds through all the affairs of men.'"

"You haven't let Ms. Sheridan's crazy get inside your head, have you? It's already crowded enough in there."

I don't take the bait, turning to Trager instead. "Are there other soldiers who've been hacked?"

"You're not cleared for that discussion."

I'm certain that answer means yes.

Inside the frame of the tablet, her fingers tap against a tabletop. "A developing theory is that one of the DCs, one deep inside our communications system, is behind the infiltration. Defense contractors used to play the short game. They made money just prepping for the next war. Then they figured out they could use their congressional reps to buy more conflicts, and sell more goods. Along the way the big DCs ate the little ones, and one of the survivors must have thought, *Why stop with the politics? Why not decide the course of battles too?*"

I frown, wondering why she's telling me this, what she's fishing for. I have no secrets. As the commanding officer of Guidance, she knows that. So maybe she's feeding me misinformation because she thinks I'm a conduit to the Red?

I answer cautiously. "This is an issue that goes beyond the army. Maybe a defense contractor did develop a system to infiltrate our communications, but I think the Red took it over. If a DC was in control, they would hide what they're doing. They wouldn't keep coming back and using me."

Kendrick says, "I agree. And no DC has the organizational integrity to pull off an infiltration at this level and hide every sign of it. At some point, somebody would make a mistake, and that hasn't happened."

"So it's the Red," I conclude.

He leans back in his chair, elbows on the armrests and fingers locked together in front of his chest. "If that's what you want to call it. Shit, why not? You could call it anything, because we don't know what it is, and we don't know how it works, but we think we know what it wants."

This startles me. I lean forward, eager to hear whatever he might say, because the Red's agenda has been an impenetrable mystery to me.

Kendrick shows his teeth in what might be interpreted as a black-humor smile. "The evidence we've gathered suggests that its purpose is to shake things up. To hammer down Goliath and raise up David, and when David gets too big, to hammer him down too."

It's a metaphor, but I don't understand it. "Are you talking defense contractors? Or countries?"

"All of it," Kendrick says. "All of us. Anything hooked into the Cloud is vulnerable. You. Me. Every wired soldier. Ahab Matugo. Any punk kid in the street steering through life with farsights engaged. And Thelma Sheridan too. She's tried to cut herself off from the Cloud, but she can't cut herself off from everyone and everything else that's hooked in."

I'm suspicious he's playing me, just to see how much shit I'll swallow, but I don't care. "So we need to get rid of it."

"Easier said than done. It's distributed all through the Cloud."

"So there's no way to get rid of it?"

"There's always a way, son, if we're willing to pay the price."

I wait, but when he doesn't elaborate, I press him. "Well? Are we?"

"The question's in committee. In the meantime, just consider it another factor in the terrain we have to negotiate as we further the interests of our country."

I can't believe what I'm hearing. "Just live with it? Is that what you're telling me?"

"Son, what makes you think you have a choice?"

*Just live with it.*

I fold up the bones of my dead sister, grab my helmet and my HITR, and head to the barracks. Dawn has started to make a reluctant impression, nothing more than a faint glow to the east, beyond the quad. Night still owns the sky, filling it up with stars and the bright, gliding sparks of satellites. Along the sidewalk, footlights cast a wan amber glow against the concrete, minimizing the presence of our facility to anyone looking in on us from above and making it hard for me to see anything farther than knee height from the ground.

So I don't notice Jaynie until she speaks. "Ransom says God is still talking to you, sir."

I peer into the dark, and after a few seconds I make her out. She's sitting cross-legged on the flat rim of an empty landscape planter that curves around the corner of the barracks. I walk over, set my rig on the ground, and sit down too, with my weapon leaning up against my titanium knee. When I stretch out my legs, my feet look like alien artifacts against the dimly lit concrete.

I tell Jaynie the consensus opinion: "God has taken the form of a rogue autonomous program that has infiltrated the Cloud. I've been hacked. I'm not the only one."

Her voice comes out of the dark: "Are you shitting me?"

"Nope."

I tell her what little I know about the Red, hoping to compromise her with what is probably restricted intel. That way, when she requests to be transferred to another unit, Kendrick will almost certainly say no, and I'll get to hold on to a skilled non-com.

"*The Red*," she whispers. "It's true, then."

"What's true?"

"That there's something out there, steering people to their doom."

A shiver runs up the back of my neck. Jaynie is solid: smart, skeptical, reliable. She's the big sister I never had, ready to kick me back into line when I start to deviate. Supernatural shit is not her thing. "Jaynie, what are you talking about?"

"You need to get out in the world more, Lieutenant. Strange things are happening. People are making choices you'd never guess they'd make. You know Moon? His sister quit her factory job out of the blue. She told him it was like a spell came over her and she knew she wasn't supposed to spend her life making sure ten million pieces of candy all had their wrappers on straight. Tuttle's mom dumped the deadbeat anchor she's been living with for nine years, after a feeling came over her that it was time to move on, so strong she couldn't deny it. Ransom's little brother was all set to enlist, but after he watched *Dark Patrol* he pulled his paperwork, packed his bag, and went off with this youth group that does charity work—giving up all chance for a paycheck. And I've heard story after story of rich kids like you signing military contracts for no good reason."

"I had a reason."

"Not everyone does." Her boot scrapes the concrete. Her tone is soft but mocking. "People say, 'I woke up to the truth.' Or, 'God made me restless in my heart.' Or, 'For the first time in my life I *knew* why I was put in the world. I just knew.'"

"Is that bad?" I ask her. "It doesn't sound like doom to me."

"It's damn suspicious. Have we all been hacked?"

"Have you?"

"Would I know it if I had?"

"Do you have any reason to think you have?"

"*Yes.* I got dumped into the closing action of your reality show, didn't I? And that shouldn't have happened. I'd just finished a combat tour. I was promised a break, but new orders came through at the last minute, and I was sent to Dassari."

"I'd been waiting weeks to get a new sergeant. We were understaffed. You know there's never enough personnel to go around."

The front door of the Cyber Center opens, startling both of us, and out of instinct I reach for my rifle—the second time I'm about to bring a weapon to bear on my commanding officer, because it's Kendrick who steps out from the bright light spilling through the doorway.

I stand up. Jaynie gets to her feet too. The morning is starting to brighten. Maybe there's enough light in the east that Kendrick can see us . . . but I'm sure he already knows we're there.

"You need to learn more discretion, Shelley," he says as he gets close, letting me know he's been following the thread of our conversation as it was captured by my overlay. I'm not surprised. I knew someone would be listening.

He turns to Jaynie. "What about it, Vasquez? You really want to buy into the cyberspook story? Start blaming everything that doesn't go your way on the Red?"

"Gotta blame someone, sir."

He laughs, a loud bark straight from the belly. "That we

do, though we used to just call it luck. Learn to work your luck, and stop scaring yourselves. We know the enemy is out there. That's a big step forward."

He goes on his way, disappearing into the barracks.

"No secrets around you, huh, sir?" Jaynie says.

I bend down to pick up my dead sister. "None," I agree. "It's good to keep that in mind."

Elliot's inside, leaning on the watch desk. Jayden Moon is on duty behind the desk, already showered and changed and looking annoyed with Elliot, who has no doubt been explaining to him the relationship between war, politics, and defense contractors.

As I come in, Moon looks at me in relief. "LT, Mr. Weber is here to see you."

Elliot turns to look me up and down, from my buzz-cut scalp to my robot feet. "Shelley. I couldn't believe that was you out there tonight. You were still in a wheelchair the last time I saw you."

I fake a smartass grin, because if I look worried he's going to ask why. "I think the prosthetics have proved themselves. I'm not a super-cyber comic-book warrior, but I can keep up. My official certification should be coming through. I'll be field qualified, and that means Kendrick's program will get a big grant." I cross to the stairs, hauling the M-CL1a and my dead sister. "So how long are you here for? You're not going back this morning?"

He falls into step beside me. "No, no. I still need to do an interview with you—a *short* interview," he quickly adds when I start to object. "Come on, it's just a human-interest piece on the star of *Dark Patrol.* The army wants it done. They're pushing this prosthetics program. It's why I'm here."

There are other reasons he's here, going back to a two a.m. phone call.

We start up the stairs. I say, "It's hard to believe you're writing propaganda pieces for the army these days."

He pauses on the landing, giving me a measuring look. "I know you've got a lot going on, Shelley, but I am not your enemy."

Maybe that's true. I hope it is. But I'm not going to let him lay on the guilt. I keep going. "Things aren't simple," I tell him. "Not with you, not with the army."

Maybe I'm getting through. "You think I've got another reason for being here?" he asks as we reach the top. "Okay. You're right."

I keep going, until I reach the door of my room. The dead sister is getting damned heavy, so I open the door and set it down inside. Then I turn back to Elliot.

He says, "I've heard a rumor—"

I hold my gloved hand up, palm out, and he stops. I tap a finger by my eye to remind him what's there. "Don't say it, if you don't want the army to know it."

"If they don't know it, they're more screwed up than even I give them credit for." He crosses his arms, lifts his chin, as if daring me to argue. "I think the idea started with *Dark Patrol*, but there's a rumor running wild, Shelley, that the linked combat squads have been infiltrated—hacked through their skullcaps."

Out of instinct, I adopt my stonewall expression. "Where did you hear that?"

"In the Cloud. No fixed point. It's one of those things people talk about . . . and it got me thinking. At Kelly AMC, when I came to see you, you weren't too sure why you'd wanted me there. You were starting to regret it. Do you remember what you asked me?"

I do, but I deny it with a shake of my head.

"You asked, 'Did I sound normal when we were talking?'"

"And what was your answer?"

He scowls. "Look, the point is, you had doubts about your own cognitive processes."

"Your answer was that I sounded normal."

"Yeah, that's right. You still do. It's only in the King David moments when things get strange." He raises his eyebrows, his gaze inviting me to explain.

I retreat instead—"I've got to get some sleep"—slipping into my room and closing the door firmly behind me.

While I'm taking a shower I dictate a report of the night's fun and games, a strategy that lets me fall into bed just as the sun makes it over the horizon. The glare outside the closed blinds is like a nuclear explosion.

I close my eyes, and the always-on icons of my overlay brighten a little, but when I ignore them, they fade again into translucent near-invisibility. I'm drifting off, seeing dream images instead of the icons, when a rectangular message box pops up in the lower third of my vision, startling me back to consciousness: *Public Network Available*.

I open my eyes again to the stripes of nuclear fire leaking in through the blinds.

Guidance put me in lockdown as soon as I entered the secured grounds at C-FHEIT, and I'm scheduled to stay locked down for three more days until I go on leave. So why am I connected to the Cloud now?

Maybe it's a reward that Kendrick forgot to mention. Or maybe it's a mistake. I don't really care. "Call Lissa," I whisper.

But there's already a call coming through, and it's her. "Lissa?" I ask in astonishment.

Her voice is in my ears, low, breathy, frightened. "Oh my

God, Shelley. Is it really you? I didn't think I'd get through, but I just wanted . . . how long have you been online?"

"Seconds. Lockdown got lifted. I was about to call you. How weird is that? That you would call me just when—"

It occurs to me how truly weird that is. "Jesus, the Red switched me on."

"The Red?"

"The Red."

I don't have to explain it to her. "So it came back," she whispers.

"King David," I confirm.

"Then the new security didn't work. No wonder . . ."

"Lissa, what do you know about new security? Tell me what's going on."

"I'm not sure how much I can say. Do you remember the army wanted to open a contract with Pace Oversight, to oversee our research?"

"Your company turned it down."

"The army came back. National security. Needs of the country. We've been working with them for weeks now, and . . . I'm worried I said too much."

"What do you mean? What do you know?"

"Every time I talk to you, Shelley, someone's listening. They're listening now, aren't they?"

I start pacing, my robot feet tapping on the floor tiles, the stripes of brilliant light raking my eyes and leaving me half-blind. "You don't have to tell me."

But I want to know.

Lissa wants to tell me. "The army liaison I've been working with—you don't know her—she called me almost an hour ago, so early that I just knew something was wrong. I was afraid for you. I don't want you set up for another slam."

"I'm okay. Don't worry."

"She wanted my best guess on how to get rid of it . . . of the Red."

"But I was just talking to Kendrick—" *About that.* I stop myself before I say too much, but she understands.

"It's a critical question," she says, "and the answer isn't easy because the Red isn't just one thing. I think it's grown up out of a collection of marketing and inventory programs—"

"Marketing? Are you kidding?" General Trager's suggestion that a DC designed it makes more sense to me.

"You think it sounds banal?"

"Yeah."

"The most complex programs in existence are used for consumer analysis. They're everywhere, watching and analyzing every aspect of our lives. The amount of data gathered on any one of us is mind-boggling—but that's only one aspect. Shelley, from what I can tell, pieces of this program, the Red, are running all over the world, and those pieces are mirrored, so it's not like anyone can just 'pull the plug.'"

Kendrick said the same thing, and when I asked if there was no way to get rid of it, he told me, *There's always a way, son, if we're willing to pay the price.*

And me, pushing him: *Well? Are we?*

"What's the price of getting rid of the Red?" I ask Lissa. "What would we have to do?"

"I think we'd have to break the substrate it lives on . . . bring down the Cloud. That's what I told the army—and I'm afraid they might decide to do it."

Kendrick said the question was in committee.

"No one can bring down the Cloud," I object. "It's everywhere, a redundant system."

"We like to think so." Her voice is soft, frightened. "It's not true. Geek interlude, baby. All nonlocal data traffic goes through a limited number of physical locations known as exchanges. Take out a handful of those—"

Her explanation cuts out in midsentence. The call has dropped—but my network icon is still green. So I call Lissa back—but the call doesn't go through.

Seconds later, someone activates the post's defensive alarm.

Rumbling thunder fills the barracks as everyone scrambles for armor and bones.

It takes me two minutes to dress and rig up. I pull my helmet on and watch the icons come up on my visor. I'm linked to my skullnet, my HITR, a growing number of my soldiers, and to the C-FHEIT network—but my link to Guidance is grayed out. Delphi's voice doesn't greet me. No one talks to me at all.

I visualize a link to Colonel Kendrick. "What's going on?"

"We're under attack. See to it that your soldiers are rigged and ready."

The helmet's tiny fans blow welcome cool air across my fiery cheeks. I grab my weapon and throw the door open.

Elliot's at the top of the stairs, dressed in boxer shorts like he just rolled out of bed. He whips around to look at me, face taut with shock, fear, his eyes squinting as he tries to convince himself that the man behind the anonymous black visor is me. "Shelley?"

Between us, the door to Major Chen's room opens and the major steps out, wearing armor but no bones. I slip past him to the top of the stairs. There's no time to talk to Elliot, but I pause anyway, touching his shoulder with my gloved hand. "Elliot, I don't know what's going on, but it's serious. Stay out of the way, and be ready for anything."

I jump down the stairs, all the way to the landing, letting the dead sister's leg shocks absorb the impact. One more jump and I'm in the lobby. It's empty, except for a private whose name I don't know, looking frightened as he maintains his station behind the desk.

The doors to the enlisted quarters are open, men on one side, women on the other. It's chaos in the hallways as soldiers scramble out of their individual rooms, still trying to finish strapping into their dead sisters while staggering toward the lobby. Some have their helmets in their hands instead of on their heads.

On the women's side, I see Jaynie, fully rigged and helmeted, step out into the fray. "Thirty seconds!" she screams offline. "You have thirty seconds to get yourselves fully rigged and assembled in the lobby or I will kick your asses!"

Sergeant Nolan tackles the men's side with similar encouragement, so I turn to the private serving desk duty. "Report."

He's a skinny kid with wide, frightened eyes. He passes me a paper printout—something I've rarely seen since I've been in the army. "General message from Fort Hood, sir."

Subject: ALERT STAGE RED:
NUCLEAR EXPLOSION DETECTED
VICINITY OF DALLAS.

Body: An explosion in Dallas County has been identified with a high degree of certainty as originating from a low-yield nuclear device. All personnel are to return immediately to their duty station. If that is not possible, personnel should report to the nearest military facility.

Details to follow.

"Form up!" I scream as soldiers pour into the lobby. The sergeants push them into lines and chaos transforms to order: four neat rows of five. My sixteen LCS soldiers are in armor and bones, their helmets on. At the end of each row is a single soldier dressed like Major Chen, in combat uniform and armor, but no dead sister, no helmet, just an audio loop. They are support personnel. There are five altogether, counting the private still manning the watch. Theirs are the only faces I can see, and all of them look scared.

I'm scared.

I want to know if only one bomb went off . . . or were there others, in other cities? Was there a bomb in San Diego? Is Lissa still alive, or did I hear her last words just now on the phone? Why the fuck were we talking about how to bring down the Cloud? I didn't even tell her I love her, and she was afraid. She was already afraid.

And my dad? Is he still alive?

And these soldiers in front of me . . . how long will they survive in the war that must surely come?

Everyone looks up as Colonel Kendrick comes down from the second floor, rigged in armor and bones, his helmet on. He walks down the stairs—a delicate operation given that the dead sister's footplates are too big to fit on each step, but he pulls it off with grace.

Major Chen follows behind him. No visor hides his stern expression. I don't doubt that he's received notice of the stage red, so I slip the printout into my pocket and snap to attention along with everyone else.

Kendrick halts his descent four steps from the bottom. The anonymous face of his visor surveys the troops. He speaks over gen-com: "Our country is under attack. Improvised nuclear devices have been detonated in the vicinity of Dallas, Miami, Alexandria—"

Discipline breaks, and sighs, gasps, and groans follow the naming of each city.

"—Chicago, Seattle, San Jose, and—"

I steel myself. I know somehow that the last city to be named will be San Diego. I desperately wish to be wrong, but he speaks the name and makes it real. Heat flushes from all my pores and the skullnet icon glows. I tell myself, *Lissa is still alive*, and I force myself to listen as Kendrick continues to speak.

"The INDs are suspected to have been vehicular bombs in the ten-kiloton range, producing major building damage within a half-mile radius of ground zero and significant burns and radiation injuries within a mile. Who the enemy is or what the goal of his attack might be, we do not currently know. But the widespread nature of this attack and the number of fully functional nuclear devices indicates he is well organized, well armed, and very likely well placed within our own security structure. Which means this is an inside job, one that has placed our country, our system, our very way of life, at risk.

"Our communications systems are overburdened. We will proceed without the expectation of one-on-one oversight from Guidance, but helmet-to-helmet communication must be active at all times.

"Your orders are to man your assigned defensive stations, and if any unauthorized vehicle or individual enters our air- or ground space—

"*Hell!* If any suspect *wildlife* shows its nose around here, blow it to glory. Move out!"

My civilian network icon is still green, assuring me I'm linked to the post's network, but my calls and queries—to Lissa and to my dad—don't go through. Maybe our civilian network is just cut off from the Cloud. Maybe the Cloud's overloaded. Or maybe it's gone.

Kendrick and Chen are linked into the military satellite system through the angel that keeps watch above us, but the rest of us remain cut off, with our links to Guidance grayed out. It's a decision made by Command. There's a real fear that excessive traffic could overwhelm and paralyze what's left of our communications system, so only high-level traffic is being allowed through.

So with my two sergeants, I take over the chores usually assigned to Guidance, patrolling the defensive posts to make sure weapons are kept ready and that no one has fallen asleep. The morning drifts past with no sign of enemy incursion. It would be almost a relief if we were attacked. At least there would be something to do besides brood over the fate of the people we love.

Just past noon Kendrick opens a solo link to me. His low voice rumbles in my helmet audio: "Shelley. Command meeting. Five minutes."

"Yes, sir!"

I have never been so happy to be included in a meeting.

I remove my helmet as I step into the conference room. It's the same room where we had our predawn meeting—an event that took place in some other age, some other world. Colonel Kendrick is there with Major Chen, but there are no virtual officers. Though the tablets are still set up on the table, they're empty, their displays switched off.

On the wall, a monitor plays what must be a satellite feed from one of the mass-media propaganda networks. The volume is muted, but the caption tells me I'm seeing a massive, gridlocked traffic jam as people flee Alexandria.

Chen looks up at me from his seat at the conference

table, his face a stern mask. "The mediots have dubbed it 'the Coma.' Seven of the country's primary data exchanges were knocked out in the blasts. All of them were built to withstand Category Five hurricanes, but not close-proximity nukes. Ground-based telecommunications have been sliced up into regional modules, most of which collapsed under the resulting load within a few minutes of time zero. Satellites have been unaffected, leaving the mediots in charge of peddling whatever propaganda they see fit, but their privileged position is under threat. Power grids are on their way down, because load balancing is tracked through the Cloud, and within the United States, the Cloud is gone."

Lissa said that to get rid of the Red, we'd have to break the substrate it lives on.

I don't want to believe the army had a part in that.

"Death toll?" I ask, still standing, rigged in my dead sister with my helmet under my arm.

Chen's eyes narrow; he shakes his head. "Numbers at this stage are fictitious. Collateral damage is presumed extensive. It's logical to assume the target wasn't just the buildings. Hundreds of technicians—highly trained to run and repair these facilities—must have been killed in the attack. God knows how long it will take to get back online without them."

"I talked to my girlfriend this morning," I confess. "Lissa Dalgaard. Right before the bombs went off. She's been consulting with the army, sharing her research on the Red. She said this was it—this was the price to bring it down. She was afraid the army would do it." My gaze shifts to Kendrick. I have to know the truth. "Did we?"

Kendrick is still wearing his armor, but his dead sister has been folded up and stashed behind his chair. Like me, he's been up all night. Fatigue lines show in his face. So does his temper. He leans back in his chair, crossing his arms over his chest as he considers me . . . as he considers whether or not to pull his sidearm and shoot me, that's my guess. One way or another, I know I'm going down.

His fist hits the table. "When were we discussing the price, Lieutenant Shelley?"

I draw myself up. "This morning, sir."

He pushes his chair back and stands up. His palm is resting on the flap that secures his sidearm. "And in your estimation, is the US Army capable of setting up a continent-wide coordinated nuclear assault on American soil—in *violation* of the Constitution of the United States—inside of one hour?"

I'm too stupid to be cowed. "You said the question was in committee, sir."

"In *committee*! Do you know the primary fact about committees, Lieutenant? They are slow! Or did your fancy *Man-hattan* private school fail to teach you any real-world knowledge at all?"

"They don't seem to have done an especially good job, sir."

"That's the fucking truth! You were assigned to C-FHEIT because you are supposed to have functional brain matter inside your skull, but if you give me another reason to think there's nothing in there but spoiled cum I will revoke your contract and hand you back to the state prison authorities who sold you to us in the first place!"

I like Kendrick. I admire his straightforward manner, but I decide it's the wrong time to say so, and for once I keep my mouth shut, standing at attention, my stony gaze fixed on the gray spot of a mosquito's corpse crushed against the wall.

Maybe that's good enough for him. He turns away, pacing the width of the room. He stops somewhere behind me. "Who is our enemy, Lieutenant? Given what you know?"

I consider it. The Cloud has gone down. It can't be

coincidence. It has to be a strike against the Red. And who knows about the Red? Who is in a position to conduct a massive strike against it . . . and is deep-dark crazy enough to do it?

"Vanda-Sheridan, sir, seems the likely candidate."

"That wasn't so hard, was it?"

He's still standing behind me. For all I know he has his sidearm aimed at the back of my skull, but I hazard a question anyway. "Is there evidence?"

"Not my department. Intelligence likes Thelma Sheridan for this one, but she's using a front of Bible-jerking jackoffs here in the local neighborhood who are calling themselves the Texas Independence Army. They have claimed responsibility for the attack and declared their intention to take the state of Texas out of the Union. And while I'm sure many of our fellow American citizens would be thrilled at this news and cheerfully wave good-bye to the Lone Star State, the president has decided otherwise."

He walks back to his chair so that I can see him again, and see that his pistol is still in its holster. He turns around, but he doesn't sit down. "The president has declared a state of emergency authorizing the army to respond to this act of insurrection, but there is a complication."

I let my gaze wander from the dead mosquito to his eyes. They are cold. As cold as anything I've seen . . . and I know suddenly what the complication is because it's what I would do if I were intent on slicing up the Union. "They didn't blow all of their nukes, did they, sir?"

"No, Lieutenant Shelley, they did not. There are booby-trapped vehicles parked in five metropolitan areas containing additional improvised nuclear devices. If any public announcement is made of that fact, or if evacuations are attempted, we are assured that some or all of the INDs will be detonated. If the vehicles lose contact with a continuous satellite signal generated by the Texas Independence Army, the weapons will be detonated."

"A dead man's switch."

"Correct."

"What cities?"

"That information is not pertinent to our mission."

I envision one of the INDs in an innocuous SUV parked in a Manhattan garage, not far from my dad's apartment building. Is it worse to guess? Or to know for sure?

Not that I have the option. "Sir, what is our mission?"

"In accordance with the demands of the terrorists, a plan is being implemented to evacuate military personnel from the state of Texas. You and I will not be going. We'll be staying behind in enemy territory along with the C-FHEIT linked combat squads, awaiting instruction.

"I am assured a massive effort is under way to locate the leaders of the insurrection. It is believed that said leaders possess disarmament codes that will neutralize the nuclear devices. Our mission—and it falls to us because we are here, on the ground in the suspected neighborhood, trained and ready—is to find and take possession of those codes without interrupting the dead man's switch and without allowing the purposeful detonation of any weapon."

By clamping my teeth together—hard—I manage not to say what I'm thinking.

Evidently, Kendrick hears it anyway. "What must be done will be done, Lieutenant. Whether it's possible or not is not our concern."

I glance at Chen . . . hoping, maybe, to see some hint that this is staged, that none of this is real. But behind the composed mask of his expression I sense despair.

A new video is playing on the monitor, showing a line of men dressed in civilian clothes and carrying automatic weapons. Most look to be in their thirties, and most look out of shape and overweight. They have armbands, blue like the blue of the Texas flag, each with a big white star. They stand with stonewall gazes in a line outside a chain-link fence with small signs wired to each section. Each sign is crudely defaced with blue spray paint not dense enough to hide the words *Property of the Federal Government.*

I can't tell if the fence is protecting a weather station or a weapons depot, but lying dead in the street in front of the men is a young Hispanic woman, legs bent back, blood seeping from her chest, blank eyes staring at the sky. A gunshot-riddled protest sign lies beside her. I can make out only the first word written on it: *Loyal.*

So the resistance has already begun. Martyrs are already dying.

"I don't get it," I say to no one in particular. "There are more guns in Texas than citizens. Vanda-Sheridan can't believe that people are just going to sit on their hands while a DC takes over the state—"

"No?" Kendrick asks. "Not when the only news comes through satellite feeds Vanda-Sheridan controls? Not when the military is abandoning them without offering a reason? There's a big advantage to controlling communications—and to owning the governor and most of the big-city mayors."

"Sir, Lissa was in San Diego when . . . when the device went off. She knows about the Red. She's been working on an army contract. She's valuable. If there's any way—"

"I already put her on the recovery list, son. There's nothing more either of us can do, except to slam Thelma Sheridan as hard as she slammed us."

"Queen-of-the-world syndrome," Chen says bitterly. "It's the doom of our species that psychopaths always want to be in charge."

• • • •

Vanda-Sheridan specializes in surveillance satellites, so our first challenge is to leave C-FHEIT without being noticed. That means no helicopters and no SUVs. We'll go on foot. Satellites might still log our presence, but on the first night of the war, the TIA will have larger concerns than a few scattered refugees in the rangelands.

We wait for full dark, hoping for cloud cover, but all we get is the usual smog layer rolling up from the gulf.

I'm rigged in my dead sister, helmet on and a full pack on my back with food, water, ordnance, and a med kit. Frag, flash-bang, and smoke grenades nest in my vest pockets, and I'm carrying my M-CL1a with its underslung barrel for programmable grenades.

There are eighteen of us: the sixteen enlisted of C-FHEIT's dual LCS, along with me and Colonel Kendrick.

As we wait together for the order to move out, Jaynie opens a solo link between our helmets.

"Lieutenant Shelley?"

"What's up?"

"You were wrong, sir."

I feel like a kid guilty of any of a number of transgressions and with no idea which one I'm being called on. "It's not uncommon," I confess. "So hit me. What exactly?"

"At Dassari you told me a story. You said a DC will never allow a war in their own country. Well fuck, sir, if what Colonel Kendrick told us is true, Vanda-Sheridan just *engineered* a fucking war in their own country. In *our* country."

"Huh. Guess I did call that one wrong."

She pushes a little harder. "You remember rule one? 'Don't kill off your taxpayers.'"

"You have a damn good memory, Jaynie. I guess I don't know what the fuck I'm talking about."

"You weren't all wrong, sir. You said at Dassari there was nothing at stake, and that was true. But it's different now.

This is a real war, and there's a lot more on the table than the fortunes of a few dragons. I just want you to know, I've got your back."

"Shit, Jaynie, you're scaring me."

"It's good to be scared, Shelley. It's healthy."

I smile to myself. "Then I've never been better. Let's look after each other, okay? And everyone else."

"You got it."

Kendrick breaks in on gen-com. I wonder if he's been listening in, but all he says is, "You've got your go-ahead, Shelley. See you on the other side."

"Yes, sir."

*"Hoo-yah!"* Ransom yells, the volume automatically dampened by my helmet.

The entire unit responds, *"Hoo-yah!"*

And I take off, because it's my assignment to go first.

Powered by my dead sister, I leave the grounds at an easy lope, angling to the northeast. A map projected on my visor shows the tiny, glowing point of my existence as it separates with excruciating slowness from the mother-ship gleam of C-FHEIT. Somewhere above me an angel is watching.

The air is still, the night ethereal in its silence. I'm the loudest thing around, crackling through the dry grass in a thudding rhythm complemented by my breathing. The moon hasn't risen yet. Behind the night's thin smoke veil stars gleam in multitudes. Satellites move among them, but no planes fly over Texas tonight.

My overlay tallies the passing seconds. It takes me three minutes and forty-five seconds to cover the first kilometer. That's when I see a second glowing point depart from the mother ship: Ransom, leaving on a slightly different heading. The rest will set out over the next hour, two to three minutes apart. Scattered across time and miles, we'll be harder to detect. So goes the theory.

A coyote howls somewhere to the west. I resist the urge to run faster. Our initial goal is to get out into the countryside unnoticed. We don't even know where we're going yet.

It's twenty-four kilometers to the perimeter fence. I make it in less than two hours—and my feet aren't even sore. I am aware of fatigue setting in, but the skullnet keeps it at a distance.

I stop beside the fence long enough to drink water and to survey the map, tallying every point in the scattered constellation of our dual LCS. If anyone gets in trouble, if their equipment breaks down or they become sick or injured, Kendrick's order is to leave them behind. I don't like it. No one does. Still, I'm guessing the Texas Independence Army is a long way from imposing their authority on the hinterlands, and that out here an injured soldier has more to fear from coyotes than from Vanda-Sheridan's treasonous militia.

I hope so anyway.

Turning back to the fence, I extend the arm hooks of the dead sister and then jump. Using the hooks to catch the top rail of the fence, I lock on. I'm hanging there, but I don't feel my weight because I'm standing on the dead sister's footplates. At the top of the fence three strands of barbed wire strung on angled braces separate me from the other side. I clip them one by one, ducking to dodge the backlash. Then I use the arm hooks to haul myself far enough up to get a knee over the top. On the ground again, I resume my lope to the northeast.

Not long after, I reach a state highway. I lie low for several seconds, listening for traffic. When I don't hear any, I vault a barbed-wire fence, bound across the road, and vault another fence. The waning moon looks old and worn as it looms over the eastern horizon. Its yellow light picks out the boxy shape of a ranch house eight hundred meters down the road. I hear a dog bark, but it doesn't sound too sure of itself.

I keep going.

At 0100, my map updates. I'm not linked to Guidance, so I assume Kendrick has pushed new orders through. I'm to bear east and south, where I'll intersect a county road 13.2 kilometers away. *Bivouac*, it says. *Wait for transportation.*

Hallelujah. We won't have to run all the way to wherever it is we're going.

Because Texas is, after all, one hell of a big state.

One hell of a big state, with a lot of military, both veterans and active duty.

By the time our LCS has reunited on the roadside, Guidance has somehow hooked up with a local kid who is home on leave after a year in the Sahel. They give him a field promotion to specialist and tell him that he is now operating behind enemy lines, without a uniform. He thinks it's cool.

He takes his dad's eighteen-wheel cattle truck, does a few experimental slaloms on the narrow road, and gets the wheels to slide sideways, leaving a beautiful skid mark that ends just short of a ditch while bringing the cab to rest on the opposite shoulder. That's something we don't learn in New York City.

A team of four from our LCS hurries to get one of the back tires unbolted. They settle it at an angle on the axle so it looks like the axle is bent. That's all the subterfuge we can manage before Kendrick barks at us to scatter.

I take off along the road, sprinting hard to my assigned position, eight hundred meters out. Powered by the dead sister, I make it in three minutes, but my organic parts do not approve. I'm shaking as I throw myself on the ground in the shadow of a thin, scrubby bush. My breath is whooshing so hard that for a few seconds my visor's ventilation system can't keep up.

Several pairs of running footsteps pound down the road in my wake, but one by one they fall silent before reaching me. Only one runner comes all the way. I check the map on my visor and confirm that it's Ransom. Brush crackles as the bright point marking his existence departs the road, opposite me. The rest of the dual LCS is spread out all the way back to the disabled cattle truck.

I am so tired I'm not entirely sure I'm going to be able to get up again. The organics hurt, and my nerves are so raw that the feedback from the prosthetics is about to cripple me. Switching from the visor to my overlay, I pull up the neural feedback bar that Joby installed, and I slide it down.

As the pain eases, I hear in the distance the low rumbling of an approaching truck. Though I knew it was coming, I'm startled anyway and I scramble for the pistol Kendrick gave me to use. It feels small and useless in my hand, but I'm careful with it anyway, keeping it out of the dirt.

A green light pulses three times in my visor, announcing a direct link to Guidance.

"Hold position," Delphi breathes in my ears.

"Roger that," I whisper. "Is Guidance hooked in everywhere?"

"Affirmative. Everyone's got a good spirit."

My lips shape a silent *Thank you*, which my skullnet picks up and sends.

Guidance exists to help us avoid fatal mistakes—and tonight, with six rookies and everyone light-headed from exhaustion, we need all the help we can get, because if there are any errors in this mission, Boston might get blown up.

I don't actually know that there's a bomb in Boston. I'm just pretending there is, because in my heart I know the first target of the secessionists is going to be Manhattan, that it has to be Manhattan. Symbols are powerful things, and the city of New York symbolizes unity, diversity, past, future . . . and a big middle finger flipped at terrorists like the Texas Independence Army.

The red veins of the skullnet icon flicker, drawing my focus back to the present and to the growing rumble of the approaching truck. It's a container truck belonging to the Texas National Guard. Intelligence has been tracking it ever since it was stolen at gunpoint by a turncoat guardsman loyal to the TIA. It's transporting artillery, which is interesting though not relevant, since none of us has ever trained in artillery. We don't want the truck for its weaponry. We want it because it's a TIA asset. If we can quietly steal it back, we should be able to ride it a couple hundred miles east without the TIA's even noticing that anything's gone wrong.

My breathing slows, and my heartbeat settles into a deep, background thud. There's no way to know how close the truck will get to our fake accident scene before it stops. If the driver is the suspicious type, he might try to turn around as soon as he sees something is wrong. But this is a narrow county road with soft shoulders. Turning around in a big rig might not be possible—and it's my job to make sure the driver doesn't have time to try.

Sound carries remarkably across the flat landscape. Minutes pass as the truck draws near. As I lie on my belly, flat against the ground, I think about Texas scorpions. I imagine them crawling all around me. Or tarantulas.

"Ready," Delphi says.

At the angle my head is turned I can just see the glow of the truck's headlights rising above the brush.

I switch to angel sight, so I'm looking down from the drone's position as it cruises slowly above the road. I watch the oncoming truck pass beneath it. The staged wreck of the cattle truck is visible in the distance, the beams of its headlights shooting past a barbed-wire fence into an empty cattle range. Amber lights outline the cab. The kid is crouched beside the "broken" wheel, but as the headlights of the guard truck touch him, his skinny figure straightens and he turns, moving his hand up and down to signal to the oncoming truck to slow down.

Brake lights on the stolen guard truck blaze in brilliant red, and then the gunning throb of air brakes washes over me. "Betcha he was half-asleep," I whisper to Delphi.

She's too professional to answer.

The air brakes stop. The truck rolls past me at not more than fifteen miles per hour. Then it stops. It sits there for most of a minute, the engine rumbling. Diesel fumes envelop me.

The kid starts walking toward the truck. The headlights show him dressed in a thin T-shirt and tight jeans. Anyone can see there's no weapon on him. He's not a threat.

Still, there's no sign of any activity in the cab. Unless the driver has a satellite phone—not very likely—he's on his own trying to figure out what to do. "Delphi, he's going to come out guns blazing. Command can't sacrifice that kid."

The kid stops. He's still over fifty meters away.

"Get ready, Shelley," Delphi says. My angel sight goes away, leaving nothing to distract me.

My position is behind the cab, in the dark beyond the road. I get my feet under me. Crouched, waiting, I pass the pistol to my left hand.

The cab's window rolls open, an elbow sticks out, and a tentative voice calls, "Howdy!"

"Howdy, sir!" the kid answers with perfect midnight innocence. "You got a truck jack, sir?"

"Geez, son," the driver whines. "You don't carry your own jack?"

Delphi says, "Go, Shelley."

I go, using all the augmented power I have. My first leap takes me to the edge of the pavement. The driver hears the impact of my footplates. He turns to look, forgetting to use the mirror. I'm already in motion.

My second jump puts me on the running board, beside the window, which is rapidly closing. The driver is so startled by my sudden proximity that he throws himself sideways across the seat, leaving the window only half-closed. I try the door handle, just in case, but it's locked, so I shove my gun hand through the remaining gap in the window while grabbing the steel loop of an outside grip with my other hand to keep from falling down.

The driver is still sprawled across the seat, but he decides to fight back, bringing his booted foot up and aiming a vicious kick at my gun hand.

I've got the pistol aimed at his face. I could kill him easily, but Kendrick said I'm not supposed to; I'm not supposed to break the window either. We want the truck to show no sign of damage. I yank my hand back.

"You kill me and you're blowing up New York," he screams.

I *knew* it.

*Fuckwad.*

Delphi says, "Reach down and to your left. Along the armrest. Hit all of those buttons. One's the power lock."

"Can't. Gun's in my hand."

I reach through anyway. The driver tries again to kick me. This time I hit his shin hard with the gun barrel. I can't get much of a swing, but the impact is solid. He gasps, and for a few seconds he's frozen in pain.

Ransom breaks in over gen-com: "LT, you need help with that door?"

"Get up here!"

He lunges onto the running board, huge in his dead sister. I can't see through his black visor, but I imagine him grinning.

I'm not.

"Get the door unlocked! I don't want blood in our new truck."

"Yes, sir!" He reaches through the open window, groping for the power lock.

I hear a click and pivot away from the door so Ransom can get it open. I'm still holding the steel loop of the handgrip as I swing around, but I've made a rookie mistake. If I'd grabbed the loop with my dead sister's arm hook, my rig would take the weight, but now it's my right arm that has to hold everything up: my body weight plus an eighty-pound pack, and the weight of my dead sister. I groan. My shoulder is close to separating as the door swings open, so I am not in a good mood as I hurl myself into the cab.

My temper doesn't improve when I see the driver has pulled a pistol that he's bringing to bear on me. Using the butt of my own gun, I hammer him in the crotch, eliciting a scream that cuts off sharply when the pain closes up his throat. His weapon tumbles to the floor. Using my arm hook, I grab him by the belt and haul him with me as I back out of the cab. Ransom catches him before he can tumble to the pavement.

"Goddamn it, Shelley!" Kendrick shouts. I can't see his face past the black screen of his visor, but I get to hear his voice twice: both live and over gen-com. "I told you to take it easy!"

We're both looking down at the driver—Guidance says his name is Troy Butler—curled on the pavement in a fetal position, moaning and clutching his crotch.

A mishmash of voices is in my ears as my helmet collects all the solo links between squad members and plays them for me at low volume. I hear Sergeant Nolan and Specialist Tuttle working to get the cattle truck put back together, and I hear Sergeant Vasquez and Specialist Harvey doing an inventory of the weapons carried in the back of the hijacked National Guard truck. They speak in clipped phrases because we're in a hurry. We are scheduled to roll in seven minutes, but Kendrick wants to interrogate the prisoner.

I still have the colonel's pistol, so I use it to gesture at Troy Butler as he quivers on the ground. "Sir, you just said not to kill him—and he's not dead."

Kendrick looks up at me. I can't see any hint of expression in the empty field of his black visor, but I have a good imagination. "Did I need to add, 'Don't emasculate him?' I thought that might be assumed."

"I didn't cut anything off. He's just a drama queen." I reach down and grab good old Troy by his arm. "Get the fuck up, cracker, before I shove this pistol up your ass."

Reality slips. *Did I just say that?* I let go of Troy's arm and step back, certain that someone I don't know just slipped inside my soul.

"Damn it, Delphi," I whisper. "What are you juicing me on?"

"Whatever it is, Delphi," Kendrick says, "back it off a couple of notches."

Eight hundred meters down the road, the engine revs on the cattle truck and Sergeant Nolan shouts directions.

Kendrick nudges Troy Butler with the toe of his footplate. "I advise you to get up now, PFC Butler, because we are all tired and cranky, and it would be really easy for my juiced-up LT to make a body disappear out here in the ass-end of nowhere."

Threats never sound hollow when Kendrick makes them. Troy Butler foregoes groaning on the asphalt and, pulling himself together, he manages to struggle to his feet. He is not in uniform, but he *is* a National Guardsman. He picks that moment to remember the fact. Straightening his spine and squaring his shoulders, he turns to Kendrick and salutes. "Private First Class Troy Butler, reporting for duty, sir."

Kendrick crosses his arms over his chest. "About fucking time."

I consider raising the pistol and bringing it down on the back of Troy's turncoat skull, but Delphi is riding me, and she whispers, *"Chill."*

"Lieutenant Shelley," Kendrick says, "I think it's best if I have my gun back now."

"Give it to him, Shelley," Delphi warns.

"Stop nagging me," I whisper between clenched teeth—but I step around Troy and return the pistol to Kendrick. Down the road, the cattle truck is slowly straightening, its taillights blazing as it begins to roll away.

Troy isn't watching it; he's watching me. Though he holds his posture at attention, his eyes roll to take me in; his hands are shaking. I still have my HITR, and I think we're both wondering if Kendrick is going to let me shoot him.

"Private Butler," Kendrick says. "I'm told you have a little sister named Trina Butler, who is currently living in Fargo? Is that true?"

Troy's not worried about me anymore. He gives all his attention to Kendrick. In a breaking voice he says. "Sir, my sister has nothing to do with this! She's got two kids—"

"Jared and Beth," Kendrick agrees in a congenial tone. "Am I right?"

"Sir, please. What I did today, it was a mistake—"

"You're goddamn right it was a mistake, Private! And when word gets out that Trina's brother is a traitor—"

"Sir, please!"

"—that he's part of the terrorist group who nuked American cities and took down the Cloud—"

"It wasn't her fault!"

"Nobody's going to care. People want blood. An eye for an eye. We took your sister and her kids into custody for their own protection."

Troy turns out to be smarter than I would have guessed. "What do you want me to do, sir?" he asks in a subdued voice.

"Exactly what you were doing. Drive the truck. Show your papers at any checkpoints that require it. Be an eager participant in the Texan revolution . . . and don't let it slip that your cargo has changed. Guidance will be watching through my eyes. If anything goes wrong—and I don't care if it's your fault or just bad luck—your sister and her kids disappear. That's easy enough to understand, isn't it, Private Butler?"

"Yes, sir. It is, sir. Thank you, sir. Thank you for a chance to make up for the mistake I made this morning. I wouldn'a done it, sir, except I seen too many movies. Those lying fags in Hollywood just make it look like fun."

"A weekend party," the colonel agrees. Then, in an undertone that indicates he's linked, "Vasquez, get out here. The LT's a little strung out, so I think we'll let him rest. You get to ride up front with me and keep an eye on our loyal Private Butler."

"Coming, sir."

It takes her three seconds to appear at the open cargo door of the National Guard truck. As she trots toward us, her inventory arrives on-screen in my visor. Just like Intelligence said, the truck is carrying artillery, along with lots and lots of shells.

I don't like being dismissed by Kendrick, but I also don't

want to share the cab with Troy Butler, so I don't argue. I just turn my temper on those soldiers walking back from the cattle truck. "This is not a Saturday stroll! Get your asses moving. We roll in three minutes!"

They pick up the pace. I throw Kendrick an ironic salute, nod at Jaynie, and head to the back of the truck to see if there is any room among the weaponry to lie down and go to sleep.

There is no room to lie down.

And we're under orders to stay rigged.

I stand just outside the open cargo doors, making a head count as our people climb in. Jaynie is beside me, waiting to close and lock the doors, while Sergeant Nolan is just inside, duplicating my count and chivvying people to move to the back and make room.

The dead sisters, so fleet and agile in the field, turn awkward as soldiers clamber over pallets of ammo and squeeze past the two big guns. The cargo container isn't loaded to the top, but there isn't much empty floor space either. I open a solo link to Kendrick, who is in the cab, keeping an eye on our prisoner. "We need to dump some of this stuff."

"Can you get all our people in there or not?"

I check my count—only Flynn, Ransom, and me still to go. Flynn climbs in; Ransom follows. I jump up next to Nolan. "We're all in now, but it's tight."

"I don't want to risk discovery. It's only going to be a couple hours, so get the doors shut and make the best of it."

Jaynie links in. "Ready, LT?"

I give her a thumbs-up. She swings one door shut and then the other. Handles are levered; locking rods slam into place.

For a second it's too dark for my night vision's photomultiplier to work. Then a couple of LED flashlights come on. Flynn's got one in her mouth as she crawls across pallets to get farther back.

"Heads up," Kendrick warns over gen-com. "We are moving in ten seconds."

"Secure yourselves!" Nolan barks.

He takes his own advice, folding into a crouch in a small open space beside Ransom, under the muzzle of the first gun. I use the same maneuver to go down. The dead sisters don't make it easy to sit, but it turns out to be possible. My back is toward the cargo doors, my robot legs bent at their artificial knees. I lean against my pack, trying to ignore the discomfort of the dead sister's back frame. The truck starts to roll. I can hear the tires grind against the pavement as Troy progresses through the gears.

I link to Kendrick again. "Air is going to be a problem."

"If anyone starts to suffocate, I'm sure Guidance will let me know."

I close the link and touch Delphi. "Still there?"

Her answer comes right away. "Until the war is over."

"Did you pick up any sign of the Red?"

"The Cloud's broken, Shelley. The Red's gone. I'm the only one messing with your headspace now."

"I don't know how much I like being an ordinary mortal."

She doesn't answer. Chitchat isn't professional.

I tell her, "When you're messing in my headspace, try not to turn me into a mean-ass gangster killer, okay?"

"Go to sleep, Shelley."

Like I have a choice. The skullnet icon flickers, and I'm out.

My head is full of dreams that vanish as I snap back into awareness. I can't recall a single image, but my brain is mired in a residue of dread. It's as if I've wakened into an awareness that we are trapped, all of us, prisoners in a pointless struggle that will never change one damn thing in the world. I fight a looming sense of panic. It's not easy to do while breathing the close, stinking air inside the cargo container, with nothing to see but darkness beyond the pearlescent glimmer of my visor's latent icons.

I need more to look at, and I need to know where we are, so I pull up a map. At first I can't make any sense of it. It's just a jumble of lines drawn on a meaningless textured background. I suck fortified water from my pack to get more calories into my system, and then I check the time. We've been on the road two hours and twelve minutes.

My helmet filters out the road noise, amplifying the smaller sounds: the scrape of a strut against the floor, the whisper of cloth against cloth, a soft cough from a dry throat. Someone—Ransom or Nolan—shifts, bumping a strut against my right footplate. I pull my foot back, and check the map again. I'm more alert now, and this time what I see makes sense to me. We've circled around, so we're well south of C-FHEIT.

Kendrick speaks on gen-com: "We're coming to a checkpoint. I'm with Vasquez, out of sight in the bunk behind the seats. We are going to try to get through without incident, so no movement, no sound, no lights—but be prepared to fight."

I slide a few millimeters as the truck decelerates, before bracing myself with my hands. I'm listening hard to my helmet audio, hoping for some hint of what's going on outside, but we're still rolling, so all I hear are engine and tire noises, and a loose rod rattling in its socket on the door.

"If we are discovered," Kendrick continues, his voice deadly calm, "we hit back hard and fast. Take out everyone at this checkpoint, and do it before our presence gets radioed in."

Really? And how is that going to work? Surely someone at the checkpoint will be sitting on the side with a radio or a satellite phone in hand. That's how I'd do it. *Take out everyone before word gets out* is superhero bullshit. I put our odds of success at about one in a hundred—and if we fail, New York gets blown up. No pressure there. God, I hope Troy really loves his sister. I hope he's good at lying.

I decide to ignore Kendrick's order to sit tight. If we're going to fight, I want to go into it as light, as agile, as fast as I can be. So I slip out of my backpack. No point in carrying the extra weight or taking the chance that it will catch on something in close quarters.

"Easy," Delphi warns. "The goal here is to avoid a fight."

I focus on the word *understood.* My skullnet picks it up and transmits it without my having to speak aloud. But just because we don't want a fight, doesn't mean we aren't going to get one.

Slowly, silently, I turn over. I get my feet under me until I'm crouched facing the cargo doors. I have my M-CL1a in hand. My finger is beside the trigger.

I think, *Prep Ransom and Nolan.*

"You got a bad feeling?" Delphi asks.

*Edgy.*

Behind me, I hear a faint creak of struts, then there's a touch against my shoulder. I check the squad map, confirming that Ransom is right behind me, and Nolan is crouched beside him.

The truck comes to a stop with the diesel engine still rumbling, the loose rod still rattling. I can't hear anything from outside.

"Three enemy visible," Delphi informs me as she switches on angel sight. "All armed with assault rifles."

In night vision, I'm looking down on an anonymous four-way intersection, surrounded by terrain that is all too familiar. Though we've been on the road over two hours, we're still stuck in the same ass-end of nowhere, with barbed-wire fences providing the only vertical relief in a flat, featureless rangeland.

By contrast, the intersection is busy.

Directly in front of our National Guard truck, two big pickup trucks are parked sideways across the road, blocking the way. A third pickup waits on the shoulder, its headlights illuminating the road on our driver's side. Enemy Number 1 is standing on the running board of our truck, looking in the driver's window, the stock of his weapon cradled in his bent arm. I can't see the muzzle, because he's got it aimed inside the cab. Enemy Number 2 stands on the road below, a man with a huge belly, his posture tense as he holds his assault rifle in a two-hand, cross-body grip. Number 3 is a slender shadow stalking cautiously alongside the truck, heading toward the back.

*More?* I ask, staring at the pickup trucks.

Delphi says, "No indication that anyone remains in the pickups, but that is *not* confirmed."

Kendrick links again to gen-com, but he doesn't speak. Instead, he pipes his audio to us so we can hear what he's hearing. Right now that's a man with a drawling, high-pitched voice, confidently explaining the facts of life:

"Listen here, Troy, my friend. I know you're a loyal son of the revolution, but the fact is, you got no manifest. So no one's gonna miss a thing if the rest of us help ourselves to a little bit of your cargo. After all, we all gotta make a living."

Troy speaks, his voice sounding louder, closer. "Sweet Jesus," he says. "Buddy, would you get that fucking gun out of my face?"

Enemy Number 3 has reached the back of the truck.

Through angel sight I watch him try the lever that opens the cargo doors; with my ears I hear the mechanism clang and bang, but a lock keeps it from opening. Number 3 retreats to where he can see the cab. There's too much engine noise, too much rattling steel to hear him, but it looks like he's yelling up to the front. Buddy confirms this when he says, "Troy, I'll get this gun out of your face when you turn over the key to the cargo."

*Give him the key*, I think—because I like Buddy even less than I like Troy.

Troy's not too impressed with Buddy either. "Just give me a fuckin' minute. The key's up top, in a locker alongside the bunk."

"Yeah?" Buddy says. "You make sure it's a key you grab, or your brain's gonna be all over the roof."

"Take it easy," Troy grumbles. I hear scrunching sounds—shoes on the vinyl seat?—and then Troy's voice gets louder. "I ain't that devoted to the revolution."

A click . . . muffled noises . . . then Troy, distant again: "Here. Have at it."

"You come on down out of the truck for a minute," Buddy says.

In angel sight, I see Buddy jump down from his perch beside the cab door. The door opens, and Troy climbs down. They walk together toward the back of the truck, the fat man with the weapon trailing behind them.

Kendrick whispers over gen-com. "Shelley, Nolan, Ransom, this is your party. Don't shoot each other, and try not to shoot Troy. Everyone else, hunker down and do not participate unless ordered to do so."

Angel sight shows me three men standing behind the truck and one more off to the side. That one is Troy, who has positioned himself outside our immediate zone of fire. He really is a lot smarter than he seems.

Buddy is holding a flashlight so that its beam shines on the back of the truck. Number 3 stoops to work the lock. When I hear steel clang, and then the grinding of a lever, I drop out of angel sight and watch with my own eyes as a single door swings slowly open. The flashlight beam reaches through the gap and rakes across my visor. All I can see in night vision is a shapeless green glare.

I shoot anyway, a short burst.

"*Fuck!*" Buddy screams as the flashlight disappears, and I know I missed him.

The door swings shut.

I launch myself at it, hitting it with my shoulder. As it slams back, I jump out, shooting a burst at the place where the fat man was standing when I last saw him with angel sight. He's still there. As my robot feet hit the pavement, he goes down with two dark holes in his chest. His weapon clatters to the asphalt, unfired.

I swivel, looking for another target, but Buddy and Number 3 are nowhere in sight. A shattering of small-arms fire comes from the side of the truck. I duck back, sheltering behind the open cargo door, but as I move, a power surge like I've never felt before makes my left leg spasm. The knee twists sideways. Searing pain shoots up my hip. I lose my balance and go down, but I'm able to roll onto my belly, with the HITR in my hands.

I'm aware of Nolan and Ransom, leaping over my head as they exit the truck, but I'm not watching them. All I'm looking for is a targeting circle in my display.

It pops into existence and I cover it, firing a burst as chips of pavement kick up beside me. It turns out my target is Buddy. The bullets hit him in the chest, knocking him into the air for a half second before gravity body-slams him to the road. He doesn't move.

"Where's Number Three?" I shout over gen-com.

"Number Three is down," Kendrick says in a calm and deliberate voice. "Where's our prisoner?"

I turn to look at the place where Troy was standing before the shooting started. Nolan's there now. "Got him, sir," the sergeant says. Troy is belly-down on the ground, his arms over his head. He must have dropped at the first shot. Smart man.

"Get him up," Kendrick says. "Shelley, you still with us?"

"Yes, sir. Are we clear?"

"We damn well better be, but I want a sweep."

"On it."

I roll over and sit up, the pain in my hip gone as fast as it came. Above me, most of our dual LCS is crowded in the open doorway, everyone labeled with a name. I pick some at random. "Harvey! Take Fernandez and Hoang. Circle around. Look for problems." They jump out eagerly and disappear around the truck. "Tuttle! You, Moon, and Wade, go check the pickup trucks."

"The rest of you get the bodies," Kendrick adds, "and load them into the back of one of the pickups."

Everyone bails out over my head, landing with rattling thumps on the pavement. More than one whispers a fervent thank-you to God for the fresh air, which really isn't all that fresh given that it's laden with the stink of gunpowder—but compared to the noxious air inside the truck, it's golden.

As they clear out, I test my left leg, bending the robot knee and flexing the ankle. This produces no repeat of the weird electric surge that knocked me down. So I get my feet under me and, moving cautiously, I stand up again. When I put weight on the leg, it's stable.

That's when I notice what looks like a bullet hole in my fatigues, just above the left knee. I lean down to inspect it, putting my little finger through it, just to prove to myself that it really is a hole.

Someone comes around from the side of the truck. My visor tells me it's Jaynie. "Are you hit?" she asks.

"It's starting to look that way."

She grabs a little LED flashlight, and squats to look. Her finger slips into the hole; she flinches when she feels the titanium bone. "I think there's a dent." She looks up at me uneasily. "Do you still work?"

I raise my left foot, put it down again. "Seem to."

My adrenaline high is draining away and I'm starting to feel shaky, especially when I consider how close that bullet came to hitting my living flesh.

Still crouching, Jaynie shines her flashlight in a circle on the pavement around us. "Gotcha." She gets up, takes a couple of steps, and picks up something from the road. "Here, I think this is yours."

I hold out my hand. Her flashlight shows the blob of a spent bullet dropped into my palm.

Dr. Masoud once implied my robot legs were better than natural. I have to admit, he might be right. I'm a faster runner now, I'll never twist a knee or an ankle, and bullets bounce off the titanium instead of shattering my natural bones.

Jaynie asks, "How many lives are you planning to burn through before you make your twenty-fourth birthday, Lieutenant?"

"I guess it depends on how many I've got."

Her voice drops. "You still King David? Is God still with you?"

I consider the edgy feeling I had in the back of the truck, but that was a hunch, lacking the raw certainty of a whispered hint from the Red.

I shove the bullet into my pocket. "Delphi thinks the Red is gone. If so, it's just luck now."

• • • •

Sergeant Nolan and two rookie privates are left behind, tasked with getting rid of the pickup trucks. Jaynie returns to the cab with Troy. Kendrick sends the rest of us back into the container truck. We cram ourselves in again among the big guns and the pallets. He closes the cargo doors, and a few seconds later, the truck rolls. Kendrick believes if we don't acquire the shutdown codes by dawn, we lose.

Guidance distributes an Intelligence briefing describing our target. The briefing includes dossiers of seventy-one individuals believed present in the facility, a number that includes the hired security. There is also an architectural diagram identifying points of resistance, and a walk-through video of the route we will follow. I look it all over with increasing disbelief.

"Delphi," I murmur.

"Here."

"Who the hell put this report together?"

"Intelligence provided the briefing."

"I *know* that. But if Intelligence has someone on the inside who can do a video walk-through, why doesn't that agent just grab the shutdown codes?"

"Negative. There are no sympathetic personnel inside. Shoot to kill, as needed. No exceptions."

"That's crazy. Somebody had to take the video. Who was it?"

"I don't know, Shelley. And you don't need to know. Just know where you're going, and know what you're looking for. You're going to lose communication with me when you're inside. So do the run-through now. You won't be able to ask questions later."

The facility is code-named Black Cross. It's a Cold War relic built with black-op funds in the 1960s, and quietly sold at the turn of the century to a Texas rancher and oilman as a thank-you for some forgotten political favor. The rancher wanted it for an Armageddon shelter, just in case God didn't actually show up on doomsday to collect the faithful.

The facility has decent security. Cameras are positioned around it. A single dirt road leads up to it. Its surface profile is a low, sprawling hill, covered in dry grass and grazed by scrawny cattle. In another landscape the hill might be a convincing natural feature, but here it provides the only relief to an unrelenting flat geometry. A satellite antenna sits just below the hill's high point. We are *not* to take out that antenna. It's the dead man's switch that sends a continuous signal of reassurance to a geosynchronous satellite, which relays the signal to the nuclear weapons in New York and other nice places. If the signal fails, the bombs go off.

Entry into Black Cross is through a set of wide double doors embedded in the artificial hillside. There are also ventilation shafts—three in all—around the hill. None are large enough to climb down, and all are secured by heavy grates and watched by cameras. They're included on the map purely for academic interest.

Guidance has decided our only way in is through the front door. We were never trained in finesse, so there will be nothing subtle about our assault. If the doors are locked, we'll blow them open, and in the ensuing confusion we will enter.

There is a staging area on the inside, designated Level 1. A large freight elevator descends to Levels 2 and 3, but we will be taking the stairs. Level 2 is an east-west tunnel with living quarters appended to it. Level 3 is a north-south dumbbell-shaped chamber with food storage on one side and a control room on the other.

Security is provided by experienced mercenaries identified as employees of Uther-Fen Protective Services. All are foreign, with poor English skills. The report speculates that this is a tactical choice. It's unlikely the TIA fully trusts their hired help. So the language barrier becomes another level of security, making it harder for the mercenaries to crack their client's secrets and seize control of the nuclear devices.

"Violence of action" is our tactic: Move fast and hit hard. Take down the enemy in the critical seconds before he can react. The scheme strikes me as even more ridiculous than our checkpoint assault. I have to admit that plan worked, but at the checkpoint we faced only three enemy soldiers, none of them well trained. Uther-Fen Protective Services is going to be a lot better staffed.

I do the walk-through several times. It's an amazingly detailed record, given that we've got no one inside. I visit every room, every closet in the facility. I survey the names and faces of every murderous traitor within, as well as the names and faces of their kids, of which there are a few.

"Delphi, what about the kids?"

"Shoot to kill, as needed," she repeats. "No exceptions. Give no consideration." Then she adds, in a softer voice, "You can accept an offer of surrender if it doesn't slow you down. Just remember, if those bombs go off, a lot more kids are going to die."

"I understand." I can't let anything stand between me and those shutdown codes. I can only hope someone loves those kids enough to pull them out of the line of fire.

Intelligence has ascertained that the codes we need are on a thumb drive hanging around the neck of the newly installed president of Independent Texas. He's a tall, thin, blond-haired, self-important yahoo, thirty years old, named Blue Parker, no doubt for his pretty blue eyes. He's the photogenic face of this revolution—and its fall guy when the independence thing fails, though I doubt he's figured that out yet.

I'm looking forward to meeting President Blue Parker and assisting him with understanding the tenuous nature of his title.

It's 0346 when we finally get to where we're going. We pile out of the back of the truck, and form up beneath the cover of a tree. Cows watch us by moonlight; some start moving away.

Delphi projects a schematic onto my visor that lays a bright green trail across the field. "This is the route you need to take," she tells me. "It's plotted to avoid the security cameras. Do not deviate."

"I understand."

I look back at the truck. Troy is still in the cab. Specialist Fernandez and Private Antonio climb in with him. Their assignment is to escort Troy as he drives the truck back the way we came, and to rendezvous with Sergeant Nolan if that's possible. Kendrick stands by the open door, looking up at Fernandez. "Do what Guidance tells you," he reminds them, speaking over gen-com. "And *do not* call attention to yourselves."

"Yes, sir."

Kendrick gives them a thumbs-up. Then he closes the door and steps away.

As the truck pulls out, thirteen of us are left behind.

"Damn," Ransom says over gen-com. "I was hoping we'd get to play with those big guns."

"Still lots of fun ahead," Moon reminds him.

"Ass-kicking fun," the colonel says as he looks us over with the empty face of his black visor. "We have two advantages tonight. One is that our enemy is distracted. The citizens of Texas have turned out to be less enthusiastic about secession than the TIA hoped, so their leaders are a little busy tonight, crushing popular dissent. Two, the TIA believes they've already won the war. They assume the knife they're holding to our throat is sharp enough that the US Army won't dare fight back. That's never a safe assumption."

Soft, assured laughter runs through the ranks.

"So check the cinches on your dead sister, get your pack squared, and make sure you have your face mask and oh-two cartridge at hand."

At this last remark, an uneasy murmur runs through the gathered troops. Kendrick ignores it. "Do *not* use your face mask before you are instructed to do so. We are going a long way down and we can't tank-breathe all the way. Now—we are only six kilometers from our target. I know every one of you is tired, and I don't give a damn. You either win this war tonight or you die trying. Is that understood?"

"Yes, sir," I say, one of a chorus of soft, affirmative mumbles, because none of us is stupid enough to yell, out here in a primal silence flawed only by the occasional lowing of a cow.

"Do not veer from the route Guidance has given us," Kendrick warns. "If there's a rattlesnake in your way, *tread on it.* Don't go around, or you run the risk of triggering a perimeter camera. Got it? Let's go."

"Lucky thirteen," Tuttle whispers off-com as I slip past him on my way to take point.

"Damn straight," I whisper back.

It's up to the thirteen remaining soldiers in our squad to win this war.

We go single file, the LCS falling in behind me as I follow the highlighted trail marked out by Guidance. After the first couple of klicks, I startle a cow that was chewing its cud in the moon-cast shadow of a tree. It snorts and takes off at a slow run, causing a commotion among its friends.

I don't like it. If anyone inside Black Cross is paying attention to the perimeter cameras, they might want to know why a cow is agitated—but shooting the cow would guarantee more attention.

"Delphi?"

"Here."

"No devil eyes looking down on us, right?"

"They do have a drone, but it's on the ground. Equipment malfunction."

"Handy coincidence."

She doesn't answer, but I'm more impressed than ever with the preliminary work Intelligence has done.

Soon, all that stands between us and the hill is a single grove of scrubby trees and a final four hundred meters of open range.

Not far from the grove are six cows. One watches us intently. It's bigger than the others, and I've got a strong suspicion it's a bull.

"Heads up for *el toro*," I say over gen-com.

Kendrick comes back with, "Ignore *el toro*. Do not break your line."

Then Lissa speaks. I know the voice I'm hearing can't be real, but her words are as clear in my ears as the first time she said them in the hospital: *Don't die, okay?*

God is back, messing with my brain.

I stop where I am, raising a hand to warn Tuttle, who's following behind me. "Hold up."

This is a bad move as far as the bull is concerned. Interpreting our sudden halt as a challenge, he snorts, lowers his head, and paws at the ground.

Tuttle crowds up to my shoulder, craning to see why I've stopped. "You got something?"

Kendrick wants to know the same thing. "What is it, Shelley?"

"I'm not sure."

The bull snorts again, and then he trots slowly toward us, testing our response, his tail switching. It comes to me that someone else is watching him, and we need to get the hell out of sight before that gaze finds us.

"Drop flat!" I order. "Down now!" And despite the threat of the bull, the entire line obeys, Kendrick included. I hear creaks and crunches and soft thuds as they go down. I drop too, and so does Tuttle. The bull stops, puzzled by the sudden disappearance of his foe. I lift my head to look through the trees, where I can just see the target hill.

Through the screen of vegetation, I see a muzzle flash. It repeats three times. I hear the slugs hit flesh—and the bull goes down on his knees with a bloodcurdling bellow. The sound of the shots arrives, and the startled cows take off running. In between the bellowing of the bull I make out distant voices, whooping in victory. Then two more shots, and the bull goes all the way down with a grunt. Its labored breathing is still loud in the night's quiet, but it's not bellowing anymore.

"Delphi?"

"A delayed report was just forwarded from Intelligence," she says, sounding quietly furious. "Two Uther-Fens are doing a walkabout on the hill."

"Tuttle," Kendrick says. "We need a sharpshooter. Go forward with the LT and set it up."

Tuttle and I creep into the trees, following the path Guidance has chosen for us. That the mercenaries are shooting cattle tells me they are bored and unsupervised, and may not have a clear concept of the extent of the war unfolding around them. It also tells me that they've got night vision, and we do not want to give them a more tempting target. We stop just before we reach the other side of the grove.

As I help Tuttle set up his weapon on its tripod, the Uther-Fen gun goes off again and another cow starts bellowing, this time off to the east. Kendrick tramps up behind us. Opening a solo link, he asks me, "What just happened?"

"I hallucinated a voice, sir. It was a warning."

"Damn it, are you telling me that Thelma Sheridan immolated thousands, took down the Cloud, and commenced a war, all to get rid of the Red, but it's *still* out there, bleeding through the ruins?"

"Yes, sir."

"*Lucky for us*," Delphi whispers, just to me.

Kendrick makes a growl of disgust. "Get yourself ready, Lieutenant. You're going in first."

"I want Ransom behind me."

"Do it."

I switch to gen-com. "Ransom, you've got ten seconds. Move up to the front of the line. Stay on the ground until you're into the trees. Follow when I go."

"Yes, sir, LT!" he says with the enthusiasm of a golden retriever.

I keep my gaze on the hill. The twisting, gnarled tree trunks obscure our infrared profile, but they don't block my view. I can see the recessed doors of Black Cross, and on the slope immediately above them, the two Uther-Fen cow killers—tiny figures standing a few feet apart, one with binoculars and one with a rifle. The shooter isn't using a tripod to steady his weapon. No wonder it took several shots to drop the bull.

Tuttle gets down on his belly. The angel has provided the exact distance and elevation for his shots, while Kendrick uses an atmospheric gauge to measure air temperature and wind speed. One of the Uther-Fens is going down for sure. The only question is whether Tuttle can shift his aim fast enough to take down the second one.

Kendrick addresses the LCS: "Be ready to advance on my command."

Tuttle's goal is to drop the two cow killers without a fuss, so that no one on the inside is alerted—but whether or not that happens, we will go on to hit the target fast and hard. Even if the defenders know we're coming, they won't have more than a couple of minutes to prepare—and it's in the confusion of battle that we'll have our best, our only chance at victory.

"I'm clearing your visor," Delphi says.

Maps and icons vanish. Nothing left to impede my view of the ground in front of me when I charge the hill.

I hear someone move up behind me. I assume it's Ransom, but I don't turn to look, I don't speak. I keep my attention focused on the hill as Tuttle pops his first shot. His second shot goes off two seconds later. I see one Uther-Fen go down as the round blows a crater in his chest. Tuttle's second shot hasn't even hit yet when Kendrick says, "Go, Shelley."

Tuttle can shoot over my head if he needs to pop another round.

I launch myself out of the grove at an all-out sprint. I still don't know the status of the second Uther-Fen, and I don't know for sure if Ransom is behind me, but I trust that he is. I trust my squad to cover me, and I trust Delphi to let me know if something changes.

I'm halfway to the hill when she gives me the news: "Two confirmed kills, but one of the bodies is visible to the security camera positioned above the doors."

I don't waste breath to answer. Nothing left to talk about. The defenders are aware of us, but it doesn't matter. Either we slam the TIA now, or we die.

Delphi starts counting down the distance I still have to go before I'm close enough to use my grenade launcher. "Fifty meters. Forty. Thirty. Twenty—

"Door is opening," she says. "Get down!"

I keep going, squeezing one word out of my heaving lungs. "*Count!*"

"In range! *Now!*"

I skid to one knee, bringing my M-CL1a to my shoulder to stabilize it. I'm not looking at the target. A blazing gold point has ignited on my visor, and the only thing that matters to me is covering that point with my targeting circle. I shift my aim. The circle slides onto the point. My tactical AI pulls the trigger, and a grenade launches from the tube beneath the rifle barrel.

"Drop, Shelley!"

I do it, going down flat on my belly, pressing my visor into the dust of an unpaved road. I link to Kendrick's helmet cam in time to see the explosion. The grenade was meant to blow the doors open, but someone from inside opened a door just as I lined up my shot—so the AI programmed the grenade to reach the interior.

The explosion goes off behind the doors, blowing them wide open and launching a body into the air like a rag doll. A cylindrical object goes spinning up through the fireball.

"What is that?" I whisper to Delphi.

"An RPG launcher that was being aimed at you."

Not something I want to think about.

I take off again. This time, Ransom is right beside me. We race each other, closing the distance to the shattered doors. Two bodies are lying in the debris. I fire a round into each of them to make sure they're all the way gone. The stink hits me as I jump over them. It's god-awful—stomach contents, explosive residue, and burning flesh.

I wave Ransom to one side of the door. I take the other. Shoving the barrel of my M-CL1a around the corner, I sweep it in a fast arc so my AI can get a look at the interior. It's a big, open, concrete-walled room. Straight ahead is a freight elevator. On my left is a fire door closing off a stairway that descends all the way to Level 3, the lowest level of Black Cross. Then I do a slow reverse scan so I can see what's there. I make out only one enemy. He's down on the floor, his smoldering body crumpled in a corner.

"Clear to advance," Delphi says.

I slip inside, with Ransom right behind me.

We didn't use an RPG to open the doors because we didn't want to take the chance of a cave-in at the Level 1 staging area. The grenade alone has left the utilitarian room glowing with heat, reeking with fumes, and nearly empty of oxygen. It's tempting to reach for the face mask secured against my chest, but Kendrick hasn't ordered us to use oxygen yet, and we've got a long way to go.

Two rounds go into the downed merc, and then I approach the steel fire door, positioning myself beside the latch. "You're going to open it," I tell Ransom.

"Yes, sir."

He backs up against the wall on the hinged side of the door.

I've got my weapon in one hand, the stock braced against the hip strut of my dead sister, ready to fire. In my other hand I've got a fragmentation grenade. If the door is locked, we're going to have to blow it open and that's going to slow us down. I hope it's not locked. Ransom takes the handle in his gloved hand. "Ready, LT?"

"Just wide enough for the grenade," I warn him. "Then get it shut and get the fuck out of here."

He shoves the handle down and pulls back. The door is not locked. I trigger the grenade, then toss it through the gap into the stairwell. Bullets hammer the door's inner face, knocking bubbles into the steel. Ransom can't get it shut against the force of impact. "Kick it," I tell him.

I fire down into the gap. Ransom takes a step back. There's

hesitation in the defensive fusillade. He uses the moment to launch a kick backed up by the full force of his dead sister's leg strut. The door booms shut. "Get out!" I scream at him.

He launches himself at the entrance, and in one bound he's through it and outside. I'm right behind him.

The grenade goes off. It's a double explosion—*boom, boom!*—one more concussion than I can credit to my little frag. The shock vibrates through my footplates. When we look inside, the steel fire door is on the other side of the room, blown off its hinges by the concussion and hurled into the concrete wall.

"Idiots tried to blow us up," Ransom says. "Blew themselves up instead."

"Looks that way."

My guess is they launched a grenade at the open door, but it never cleared the stairwell. It's going to be seared and shredded meat down there.

I scramble back to the blackened door frame and stick the muzzle of my weapon around the corner. There are two bodies on the landing below. That's as much as I can see because a solid wall stands between the flights of stairs.

"Clear to descend," Delphi says quietly.

Two or three flights down, I'm going to lose my connection to the angel. "Bye, Delphi," I whisper, and I jump all the way to the blood-slick first landing, letting the shocks of my dead sister take the impact as I come down between the two bodies. I back up against the hot concrete wall, getting out of the way as Ransom comes down behind me.

A glance at the map shows Vanessa Harvey above me at the top of the stairs, Jayden Moon a step behind her, and the rest of the LCS still coming in.

I ease forward to look down to the next landing. I don't see anyone, so I pivot and jump again, with Ransom following. Our tactic is to move fast and deprive the enemy of a chance to set charges—but Level 2 is deep underground. We've got six flights of stairs to transit and we will meet enemy fire before we get that far.

Blue Parker is huddled somewhere downstairs. He knows we're coming. I try to imagine what's going through his head. The nukes are his only leverage, so I don't think he'll blow them until there's no doubt left that he's going to lose. Even then—well, he's a true believer. Reality can smack up against a mind like that and bounce off without effect—which is fine with me. The longer he takes to understand what is happening to his glorious revolution, the more time we have to win.

Ransom and I hit the third landing and we're met by gunfire: a maelstrom of bullets pounding into the walls, the roof, and the base of the concrete stairs above us, spewing fragments in every direction.

I throw myself back into the corner. Ransom drops to his belly. Vanessa Harvey jumps down from the landing above, turns—and a bullet hits her visor. She slams back against the wall, just a meter away from me, sliding down to a sitting position. Her visor is dented and spiderwebbed, but it's not perforated, so no bullet is lodged in her brain. Her chest heaves as blood runs from behind her visor onto her chest. "Talk to me, Harvey," I say.

"Fucking broken nose," she growls over gen-com.

Kendrick's voice cuts in: "Clear the way, Shelley."

No way out but forward.

I check my display. My link to Guidance is gone. Communication is helmet-to-helmet. My tactical AI will still help me aim, but without oversight it won't fire. So that duty falls to me.

I put my finger beside the trigger for the grenade launcher. "Fire in the hole!" I announce over gen-com. I don't know how far the signal will travel inside the stairwell, but my nearest soldiers will know what's coming.

I jump across the landing, jam the muzzle of my weapon down past the curve of the rail and, without looking, I launch the grenade. Ransom grabs my pack and pulls me down to the floor beside Harvey. The grenade goes off.

Only the helmet keeps me from losing my hearing in the concrete confines of the stairwell. A wall of fire shoots past just above us, rising up the chimney of the stairwell. On the landing above figures drop flat and dive for corners.

The fireball lasts only a couple of seconds. Silence follows it, but again we've managed to burn out most of the oxygen. No choice now but to get all the way down to Level 2 as fast as we can.

"Get Harvey's arm," I tell Ransom.

We haul her to her feet. "I'm good!" she snaps and, twisting free of my grip, she jumps through the fumes, down to the next landing. I follow, and Ransom comes after me. With no active resistance, it takes only seconds to reach Level 2. The concrete walls are cracked from the blast, and there are two more bodies on the floor, both wearing black Uther-Fen uniforms. The fire door is askew in its frame.

Our goal is Level 3, but I want air, so I kick the fire door open, covering the hallway beyond with my weapon—but no one's in sight. I pick up an empty magazine from the floor and use it to jam the door's hinges.

This is the residential level. Doors line the hall, all of them closed. Kendrick jumps down from the flight above, landing behind me. He catches Harvey by her arm strut before she can take off again. "You're staying here." He shoves her toward the open door to get her out of the way as Moon jumps down. "Hoang! Johnson! Assist Harvey to secure Level 2."

"Yes, *sir*," Harvey says, biting off each word. She's furious at being taken out of the action.

Ransom disappears downstairs. Moon takes off after him. I turn to follow, but I stop at the rumble of a muffled explosion. "What the hell is that?"

Kendrick says, "That would be Vasquez disabling the elevator shaft."

Only one way out now.

I move out, following Moon and Ransom.

It's another three flights down to our goal. Jumping in the dead sisters, we get there fast. Only 110 seconds have passed since we entered the staging area on Level 1.

Another fire door stands in our way. I can't hear anything beyond it, but I'm certain there are at least a dozen well-armed mercs on the other side, waiting to greet us.

According to the map, the stairwell opens onto a fifteen-foot-wide hallway joining the two halves of the dumbbell that make up Level 3. Across the hallway is the freight elevator that Jaynie just disabled. The storage lockups for food and water are on one side, the control room on the other.

I'd like to blow the fire door open, but that would chew up what little oxygen is left in the stairwell, it would risk damaging the power supply to the control room, and it would take too much time. So I position myself beside the door and get ready to open it by hand. Ransom moves in behind me, where the wall will protect him when the shooting starts. Moon takes a position on the opposite side of the door. PFC Layla Wade comes down next. I send her to stand behind Moon. There isn't room to fit anyone else without putting them right in front of the fire door.

"No one else come down!" I order over gen-com.

I reach for the door handle. I need to unlatch it, and then kick it open.

"Hold up, Shelley!" Kendrick calls over gen-com. He ignores my last directive and vaults down the final flight of stairs, filling up the space in front of the fire door. Then he turns to look back up. "Everyone, face masks on! Once your face mask is secure, *stay put*. Do not descend to Level Three until instructed."

I shoulder my weapon and get my face mask out of its titanium case. Sliding my hand up under my visor, I hold the mask against my nose and mouth, giving the engineered tissue the required ten seconds to adhere to my skin, cursing the lost time. When oxygen starts to flow, I take my M-CL1a in hand again—but now that I've got more $O_2$ in my system, I start to think.

I'm 100 percent sure that when I open the fire door, a fusillade of defensive fire will erupt from the other side.

I really don't want my hand shot off.

I look at Kendrick. He's taking off his backpack. He gets his oxygen cylinder out of it, stuffing it inside his vest.

I *really* don't want my hand shot off. So I use the time to uncinch my right leg from the frame of the dead sister.

Kendrick sees what I'm doing. "Shelley, what the fuck?" His voice is muffled by the oxygen mask.

So is mine. "Using the resources, sir."

The cyborg foot can bend in multiple directions and grip with the strength of a hand—but unlike my hand, it's replaceable. Balancing on one leg, I bend the other until I can grab the door handle with my foot.

"Well, fuck me," Kendrick says.

Then he makes Moon back up a couple of steps and takes over his place on the other side of the door. This forces Wade to move all the way back to the bottom step. "Crouch low," I tell her.

Kendrick crouches too. "Ransom," he says. "Moon—as soon as the door is open I want you both to pitch a flash-bang into the hallway. I'm going to use my backpack to prop the door. Got it?"

"Got it, sir." Ransom gets a grenade from his vest pocket. I get hold of the door handle again with my robot foot.

"Okay, Shelley," Kendrick says. "Let's do it."

The door opens outward. I shove the handle down and kick as hard as I can.

It flies open, swinging 180 degrees as a chorus of automatic weapons thunders death into the stairwell. At least one of those bullets strikes my titanium foot. The impact knocks me off balance, sending me spinning into Ransom. He jams his shoulder against my chest, pinning me to the wall so I can't fall down while he pitches his grenade past me. From the corner of my eye I see Kendrick lob his backpack through the doorway. The door swings only partly shut as the grenades go off with dizzying concussions.

Ransom rolls back against the wall while my visor darkens to hide my eyes from the glare. Even before it clears I drop into a crouch, moving as fast as I can to resecure the cinches on the leg strut of my dead sister. I'm getting a red-hot feedback from the limb. The foot didn't shatter, but the joints don't fit right anymore, and I can't make it completely flat.

*Screw it.* Joby can always make me a new one.

And in the meantime, Moon, Ransom, Kendrick, and Wade are pouring bullets into the chaos of Level 3.

I join them. Still crouching, I hold my HITR so the muzzle is out the door and, using the targeting cam, I shoot anything that moves. Smoke and screams fill the hallway outside. Ransom is leaning over me to shoot, so I hear him grunt when he gets hit. He disappears from my field of view, knocked back into the stairwell. On the other side of the door, Moon gets slammed backward into the wall. Screams erupt behind me, but they're not coming from Moon or from Ransom. It's a woman. I glance over my shoulder to see Wade down, her legs shattered and pumping blood.

*Fuck.*

"Nakaoka!" I yell. She's the closest thing we have to a medic. "Up front! Wounded!"

"On my way, sir!"

Ransom is back, leaning over me again, though he's hurting. He's got his shoulder braced against the door frame, his breathing is fast and shallow, and he's dripping on my gloves. I glance at my hands, reassured to see it's sweat, not blood. His armor must have saved him.

Wade wasn't so lucky. Her status goes critical, posting automatically in bold red on my visor: heart rate 210; brain function declining.

"Vasquez!" Kendrick bellows. "Now would be a good time."

"On my way, sir!"

I run out of targets. The shooting stops. We've won a lull in the defense . . . and Wade isn't screaming anymore. Nakaoka bounds down the stairway as Wade's chest spasms in shallow, panicked breathing.

"Moon," I bark. "Status?"

"Ambulatory. Noncritical."

"Same," Ransom says before I can ask.

Jaynie appears on the landing above with a bigmouthed gun in her hands. Nakaoka and Wade block the bottom of the stairs, so she vaults over the rail, coming down right behind me.

The gun she's carrying is illegal, a chemical weapons dispenser that we are not supposed to have. "Kendrick! Where the hell did that come from? I didn't see it in the battle plans."

I thought he'd ordered face masks to protect us from enemy assault; I didn't think we'd be the ones to violate international law.

Jaynie shoulders past me. Kendrick says, "Need-to-know, Lieutenant." The chemical gun goes off with a sound like popcorn as Jaynie sprays a fan of cylinders into the smoke-filled hall. "Need for secrecy."

Wade's status on my visor updates: heart rate, zero; brain function, flatline.

"Advance!" Kendrick orders.

I wheel and lunge into the hall.

Smoke clouds the air. I look right, left, right again. No one's moving. No one shoots. Blood pools the floor, seeping from bodies in Uther-Fen uniforms. Not one of them screams. Not one of them groans. Surely they can't all be dead? What kind of nasty gas did Jaynie have in those cylinders?

"Tuttle!" Kendrick bellows over gen-com. "You, Fevella, and Flynn! Down to Level Three." He shoots out two camera buttons near the ceiling.

I don't see any civilians among the fallen, but steel doors guard both ends of the hallway. I'm contemplating what it will take to blow the door to the control room off its hinges without bringing the ceiling down when a large gray rat falls from overhead, landing with a plop in the blood. I look up to see neat ductwork and piping suspended from concrete. Then I nudge the rat with the toe-end of my footplate. A camera button is stuck on its narrow forehead. A whip-wire antenna sticks out of the back of its skull, lying flat against its spine. The mystery of how Intelligence knew exactly what was going on down here is solved.

Ransom leans over to look. "God-*damn*," he says in a voice muffled by his face mask. "Is that a robo-rat?"

Kendrick glances at it as he steps past to survey the fallen mercs. "Sucker's rigged up just like Shelley. Skullnet, camera, transmitter. The rest of us are fucking obsolete." He points at a body with its throat shot out. "This one! Moon, Ransom, haul this carcass to the end of the hall."

They grab the body by the shoulders and drag it to the control room door, making trails of blood and bloody footprints. It's no worse to look at than any of the carnage I saw on the way down, no worse than the torn-up bodies sprawled at my feet, but the sight of those blood trails hits me and I freeze, gripped by a sense that none of this is real.

Someone nudges my arm. "LT," Jaynie says. "You still with us? Better take some fluids before you drop."

She trots after Kendrick. I grab my water tube, slide it under the oxygen mask, and suck in a mouthful. Tuttle, Fevella, and Flynn burst out of the stairwell, one after another, their weapons in hand, heads turning as they look for a target. I gesture toward the control room. "Go. Follow the sergeant."

Nakaoka steps out next. She's armed and ready too. "Nothing I could do, LT."

"I know."

I take another mouthful of fortified water, then shove the tube back under my armor. I'm light-headed, almost dizzy. Maybe my face mask is leaking. Maybe it's cerebral exhaustion. That happens. Brain cells run out of raw materials, waste products build up, thinking gets confused, and the skullnet can't fix it. Only time can, and we don't have time. Gathering my wits, I crook my finger at Nakaoka, and we trot to the end of the hall.

We've got a total of nine personnel jammed together at the control room door. Jaynie is organizing them, shoving people into lines so we don't crash into one another when we storm the room. I make my way to the front, conscious of each second ticking past. Kendrick is holding a DNA scanner that's leashed to the wall. The shell of the scanner is plastic: flat, white, and teardrop shaped, with a micropoint at the narrow end. "Try it under the jaw," Moon says, holding up the corpse that Kendrick wanted. "There might be blood pooled there."

Kendrick does it, and then he glances at a display. "Good call." Moon and Ransom haul the body out of the way, while Kendrick turns to a keypad. "Prep the troops, Shelley," he says as he punches in a code.

My brain is still lagging. For about two seconds, I have no idea what we're supposed to do on the other side of that door. "*Fuck*," I whisper. Kendrick turns his visor in my direction, his hand poised above the enter key.

"Blue Parker!" I bark. "Take him alive. The codes we need are on a thumb drive around his neck. Do not destroy the equipment! We need that too. Shoot to kill, as needed. *Aim carefully!*"

Kendrick presses the enter key.

The door unlatches with a loud click, opening inward. Moon pushes it a couple of inches, then ducks back as a bullet flies out. Jaynie reaches around the corner with her bigmouthed gun, jams the muzzle into the opening, and shoots.

I glance up at the ducting. It runs right through the concrete wall. The gas from our initial assault should have been sucked into the room. If people are awake in there, it's because they've got face masks.

And we've got no time.

I kick the door and turn right, to where the shooter has to be.

The room is big. I already know what it looks like from the Intelligence report. The back half is boxes and canisters: food, electronic parts, weapons. Cubicle dividers screen that part off from the front. On one side are two small, glass-walled offices. At the center of the remaining space there's a server tower, with twin consoles on either side of it, though only one gets used; the other is backup. Big, bright monitors loom above the consoles. Opposite the offices is a little kitchenette, with a fridge and microwave, a table, a couch, and more monitors tuned to the talking heads of mediots overseeing news feeds.

Daylight bulbs fill the space with a clean white light that clearly illuminates the shooter. She's a young girl, blond haired, with an old-fashioned gas mask strapped to her head. I recognize her from her dossier. Her name is Allison, she's fourteen years old, and she's lining up on me with a big fat pistol, murderous fury in her eyes.

We both pull the trigger at the same time. Her round hits like a fist against my chest. It knocks me into the wall, while she goes over backward with a red flower blooming in her throat.

I can't breathe.

I'm utterly calm anyway—and it's all on my own. The skullnet icon is not even glowing. My brain is exhausted; my emotions are too.

My gaze sweeps the room, taking in the bodies scattered across the floor. Not as many as I expected. Defenders must be hidden in the lanes between the stacked supplies.

How many have gas masks and guns?

Tuttle grabs my arm. "You okay, LT?"

My chest spasms, and I suck in a whooping breath. The slug is a dull silver coin, pancaked in my armor. "Find Blue Parker," I tell Tuttle. And then I scream it over gen-com: "Find Blue Parker. *Now!*"

We flip the bodies over—not gently—logging names and faces. Most are still alive. A few I'm not too sure about. Specialist Fevella checks them off a list he's keeping. We add in everyone we know about: the civilians in the main section of the control room, the dead mercs, thirteen kids that Harvey found on Level 2. The total comes to fifty-nine, but seventy-one individuals are known to be at Black Cross. So we sweep the storage aisles and find seven more sleepers. That leaves five civilians unaccounted for, including Blue Parker.

When I get back to the main section of the control room, I see Kendrick, sitting at a console. I do a double take because he's not wearing his helmet. He's still got his face mask on, but his helmet is sitting on the floor at his feet.

From boot on up, it's drilled into us that during combat operations the helmet *does not come off.* Period. End of discussion. Remove it during a field exercise and you will get to start your training all over again. Kendrick's helmet is off because he's talking on a Black Cross satellite phone. When he sees my visored gaze fixed in his direction, he flips me the finger.

I go listen anyway, cranking up the volume on my helmet's external pickups so I can hear the voices on the other end of the line. He's talking to Intelligence. They confirm that the outgoing signal to the INDs is still being generated, so at least we know the dead man's switch hasn't been thrown yet. But what if the bombs can be set off from some other location?

It's been less than six minutes since we launched our assault, but if we don't find Blue Parker, if we don't send the shutdown codes, it's for nothing.

Kendrick moves the phone away from his mouth. The volume in my audio pickups drops automatically. "Shelley, take as many people as you need to make a data relay and get up to the top. Download coming in."

"I'll go with you, sir," Ransom says.

"No," Jaynie counters. "I need you here. Fevella, Flynn,

Nakaoka, go with the LT. Shelley, can you pick up Hoang on Level Two? Harvey doesn't need him."

"Yes, ma'am," I say with only a tinge of sarcasm. My sergeant has taken over my command, but I don't confront her, because time is critical and she's made the right call. With my assigned team, I sprint for the stairwell.

Fevella stays at the bottom. I call ahead, get a link to Julio Hoang on Level 2, and have him take a post in the stairwell. Nakaoka drops off a couple of flights above Hoang, and then I leave Flynn behind. Even with the dead sister, sprinting up that many stairs is a challenge, and by the time I leave Flynn I've burned out my oxygen cylinder. I peel off my face mask as I haul myself up the second flight from the top, gasping at hot, stale, stinking air. A breeze is chasing me up from the bottom. God knows how much toxin is still in it. I'm not feeling too good, though whether it's poison gas, cerebral exhaustion, oxygen-deprived air, or me psyching myself out, I don't know.

But I get a break. I'm one flight above Flynn, one below the top, when my helmet links up with our angel and the download drops in. I forward it to Kendrick. It relays through the helmets of the soldiers waiting on the stairs, and a second later, Kendrick's voice speaks in my ears: *"Received."*

I look at the download.

It's just a photo of the storage area at the back of the control room. One of the robo-rats must have taken it and relayed it out, right before the gas seeped in through the AC. It shows a man with a gas mask climbing into a spider hole under the crates. Two civilians stand by, ready to lock him in I guess. I know the man is Blue Parker because I can see the data stick still hanging on a chain around his neck. In his hands I see a tablet.

A cold sweat flushes out of my pores, because now I

know what their plan is. If all is lost, Blue pops the data stick into the tablet and sends the codes remotely.

I want to go back down to Level 3, but I don't have any more oxygen and it will all be over one way or another by the time I get there.

I don't want to stay where I am, because there are two burned bodies on the landing, and the stairwell reeks of gunpowder, vomit, shit, and blood.

So I climb up, one stair at a time.

Now that I'm in touch with the angel again, Delphi's back in my head. "Stay at the stairwell. We need you to relay." She's trying to sound stern, but there's a quaver in her voice, just like that day when I had my legs blown out from under me.

I lean against the frame where the fire door used to be, staring out past the main doors of the Level 1 staging area. Within a twisted and shattered frame, they hold a pastoral image of a Texas night—dried field and gnarled trees, rendered in night vision. Only a few minutes have passed since we blasted our way into Black Cross.

I wonder, is it worse to know? Or not know?

"*Fuck it,*" I whisper, and I link through our daisy chain to Kendrick's helmet cam. I pick up the feed just as Ransom is pulling the trapdoor open. Tuttle shines a light into the hole.

If we had something to interfere with the wireless signal from the tablet, we'd be okay.

But we don't.

The only equipment we have is what was available to us at C-FHEIT.

"Get him out," Kendrick says.

Jaynie and Tuttle grab Blue Parker under the arms and haul him out of the spider hole. He's clutching the tablet in his right hand. The data stick is no longer around his neck.

It's inserted into one of the ports on the tablet.

The fuckwad starts shrieking threats: "I'll blow it! I will! I will! I will!"

I shudder and shiver and close my eyes, hating him, hating every mad syllable he screeches in a voice pushed high by panic and fear.

"I'll blow it! I'll blow it! Don't touch me! I'll blow it!"

*So why the fuck doesn't he?*

It all goes quiet.

I open my eyes again, to see Blue Parker with a pistol jammed under his jaw.

"Now," Kendrick says in a voice pitched so low I expect my eardrums to start buzzing, "you and I both know that you didn't really want to murder tens of thousands of people yesterday. I bet that wasn't even your idea. And I know you don't want to add thousands more to the body count, because you *will* go to hell for it, for all eternity, and after the Devil has flayed off your skin, he'll fuck you while you're lying on a bed of coals."

Kendrick is not even talking to me, and I start to sweat. When the colonel makes a threat, it's not hard to believe it. Blue Parker believes it. He starts to cry.

"Give me the shutdown code," Kendrick says.

"It's on the stick," Parker answers in a broken voice. "It's labeled."

Jaynie takes the tablet from Parker. The screen is black, locked down with a passcode.

"It's four, three, two, one," Parker tells her in a trembling voice.

"And then boom?" she asks him.

"No! I swear."

Kendrick looks over her shoulder as she enters the digits. A file listing blossoms on the screen. Everything is right there, in alphabetical order:

ATLANTA LAUNCH
ATLANTA SHUTDOWN
DENVER LAUNCH
DENVER SHUTDOWN
NEW YORK LAUNCH
NEW YORK SHUTDOWN

"New York first," I say.

"Go ahead, Vasquez," the colonel says. "New York. Make the LT happy."

What if it doesn't work? What if New York blows up first? I squeeze my eyes closed as Jaynie launches the shutdown program.

"Delphi, tell me."

"No report yet."

Seconds tick past. Then Delphi speaks to everyone over gen-com. "The New York device has disarmed itself." Screams of joy echo in the stairwell, followed by faint cheers from far below.

Jaynie's graceful fingers free Atlanta next, and when the thumbs-up comes through on that, she shuts down the cancer in Denver, in Philadelphia, and in Phoenix.

It's all over, isn't it? We slammed the TIA.

I want to believe it, but I hear something. I hear jets outside.

It sounds just like Africa, fierce engines roaring on the edge of hearing. They don't scare me, though, because I know they must be ours—and I want to go see them. I want to go outside and be under the stars and know that the world isn't dead. It's a compulsion. My hands start shaking, I want it so bad. Going off-com, I yell down the stairwell to Flynn, "Tell everybody to move up one flight. Spread the word off-com."

"Sir?" Flynn calls, incredulous.

"Off-com," I repeat. "Don't clutter gen-com. I'm just going outside."

She calls the order down. I hear it repeated by Nakaoka. As Flynn clomps up the stairs, I leave my post at the top of the stairwell and move to the door.

The jets are a lot closer now. I can't see them, but their roar builds with incredible speed as they sweep in from the west: low, fast, and dark. My helmet filters the engine noise, but it still vibrates in my bones and shakes the world. For a second I think I hear Delphi screaming at me, but it has to be my imagination . . . that way we sometimes hear voices in white noise.

A light flicks on in the east. Bright white. It's not the sun. It's a rocket—a huge, multistage rocket, an anomalous tall tower of propulsion lifting off from out of nowhere. It's got to be at least ten miles away, but the glare of its first stage chases back the night.

Vanda-Sheridan not only makes satellites; the company launches them too.

The rocket climbs straight up. I have no way to tell how far.

The jets pass my position. Fighter jets: I see the glow of their afterburners as a sonic boom slams across the land. And then they release two missiles, with blazing trails that outrun the fighters and arc upward on a course to intercept the rocket, which has begun a slow turn north.

The missiles chase the rocket, but it's hopeless. They will never catch it.

Then the rocket's guidance system fails. I think the fighter pilots are jamming it, interfering with its navigation. It flips over, nose down, and it explodes.

For some tiny shard of time, I look at the fireball, but I can't really see it. It's like God, or the seed of a new universe blossoming—something that is just not meant for human eyes. Terror kicks out my higher brain functions and instinct takes over. My eyes close. I wrench backward, diving into the sheltering darkness of Level 1. I land on my forearms. The struts of my dead sister take the initial impact, then my chest slams into the concrete, and then my visor. Pain shoots into the back of my skull, a black, lightless pain . . . there's no light anywhere. I can't see a thing, not even with night vision, but I don't need to see. I know where the stairwell is. Flynn is just one flight down. Nakaoka's below her, then Hoang, and Fevella.

Why don't I hear them on gen-com? Why don't I get an icon? I can't see any output, not from the visor and not from my goddamn overlay.

*Screw it.* I scream instead. "Flynn, get downstairs! Go down! Go down! Go down!"

I scramble to take my own advice—or I try to, but the dead sister won't move. Its joints are frozen and suddenly it's Africa all over again, and I'm stuck in a broken rig.

The blast wave hits.

A roaring white noise slams through my brain, the concrete floor shudders, there's a tearing screech that sounds like a steel world caving in, and then the fragments of that world pepper my back and crack against my helmet.

I want to get to the stairwell. I'm desperate to get there. So I put all my strength into my right arm, fighting the dead sister's frozen elbow joint, forcing it to bend, until I can reach a cinch on my left arm. I yank it loose and grab the next. My left hand comes free, and then it's easy to pop all the other cinches and roll out of the rig, leaving my pack behind with it.

But my robot legs aren't working any better than the dead sister. I get nothing from them. No feedback at all.

*Screw it.*

I drag myself across the floor. I can't see a thing, but I want that stairwell.

By the time I reach it, it's getting quiet outside. I taste dust in the air. I grab the door frame and pull myself to a sitting position. My robot legs are dead weight and there's still no sign of life in my overlay. Still nothing on gen-com, and the screen of my visor is dead, dead, dead. I should be able to see through it if all the electronics are blown, but I can't. And I can't hear much of anything. The audio pickups aren't working.

So I break the prime directive of field operations, and I take the helmet off.

I still can't see anything, but now I hear Ransom's big southern drawl: "*Landing five, stairwell's open.*"

I hear the clomping feet of at least two dead sisters climbing the stairs.

"*Landing six, stairwell's open.*"

"You don't want to come up here!"

I try to yell it, but my voice is so hoarse the words come out as a growl that reverberates against the concrete. "A fucking nuclear bomb just went off outside."

"Shelley?" Ransom yells, so loud I swear more bits of the ceiling rattle loose and hit the floor.

Ignoring my advice, he runs up the stairs. He's not alone. I see a glimmer of light at last, blue-white in color like the beam of an LED flashlight, but the light is shattered into a hundred broken pieces, like gleaming shards of glass.

"Goddamn it, Shelley!" It's Kendrick and he's furious. "Why the fuck isn't your helmet on your head? Why aren't you on gen-com? Where the hell is your rig?"

I can't take my gaze away from those shards of light. I've never seen anything like it before. "What the hell kind of light is that?"

"What?"

"How can you even see where you're going with the light all fractured and scattered like that?"

I hear a faint sigh from the joints of his dead sister. By the sound I know he's right in front of me, but all I see is that crazy light—splinters and facets. "It's like looking through fly eyes."

Then the light shoots straight to the back of my brain like a red-hot needle. My eyes squeeze shut in agony and my head jerks back, cracking against the door frame. "*Fuck.*"

"You're supposed to be wearing your goddamn helmet!"

"It's broken! I can't see or hear anything with it on!"

"What's wrong with him?" Ransom asks.

I'd like to know that too.

"How do you know it was a nuke?" Kendrick asks.

"I saw the fireball."

"You looked at it? *Jee*-sus." Each syllable is a beat of his anger. "I need to shine the light in your eyes. Look past my shoulder, and don't blink."

"I can't fucking see your shoulder."

"Guess."

I force my eyes open and the light comes again, but it's not as bright this time. "Ho-ly *God*," Kendrick murmurs. "You are one lucky son of a bitch. I think it's your overlay. The surface is crackled like shattered glass."

Ransom says, "You can get new lenses, Shelley. Get it fixed."

"Yeah." Assuming there's still a world out there. I lean back against the door frame and try not to think about that. "How's everybody downstairs?"

I hear the whisper of Kendrick's bones as he stands up again. "You know we lost Wade. Otherwise, minor injuries, and no cave-ins from the nuke. Those Cold War boys, they knew how to build a bomb shelter."

I tell him about the rocket, and the fighters that came to stop it out here in the middle of nowhere. "Those pilots—

if they hadn't been here, maybe she would have hit Austin, or San Antonio, or someplace farther away, but they didn't let it happen. They sent that rocket down. And she could have just let it crash, but she didn't. She blew the nuke. Sir, she vaporized them."

Kendrick spends about twenty seconds softly swearing. Then he reins in his temper. "Can you get up?"

"No. My legs are dead—just like the helmet and my rig."

"EMP," Kendrick growls. "That nuke blew out your circuits. You're too damn vulnerable. You need a redesign."

"I'm feeling like the skullnet's gone too."

"If it is, it's not going to do you any good to think about it. I want you stripped down, in case there's any radiation contamination on your clothes."

The armored vest, the jacket, and the T-shirt are easy. They help me with the pants.

"Okay, Ransom," Kendrick says. "Let's get him downstairs. Take his other arm."

"You're going to regret hauling me down there when you have to carry me out again."

"We'll make do."

They haul me down six flights to Level 2, where the surviving terrorists are being held. The lights are still on—low-energy LEDs emitting a cheerful semblance of daylight. "Looks like a fucking Picasso painting."

They put me down on the tiled floor of a shower. Someone turns on an icy stream of water that sprays over my head and shoulders.

"*Fuck.*"

A plastic bottle gets shoved against my hand. I grab it. "Wash everything," Kendrick orders. "Ransom, make sure he does it."

"Yes, sir."

Thank God the water is warming up.

• • • •

A few minutes later I'm in one of the rooms on Level 2, sitting up in someone's bed with a bottle of water in my hand that Ransom scavenged from some Black Cross stash. I twist the cap off and take a sip. It's cold and nonfortified and hurts like hell as it slides past my raw throat. My eyes are starting to hurt like hell too as the ruined lenses of my overlay distort the tissue beneath. And the bruising I took from a little girl's bullet makes my chest hurt every time I breathe.

"Hey, LT."

It's Flynn.

"I stole some clothes for you."

"Not an Uther-Fen uniform?"

"No, sir. Civvies. Keep you warm when we're evacuated."

Since I can't see what I'm doing, she helps me out. There's a knit pullover and soft trousers. "This is a coat," she says, laying a length of textured fabric in my lap. "For when we're ready to go."

"Any word on when that is?"

Kendrick answers, his voice coming from the vicinity of the doorway. "It won't be long. Intelligence is going to want to take this place apart, which means we get evacuated ASAP."

"My rig. My pack, my weapon, everything—it's still up on Level One."

"We're going to leave it, in case it's contaminated. How's your head? You going down?"

"Yeah." There's no doubt now that the skullnet is dead. It's supposed to regulate my brain chemistry, but it's not doing that and I am not okay. I'm going down fast, falling through some inner dimension into a darkness that weighs heavier with each passing minute.

"I don't have any tranqs," Kendrick says. "You're going to have to hold out."

"Yeah . . . you know, it's a fucking miracle we only lost Layla Wade."

"Yeah, it is. Listen, I don't know if you heard, but Blue Parker admitted this viper nest was funded by Ms. Thelma Sheridan. He's offering to provide evidence, if he can get a deal."

"So there's proof." I want to believe Sheridan won't get away with it, but money can distort facts or make them disappear. "Do you think she'll still be able to buy her way out of it?"

"She'll try."

"Colonel, we can't let her do it."

"Take it easy. You've done enough for tonight."

"Yeah. I killed a whole lot of people, I don't even know how many. I killed a kid. I had to do it—because Sheridan decided to start a war. A fucking war. Because money really can buy anything."

"Anything at all," Kendrick agrees. "Nukes, revolution, mindless followers."

I think about fourteen-year-old Allison, who did her best to put a bullet in my heart. "You think money can buy clean hands?"

Kendrick snorts. "Guilt doesn't stick to a dragon. If it did, they wouldn't be where they are in the world."

I meant my hands, but I think he knows that.

"We did a good thing today, Shelley. And when we get you wired up again, the guilt will go away."

Reinforcements arrive. The civilian prisoners are evac'd, and then Kendrick turns over control of Black Cross to an Intelligence team. Ransom tells me they're all wearing radiation dosimeters. He and Tuttle get to haul my ass six flights back up to the top. They're both big men. With my added weight their dead sisters are starting to slip at the joints, but they get me in through the back gate of a waiting Chinook. I do not want to be carried even one more step than necessary, so I tell them, "Put me down at the end of the bench."

Tuttle says something, but I don't have a helmet anymore, nothing to boost my hearing, so I can't make out what he's saying over the roar of the engines. "Goddamn it, *speak up*!" My skullnet's dead, and my temper is as sharp as shattered glass. "Think I can hear you over this noise?"

"Just saying, plenty of empty seats forward!"

"The squad can climb over me. Put me down."

"Right here," Ransom says. "Let's do it."

They settle me on the end of the bench. One of them clomps back down the ramp. "You doing okay, LT?" Ransom asks, revealing who has stayed behind.

"Yeah," I lie. "How about you?"

"Hurts to breathe, but no broken ribs."

"If you were carrying me up those stairs with broken ribs, I'd kick your ass."

"Yes, sir."

There's a thud as he shoves his pack under the bench. I hear him stripping off his bones in preparation for the flight—technically he's supposed to do that outside the helicopter, but I don't say anything.

Footsteps and tired imprecations let me know that more soldiers are filing in. Packs hit the floor with solid thumps. The overhead racks rattle and clang as the folded-up carcasses of the dead sisters are loaded into them. Then the bench shifts as Ransom sits next to me.

"Keeping an eye on me?"

"I got your back, sir. That's all."

"Same—not that it will do you much good right now."

"You were a demon from hell down there today, sir."

I guess that's a compliment. It feels like a gut shot.

Out of habit my gaze shifts to check the squad's status on my visor—which of course I'm not wearing. I swear softly. Being cut off from gen-com means I don't know where people are or what's really going on, and I can't put out a general query—but I'm still an officer and I can make myself a pain in the ass if I want to. I raise my voice and communicate the old-fashioned way. "Call out! Who's here?"

A woman says, "Sarge is already doing a head count on gen-com." Her voice is low and nasally, and for a second I don't recognize it. Then I realize it's Specialist Harvey, speaking with a broken nose.

"Goddamn it, Harvey! I said we're doing a roll call."

"Yes, sir."

"So where's Kendrick?"

We have a designated order for roll call, by descending rank, ascending name.

Jaynie answers from the open gate. "The colonel will evac later."

"That makes you next, Sergeant. Call out!"

"Vasquez."

"Fevella."

"Harvey."

"Moon."

"Nakaoka."

"Ransom."

"Tuttle."

"Flynn."

"Hoang."

"Johnson."

There's an interval of silence when Wade should have called out. Then I hear the rattle of another dead sister going into the overhead rack, the thump of another pack being stowed under the bench. "Can you slide over, sir?" Jaynie asks.

I get closer to Ransom, making room for her on the end of the bench. "All the equipment's properly stowed?" I ask her.

"Yes, sir."

Gears whine as the back gate closes. The Chinook's engine cranks up.

I lean toward Jaynie. My forehead hits her helmet. "Have we got a status on Sergeant Nolan's group?" Nolan and two privates were left behind at the traitors' checkpoint, tasked with getting rid of the pickup trucks.

"I haven't been able to check in with Guidance, sir."

"So no status on Fernandez and Antonio?" They were sent with Troy and the National Guard truck.

"Not yet, sir."

"Geez!" Ransom exclaims from my other side. "I thought I only got hit twice, but there's three bullets pancaked in my armor! And that's just the front side. I bet there's shrapnel in the back." I feel him lean across me as the Chinook begins to lift. "Hey, Sarge—how many do you have?"

"I wasn't frontline assault," Jaynie calls out. "I don't have any."

I remember being shot once in my robot foot and once in the chest by little Allison. I touch my chest and wince at the pain of the bruise, follow it to its center, where the tissue is swollen. The bullet hit a lot closer to my throat than I thought. If it had hit just a little higher I wouldn't be here.

Just bad luck, I guess.

*No.* That's not what I'm thinking. I don't want to die. I don't.

I need to know that Lissa is alive. I want to see her again, and my dad, and Elliot. But my skullnet is dead, and there's nothing to hold back the black void seeping into my chest.

I feel Jaynie lean against me. I'm startled by the humid warmth of her breath against my ear.

"You got your helmet off, Sergeant?"

"I've got to ask you off-com, sir. Why did you go outside?"

Everyone in the squad is wearing a helmet that can filter a whisper out of the engine noise. "We're not off-com."

"Everyone has shut off audio enhancement, sir. It's just you and me. So why did you go outside? The colonel was screaming at you to stay in."

Delphi was screaming at me too. I heard her voice in the white noise of the jets.

"My audio wasn't working right. Maybe there was interference from the jets."

Jaynie pushes me harder. "So why did you go outside?"

"I just wanted to."

I really, really wanted to.

Jaynie says, "Too bad God got sucker-punched. He might have warned you to stay inside."

A shudder runs through me. Jaynie doesn't know the Red came back to visit me on the approach to Black Cross.

The Red has always been on my side, whispering premonitions of danger . . . but when I heard those fighters coming, something in my head *demanded* that I go outside. Why?

I think I know. Right up until the blast everything I saw was relayed out through the angel, saved for posterity.

To Jaynie I say, "It made good drama, don't you think? A kick-ass end to episode two when I witnessed those pilots get vaporized?"

I hear an edge in her voice: "It's not a fucking joke, sir."

"I'm not joking. The Red's back, Jaynie, and it was fucking with me. It was fucking with my equipment. It walked me out that fucking door."

I feel her pull away. She thinks I'm crazy. Maybe I am.

But a few minutes later, I feel her breath in my ear again. "I don't want to be a puppet. We need to take it out."

"The Red? This whole fucked-up episode is because Thelma Sheridan tried to take down the Red. She murdered thousands of people and nuked the country—and the Red is still here! You want to get rid of it? Then you're going to have to play a harder game than a dragon. Can you do that?"

"I don't want to live with it."

I ask her what Kendrick asked me: "What makes you think we have a choice?"

She doesn't answer. She doesn't talk to me at all after that.

Eventually, we land somewhere.

The engine winds down; it's getting easier to hear. Jaynie gets up; so does Ransom, but he's left his helmet on the seat—a fact I discover when my elbow bumps against it. The overhead racks rattle as the dead sisters are pulled down. From the chatter, I deduce we've been delivered to San Antonio and that permission was given to remove helmets. An announcement must have gone out on gen-com, but I'm not linked. Can't hear the Cloud. Can't see the world. Can't walk. I want to punch something.

The smooth growl of an electronic mechanism is followed by a puff of air that smells like dust and jet fuel as the ramp opens. In a clipped voice, Jaynie says, "Harvey, take care of Lieutenant Shelley."

Not hard to figure out that she's still pissed at me.

"Yes, Sergeant." Evidently it's Vanessa Harvey standing right in front of me. "Bring it up!" she yells. Then in a softer voice, "LT, you aren't going to believe this."

"What?"

"They brought a wheelchair for you."

It's an old-school model—no electronics—but they've sent an attendant to push it.

Dawn has come. I can tell from the purple shards of light, so dim they don't hurt my eyes at all as I'm wheeled across the tarmac. The tramping footfalls of my soldiers following me are a comforting sound. A white artificial light appears ahead. It gets brighter, chasing back the dawn with luminous fragments so intense I duck my head. The chair's wheels roll over a bump and the air becomes stuffy and still. I'm indoors, and the AC is not working. There are a lot of people around. Camera shutters click and flashes go off in my face. I duck my head farther and cover my eyes with my hand.

"What the fuck is going on?" I growl at no one in particular.

Tuttle answers, "Photo op." Then fear enters his voice as he whispers, "Shit! *Generals!*"

Now I really want to punch something.

People are moving all around me, talking in low voices. I'm still hiding behind my hand when my wheelchair comes to a stop.

"Lieutenant Shelley," a man's voice says—one that sounds suspiciously familiar. "I want to thank you and your unit for what you did tonight. Uncounted lives have been saved by your heroism, and all of you have the thanks of a grateful nation."

It's the goddamn president.

Not that I voted for him.

But Kendrick will kick my ass if I mouth off or fail to conduct myself with the dignity inherent to an officer in the United States Army. So I drop my hand to the armrest, sit up straight, and open my eyes to the pain of the overhead lights. There's a gasp and a twitter around me that tells me my eyes must look pretty bad, but I ignore it. I stare in the general direction of where the president must be and I say, "Thank you, sir," in a voice that's still hoarse and dry.

Someone touches my right hand. I'm so startled, I jerk back in the chair.

Jaynie hisses in my ear, "Shake the president's hand."

*Fuck.* But I do my job. Composing myself again, I look up. This time I have more to say. "My apologies, sir. Our LCS communicates with gen-com bulletins, but I'm not hooked in anymore. Equipment failure. And my sergeant hasn't had a chance *to brief me on our agenda.*" This last I say through gritted teeth to let Jaynie know that I don't care how pissed she is, I'm going to kick *her* ass when we're out of here. And then I hold out my hand.

The president grasps it. "No need at all to apologize, Lieutenant Shelley. It is an honor to meet you."

Next item on the agenda turns out to be *Get the crazy cyborg out of sight,* which is fine with me. The attendant pushes my chair past shattered ghost shapes that I interpret as people. Behind me, cameras continue to click and flashes go off as the president moves on to greet each remaining member of our dual LCS, thanking them for their service.

The sounds of the ceremony soon fall behind. I hear the soft hiss of wheels against floor tiles, the astonished whispers of my soldiers as they escape the photo op, and the tramp of their boots. The attendant turns the chair to go around a corner. The air gets a little colder. My soldiers don't follow. I hear them as they continue down the hall. It scares me to be apart from them. "What the hell is going on?"

From in front of me a voice says, "Shelley, it's me."

I think my mouth falls open—which works out all right because Lissa puts her lips against mine, and with her hands behind my head, she gives me a long, long kiss. Of all the things I could be thinking, the one that pops up first is that I'm really glad Kendrick made me take a shower.

With my lips brushing hers, I whisper, "Lissa, I didn't know if you were even alive. Kendrick said someone would try to get you out—"

"They did. I'm okay. They brought me here." She pulls back. "Major Chen's here."

He reveals his presence by speaking in his level, pragmatic voice. "I want to commend you, Shelley, for doing what needed doing."

"Thank you, sir, but it was Colonel Kendrick's victory."

In my mind, I go back to Black Cross. I hear the jets again and I want to go see them—I *need* to see them, so I step outside—and I watch the rocket begin to fall. "I fucked it up at the end, Major. But I want to thank you for getting Lissa out."

"That was Kendrick's victory too."

The door closes with a soft click. I'm not sure if Lissa is still with us.

Chen says, "Shelley, I need to be very clear with you. Everything that happened, everything you witnessed over the past twenty-four hours, is classified, subject to a need-to-know basis. You will say nothing to anyone without my approval."

"I understand, sir. Where's Lissa?"

"I'm here, Shelley."

"You will say nothing to Lissa."

"Yes, sir. I understand."

Chen steps closer. I tense as he takes my wrist. "This is for you." He puts something made of cloth in my hand. I explore its familiar shape: the smooth, strong fabric, the embedded microwire net. It's a skullcap. "It's preloaded with your profile."

I sit there with it in my hands, afraid to put it on. What

if it doesn't work? If the EMP blew out the microbeads in my brain, then a skullcap isn't going to do me any good at all. I'd need to have the microbeads reinstalled. I don't think that's ever been done before. I don't know if it's even possible.

"Shelley?" Lissa asks, her voice taut with worry. "Are you okay?"

But the beads are organic, aren't they? And organic structures are immune to EMP.

*Stop screwing around,* I tell myself. *Just fucking try it.*

I duck my head and slip the cap on, pressing it close to my scalp. I can't get it as close as I'd like—I've got a quarter-inch of hair on my head—but if even a partial signal gets through, I'll know the beads are working.

I hold my breath. Two seconds, three . . . and I feel a sense of lightness rising in me, countering the weight of the shadows in my head. Relief flushes through me. And gratitude.

I run my gloved hands over the cap one more time. And when I'm absolutely sure? I give Lissa a smile. "I'm okay, baby. I'm doing fine."

# LINKED COMBAT SQUAD

---

## EPISODE 3: FIRST LIGHT

LISSA AND I HUDDLE TOGETHER IN THE BACKSEAT of an army SUV. Chen is up front with the driver. We're one vehicle in a well-armed convoy taking our C-FHEIT soldiers to Kelly Army Medical Center. Twenty-four hours have passed since the bombs went off. An enforced quiet presides in San Antonio's streets. Lissa describes the barricades and checkpoints she sees, controlled by National Guard troops and curtailing all civilian traffic. Only military, police, fire, and ambulances are allowed to move.

She tells me of damaged cars littering the streets, some still with mournful families waiting in them—the flotsam left behind from yesterday's flood of traffic as a million people tried to flee the city.

Traffic lights aren't working, none of the stores are open, and scattered plumes of smoke stain the dawn sky. "But I don't see any big fires," she says. "And no looting. It was worse in San Diego. Here, except for the wrecked cars, there's hardly any damage."

But there's damage under the skin, in the city's nervous system, in its collective cyber mind. San Antonio is deep in the grip of the Coma.

• • • •

"Oh God," Lissa says. "The hospital's turned into an armed encampment."

We're barely moving now, rolling forward at maybe ten miles an hour.

"There's razor wire, and MPs with dogs . . . and hundreds of civilians. They're all standing in a long line like they want to get inside."

"They'll be taken care of," I tell her, hoping it's true. "Anyway, you're not going to wind up out there. You're staying with me."

Major Chen is on the phone with hospital security. He arranges for two MPs to meet us beside the car. An attendant is there too. She puts a monitoring sleeve on my forearm even before I get out. I'm moved into a wheelchair, and then the MPs escort us inside.

The power is on, evidenced by air-conditioning, and overhead lights that break into bright fragments in my vision. The lobby sounds packed, people on all sides, questions being asked and answered, a groan of pain, and one high, frightened voice.

"Are they wounded?" I ask.

The attendant answers. "Mostly civilians with minor injuries, sir. A lot of them are still here because they don't have any way to get home."

We move quickly through the lobby and onto a waiting elevator. "Lissa?"

"I'm here."

The elevator doors open and we proceed, passing rooms or offices, I don't know which, but I hear people talking, discussing patients, discussing strategy. The attendant tells me, "We've got you on a priority schedule, Lieutenant Shelley. Right now we're going to do a medical assessment, and then we'll commence with your course of treatment." The wheelchair comes to a stop. "Ma'am, you'll have to wait outside."

"No." I sit up straight, gripped by a sudden fear that if Lissa slips away from me again, she might disappear forever. "Lissa stays with me!"

"Take it easy, Shelley," Major Chen warns in a stern voice. "You do not need to worry about Lissa. We didn't pull her out of San Diego just to lose her on the streets of San Antonio."

She says, "Shelley, I'll be okay."

My heart is pounding in my ears, but I'm wearing a skullcap that doesn't allow me to harbor irrational fears for very long. Lissa kisses my cheek and whispers, "Don't worry."

I'm taken into a room. The door closes. I know someone is with me, though I'm not sure who, until Major Chen speaks. "Shelley, you're going to be here at Kelly AMC for at least a week while you get put back together. During that time you will exercise extreme caution in all contacts."

"Yes, sir. I told you, I understand the security requirements."

"I require absolute compliance."

"Major—"

"You will not mention the Red—you've never heard of it. You will not discuss the mission to Black Cross with anyone, not even Lissa. You will not mention Thelma Sheridan's name or the name of her company, nor will you suggest knowledge of her involvement in the insurrection. So far as you're concerned, you don't know her, and she isn't involved. Is that understood?"

"*Yes.*" I do understand the need for silence, but I'm exhausted and crippled, hunger is grinding at my belly, and every muscle I still have is aching. I don't need to hear his doubt on top of that. "What the hell makes you think you can't trust me? This isn't going to turn into a whitewash, is it? Colonel Kendrick said we had a confession from Blue Parker."

"We have a confession, this is not going to be a whitewash, and you will not mention either of those subjects again."

"Okay." Time will prove the truth. For now I have another concern. "Lissa knows about the Red."

"I believe it's her theory," Chen says, a sardonic note in his voice.

"She'll want to talk about her theory. I'll want to listen."

"Understood." His tone softens. "Layla Wade will receive a posthumous promotion to specialist. C-FHEIT will hold a memorial service for her the day after tomorrow. I know you'd like to attend, but you need to be here."

"Wait, can't I—"

"No."

"I'm not even wounded."

"You hope you're not wounded, but we don't know the condition of your eyes yet. We need you put back together, ASAP, so we're flying in an eye surgeon tonight who specializes in overlays. She'll see you first thing tomorrow morning."

He takes my hand and puts a phone into it. "From Guidance. They say it's voice trained. Keep it with you and answer if it rings. Service is spotty, so no guarantees, but we'll try to hook you in during the service."

He leaves the door partly open when he goes out. I hear him tell Lissa, "He's got a full schedule of appointments. It'll be a while." Their footsteps recede, and for the next two hours I'm weighed, measured, and analyzed. They tell me I'm not radioactive and that I was far enough from the blast not to suffer significant biological effects, but they won't let me eat until I take another shower.

The skullcap fits better when my hair has been washed away.

I still don't get to eat, though. I dress in T-shirt and shorts, and then I'm met by Specialist Bradford—the same CNA who took care of me before. "Lieutenant Shelley, didn't expect to see you back here so soon."

"Didn't expect to be here. How have you been?"

"Oh! You're gonna wish you didn't ask that," she says, taking the handles of my wheelchair. "But let's get you on your way. Sorry to be the one to tell you, but his royal majesty has asked you to come visit."

"You mean Dr. Masoud?"

"Isn't that what I said?"

We pick up the tramping footsteps of the two MPs as she whisks me into the chatter and traffic of a hallway. "Anyway, it's been a nightmare around here. A third of the staff not coming in, patients flown down from Dallas, civilians at the emergency clinic. There's not enough of anything—you've probably noticed you didn't get the luxury-model wheelchair this time around? And there's not one empty room. We had to put three beds together to open a room for you."

"Sorry about that."

"Oh, no, no. Special orders for you. Special escort too."

It occurs to me how it looks. "I'm not a prisoner."

She chuckles. "Uh-huh. All our patients like to think that way."

We get on an elevator. The MPs don't let anyone else get on with us. "Please wait for the next elevator," one of them says as the doors close. I'm not sure if they're here to protect me from reprisals or to make sure I keep my mouth shut. Probably both.

• • • •

Masoud is waiting for me, and he's not in a good mood. I can't see him except as an undefined shadow that blocks the light. He says very little as he checks out the bioelectric interface in my legs. His hands are steady and gentle as always, but I smell anxiety in his sweat. I brace myself for an explosion of temper when he decides it's my fault that he's not going to get his Nobel Prize.

A series of little electric temblors shoots up through the stumps of my legs—and then Masoud makes a happy grunt deep in his throat.

"The interface is undamaged, Lieutenant. It's Nakagawa's unshielded processors that failed." He's so happy, he actually chuckles. "I'll let him know."

"He's not going to take it well, is he?"

Masoud outright laughs. "Joby does not like to admit he can make mistakes."

A few minutes later I'm in the basement, in a dentist's chair, staring at the weird patterns cast by the ceiling light while Joby's technician swaps out my legs again. Joby's office is across the hall, but he doesn't come to see me—not that I'm complaining.

"Are you putting back the old set of legs?" I ask the technician.

"Joby says it's a temp fix. He can't put together new limbs overnight."

I shrug. "The old set worked fine."

When she starts snapping together the electrical connections, a searing pain shoots up my spine, but it settles quickly to a vague burn.

The tech says, "I've turned the sensitivity way down, since you can't adjust it yourself anymore."

I stretch the leg out, pull it back up again. "Let's do the other one."

I can't see anything but fractured lights and shadows,

but I still manage to walk out to the hall, where Specialist Bradford is waiting. "Look at you, Lieutenant Shelley. Now what am I going to do with this wheelchair?"

Turns out Lissa is there too. "Oh my God, Shelley! You're walking!"

Behind me, the tech snorts. "Replaceable parts. Makes him easy to fix."

Major Chen said something like that, back at C-FHEIT. I don't doubt that Command is taking notes.

I reach out my hand and Lissa grasps it. Then I turn to where I think Bradford is standing. "Any chance of getting some food?"

"How does fortified water sound?" she asks cheerfully, because next on the schedule is a surgery to repair and upgrade my skullnet, local anesthetic only. I complain about that: "I'm exhausted. Can't you just put me under and let me sleep?" The answer is no, so I'm sitting up the whole time, my head bolted into place and my empty stomach coiling into an angry knot. But it's over within an hour. The surgeon glues my scalp back in place, a nurse watches over me for another hour, and then I'm finally allowed to go to my room.

Lissa meets me there. While I blindly wield a fork to devour the meal brought to me by a CNA, she sits in a chair beside the bed and tells me her news: "Major Chen wants a modification of the Pace Oversight contract, requiring me to work on-site in a secure facility up in Austin."

"That's good. I don't want you going back to San Diego."

The MPs are stationed in the hallway outside, but the door is closed, cutting off most of the noise of carts rolling by, and conversations spoken in passing.

"I'm afraid for you, Shelley."

I pause with a forkful of rice halfway to my mouth, wondering what she's been told. Even before the bombs went off, she'd guessed the Red was back in my head. Post-Coma, it still exists. I should be afraid of that, but I'm not.

I finish conveying the fork to my mouth, and chew slowly on the rice. "What's going on in the rest of the world?" I ask her. "Have you heard anything? Were any other countries targeted?"

"I don't think so. Whoever did this was trying to isolate the United States, knock us out of the Cloud."

"And it worked."

"Only partially. There are still satellite uplinks, if you can afford them, and data networks can still function in local areas . . . at least if there's power. No, if this was an attempt to lock out the Red, it was a clumsy one."

I hesitate, unsure how much I can say, finally settling for what she already knows. "The Red has kept me alive. Mostly, it's been on my side, but I don't know why. I don't understand what it's for. You said it was a marketing program. But what does that mean? That the Red just wants to sell us stuff?"

She laughs. It's a brittle, cold sound, like the crack of glass that doesn't quite break. "Sure, maybe. The thing is, it *knows* us." I hear her stand up. She touches my shoulder, her fingers moving in a slow stroke down my arm. "Imagine it has data tentacles everywhere, reaching into browsing and buying records; game worlds; chats; texts; friend networks; phone conversations; airline, banking, utility, and entertainment records; GPS locations; surveillance cameras; *whatever*." Her fingers return to my shoulder. "It could know more about us than a spouse or lover knows. It could figure out who we really are, and what we really want—down to the dreams we won't admit to ourselves—and then steer us in that direction, onto new paths that optimize who we are, that lead us toward the lives we're best suited to live."

"That's what Jaynie was talking about," I realize. "Right before the Coma, she was telling me about all these people who just suddenly decided to strike out in new directions."

"That's what I think it's about." Her voice is trembling.

"Lissa?" I reach for her hand, take it in mine. I reach up to find her smooth cheek, and feel tears there. "Baby, what's the matter?"

"You, Shelley," she says with an edge to her voice. "Look at the path you've taken. Look who you've become."

I've already done that so many times, and it's true that I never planned this life. That spring in New York . . . I already had my applications in for graduate school. Internships would follow, and eventually a place in my dad's company. It never occurred to me to go into the military. I would have laughed at anyone who suggested it. Then I uploaded that video, and my life changed. "Baby, that wasn't the Red. It was too long ago. That was just me, pretending I could make a difference."

"That's what you tell yourself."

"Come on, Lissa. My dad wants to blame Elliot for what happened. Now you want to blame the Red. Both of you need to accept that it was me. I put myself on this path."

And I don't need anyone—or anything—to blame.

I think Colonel Kendrick was right when he said I belong in the army, that I'd been lucky to find my place, but it wasn't lucky for Lissa. I betrayed her when I took up this life.

I want her to kiss me, but she pulls away. She's angry with me, and that is not what I want. "Lissa—"

"You don't regret anything, do you?"

It's like she knows what I'm thinking.

"I regret a lot of things, but it wasn't the Red that put me on this path. That's all I'm saying. The Red is new. It didn't exist before this year. I think it saw first light around the time I transferred to the Sahel."

"Uh-uh. That's just when you woke up to it."

"No. That's when it got real. I still don't get it, though. What's its purpose? Why is a marketing program messing with our lives?"

She answers with a sarcasm that's rare for her, "Well, I can't know for sure, but penniless fuckups make lousy customers, don't they?"

It's so absurd I have to laugh. "So the Red makes optimized customers? Happy little consumers who buy more shit?"

The silence is so cold it crackles. She's going to walk out on me; I know it. "Lissa, I'm sorry—"

I hear a little snort, and then a giggle. "You know, when you put it like that it does sound kind of silly and shallow." She sighs. "But that's what it looks like to me . . . and people who threaten the system, like those fanatics who cut us out of the Cloud—"

"Those people get slammed."

She returns to the bedside, takes my hand, and kisses it. "You work for the Red, Lieutenant."

I slip my arm around her and pull her in next to me, hoping we don't knock over the tray. I kiss her cheek. "Yafiah and Dubey sure got a rotten deal." I don't tell her about Allison, the little girl I shot down at the bottom of Black Cross, but she got a lousy deal too.

"No one of us matters all that much," Lissa says. "Not measured against the backdrop of an entire world."

"So you told all this to Chen?"

"Most of it."

"When do you go up to Austin?"

"I told him I'm not going. Not so long as I can stay here with you." She turns her head; her lips brush mine. "He said we probably have a week."

"Yeah, that's what he told me too."

"After that I'll go to Austin. I think this research is my new path in life."

That night, we go down to the cafeteria, where we can watch the news-propaganda stations while we eat—or anyway, Lissa watches. I just listen. The MPs are with us—a new shift. Lissa whispers in my ear that they act like secret service agents, their eyes constantly assessing the staff and visitors crowding the tables. The volume on the televisions is turned up loud so it can be heard over the low, continuous buzz of conversation.

The mediots spend a lot of time interviewing refugees and politicians. They talk about the different blast sites. And then they cut to a video of the White House press secretary, reading an official statement. "In the early hours of this morning, in South Texas, an army unit stormed an underground bunker known as 'Black Cross,' believed to have been the headquarters of the Texas Independence Army. Blaise, aka 'Blue,' Parker, alleged leader of the TIA, was found at the facility and taken into federal custody."

Lissa takes my hand, gives it a worried squeeze. Major Chen would have told her that I can't talk about where we were or what we did. That doesn't mean she can't figure it out.

The press secretary doesn't take questions, saying only, "Additional, detailed information will be released very shortly, as soon as it is confirmed." The disarmament codes are not mentioned, and neither are the unexploded nukes. The president is holding back on that news, which is understandable: There's a real risk of igniting a fresh panic.

The mediots move on in their coverage. They talk about the radiation, the upcoming trials, the congressional investigations, the displaced families, the death toll. They try to sound sincerely concerned, but now and then the mask slips. Behind their sympathetic tone, I hear a giddy excitement. They love this new world in which they get to control the flow of information throughout the country. So long as the Cloud is down, they rule America via satellite; they get to tell us what the facts are, and they get to hide the facts they don't like. They get to write history. And the history they're writing says that Blue Parker was the mastermind behind the Texas Independence Army. There's not a whisper of Thelma Sheridan's involvement, not a mention of her company. I assume the mediots don't know about her. The government is probably keeping her involvement quiet while they pursue an arrest.

Then I hear her speaking—Thelma Sheridan. She's on the television. Not hiding at all, not evading arrest. A mediot is interviewing her, asking her opinion: "Vanda-Sheridan specializes in surveillance and security. Do you have any insight on what went wrong? How these nuclear weapons fell into private hands?"

"None of us will know for sure until the investigation is complete," Sheridan says. "But security issues almost always resolve to one cause—a lack of sufficient funds to support the security infrastructure. With Congress continuously calling for cuts in the defense industry, it's likely we'll see even more heinous acts of terrorism by unbalanced people, until our leadership takes responsibility for fully protecting this country, as they are obligated to do."

I think of those two fighter pilots, who gave up their lives to stop a rocket from reaching San Antonio. I'm glad, suddenly, that I went outside to witness it. Somebody needed to. "Shelley?" Lissa says. "Shelley, are you okay?"

Lissa doesn't know about Sheridan's involvement.

What if Thelma Sheridan has bought her innocence? What if she's paid off enough government officials and congressional zombies to ensure that she will never be arrested, that any investigation will be only a façade?

Major Chen promised it wasn't going to be a whitewash, but maybe that's just what he was told.

"Lissa? I need to go back to the room."

I hold her arm and she guides me there. The MPs take up posts outside the door, while I get out the phone Chen gave me and ask it to call Colonel Kendrick. It works like a charm, ringing three times before he picks it up with a groggy, "What the hell—? Shelley? Why aren't you asleep? Like I was until a few seconds ago?"

"Has she bought clean hands?" I ask him.

"*Shit.* You know my problem with you, Shelley? You don't know when to sit tight and shut up."

"That's how it came to this, sir. Too many people decided to sit tight and shut up, even when they knew shit was going down around them. And if one person, one organization"—I turn my back on Lissa, cup my hand over my mouth, and whisper—"has enough concentrated wealth to buy a domestic war, nuke seven cities, bring down the Cloud, *and get away with it*, then how long can it possibly be until some asshole who's even crazier blows us all to vapor?"

"She *will not* get away with it," Kendrick says, biting off each word. "And if you want to be part of it, you will shut the fuck up right now."

The line goes dead.

I stand there a few seconds, before lowering the phone from my ear.

"Shelley?" Lissa asks. By the sound of her voice, she's retreated to the door.

"I'm sorry, baby." I turn to her and hold out my arms. She comes to me. We hold each other and I'm shaking, because I'm thinking how close I came to losing her. If she'd been closer to ground zero in San Diego, she'd be dead now. So many people *are* dead, because for decades citizens like me and my dad, my uncle, and Lissa's parents—good people—quietly financed war after war because it's easier to pay our taxes than to risk our livelihoods by trying to change the system. Our silence let wealth accumulate in the hands of people like Thelma Sheridan, people who came to believe they could buy absolutely anything, even innocence.

But not this time.

In the morning I go to my appointment with the eye surgeon who was flown in from California. As I walk into her borrowed suite, with Lissa guiding me and another shift of MPs following in our wake, I'm greeted with starstruck enthusiasm. "Lieutenant Shelley, sir. I didn't know it'd be you I was treating until just a little while ago, when I saw your record." She's well spoken, with a youthful voice, and a West Coast accent. "The army told me I'd be treating a war hero, but they didn't say it would be the Lion of Black Cross."

"The what?"

Lissa guides me into an exam chair, and I sit down.

"That's what they called you in the documentary—"

"What documentary?"

Lissa is puzzled too. "The only documentary we've seen is *Dark Patrol*."

"This is a new one. It just came out last night on a premium channel. It's called *Bleeding Through*, because corruption bleeding through so many levels of our government is what led to Black Cross. I . . . I couldn't believe what you and your men had to do down there in that ancient bomb shelter. Lieutenant Shelley, I want to thank you for your service, your courage, and for stopping those bombs from going off. If you hadn't gotten those disarmament codes . . ." There's a catch in her voice. "One of the unexploded bombs was within half a mile of my parents' home."

So episode two is already out. I guess Black Cross isn't a secret anymore.

"It'll be on mass media tonight," the eye surgeon adds.

What was it Ransom said? *You were a demon from hell down there, sir.* Ransom meant it as a compliment, but I don't think my dad's going to see it that way. I'd save him from that knowledge if I could.

The surgeon gets to work, propping my right eyelid open before teasing loose the ruined lens of my ocular overlay. When she lifts it away with tweezers, I can see again.

"*Holy God,*" I breathe, taking in the astonishing sights of inspirational posters on the walls and the surgeon's smiling face.

She's slight, slender, pale, and young, with black hair in a neat braid down her back, and black eyes. From the shape of her face, her lips, my guess is pure Japanese ancestry.

"Is that better?" she asks me.

"Hell yes."

I turn to admire Lissa, waiting by the door. She's dressed in a white shirt and gray slacks. Her black hair is tied back, and there's an anxious smile on her face. "You look gorgeous," I tell her, with a wide grin.

After both lenses are off, the surgeon examines my eyes. "You're very lucky, Lieutenant, that you had your visor down when you looked into that inferno."

The visor is always down. It's impossible to lift it, but I don't tell her that.

"Your corneas are going to need a few days to heal before we replace the overlay, but it doesn't look like there's any permanent damage."

Afterward, Lissa tells me that she doesn't want me to get

the overlay replaced. "If you don't have it, then Guidance can't be looking through your eyes, and the army can't own you every minute of your life."

"I have to have it—"

"Do this for me, Shelley."

"Lissa, I *can't.* I need the overlay. It lets me control the feedback from my legs—"

"You can do that with farsights."

"I can't wear farsights in the field!"

"Then stay out of the field! You've seen enough fighting already. You've had your turn, you've served your country. Let someone else play the hero's role."

"It's not a role, Lissa. I didn't ask for any of this."

"Like hell you didn't. What did you tell me this afternoon? You said *you* put yourself on this path. You chose it, Shelley. You had a quiet, prosperous, *peaceful* life lined up in front of you, and you didn't want it, but you weren't man enough to admit that, you weren't man enough to tell your dad 'No thanks' and walk away. That's why you posted the video. It wasn't about civil rights. You just wanted to shake things up, change your path, wake up a dragon—and get to play the hero's role guilt-free. And it worked. You're the Lion of Black Cross—"

"Jesus, Lissa. We haven't even seen the show yet. I don't even want to see it."

"Of course you don't. You've already played that role. On to the next one. Right?"

"It's not a role! It's a duty."

I get the last word, because she walks out on me.

I don't follow.

Later that morning, Major Chen calls from C-FHEIT, and I get to watch Layla Wade's memorial service on the screen of my phone. Afterward I ask him if he knows about *Bleeding Through*.

"Can you believe how fast that was put together? Command hosted a showing early this morning, but you should be able to watch it tonight. It's really well done, Shelley. Something to be proud of. Something the country can rally behind."

"But, Major . . . the Lion of Black Cross? Really?"

"What can you do?" he says. "You just have to accept it. The country needs a hero."

Lissa comes back just after lunch. I'm half-asleep, but when the door swings open, I sit up. The blinds are drawn. The lights are off. I can't really see her face in the shadows, so I can't tell if she's come to stay or if she's come to say goodbye. "Lissa . . . ?"

Softly, she says, "I stand by what I said."

"So do I. I need the overlay, and I will be going back in the field."

"Shelley. I get angry because I want you to be safe. But it's stupid. There isn't time enough to be angry, and there isn't any way to keep you safe. We have six days. Will you forgive me?"

I smile. "Isn't that supposed to be my line?"

"Dickhead."

We try, very quietly, to forgive each other. At least for now—until I get a new overlay—no one's watching.

*Bleeding Through* plays that night, and Major Chen is right—it is well done. Our assault is mission critical. We get the disarmament codes. We save five cities. We're heroes . . . and there's not a mention of the Red or any whisper of Thelma Sheridan's name.

That doesn't worry me anymore.

In the days that follow, the MPs stick close to me. I'm grateful to have them. Kelly AMC is a busy place, crowded with staff, patients, visitors. People recognize me when I'm out in the halls. They stop me to shake my hand, they thank me for my service, but when they start asking questions about Black Cross, the MPs politely intervene with a rehearsed response: "Due to national security concerns the lieutenant is unable to answer questions at this time." Then they hurry me on my way. They don't have to deal with protesters, persistent journalists, or civilian unknowns, because Kelly AMC has been closed to all but authorized visitors. It makes the situation easier for me.

The downside is that the MPs won't let me leave the hospital grounds. "Sir, emergency restrictions require you to remain within a secure zone—for your own safety."

If I had something to do, I wouldn't complain, but I don't have any appointments. My main assignment for the week is to let my body heal.

I call Colonel Kendrick to plead my case, but he doesn't answer. I call Major Chen. "I just want to walk around outside, see what's going on, help out if I can." I know that Kelly AMC is a bubble of light, power, and three meals a day. It's different beyond the razor wire.

Major Chen won't consider it. "You have to accept that you're a target of TIA sympathizers and every rabid journalist who managed to get a ticket to San Antonio. Don't fight it, Shelley. You've got Lissa with you. Enjoy the respite while you can."

I do my best.

Seven days after Black Cross, the eye surgeon from California installs my new overlay. I download software and get all my accounts set up, while the audio nodes in my ears are being replaced. Late in the morning, I get a priority text from Joby's technician telling me to come down and get my new legs.

The new prosthetics look thicker and stronger than the originals, though they install in exactly the same way. "Are these heavier?" I ask the technician as I take some test paces around her office.

She smiles at me. Then she uses her farsights to link with Joby. "The lieutenant's complaining about the weight of the legs. I told you he'd notice."

"I'm not complaining. I was just curious—"

She shrugs. "Joby's coming over."

The door bangs open. Joby's face is flushed; his eyes are furious. "*Fifteen* grams," he yells at me. "*Each* leg. You're complaining about a difference of fifteen grams? You can't even detect it! The limbs are *not* meaningfully heavier. They only look more robust because the processors are wrapped in an electromagnetically opaque insulator."

"Is that right?" Suddenly I want to know just how angry Joby can get—so I go after the quality of his work. "This insulator—it's some candy-ass material that's going to snap the first time I put any real torque on the legs, isn't it?"

It's possible I've gone too far. He stops breathing. He stands frozen, giving me a killer's stare. I watch his hands. I don't think he's armed, but I don't want to find out the hard way. When he finally gets enough control to speak, his voice is low and husky. "Double-walled titanium. I double fucking dare you to break those legs. Go ahead and do it. Just know that your organics will be toast long before the legs give out."

I nod. "I'll keep that in mind."

He does an about-face and stomps back across the hall. The door of his lab slams shut with a concussion that makes every piece of equipment in the technician's office vibrate, and induces someone in the morgue down the hall to open a door and look out.

The technician is rocking in her chair, her arms crossed over her wide, soft chest, and a huge grin on her face. "He's kind of touchy about his work," she tells me. And then she laughs.

So that's it. I'm repaired. I'm ready—and Kendrick knows it. He calls as I'm heading up to my room. "You have civilian clothes." It's not a question. I don't doubt he knows everything about me. "Put them on. Pack up your stuff and check out. I'll pick you up out front in thirty minutes."

"Where are we going?"

"To lunch."

"And then?"

"Still to be determined."

My heart is hammering, because I know this is it. Kendrick promised that Thelma Sheridan would not get away with what she did, and that I could have a hand in bringing her justice. I want that. I want to be part of it.

Lissa doesn't link when I call her, but a few seconds later she texts that she's in a meeting with Major Chen. I text back that I need to see her. Then I call the hospital administration to let them know I'm leaving, but Kendrick got to them first: I'm already checked out. I put on the civilian clothes I picked up in the hospital shop—a collared shirt and khakis—and the shoes with their inserts that Major Chen sent down from C-FHEIT so I don't traumatize the civilians. Then I pack my things.

There isn't much. I've got a couple of army T-shirts and shorts, a hoodie, and a new combat uniform. They go easily into a small duffel, with room to spare. I try Lissa again, but the call goes to voice mail.

That's when Elliot Weber walks in. I can hardly believe my eyes. The last time I saw him was at C-FHEIT, the day the Cloud came down.

"Elliot! Where the hell did you come from? And how did you get past my MPs?"

He stands there with a troubled smile. "Kendrick issued me a pass."

"Kendrick did?"

"Yeah. I've been stuck up at C-FHEIT since the revolution. Kendrick brought the troops back, but you weren't with them. That scared the shit out of me, but he finally told me you were still alive."

"I took some damage."

"I know. Kendrick let me watch TV. I saw episode two. You know what they're calling you?"

"Yeah, I know."

"The Lion of Black Cross."

"It wasn't my idea."

"Shelley, I want to thank you for what you did that night . . . you and the rest of the squad." He holds out his hand. I take it by reflex—a brief, formal handshake—but I'm puzzled, unwilling to accept that Elliot approves of our brutal, violent mission.

He adds, "It doesn't change my opinion of manufactured wars."

I smile, more comfortable on familiar ground. "So how did you finally make your escape from C-FHEIT?"

"Kendrick. He offered me a ride. Did you know that guy flies helicopters?"

Suspicion bites down hard. Why would Kendrick bring Elliot down here, today of all days?

"Shelley? What'd I say?"

Maybe I'm reading too much into it. Maybe this really was the first chance to evacuate Elliot from C-FHEIT, and

Kendrick was just taking care of loose ends before our next operation.

But it hits me that this is my loyalty test, a measure of my commitment to a mission on which there will be no room for divided loyalties, or for doubt . . . but this is not Dassari. This is the real thing. I won't be talking shit on this mission. There is no conflict in my mind. Bringing justice to Thelma Sheridan is the right thing to do. I think even Elliot would approve. Before today, I never heard him say a word in support of military action—but when the story is set up right, even the cynics are persuaded.

I smile an apology and grab my duffel. "Your timing is the worst. I have to go."

He catches my arm. "Hey. I know you're the big war hero now, but give me just a minute, for old times' sake."

That catches me by surprise, and not in a pleasant way. I drop into my stonewall expression. "You want to lay guilt on me?"

"I want you to listen. I want you to think about who you are, and where you are, because you're trapped here"—he makes a sweeping gesture—"inside this military fantasy land, where everybody thinks like you do."

"What are you talking about?"

"Information flow. I was doing some digging before the Coma. A group in Austin showed me a preliminary report, along with the 3-D model they produced from their data. And you know what? There *wasn't* a whole lot of flow. Not while the Cloud was still whole—"

"Look, I really don't have time for a science lesson."

"Hear me out, Shelley. This is important, and it's about you. In theory, publicly available information should be able to flow freely in the Cloud, but it doesn't work that way because people filter what they hear. So the Cloud gets divided into millions of bubbles"—he presses his fists together—"and information has a hard time moving between them. Filters let some ideas through, but block others—"

"So? No one's got time to listen to it all."

"—and every one of us winds up trapped in our own little realities. Shelley, when you look at how many filters there are, it's kind of amazing that most Americans can even tell you who the president is—but some people don't even know that, and it's not a language barrier—"

I try to cut him off. "It's where you live and who you know."

"And who we *choose* to know."

"We pick the friends who share our beliefs and interests. That's been going on forever."

"More so now—or before the Coma, anyway. Traditionally, it was hard for people to move between groups. Now it's easy. Move to the big city. Move south, move north. Search the Cloud until you find the people who understand you. Fit in better by adopting new beliefs and abandoning old ones."

Maybe he's talking about me, I don't know, but this is not a conversation I need to have. "I've got to go downstairs."

He puts out an arm, as if to block me from the door. "Step back and look at yourself, Shelley. Don't you see how hard you're trying *not* to hear what I'm telling you? It's like you're afraid of what I might say."

Am I?

Elliot takes my hesitation as an invitation to continue. "It's not a static situation. The filters are getting stronger. People are dividing into smaller and smaller groups, while the number of widely shared memes—ideas or facts known to just about everyone in a large, related group, like the population of the US—is in steep decline, or it was, until the Coma. It sounds strange, but I think there's more shared information in America now, than when the Cloud was whole."

"Because the only information we get is from the mediots." I maneuver past him to the door, hit the button to open it. "I really do have to go."

"I'll walk with you."

The MPs look relieved. "Sir," one says, "we have orders to escort you downstairs."

"Come on, then. Let's go."

The frantic pace of nurses and CNAs moving through the hallway hasn't slowed, but the presence of the MPs tends to clear the way. I don't want to announce that I'm leaving, so I just nod and smile at the faces I know. Elliot's wrapped up in his explanation and ignores everyone. "It's about perspective. It's not that what we know is necessarily wrong or incomplete. It's that what we know and what we believe to be apparent to everyone, *isn't*."

Two young female CNAs are waiting for the elevator. One I've met. She smiles and whispers underneath Elliot's monologue, "Hi, Lieutenant Shelley," while the other looks at me with starstruck eyes. One of the MPs looks them over with a bored expression, while Elliot has forgotten that other people can hear him. "Think about the Texas Independence Army," he tells me. "They were convinced the people of Texas shared their beliefs—"

"No one shared their beliefs!" the first CNA says with real passion. "And Lieutenant Shelley made sure they got what they deserved."

Her anger rattles the MPs. They move between me and the women, while Elliot just looks puzzled. The elevator arrives. "Lieutenant," one of the MPs says, gesturing for me to board. They tell the women to wait for the next car.

"The Lion of Black Cross," Elliot says again as we descend. "I guess fame has its privileges."

"Leave it alone."

The doors open again. A week after Coma Day, the refugees in the lobby have all been moved out. Unlike the upper floors, it's quiet, with just a few people around. I check the time on my overlay. Three minutes until Kendrick gets here, and I haven't seen Lissa yet.

Elliot sounds dejected as we cross the lobby. "I haven't gotten through to you at all."

"Sure you have. You've given me plenty to think about." I drop my duffel in a chair near the glass doors and turn to the MPs. "I hope your next duty is a little more interesting."

"Yes, sir. Thank you."

"It's been an honor, sir."

Elliot says, "If you're waiting for Kendrick, he's driving a silver sedan with government plates."

I don't say anything.

"Damn it, Shelley!" His angry tone puts the MPs on alert again, but his filters are up and he doesn't notice. "You're scaring me. People cutting themselves off from everyone but their tribe—that scares me. We all know where that goes. But it's worse, because the filters that go up around us aren't necessarily our choice. It's like an external agent is working to engineer the distribution of information, and divide us from each other."

I look at him in surprise. "An external agent?"

"This is going to sound crazy—well, maybe not to you. Maybe you've already heard of it? A digital entity in the Cloud? An autonomous program, controlling information flow to tailor our perceptions of the world?"

I have never mentioned the Red to Elliot and there was no reference to it in episode two. He's worked it out on his own. I'm thinking a lot of people have.

I turn away from him and look again through the glass. I don't say anything, but silence can be an affirmation.

"The rumors are true then," he concludes. "You have been hacked. That's the explanation for King David."

"I don't know what you're talking about."

"A lot of people are asking questions, Shelley. This report I've been telling you about? It was commissioned by Ahab Matugo."

Ahab Matugo . . . who sent fighter jets that he wasn't supposed to have, to slam the border forts and upset the status quo of the war in the Sahel, forcing a cease-fire and new peace negotiations. I should hate him, but I don't, and it's not the skullnet that gives me my halo. It's knowing that I would have done the same damn thing in his place.

A silver sedan comes in past the perimeter guards.

"That's Kendrick," Elliot confirms.

"Okay. I hope you can get back to New York without too much trouble."

The doors slide open; the MPs salute. "Don't do anything stupid," Elliot pleads.

"I don't intend to."

I still haven't seen Lissa, but I tell myself I'll see her later. I toss my bag in the backseat, and get in the car.

Kendrick is wearing civilian clothes. His farsights, usually so clear they're nearly invisible, have darkened to a band of smoky glass to shade his eyes. He's got a couple of days' growth of gray hair on his head. He's not wearing a skullcap. "Cut it," he says in his deep voice as the car slides forward. He's not talking to me.

An icon flares in my overlay, then fades.

"You're on leave," Kendrick informs me as he guides the car past the perimeter guards. "Not an easy thing to achieve in a time of crisis, when the nation requires the service of every soldier in the US Army. But you're on leave, your overlay is no longer recording, and Guidance is not looking through your eyes."

It's not just the recording function that's been switched off. The network icon is a red X. "I'm locked down again." This time, there's not even a link to Guidance. I have access to onboard systems only.

"Get used to it."

If I have to, I will.

I make myself relax, leaning back in the seat. The refugees who gathered outside the hospital on the day after are gone now. Alongside the sleepy street, the concertina wire protecting the grounds looks like overkill.

"Did you hear what Elliot had to say?" I ask Kendrick.

He shakes his head—not in denial, but in disgust. "I've been hearing that for a week. He thinks everyone with a skullcap is a fucking puppet. What do you think?"

"I'm not here because I'm a puppet."

The American Coma is real, and it's not going to lift any time soon. From newscasts I know the economy has tanked. Fuel is in short supply, and goods aren't flowing for that reason and because no one knows where they should go. Kelly AMC is an oasis, running on photovoltaics and generators, but out in the real world, power outages happen every time load-balancing fails. Air traffic is restricted and only the wealthy can afford the escalating satellite data charges. More Americans are losing their jobs every day—while the rest of the world learns to go on without us.

Thelma Sheridan engineered this.

I turn to Kendrick. "So she bought clean hands? You know that for sure?"

He nods, his gaze fixed on the road ahead. "Yes."

"You promised she wouldn't get away with it."

He glances at me. "You ready to do something about that?"

My voice is calm, but my heart is racing. "Yes."

He gives me a dark, disapproving look. "The Lion of Black Cross, ready to jump in with his gun blazing!"

"Yeah, we pulled off that tactic at Black Cross, but I'm not sure it's going to work a second time."

"Think hard, Shelley. Why do you want to do this?"

I see those jets again. I see their pilots forcing Thelma Sheridan's rocket to the ground before it can reach San Antonio, or Austin, or some other place full of people just living their lives.

"It needs to be done."

"There's no going back from it."

"I understand that."

"Do you? We're setting out to slam a dragon. Do you understand that no matter how successful we are, this will always be hanging over our heads?"

"It is a rogue operation then? I wondered."

"This is what we've come to. The president is a performance artist and the congressional zombies do what their masters tell them and nothing else, while no one in the ranks above us has the authority to insist that justice be served." He shrugs. "Well, that's as it should be. The people have to claim justice for themselves. So yes, it is a rogue mission. If we go, we go on our own authority. We will not represent the army. We will not be funded by the army. We will not be defended by the army. We will be entirely on our own." He glances at me again. "Still sure you want to play?"

There's a gas station ahead on the right, one of those massive ones with six islands of pumps, but only one island is open, and the line of waiting cars extends around the corner and down the block. Some of the drivers turn to watch us with wary expressions as we pass by. Then one man recognizes me—I see it in his eyes. His mouth opens as if to cry out, *Hey, are you—?*

The fucking Lion of Black Cross, yeah. There's propaganda value in it, and not just for the army.

"Sir, if the army's not funding this mission, who is?"

"Private sources."

I wait for more, but it doesn't come. He keeps his gaze fixed on the road ahead, letting me think about things. I asked to come in on this, and he's trusted me, this far. I want to know more, but the real question is, do I *need* to? Or do I trust him? "Colonel, how much do you know? How deep in are you?"

He nods as if to himself. "Core."

He's only a colonel, but he has influence, power, and discretion—more than anyone of his rank should have—and he risked it all in the assault on Black Cross. He risked his life.

"Okay, then. I'm in." I glance in the side-view mirror, half expecting to see MPs following, lights flashing as they signal us to pull over, but there are only a few cars behind us, all civilian.

"See any federal agents back there?" Kendrick asks as he brakes at a red light.

"No, sir. Not yet." I watch the cross traffic pass in front of us: one police car and seven civilian vehicles. That's it. The light changes and we cross the intersection. Kendrick moves into the right lane. "What is our plan, sir?"

"Our plan is to arrest Thelma Sheridan and bring her to trial. A *fair* trial. One that will actually consider the evidence against her."

"But if she's already bought clean hands—"

"The trial won't happen here. There *was* an initial investigation. I talked to the agent in charge, and the evidence her team compiled is incontrovertible, but Sheridan got it buried under a top-secret classification. So we have no choice. We're using a legal principle known as 'universal jurisdiction.' It's a snake pit. We'll be yielding sovereignty and establishing a precedent we are going to regret, but it's all we have."

"*Universal jurisdiction*," I murmur, eyeing the encyclopedia icon on my overlay. The encyclopedia whispers back to me a summary definition. I learn that universal jurisdiction is a legal concept reserved for crimes so serious they are effectively crimes against the world. It allows any state or international organization to prosecute, regardless of where the criminal act took place.

"Got it figured out?" Kendrick asks me.

"It means we're taking her to a foreign court. Is it in the Hague?" I know in a vague way that fallen dictators have been brought to trial there on the authority of the United Nations.

"That was our first choice. It didn't work out."

"Where then?"

His eyes narrow; there's something bitter in his smile. "We found only one head of state with the spine to do it. Ahab Matugo has agreed to put her on trial for war crimes and humanitarian crimes. The documented evidence has been submitted. An international panel of judges is being assembled. Our part is to deliver Ms. Sheridan. In doing so, there are requirements we must fulfill. We have to prove her identity with DNA evidence. And she cannot be harmed. There can be no indication of torture or abuse, or Matugo will refuse to accept her, or to hold the trial."

I'm stunned by what he's telling me—and relieved too. "I had no idea. This is something at least . . . creditable. I thought we were just going to . . ."

I don't really want to say it, but Kendrick knows what I was thinking. "You thought we'd just assassinate her?"

He looks at me, but I won't meet his gaze. "So who's in it?" I ask.

"You, me, Vasquez—"

"Not Jaynie. She wouldn't step outside the lines."

"Yes, Vasquez. And your pal, Matt Ransom."

"This is for the fucking reality show!"

He checks the mirrors and takes an on-ramp to a freeway. "So I've been told. Episode three. I don't know whose dumbass idea that show was, but it's worked for the army and it can work for us."

"You *want* people to know what we're doing?"

"Hell, yes." Traffic is light—there's no reason for most people to be on the road, so much of commerce has shut down—and within seconds we're doing seventy. "We're doing the right thing. If we keep it secret, nothing will ever change."

I shake my head in disbelief. "Who else is in?"

"Other C-FHEIT soldiers."

"Chen told me you hand-selected everyone there."

"He trusted you with that?"

"It's true, then?"

"We're a special crew. We share certain personality traits, among them a concern for justice that is not as common as you might like to believe."

"Justice over loyalty?"

"There's no honor in being loyal to a corrupt system."

"You've been getting ready for this for a long time. Long before it happened."

"Not just me."

"Who else? Who's behind this?"

"I'm not issuing a roster."

"Is Chen part of it?"

"Yes."

"I'm guessing the Red was never part of your plans."

He scowls. "The Red is the joker in the pack. There's nothing I can do about it, except hope like hell it's on our side."

"Sometimes it is," I muse, "and sometimes it isn't. But I think for now, our goals are the same."

He gives me a questioning look.

"It's what Lissa said about what its purpose might be—to develop an optimized world with peak consumer potential across the population. That won't ever happen if a psychopath like Thelma Sheridan blows everything to vapor."

"Yeah? I hope you're right. You won't hear me complaining if we get a little supernatural help."

He flips the turn signal, and takes an off-ramp to the center of town. There's actually traffic in the streets.

"Where are we going?"

My question is answered when he turns into the driveway of a luxury hotel. "The mission starts tonight, and we may not be coming back." He pulls into a parking stall. "So I'm meeting my wife. Lissa is here too."

That's all I need to hear. I reach for the door handle.

"Hold on." The band of his farsights has gone transparent. He studies me, one hand cocked over the steering wheel. "I want to make sure you understand, all the way down to your balls, that this mission is not a game. It's dangerous, and not just for us. If and when it gets out who we are, there are dragons who *will* come after us, and they'll come after the people we love."

"Oh fuck." A cold sweat breaks out across my body. I know he's right.

Kendrick says, "My wife knows what to do. We've talked about this for a long time. We have friends. You have friends too. They'll be looking after your father. And Lissa will be safe, because she'll be working with Keith Chen in a secure facility. And no, I'm not going to tell you where. The less you know, the safer for everyone."

"Okay."

"So are you still with us?"

*Fuck.*

"Could I back out if I wanted to?"

"Technically, no. Unless you plan to go straight to the FBI, you're already a party to the conspiracy. So what's it going to be? You going to try to save your ass as a government witness?"

What would he do if I said yes, I wanted out? Would he try to stop me? I don't see a weapon on him. But it's an idle question, irrelevant in the circumstances.

"Sir, there is no way I'm staying behind. This mission is bug-fuck crazy, that's for sure, but it's still the right thing to do—and it needs to be done. I want to be part of that. I want to see justice done, no matter what the consequences—"

I stop myself, realizing what I sound like. "Ah, shit. Listen to me. I guess every fucking terrorist in the world has said pretty much the same thing."

"Probably."

"You know, this is exactly how I got in trouble in New York."

"Taking a stand?"

"Yeah. Fuck me."

"No thanks. Not my job. Now get out of here. We meet back at the car at midnight."

I grab my bag and we head for the hotel.

There's a propane fireplace at the foot of the bed. Lissa and I live that night by its flickering light. We don't talk about anything that matters, not at first. It's all fun and games, sex and room service—a limited selection, post-Coma, but still not bad. I'm not drinking and neither is she, but we're both as giddy and wild as if we've just knocked off a bottle of wine.

I don't want to waste time sleeping, but I do anyway. When I wake up, she's watching me with a smile on her beautiful face. We shower together, and then we get back in bed. I don't need to hide my prosthetics under the sheet. We've gotten past that.

We kiss for a while. Then she pulls back, propping her head up on her hand. From her expression I know it's about to get serious.

"Keith told me you've got a new mission and that you'll be away for a while."

"Keith?" I ask with honest confusion.

She arches an eyebrow. "That's Major Chen to you, soldier."

"Oh, right."

She stares at me, her gaze demanding additional information.

"You know I can't tell you what we're doing."

She waits, watching me with the patience of the sphinx. I don't want to piss her off, so I tell her just enough to hopefully give her some comfort. "This is just temporary duty. It's a specific task, and then we should be back home again."

"How long?"

"I don't know. Maybe a few days. If it's longer, I'll get word to you. I swear."

"You damn well better."

I feel like I just dodged a bullet. "So what are you going to be doing for 'Keith'?"

"A lot of statistical analysis looking at event triggers and ensuing pattern development in Cloud-based semi-autonomous systems." She sighs and looks regretful. "Beyond that, mister, I can't tell you."

I grin and grab her and we roll around laughing, but it's getting late. The midnight deadline is slouching closer, bringing with it a sense of desolation.

"Lissa." We're lying face-to-face, her eyes inches from mine. I touch the beautiful curve of her cheek. "Things have gotten kind of crazy, you know that. When you're working with Major Chen . . . if you're ever uncomfortable with what he's asking you to do, if you ever have any questions about the legality, the ethics of it, I want you to back out, okay?"

I swear, every molecule in her body ceases to move. Time stops as she stares at me with her black-body eyes—dark marble, radiating heat—a gaze that extracts from my mind things I haven't said. Time starts up again as she confronts me with it: "You're planning to do something stupid, aren't you? Just like before."

I can't deny it, but I can't confirm it either. The only thing left for me to say is, "I love you. I always have. I always will."

"And you're a dickhead! Always have been. Always will be."

"Lissa—"

"I love you anyway." Her voices breaks as she says it; tears start in her eyes.

We kiss, and we hold each other, we press our bodies against each other, skin to skin—cheek, chest, belly, crotch, and thighs—down to the boundary of my prosthetics. We can't get any closer. It's a moment I save in my mind. I don't want to think. I just want to be with her, but midnight is coming fast and I'm feeling afraid. "Lissa, there's one more thing. I need you to remember that it's the dragons who control the mass media, especially now, and you might hear things . . ."

I hesitate, uncertain how much I should tell her.

"What kind of things?"

I kiss her ear. "The kind of things you don't want to believe. If you hear those things, know they're not true. Promise me that you won't believe them."

She doesn't have any idea what I'm talking about, but she agrees to it with a nod of her head, saying, "I'll be here. I'll wait for you."

Subject: New assignment

Hey, Dad. I've got a new mission. Overseas again. I'm supposed to let you know that because of the way things are—the Coma—I might not be able to talk to you for a while. But don't worry. You understand? You are not to worry. I'm coming back. I promise.

Love you,
Jimmy

"We're going to die tonight," Kendrick says.

"What? Wait." I know that Lissa can get the true facts from Major Chen, but . . . "My dad can't think I'm dead. I can't do that to him."

It's 0121, and I'm sitting in the front passenger seat of Kendrick's old MH-6, outside the army hangars. Occasional flights are leaving from the civilian runway; I hope Elliot has found his way onto one of them.

Kendrick is piloting. He's finished his initial checks, and above the cabin, the blades are coming up to speed. We're wearing flight suits and our LCS helmets, but we're not linked into Guidance, and we're flying without bones or armor. We don't need them, because this is just a quiet flight up to C-FHEIT—in theory.

"Tonight's incident is not going to be announced to the media," Kendrick assures me, his low voice rumbling through my helmet's audio. We're using gen-com on a helmet-to-helmet basis, with a custom encryption to keep our conversation between ourselves. "The president will not let it get out that the Lion of Black Cross was assassinated by grudge-holding insurrectionists. But the people who need to know, they'll hear about it. And when they're trying to figure out who hit Vanda-Sheridan, our names won't be on the initial list of suspects, because we'll be dead."

"The truth is going to come out eventually."

"Shit, yeah. But until then, it's an extra layer of distance to protect the people who matter to us."

He talks to the tower and gets clearance. "Go ahead and put your overlay into recording mode."

I do it, though I'm still locked down.

We head out into the night, climbing swiftly so that we pass high above the suburbs. There's a cloud deck tonight, and after a few more minutes we pass through it. On the other side the stars are brighter and more abundant than I've ever seen them, even in Africa, and they're inhabited. I count three satellites passing overhead, but only one airliner.

Reaching behind the seat, I grab two nylon bags. Each contains a rappelling harness. I take one out, make sure it's untangled, and hand it to Kendrick.

I wanted to put the harnesses on while we were still on the ground, but he said no. He didn't want anyone at the hangar asking questions. I help him slide the harness up over his legs while he continues to pilot the helicopter, and then I secure the buckle at his waist.

"Make sure you're not squeezing your balls," he advises as I put mine on.

"Yeah, I have pretty clear memories from boot."

I should be nervous, but I'm not, and it's not because the skullnet is working overtime—the icon isn't even showing—it's more a state of disbelief. Deep down, I'm not convinced any of this is real. That's especially easy to believe here, floating in a dimensionless interface between darkness and stars.

"Here we go," Kendrick says. He's focused on the controls, concentrating on holding us stationary.

I look around. We're expecting to rendezvous with another helicopter, but I don't see it.

"Grab the cable and latch it," he tells me.

We're hovering in the void, the rotors thrashing above us, and darkness below. Tentatively, I open the door. Cold air rushes in. I glance down, but beyond the skid there's nothing to see, no sense of height. I push the door wider. The night is calm, so the only wind I have to contend with is the rotor wash. Leaning out, I look back. Even without switching my visor to night vision I see it: a black line of cable like a snake's head. It's moving, questing, searching for the hookup point. With one gloved hand tight on a grip, I lean out and grab it, and then shove it at the faintly luminous hookup portal. A mechanism in the cable shifts and it locks on. I yank on it, just to be sure.

"Secure," Kendrick confirms. "Go."

My gaze follows the cable back. I can see only the first few feet. I focus on the term *night vision*. My skullnet picks it up, translates it for my visor, and darkness washes away, revealing the stealth helicopter at the other end of the cable, and the side door standing open for me.

Grabbing the tether dangling from my harness, I reach out and hook it onto the cable.

The cushion of my seat dips. I glance over my shoulder to see Kendrick crouched behind me, ready to follow.

Nothing feels real.

I jump.

I fall only a few feet before I hit the end of the tether, and then I'm sliding along the cable. Fear kicks in, but at a distance. The air is thin and cold, but sweat dumps from every pore. There's a lurch. That has to be Kendrick, coming behind me. If it was the cable coming undone I'd be falling straight down. Instead, I slide sideways into the bay of the stealth helicopter. My robot feet click against the floor, and I run a few steps, dumping momentum. One of the flight crew, anonymous in his visored helmet, is there to unhook my tether from the cable.

"You're clear!"

I stumble out of the way as Kendrick shoots in behind me.

"Two on board!" the same voice says. "Disengaging cable."

I turn to look out the open bay. Our helicopter, brilliant with navigational lights, is flying itself. It drops away from us, descending toward the cloud deck and then disappearing through it. The cable is still winding back into the stealth helicopter when an explosion rips in orange fire beneath the clouds.

Kendrick sends me a document. I open it in my visor. It's titled:

MISSION BRIEFING
CODE NAME: FIRST LIGHT

"First Light?" I ask him.

We're strapped into the helicopter's passenger seats, our backs to the bulkhead. The crew is up front.

"I'm told it's a propaganda choice. This is the first overt action taken by the organization—though it is not, by any means, the first action planned by the individuals involved."

I scan the mission briefing. I learn that while Thelma Sheridan is a Texan, she chose the rugged, ice-bound coast of the Gulf of Alaska for the site of her Apocalypse Fortress. I admire her for that. No self-respecting survivalist should ever opt to watch the world die from the cushy shore of a tropical island.

The fortress sits on a low ridge. It has a curved face and a sweep of windows overlooking the sea. From a passing plane or a boat offshore it looks like a modest structure, remarkable only for its isolation—but most of its structure is underground.

The fortress is only one part of Thelma Sheridan's wilderness holding. A road switchbacks down the ridge, descending to a private airfield with a three-thousand-foot runway scraped from the valley floor. Alongside the runway are a fuel tank, two large hangars, a garage with a fleet of snowplows, and a three-story cube built of concrete where a dozen employees are housed.

One of those employees is described in the mission briefing as Lucius Perez, a twenty-seven-year-old engineer who oversees security around the Apocalypse Fortress. Perez is part of our conspiracy. So far as I'm concerned he's the most important part. He's going to help us get in, and he's going to help us get out again.

I go back to the beginning, and read the briefing over again. I like the plan that it details. I like it a lot better than the head-on assault we pulled off at Black Cross. Treachery isn't exactly heroic, but it works.

• • • •

The organization—Kendrick won't refer to it as anything else—demonstrates a talent for logistics as we move north. At a private airfield in West Texas we change into civilian clothes and then transfer to a twin-engine turboprop, which Kendrick flies to Albuquerque. There we're met by a woman Kendrick introduces as Anne Shima. She's slim, slight, and white haired, with a military bearing.

She looks me over. The robot feet only warrant a brief glance; it's my eyes that hold her gaze. It's like she's trying to see past them, to what's inside my head. "You can't see the Red," I tell her. "Most of the time it isn't there."

She acknowledges this with a nod. "The Red is a factor we can't control for. That irritates me, but I supported your inclusion in this mission. I've watched *Dark Patrol* and *Bleeding Through*. For whatever reason, there is a narrative around you that's still playing out. There's no way to know for sure, but I think your presence will benefit this mission. We're living in strange times, Lieutenant Shelley. We need to adapt to them." She extends her hand. "I wish you every success."

"Thank you, ma'am."

We transfer to a tiny private jet with seats for five. Shima serves as pilot. Kendrick and I strap into the passenger seats and use the time to sleep. He pulls on his skullcap and is out before we reach the end of the runway. I wait until we're in the air before I think, *Sleep*. Then I'm gone too. On the way to Juneau, we land twice to refuel. The biggest miracle of the journey: Despite the scarcities and hardships of the Coma, a fuel truck is waiting for us both times.

The weather cooperates, and we're able to fly a single-engine aircraft north from Juneau, landing in a snow-covered field that Anne Shima optimistically terms a runway. We tramp through snow to the water's edge, where we board a small boat moored beside a floating dock in the middle of a cold nowhere. Shima takes the helm, instructing us to cast off.

The sea is glassy and dark. This far north, this late in the year, the day retreats early. Night gathers around us as we parallel the coast. Through the torn veils of low-hanging clouds, a few faint stars gleam.

After an hour, the boat nudges up to another dock, this one slick with ice. A figure is waiting for us, a lantern gleaming at his feet. As he leans down to catch the mooring rope that I toss to him, I recognize Sergeant Aaron Nolan, dressed like us in civilian hiking gear, but still wearing his army skullcap.

"Evening, Lieutenant Shelley, Colonel Kendrick."

"Good to see you, Sergeant."

We grasp tight to our titles, holding on to the structure of the past here in our tenuous present.

With the boat secured, we grab our gear. Nolan goes first with the lantern. I follow, with Kendrick behind me. Shima trails after us with a flashlight. A path has been trampled through fresh snow to a sportsmen's lodge. It's a modern, one-story building with dark siding and wide windows. Only a faint gleam of golden light leaks past the blinds.

Nolan pushes the door open. We're in a mudroom lit by an LED. As I push open the second door, a blast of oppressively warm air hits me, along with an enthusiastic chorus: "*Hoo-yah!*"

This shouldn't be fun, but when I look around, I can't help grinning. Matt Ransom, Jaynie Vasquez, Mandy Flynn, Samuel Tuttle, Vanessa Harvey, and Jayden Moon—they're all here. With Kendrick and me, we've got two-thirds of the surviving veterans of Black Cross. Nolan wasn't with us on the assault—he stayed back, tasked with hiding the evidence of the checkpoint firefight—but he did his part. He's one of us.

There's only one person present whom I don't know: a tall, broad-shouldered, white-haired man. My overlay logs his face, but I'm still locked down and can't launch a search to identify him. Way out here, there's probably no cell network anyway, but Kendrick introduces us. "Shelley, this is Colonel Trevor Rawlings, retired from the US Army after thirty-two years. The colonel is handling the mission's initial staging operation and will be our first point of contact throughout the mission."

Rawlings offers his hand and I take it. "It's a brave choice you've made being here, Lieutenant. I commend you for it."

"It's the same choice we've all made, sir."

The lodge is decorated with a clean minimalism—white walls, blond woods, and steel accents—but the effect is overwhelmed by the quantity of gear and weapons laid out on the heated floors and the honey-colored tables. I make my way around the room, trading handshakes and greetings. We're not used to seeing one another in civilian clothes. We exchange doubtful looks and try not to laugh. Ransom catches me by surprise in a bear hug, so I slug him in the shoulder, which he seems to appreciate.

Then I turn to Jaynie, who greets me with a coy smile. "Episode three, sir?"

"That's what I hear. Why the hell are you here, Jaynie?"

Of all the C-FHEIT veterans, Jaynie's participation surprised me the most. She'd been on track for officer candidate school, and in another world, in some happier alternate history, she would have become an exemplary officer. But in our world? Her career was probably dead before it started, fatally tainted by her association with us.

Her smile widens. "Colonel Kendrick promised me a big bonus."

That takes me by surprise. "You're doing this for bonus money?"

"Money, sir?" Beneath the rim of her army skullcap, her face is a picture of wide-eyed innocence. "I'm doing this for the bonus of slamming a gold-shitting DC."

I shake my head. "Shit, Jaynie. I thought you were the sensible one."

Her good humor switches off. She eyes me with that questioning look I saw all too often in the few days we spent together at Fort Dassari. "Is the Red still haunting you, sir?"

"It's still out there, Jaynie, if that's what you're asking, but it hasn't messed with me since Black Cross . . . not in a way I've noticed."

"Kendrick said people are working on it. Not just here in Coma-land. Outside too, where there's still good information flow. But you want to know what I think?"

"Yeah," I say in surprise. "I do." Jaynie doesn't offer her opinion often, and she's a hell of a smart person.

"I think most of the people who know anything about this stuff don't want to get rid of the Red. They want to control it, because whoever figures out first how to do that gets to run things."

I nod. This makes sense to me.

She goes on. "Even if you couldn't control it . . . if you could analyze what it does and predict what it might do next, then you'd know when to launch your assault and when to hold it back."

I flash on Lissa, submerged somewhere in a secure facility, trying to understand the Red. Kendrick advised me to learn to live with the Red . . . but Jaynie's right. It would be a better trick to learn to use it.

• • • •

We will be operating as an LCS, so the equipment gathered in the room includes everything necessary to rig an LCS soldier in the Alaskan winter—insulated camo, insulated footwear, self-heating gloves, armor, helmets, HITRs, ammo, explosives, and of course, exoskeletons. There's even an angel, adrift above the lodge, waiting to accompany us on the mission. All of the equipment provided to us is new, and none of it is army. None of it is even marked as belonging to any particular outfit. We will be anonymous, just like the organization behind First Light.

The only army equipment the squad will be using are the skullcaps. Everyone brought their own. I have my skullnet of course, and the robot legs, but those are part of me now.

"Hey, Shelley," Ransom says. "Take a look."

He's got a small plastic box, maybe eight by four inches in area and three inches high. He's careful to keep it level. Perforations run around the sides. He holds it in front of a light while I peer inside. Something's moving in there. I hear the skittering of feet.

"Robo-rats," Kendrick says, taking the box. "Three of them—though whether they'll survive the cold, we don't know."

The temperature is predicted to drop to zero before dawn.

Shima helps us organize the gear, making sure everyone gets the equipment sized for them. I dress in insulated fatigues printed in a white-and-gray camo pattern. My backpack is the same material. I load it carefully, every item precisely placed. We've been provided with abundant ammunition and explosives, so I take as much as I can practically carry. Kendrick orders each of us to take three days' worth of rations, just in case. We're also provided with a summer-weight uniform, to change into sometime on the flight to Africa.

My primary weapon is still an M-CL1a HITR, but Rawlings has gifts for all of us: compact Berettas, just in case. I hold mine under a light and examine it. There's no serial number, nothing to trace it back to our benefactor.

Only a few of us are putting our names on this action.

I have no idea how deep this conspiracy runs, how wide its reach might be. Kendrick said he's at the core of the organization, but the only thing he would say about the money was that it came from private sources.

I look up, to find Rawlings watching me.

He nods at the gun. "You're asking yourself who's financing us. Who paid for all this equipment? Who could afford it?"

I would have sworn everyone in the room was focused on packing, but as he says these words, silence falls.

Better to clear up the issue now, than to go forward burdened with doubt. "It would make some sense if we were being outfitted by a rival defense contractor."

"It would make sense," Rawlings agrees. "But there is no corporate money in this room. We are funded by the donations of individuals who still believe we should have a government by the people, for the people—not one hijacked by the global elite. For three years we've done nothing but talk and plan and talk some more, but by God, the talking is done. When the mechanisms of justice fail, justice must be served by other means. That's our mission, Lieutenant. That's *your* mission."

It's easy to be cynical when pretty words are deployed, but I believe Rawlings is sincere, and besides, I've already made my choice, I'm all in, so his pretty words sound right to me. "Yes, sir. We are here to take Thelma Sheridan to trial." I return the Beretta to its clip-on holster, stowing it in the top of my pack. "That's all that matters now."

Rawlings nods his approval. "Keep your goals clear and you'll have a chance to achieve them."

Kendrick calls me aside. Shima joins us, carrying a tablet. Kendrick says, "Shima's got software for your overlay that will let you link it into gen-com. Treat it as a backup system. We've also authorized the drone to accept the standard feed from your overlay, and to relay links from you to Colonel Rawlings."

"Yes, sir."

Shima looks up from her tablet. "While the mission is under way, the angel will be the *only* point of contact for your overlay, and it will only link you to Colonel Rawlings. There's no need to worry about the security of the connection. Just like with the helmets, all your communications will be encrypted and anonymized before they're passed through a satellite link."

She slides an icon on the tablet. A link wakes up in my overlay. "Connection to the angel confirmed," she says.

"Gen-com?"

"Coming up."

I see a new icon wink into existence. "Got it."

Shima sends me a sound test; I send one to her. "Working," she concludes.

"Good," Kendrick says. "Now shut it off. We will be maintaining EM silence at the start."

We strap into the dead sisters that have been provided for us, adjusting the length of the struts and testing all the mechanisms. Our helmets go on next. I link to my skullnet, to my HITR, to the angel waiting outside in the night, and to everyone else in the squad. Only Delphi is missing. We'll be operating without Guidance—but then we had to do that inside Black Cross too.

We're ready to go. We shake hands with Anne Shima and Colonel Rawlings, who says, "Godspeed."

Then we file outside. We're a rogue militia, nine in number. That's more than I had at Dassari. I tell myself it's enough.

It has to be.

We leave the lodge at 2107. The sky is cloudy, keeping the temperature above five degrees. We're lucky there's no wind. Twenty-seven kilometers lie between us and the Apocalypse Fortress. I put Jaynie out front. It's a good decision; she sets a determined pace. We stay a couple hundred meters inland, paralleling the coast, going single file and keeping under the trees when we can, but snow is predicted for later tonight, so I'm not too worried about leaving a trail.

Despite the still air, it's fucking cold. The cyborg legs aren't affected, but they're affecting me. They're a heat dump. It doesn't matter that I'm wearing snow boots and insulated fatigues. Without body heat, without blood circulating into the legs, they take on the temperature of the air from the foot up to the knee. Above the knee, I feel like I have rods of ice jammed into the stumps of my legs.

At least I'll never get frostbite in my toes.

For most of the first hour we hear wolves howling, not all that far away. It's a haunting sound that keeps me alert. But when snow starts falling, the night goes quiet and my senses contract. Night vision shows me where to step, and it shows me Vanessa Harvey six paces ahead, but that's all I can see. For the next two hours we stride through a collage of trees and snow that looks so much the same everywhere we go, it's easy to feel like we've gone nowhere at all.

But high above us, an angel watches. If anyone wanders more than a step or two off the line, a red warning dot pulses on the map of our route that I keep projected onto my visor. So no one can get lost—but going mad from boredom? By the time we've done sixteen K it seems like a real possibility.

At twenty-two K, the angel detects an electronic signature that doesn't belong to us.

We all drop into a crouch, our weapons ready.

Arrays of electronic sensors keep watch in the Apocalypse Forest, on guard for movement, heat, electromagnetic events . . . but the engineer, Lucius Perez, controls them, and tonight, for a window of a few hours, his task was to switch them off.

If he's failed to do that, our mission is doomed.

My heart is hammering as I wait for the angel's analysis of the signal. I miss Delphi's voice; I miss Guidance.

An update scrolls across the screen of my visor: The transmission came from a small fishing boat passing just off the coast. With luck, it has nothing to do with us.

Midnight finds us clambering around the foot of a ridge, just steps from the ocean. Snow is still falling, accumulating on the steep slope and weighing heavily on the trees that tower above us. We go quietly, because we're close.

Before long, the coast levels out again, and soon we come to the verge of a road covered in deep snow. Jaynie raises a hand, and the signal to stop gets passed back down the line. We're staying off-com, passively receiving only, to minimize our EM signature.

I make my way to the front, with Kendrick following. We stand with Jaynie, looking back toward the ridge we just skirted. Two long switchbacks climb its side. Up there somewhere, the Apocalypse Fortress looks out on the sea, while in the other direction, the road follows the coast for eight hundred meters to the airfield.

I hear waves lapping against the shore, but they're not loud enough to drown out a distant rumble of engines. Looking through the angel's camera eyes, I'm expecting to see a snowcat maybe, or a plane daring the snowstorm. But the rumbling engines belong to two robotic snowplows driving up and down the runway at midnight, working to keep it clear.

We stormed Black Cross because on that night every minute mattered. If we have to, we'll storm the Apocalypse Fortress too—but with our ally Lucius Perez helping, we're hoping we can lure Thelma Sheridan outside. Finding a traitor to roll back security is always a factor in the best assault plans.

Kendrick gets the robo-rats out of his pack and hands the box to me. "Take them up to the top of the ridge. Don't worry about getting close to the house. The risk isn't worth it. Release them, and get back down here before the snow stops."

I debate who to take with me. Ransom is too big for sneaking around. Flynn is too small. Kendrick needs both sergeants with him, so I tap Moon on the shoulder—he's closest—and crook my finger. On the map displayed on my visor, the angel draws me a path to follow. I look at it, and feel the hair rise on the back of my neck.

Signaling Moon to wait, I wade through the snow until I can tap Kendrick on the shoulder. "Colonel."

He turns the blank face of his visor in my direction. "Why are you still here?"

"We're not hooked into Guidance, and we're passively receiving only, so who the hell told the angel to plot me a route up this ridge?"

Several seconds pass before he says, "We need to move. It looks like a good route . . . and if the Red's looking out for you, all the better."

He's right, although I can't forget it was the Red that walked me out the door at Black Cross, and not because it was looking out for me. I think it wanted a witness to the last moments of those two fighter pilots and I was the only available option. I know the Red is not on my side or anyone else's, but I've trusted it in the past and lived, so what the hell.

I grab Moon again and we follow the plotted route.

Our dead sisters make it an easy climb.

A light comes into sight above us as we near the top of the ridge. I signal Moon to slow down. We creep another three or four meters. Ahead of us the trees thin out so that I can see the light is coming from the curved bank of windows on the sea side of the Apocalypse Fortress. There are no blinds, no privacy tint. I can see inside to where a fire burns in a hearth, white in night vision. Someone sits in a cushioned chair beside it, head bent, reading a tablet. I imagine it to be Sheridan, peacefully contemplating the deaths of millions while her husband, Carl Vanda, recovers from his injuries in a hospital bed somewhere in an underground room.

Moon puts his helmet close to mine. "You want to go farther?"

"No." I can't risk being seen. If we lose the element of surprise the mission will fail, leaving us to face a robust counterattack, with no means to evacuate from the Apocalypse Forest. "We'll let the rats go here."

If Kendrick knows how to control the rats, he hasn't told me. I don't know anything about them. I'm just hoping they're trained to perform certain behaviors. We kneel on the snow, set the box down between us, and open it. Three rats show their snuffling noses. I tip the box, dumping them onto the snow. Just like the rats at Black Cross, each has a camera button between its eyes and a whip-wire antenna sticking out of the back of its skull. The rats will violate the EM silence of our operation when they uplink to the angel, but in the vicinity of the house, with all its electronic equipment, their signals won't stand out.

Watching them, I'm not sure they'll make it to the house. They really don't like the cold. One stands on its hind legs; another runs onto Moon's boot. "*Son of a bitch!*" he whispers as he shakes it off and stumbles backward.

"Don't step on them!"

They cluster close together, shivering.

*Should I try to take them closer to the house?* I crouch, and cautiously extend my gloved hand. They don't act shy, so I pick one up. Its head turns; its tiny black eyes fix on the light from the building and I hear a faint squeak. "Hey, I think it's attracted to the light."

I put it down again. From the ground it can't see the house lights, but it must remember where they are, because as soon as it feels the snow underfoot, it takes off, scampering away up the hill. The other two rats follow.

Movement draws my eye to the side of the house. Is there something in the shadows? Even with night vision, I can't really make it out; it's just motion, an undefined shape. I switch to the angel's view, but the drone is near the airfield, too far away to get a good look at the house.

"Do you see that?" I whisper to Moon.

"Is that a dog? It looks like a huge dog . . . only weird."

At least there's no wind to carry our scent uphill.

"Come on. Let's get out of here."

Moving as quietly as we can, we retreat.

We're halfway down the ridge when I hear a loud *crack* from below: the snap of a branch breaking under the weight of snow? Or a muffled shot? Concerned that we've been discovered, I hold up a hand for Moon to stop. Gripping an icy branch, I lean out over the slope to look down. The angel has drifted partway back from the airfield. It tracks each soldier by sight, marking their positions on my display, whether or not they're hidden beneath the trees. All seems calm. Only Nolan, Tuttle, and Flynn are in motion, moving away from the road at an easy walk—and then I make out a glimmering thread strung across the road.

"We're okay," I tell Moon. "They're stringing the spiderline." The crack we heard was the bolt, shot from an air gun, embedding itself in a tree.

When we reach the base of the ridge, we find Flynn sitting balanced on Aaron Nolan's shoulders while she secures the near end of the spiderline high in a tree. The objective is to transfer most of our squad across the road without leaving footprints.

Nolan's team needs to cross first. He's tasked with leading an advance group to the airfield, where he'll be in a position to take control of the concrete blockhouse, securing the on-site employees who are housed there, to preempt any resistance. He'll also make contact with Lucius Perez. So as soon as the spiderline is taut, Flynn, the first of his team, zip-lines over.

I catch Nolan's arm strut, tugging him around so we can conference with Kendrick. Jaynie steps forward to listen. "Moon and I saw something moving just outside the house. It looked strange. At first I thought it was some huge dog—but I don't really know what it was."

"Stay alert," Kendrick says. "If it comes down here, blow it up."

Tuttle zips across, and then Moon. I boost Harvey, and she goes next. Kendrick has his helmet next to Nolan's, imparting last-second instructions. "Remember, hunker down but keep your eyes open. Do not announce your presence. But when the shit hits, you need to hit back hard and fast."

"We will, sir."

"And if you get in trouble, we're just a few minutes behind you—but don't get in trouble."

"Got it, sir."

I help Kendrick boost Nolan up. He slides across. As soon as he's on the other side, he takes off through the forest, with his team following single file.

Ransom and Kendrick cross next, taking up a position on the other side of the road. That leaves Jaynie and me. I boost her into the tree to unhook the spiderline. Across the road, Kendrick gets out a string of explosive charges—small white packets distributed along a length of white wire—which he secures to the end of the spiderline. Jaynie reels the line in, and a row of explosives is laid across the road, invisible against the snow.

I check the time. It's 0053. The next step in the assault is to lure Sheridan out of the Apocalypse Fortress. This task falls to Lucius Perez. In exactly fourteen minutes, he will call her to ask if her husband—injured ex-mercenary Carl Vanda—is asleep.

She will say yes. She will remind him that her religious beliefs forbid a divorce, and then she will get into her snowcat and come down to the airfield to spend a stolen hour in his company . . . because even a dragon's reptilian heart can revel in the passion of a secret lover.

It won't be the first time an empire falls over an indiscretion.

The snow has stopped but the clouds linger and there are no stars to be seen as I stand motionless, waiting in the shadow of the trees. The angel shows me the airfield. The runway is clear of snow, and the robotic plows are on their way back to the garage. Nolan is making his way through the last stretch of forest verging on the hangars; Harvey, Tuttle, Moon, and Flynn follow close behind him. Across the road, Kendrick and Ransom wait out of sight, while Jaynie holds a position beside me. There is no chatter. We know our roles. It's only a matter of time.

At 0102 I check the feeds from the robo-rats. The first feed shows only a black screen. Using my gaze to highlight commands, I run the video backward at speed until I get an image. It shows a viewpoint high in a tree. Running it back farther, I see the house and surrounding snowfield dropping away as the rat is carried into the air. An owl must have taken it.

I switch to the second feed. This one shows what I think is snow, close up, with the horizon running vertically. My best guess is that the rat is dead. When I run the feed backward, it's clear the rat didn't get more than halfway to the house. Whether the owl killed it, or the cold, or something else entirely, I don't know.

Judging from the trembling of the image, the third rat is still alive. It's backed into a crevice, outlined as a black triangle around the view frame. The camera it carries is pointed across a snowy field. I think it's reached the house and has hidden in the masonry below the bank of windows so that it's looking back at us. As I watch, something slides past at the bottom margin of the video feed. I can't tell what it is.

I check the time: 0107.

Lucius Perez should now be making his call. I wonder if he ever loved Sheridan, or if he only pretended to love her to further his career.

The digits on my clock shift, increasing minute by minute, until it reads 0111.

Through the feed from the surviving rat, I hear an engine rumble. Lights shoot into the treetops and then swing down across the snow as a vehicle climbs up a ramp from an underground garage. I turn and look up at the ridge just as headlights appear on the road.

Sheridan believes herself safe. She bought her innocence, spreading enough wealth and favors around to keep her name out of all official accounts of the Coma, and anyway, this is the Apocalypse Forest. She knows that a squirrel couldn't scamper here without a sensor detecting it. She will have no reason to suspect an ambush.

The snowcat's engine growls louder as it reaches the bottom of the ridge. As it levels out, its headlights sweep the road in front of me, flaring in my night vision. My visor compensates, and I can see Sheridan inside the glass-enclosed cab. She must have the heater cranked up, because she's not wearing a parka, just a light, long-sleeve pullover, ghostly white. She drives at a cautious pace, spraying feathers of snow behind the cat's fat tracks. Just as she reaches our position, Kendrick blows the explosive charges.

A blinding flash, a geyser of snow, flaring brake lights, and the cat rocks forward, sliding down into a channel blasted out of the snow. We've only slowed the machine, though. We haven't stopped it. In seconds Sheridan will coax the cat to climb out of the ditch—or she'll put the vehicle in reverse and back out.

I sprint. With the dead sister powering me, it's easy to bound through deep snow. I launch myself at the snowcat's passenger window, hitting it with the elbow joint of my dead sister. The window explodes inward as Sheridan swings the muzzle of a large-caliber pistol in my direction. Fragments of safety glass spray in her face, causing her to flinch back just as she pulls the trigger. The bullet rips through the snowcat's roof.

Ransom pops up on the other side of the cab. He hammers with his arm hook at the driver-side window. Sheridan ignores him long enough to fire two more rounds meant to discourage me, but when the window shatters behind her, she twists around to aim her weapon at Ransom. I reach through the broken window, unlock the door, wrench it open, and drop, kneeling, onto the seat.

Wearing the dead sister, it's cramped in the cab. I move carefully, but I move fast, seizing Sheridan by the wrist just as she swings her weapon back toward me. Her finger is still on the trigger. She fires off two more rounds that go through the roof. My helmet's audio muffles the bangs, but it conveys the wail of a siren screaming up on the hill. Sheridan must have hit a panic button when the explosives went off.

Keeping a tight grip on her wrist, I use my other hand to wrench the pistol away. Ransom gets the driver-side door open. He's shuffling to stay in place on the moving track, but he still makes quick work of grabbing her in a bear hug. "Take her out!" I order, letting go of her wrist. He jumps backward, hauling her with him out to the snow.

I crawl into the driver's seat, where I pop the cat into neutral and set the brake.

Gen-com activates in my visor. No point worrying about EM signatures anymore, so Kendrick has switched us all on. We can send and receive again.

I jump out the driver-side door.

Ransom has Sheridan facedown in the snow. He's kneeling beside her, holding her wrists pinned against the small of her back while Kendrick works to secure her in plastic handcuffs, but before he can get her trussed, Jaynie is yelling over gen-com. "Cover! Incoming!"

I look up, to see a fleet of tiny rockets illuminated by fiery tails—I count six—arcing toward us from the top of the hill.

"Expect a surprise package!" I warn. "Those probably aren't explosives." Because if they were, they'd be just as likely to kill Sheridan.

"Fall back!" Kendrick orders.

He hasn't got Sheridan cuffed yet, and there's no time now. He and Ransom each grab one of her arms. They haul her to her feet and carry her into the trees.

I'm about to follow when something else catches my eye, something on the ridge: a metallic sheen racing down the steep slope at incredible speed, not following the road at all.

"Enemy on the ground!"

Using the leg strength of the dead sister, I make it to the trees in one jump. Jaynie is there ahead of me, maybe fifteen feet away. We both turn and look up as rocket glare sets the snow in the road ablaze in night vision. No explosion though. Just a series of pops, like the sound Jaynie's chemical gun made at Black Cross.

"Face masks!" I bellow, but as I reach for the pocket of my vest where I keep mine, a buzzing whine fills the air, and I know I'm wrong. The rockets haven't delivered chemicals. "Microdrones! Prepare to defend!"

Goddamn all defense contractors and their experimental weapons.

The face mask stays in my pocket. I grab my rifle instead, raising the muzzle as three, then four, then five little helicopters descend below the tree branches. The drones have a narrow, cylindrical body suspended under a rotor with a three-foot diameter. Beneath the body, which I assume contains the power source, is a rotating gun. I see two muzzles turning to bear on me.

I pick one and shoot it. The microdrone goes up in a blinding white explosion—but at the same time, a round slams into the top of my helmet, putting me down on my ass in the snow. I hear another explosion and another, along with an ongoing fusillade of shooting. A round pings off my leg. Another pancakes into the armor over my shoulder. I'm screaming incoherently because it fucking *hurts*, but I keep my head up, and when a targeting circle appears, I cover it and shoot. Another explosion. I aim again. Shoot. There's a double *whump* . . . and I can't find another target.

"Status!" Kendrick barks. "Shelley?"

I flounder in the snow. It takes me a couple seconds to get on my feet. "We have an enemy on the ground!"

"Are you hit, Lieutenant?"

"Mule kicked! It's coming, sir!" I hear it in the forest, charging toward us, crunching in the snow with the rhythm of a running horse.

"Blow it up," Kendrick says. "Vasquez, you hit?"

"*Bruised.*" The word is a whisper from between clenched teeth. Then she adds, "*Goddamn*, what the fuck is that?"

She fires a grenade into the trees.

My visor goes black against the ensuing explosion. A large-caliber weapon hammers an answer. I drop flat in the snow, but I keep my head up, my weapon roughly aimed, and when a targeting circle appears, I cover it, and launch my own grenade.

In the second and a quarter before the grenade goes off, I get a good look at what's coming for me. It's a four-legged robotic monster, standing taller than a wolfhound. I've seen prototypes of things like it, but none that moved with the agility this one displays. It looks like a mechanical wolf skeleton, though there's no true head, just two cross-braced struts with camera eyes. The guns mounted on either side of its spine swivel, one toward Jaynie on my left, one toward Kendrick and Ransom, who are protecting Sheridan somewhere on my right, deeper within the trees.

The robo-wolf jumps sideways an instant before my grenade goes off.

It jumps straight at Jaynie.

The explosion blackens my visor. By the time my vision clears, I'm back on my feet. Branches and chunks of snow are falling down between the trees, and Jaynie is lying on her belly, shooting at the oncoming monster—*bang, bang, bang, bang*—a steady rhythm, each shot striking the wolf and sparking off its frame without slowing it down at all. It leaps in the air, its gun turrets swiveling down to target her.

"Blow it up!" Ransom screams. He sounds like he's desperate to get into the fight—fighting is what he knows—but he's responsible for Sheridan right now. I'd love to blow up the robo-wolf for him, but it's already too close to Jaynie. So I switch triggers.

*The eye*, I think, hoping my AI can figure it out. The targeting circle appears. I shoot.

And the monster's camera eye, the one closest to me, blows out. The wolf fires one of its guns, but the rounds strike the snow beyond Jaynie.

It's almost on top of her though—she's about to be trampled—when she slams her arm hooks and footplates simultaneously into the snow, launching herself sideways and then bouncing to her feet, bringing the muzzle of her weapon around to target the wolf one more time.

Now we're both on its blind side. I can't shoot because Jaynie is in the way. Jaynie doesn't shoot because bullets don't help and she's too close for another grenade. The wolf swings its head away from her as it turns around. She backs up to stay out of sight of its good eye. I jump, moving sideways to get a clear line of fire—and for the first time since the shooting began, I see Kendrick. He's come forward, leaving Ransom alone with the prisoner. He's standing with his weapon ready, a few feet away from me, between the trees.

"Move your ass, Vasquez," he warns.

She jumps, all the way back to the road, while the robot swings around fast, drawn by Kendrick's voice. He squeezes the trigger of his HITR, launching a grenade. I do too, while the robo-wolf targets us both with synchronous fire from its spinal guns. I see the muzzles swivel, and I drop again to the snow. Kendrick tries to, but he's not fast enough. The heavy rounds catch him in the belly—and then the grenades go off.

As soon as the dual concussions slam past, I'm up. I look first for the robot. It's crumpled, unmoving, half-buried in snow. I look for Kendrick next. He's down too. From the ridge, there comes the roar of a snowmobile. "Jaynie, watch the road!"

"On it!"

I bound through the snow to Kendrick, crouch by his side. Two holes in his armor are filled with blood that's spilling over into the snow. I shrug off my pack and dig for the trauma kit.

Ransom comes out of the woods, still with Sheridan in his custody. Her hands are cuffed in front of her, and he's half carrying her, half dragging her toward me. "LT!" He's off-com, fury in his voice like I've never heard before. "What the fuck happened? Where was King David? Why didn't you warn the colonel? You had to know that thing was coming!"

I can't believe what I'm hearing, and I don't want to hear it now. "Shut the fuck up and get the prisoner into the cat."

I get the wound putty out.

"You had to know!"

"I didn't fucking know, okay?"

Moving as fast as I can, I peel back Kendrick's armor, open his jacket, pull up his T-shirt. Two bloody craters in his belly.

Out on the road, Jaynie fires a grenade. It goes off at a

distance, somewhere near the base of the ridge. "We've got another minute," she says.

Ransom still hasn't moved. "Shelley, you *had* to know."

"Shelley?" Sheridan asks, seizing on my name. "*Lieutenant* Shelley?"

The composure, the authority in her voice, makes me look up. She's watching me from a couple steps away, shivering in Ransom's grip, wearing only a knit pullover and a long skirt over thin house boots. The cold has drained her face of color, but her voice conveys no trace of fear as she tells me, "God gave you no warning of what waited for you here, Lieutenant Shelley, because it's not God who speaks to you—"

"Shut up!" Ransom screams at her, like he knows what she's going to say next.

I turn back to Kendrick, my hands shaking as I jam putty into his wounds.

"—it was the Devil, and the Devil's betrayed you."

"Shut *up*!"

Kendrick's visible bleeding has ceased, but Ransom has gone fucking crazy.

Jaynie strides up, and lays into him. "Specialist Ransom, you will conduct yourself as befits a soldier in the United—" She falters, because after all he is *not* a United States Army soldier, not right now.

I turn Kendrick onto his side and use the patch on his exit wounds.

Jaynie tries again. "Give me the prisoner, Ransom. You assist the lieutenant."

I glance up. Ransom is not complying. He's not defying, either. I don't know what he's doing. He's just standing there, holding on to Sheridan. I wish I could see his face.

I settle Kendrick back onto the snow and get up. Sheridan's shivering is getting worse. She's well on her way to hypothermia, maybe frostbite, and if she shows up for the trial bruised, or with blackened fingers and moldering ears, Ahab Matugo will not accept her—but Sheridan isn't ready to surrender. She looks at me as if she can see my face through the black screen of my visor and says, "I warned you a reckoning was coming. The Red sent you here. It controls you. You *are* the Devil's servant. All of you are, and you will be cast down!"

I'm rattled, hearing her call it "the Red"—the same name I use.

Ransom is rattled too, but not for the same reason. "Don't you talk to Shelley like that," he says, giving her a shake. "It's God who's kept him alive."

"Goddamn it, Ransom, it doesn't matter! Jaynie, take her!"

"It does matter, sir! It does!"

Jaynie reaches for her, but Ransom wrenches her away. Kendrick proves he's conscious by whispering, "Fucking do something, Shelley." I try to take her—"Ransom, give her to me"—while Sheridan spews more crazy words, getting deeper under his skin. "You're tools. Each one of you. Tools to be used by Satan before you're cast into the abyss!"

"Shut *up*!"

I grab Ransom's shoulder. He elbows me in the chest using the strut of his dead sister. I know he doesn't mean to hurt me. It's just that he's too angry, too scared to think.

It fucking hurts anyway. It knocks me off balance, knocks the air out of my lungs, and I swear to God my ribs would be broken if I wasn't wearing armor.

I never took Ransom's King David fantasy seriously, but I guess he did. It's like I betrayed him by failing to foresee the wolf, by letting Kendrick get hit. And then Sheridan, taunting him. He's so shaken by her accusation that it's not God but the devil who's protected us that he's out of control. He slams Sheridan facedown into the snow. Then he pulls out the pistol Rawlings gave him and points it at her, taking the most direct route to silence his doubt.

I don't have any breath to yell at him. I lunge instead, powered by my dead sister. Jaynie goes after him too, but I hit him first. I hit him in the shoulder. We both go down, and the pistol flies out of his hands, spinning through the air and landing just beyond Sheridan. I'm lying on my side, trying to hold Ransom down, when I see it happen: Sheridan scrambling on her knees in the snow, scooping the pistol up.

I don't know why her hands are cuffed in front of her . . . maybe because fifty-year-old women aren't dangerous? This one is, and I'm not allowed to shoot her. I can't even hit her, because Ahab Matugo will not take her if she's hurt.

I let Ransom go and scramble to my knees. Sheridan swings the gun toward me. She's shaking with cold. I don't know how well she can aim. There's a good chance she'll miss, and if she doesn't, my armor might protect me. So I lunge for the gun—but Ransom is already on his feet. He shoves me aside just as the shot goes off.

The slug impacts his armor, knocking the wind out of him and turning him half around. Sheridan closes on him while he's off balance, moving as fast as an AI made flesh. Jaynie can't stop her. Neither can I. And Ransom is not thinking straight. He'll kill her, I know it, and the mission will fail.

"Ransom, don't hurt her!"

He looks at me, not at her, and she uses the opening. Ransom is wearing body armor. His helmet and visor protect his head, but Sheridan is a DC. She knows how the gear works. She knows where it's vulnerable. She just steps in next to him, jams the pistol up under his jaw to steady her shaking hand, and pulls the trigger. His head jerks back. Blood sprays over Sheridan's upturned face and peppers the snow. She puts two more fast shots into his brain before I can grab the gun, before Jaynie can grab her.

Ransom collapses, his status flashing on my visor like it's some fucking video game: *Matthew Ransom, deceased.*

*"Fuck!"* I scream. "God-*damn*, God-*damn*, God-*damn*."

I'm a millimeter from meltdown. The skullnet can't keep up with my fury, my despair. Jaynie knows it. She scoops up Sheridan using the strength of her arm struts, and tramps off through the snow, carrying her to the snowcat.

*"She fucking killed him!"* I scream at Jaynie's back.

Ransom is at my feet, his blood pooling in the snow. I look from his body to the pistol I'm holding. I want to jam its muzzle against the back of Sheridan's skull; I want to put a bullet right into her brain.

"You fucking idiot, Ransom," I whisper off-com.

But I can't roll back time, and the mission is not over yet. We need to move. So I hook my arm strut in the frame of Ransom's dead sister and haul him across the snow, dropping him close to Kendrick. I gather my gear. The pistol goes into my pack; the pack goes over my shoulder. I pick up my HITR and shoulder that too. With the gear secured, I turn to Kendrick. One arm hook goes around the shoulder bar of his dead sister; the other I use to hook Ransom. Then I set out across the snow, hauling both of them with me.

Four minutes and forty-five seconds have passed since we launched our ambush.

"More vehicles coming down the hill," Jaynie says over gen-com.

"Roger that."

Sheridan is in the snowcat's front passenger seat, her hands tied behind the seat, her feet tied together and tied down.

Jaynie helps me get Kendrick stripped out of his rig and settled into the backseat. His blood pressure is low, but he seems stable. "Colonel, clear your visor, please. If you can."

He does it. His eyes are half-open, his lip curled in disgust or in pain, I don't know. "Get us the fuck out of here," he whispers.

"Working on it, sir."

I jump down and close the door. The plan was for Kendrick to drive. I can do it if I have to, but I want to hold a weapon.

"Jaynie, can you drive this thing?"

"I had a lesson this morning."

"It's yours then."

I throw Kendrick's rig and his weapon into the cargo bed, and then Jaynie helps me load Ransom. She returns to the cab, puts the cat into gear. I hear what sounds like two more snowmobiles. Trees block my line of sight to the switchbacks, so I access angel sight, and I see them, speeding down toward the bottom of the hill. Another snowcat is farther up.

Behind me, Jaynie coaxes our hijacked snowcat across the ditch that we blasted in the road. "You coming, Shelley?" she asks over gen-com.

"Yeah." I turn and bound over the ditch, then haul myself into the snowcat's cargo bed, alongside Ransom. "Go."

The snowmobiles reach the bottom of the ridge just as she lays on the speed. Rooster tails of snow are thrown up behind us, making it hard to see exactly where they are. I've got Kendrick's and Ransom's weapons in the back with me. I grab one, salvaging two grenades from its magazine, transferring them to mine. Then I aim straight down the road and fire.

"Status?" Jaynie asks.

I can't see much past the rooster tails, so I switch to angel sight. I don't see either snowmobile on the road, but then I pick them up in the forest. "They're trying to flank us."

But weaving through the trees has slowed them down, and the airfield is not far away. I hope like hell Sergeant Nolan has got it secured. I push through a link.

"Nolan, status?"

"LT! Are you going to make it?"

"Status!"

"We're on schedule. Lucius Perez has identified himself. Flynn's with him. They're working with the pilot to get the plane ready. We've located and secured twelve Vanda-Sheridan personnel on the top floor of the blockhouse."

"Were they mercs?"

"Four Uther-Fen . . . two of those might not live."

"The rest?"

"Maintenance personnel. A little roughed up. Nothing serious. They told us there were four more mercs living on the hill."

"We made the arrest, but the enemy is coming after us. Two snowmobiles in the forest, either side of the road."

"Harvey and Tuttle are stationed at the end of the road. They'll cover you. Got that, Harvey?"

"Roger that," she says.

I'm still watching the snowmobiles with angel sight. The one on the ocean side of the road is almost parallel with us. "Harvey, one of the mercs might get to you before we do."

"Hope so, sir."

"Don't let them get past you. They could try to crater the runway, or blockade it." That's what I'd do: make it impossible for the plane to take off. "Nolan, when's the plane going to be ready?"

"They're moving it to the end of the runway—the inland end. Because of the mountains, we need to take off over the sea."

"Got it."

"LT, about the pilot . . ." The hesitation in Nolan's voice

tells me bad news is coming. "So far she's cooperating, but she isn't part of our operation. She doesn't know what's going on. Perez woke her up, told her she's got an emergency flight—that's all she knows. She's thinking it's a hijacking."

"Perez said he had a pilot lined up."

"Yeah. Guess he forgot to tell her about it."

So we get to kidnap an innocent woman.

I decide I don't like Perez. He betrayed Sheridan, he betrayed the pilot, and for all I know, he's planning to betray us too.

"Stand by." I link to Flynn. "Consider Perez to be hostile. Don't let him near the controls. Cuff him if you have to. How's our pilot holding up?"

"Perez is sweet-talking her. I think she wants to slug him, but she keeps eyeing my gun. She respects that."

"If she doesn't cooperate, shoot Perez. We don't need him anymore."

"Yes, sir."

The map on my visor puts us two hundred meters from the airfield when a fireball explodes behind one of the snowmobiles. Three quick bursts of automatic-weapons fire follow, sounding like a HITR. "Status?" I demand.

"One snowmobile down," Harvey says.

Tuttle adds, "The other one's pulled back."

The pursuing snowcat is still on the road behind us, but it's not catching up.

With angel sight I see Harvey and Tuttle on foot, where the road joins the airfield. I can't see Nolan and Moon, but the map places them near the first hangar building. "Who do I need to pick up?" I ask.

"I'll take care of it," Nolan says. "I've acquired a vehicle that's faster than that thing you're in."

"It's going to take us a couple minutes to transfer the prisoner and our wounded onto the plane."

"Sir, it's a damn big plane. Suggest you save time and just drive on board."

I have to think about that for a few seconds. "What kind of plane are we talking about, Sergeant?"

"An old C-17 Globemaster. DCs have all the best toys."

"You listening, Jaynie?"

"Yes, sir. Drive on board."

The trees open up. I look ahead, to see the hangars and the three-story blockhouse where employees live. The buildings stand alongside the runway. The snowplows have done their job. The runway is clear, along with the tarmac in front of the hangars. There's not even a fence to get in our way.

"Hold on tight, Shelley," Jaynie warns.

I feel her downshift. The snowcat tilts up as we meet a berm of plowed snow. We climb, and then the snow gives way beneath the tracks, sending us lurching down again, riding a tiny avalanche onto the tarmac.

I don't know how well the snowcat will do on pavement, but we're about to find out. Jaynie makes a ninety-degree turn, and we're paralleling the runway. In the shadow of the hangar, I see a pickup truck begin to move. Night vision shows me the driver, identified as Nolan in my visor. The figure in the cargo bed is Moon. No lights are on. We pass the truck, climbing back through the gears. The tracks hammer the pavement, setting the snowcat vibrating so hard I feel like my bones are going to shake loose. "Wha' fuck kind of suspension is this?" Kendrick whispers over gen-com.

"Won't be long, sir," Jaynie says.

I prop a foot over Ransom to make sure his body doesn't get bounced out.

Angel sight shows me the pursuing snowcat, stopped two hundred meters back along the road, just out of Harvey's line of sight. I don't know where the second snowmobile has gone.

The angel tracks me. It's moving ahead to the inland end of the runway, where a monster plane awaits us, its wings, belly, and tail defined by navigation lights blazing in night vision.

Over the rattling of the snowcat, I hear a grenade go off. A fierce exchange of small-arms fire follows. Then Nolan's voice: "Tuttle, report."

"Fucking sons of bitches," Tuttle swears in a pained whisper.

This pisses Nolan off. "Report now! Are you wounded?"

"Mule-kicked! Two enemy down, Sergeant. Two more possibly at large near the hangar."

"Leave them," I say. "We're getting on that plane now."

Jaynie questions me. "They could hit us with a rocket on our way out, LT."

"Fuck 'em. We've got their queen. You think they're willing to burn her?"

"I guess we find out."

Nolan swings around in his pickup truck to collect Harvey and Tuttle. A few seconds later, he blasts past the snowcat. By the time we reach the plane, Harvey and Moon are on the ground, ready to shoot anything besides us that moves. Tuttle is inside the plane, while Nolan waits at the foot of the ramp, light from the interior blazing around him. I jump down from the snowcat's cargo bed as Jaynie lines up her approach to the ramp.

The angel is above us. I take a last look through its camera eyes. The pursuing snowcat has reached the end of the road. I don't see anyone else. Tuttle reported two possible at large, but I haven't seen them yet. On gen-com I announce, "I'm calling the angel in." Then I issue the order for the little drone to descend.

The snowcat rumbles up the ramp.

"Harvey, Moon—inside now." They come at a trot. Their footplates bang on the ramp. I follow them, and behind me, the three-foot-long crescent wing of our angel drifts in—the last member of our LCS.

The snowcat looks small within the cavernous space of the C-17's empty cargo hold. Fold-down seats line the walls, with equipment racks above them. Above the racks, banks of white, rectangular panel lights shine so brightly that my helmet switches out of night vision.

"Roll call," I say as gen-com automatically filters out most of the engine noise.

The answers come in designated order:

A whisper: "*Kendrick.*"

"Shelley," I say.

"Vasquez."

"Nolan."

"Harvey."

"Moon."

"Tuttle."

We all freeze, waiting for a response from Flynn. Fear grips me when it doesn't come. "Private Flynn! You there?"

"Yes, sir. In the cockpit. But we skipped Ransom—" Her voice catches. "Oh shit. I'm sorry, sir."

"Tuttle!" I bark. "Get the ramp up. Nolan, you're up front. Make sure the cockpit's secure. If either the pilot or Perez is not cooperative, let me know. And tell the pilot to get us the fuck out of here."

"You got it, sir." He starts to go, but then hesitates. His hand disappears into his pocket, comes out again with a high-end tablet phone. "Almost forgot. I took this off Perez." He hands it to me, then bounds up the length of the empty cargo hold, the footplates of his dead sister banging on the aluminum deck. He disappears up the ladder to the cockpit.

I look the phone over, confirm it's off, then slip it in my pocket.

We're depending on the pilot now—and on how much Thelma Sheridan's remaining mercs value their employer's life. The plane vibrates as we begin to move; the engine noise ramps up.

Tuttle is directing Moon as they put tie-downs on the snowcat. "When you're done with that, get a litter set up for Kendrick."

"Yes, sir."

"Jaynie, you and Harvey get the prisoner out of the snowcat. Make sure she is secured, hand and foot."

"On it."

I go to see Kendrick, still in the back of the snowcat. He's taken his helmet off. It's on the floor at his feet, but he dug the audio loop out and has it hooked over his ear so he's still linked to gen-com. He's limp against the seat, sweating despite the cold. His eyes are only half-open, but they shift to look at me.

"How you doing, sir?"

"I'm fucked. Why aren't you up front?"

"Nolan's on it."

"You don't know if we're on the right course."

"I'll check on it when we're in the air."

Sheridan is trussed in the front seat, but she's half turned around, watching me, looking a little worried at last, her pensive face splattered with Ransom's blood. Jaynie opens the front passenger door and climbs in. She's taken off her pack and her dead sister so she can move easily in the confined space. Sheridan whips her head around to look at Jaynie, while the vibration of the plane amps up as we speed down the runway.

If Carl Vanda is going to try to stop us from taking off, he has to do it now.

I watch Jaynie cut the plastic shackles that hold Sheridan to the middle seat. I'm ready to intervene if I have to, but Sheridan's not stupid. There's nowhere for her to run, no one to come to her rescue. Not yet. So she cooperates, climbing down from the snowcat as the C-17 lifts into the air.

"We're away," Nolan says over gen-com.

No one cheers.

Jaynie and Harvey take hold of Sheridan's arms and walk her away from the snowcat.

"Your turn, sir," I tell Kendrick. Using the strength of my arm struts, I lift him out of the backseat. He groans in agony, but there's nothing I can do. Tuttle and Moon help me get him to the litter they've set up. "Moon, you stay with him. Do what you can."

"Right, sir." He doesn't sound confident.

I take Tuttle with me. First we stop to check on Sheridan. Jaynie has her in one of the fold-down seats. Her hands are loosely cuffed behind her back. Her ankles are cuffed to the seat supports. "My shoulders are aching," she complains to me in a firm voice easy to hear over the engine noise. I don't say anything. Harvey is standing by, fully rigged, keeping watch.

I signal Tuttle. We return to the snowcat for Ransom's body, laying it out on the side of the cargo hold. With Jaynie's help, we get the rest of the gear out.

I link to gen-com. "Nolan, we haven't made our turn north yet, right? We're still over the ocean?"

"Yes, sir."

"Tell the pilot I'm going to open the aft ramp."

We're flying halfway around the world. I want to max out the distance before I have to worry about refueling, which means I'm not going to carry unnecessary cargo.

Jaynie helps me remove the tie-downs on the snowcat as Tuttle lowers the ramp. She climbs into the driver's seat, puts the snowcat in reverse, and jumps down. Together we watch it roll backward. It reaches the end of the ramp, tips over the edge, and drops away. I watch it in night vision, spinning and tumbling as it begins its long fall to the Gulf of Alaska.

Ever since Kendrick fired the string of explosives that initiated our assault, we've moved so fast, I've been only half-conscious of rising pain: a deep, merciless throbbing from the impacts I took during our shootout with the microdrones, and a low burn of feedback from the robot legs. The skullnet modulates my perceptions, but it can't knock everything out . . . and I start hurting a lot worse as my body cools down during those drawn-out seconds while I'm watching the snowcat drop away.

I'm not the only one hurting. We'll need to do a squad-wide injury assessment, and distribute painkillers if we can sweet-talk Guidance into—

*Fuck.*

No Guidance. No Delphi. We're on our own.

Nolan speaks over gen-com. "Sir, incoming call on the plane's satellite phone. Caller ID is Carl Vanda."

Tuttle brings the ramp back up, as Kendrick speaks in a whispery voice that's beginning to slur. "Get your ass up front, Shelley, and lead."

The cockpit is dark, except for the dim glow of instruments and tiny spotlights. The light illuminates four swivel seats: two in front for the pilot and copilot, and two behind for crew. In the pilot's seat is a thin, pallid, sharp-featured woman with short, light-colored hair flattened under her headset. She turns to look at me with wide, frightened eyes. Even in the dim light I can see that her hands are shaking.

Nolan is in the copilot's seat. He's taken off his rig, but his helmet is still on. Behind him I recognize our ally, Lucius Perez, from his picture in the mission briefing. He's wearing a headset just like the pilot. Opposite him, anonymous in her helmet, is Flynn. I want to kick Perez out of the cockpit, but I don't want Sheridan to see him, so I'm stuck.

Nolan gestures, indicating the pilot, and over gen-com he tells me, "Sir, this is Ilima LaSalle. Retired Air Force."

I route gen-com to my overlay, and then I take off my helmet so I'm something more than an anonymous goon in her eyes. Nolan hands me a headset to muffle the engine noise, and to allow me to speak easily with Ilima. I adjust the position of the mic. When I look up, Ilima is staring at me with stunned recognition.

"You're James Shelley," she says over the intercom.

I'm not above using my celebrity status. "Which show did you see, Ilima? *Bleeding Through*?"

"I saw them both."

"I want you to know that everybody here is a veteran of Black Cross. We are not here to hurt you, and I am personally apologizing that you've been caught up in this mission. We were led to believe that you agreed in advance to help us."

"I didn't. I don't know what's going on, and I don't know why you're here."

"Our mission is to bring Thelma Sheridan to trial. Ilima, she supplied the nuclear devices that caused the Coma."

Ilima looks away from me. There's terror in her eyes, but strangely, she doesn't look surprised.

"Did you suspect it?" I ask her.

"No! But I've . . . carried cargo before that I've wondered about." She turns to me again. "What's going to happen to me?"

"We need you to fly this plane. You're the only one here

who can, so I have to require your cooperation. I will not let this mission fail. But when we've delivered Thelma Sheridan, you'll be released unharmed. Understand?"

"Yes, sir. Yes, sir, I do."

We're heroes, so it's easier for her to believe we won't kill her.

"Where's the satellite phone?" I ask.

"You've got the headset on. I just have to connect you."

"No, not me." I don't want to give Carl Vanda my voice print. So I turn to Perez. "You're going to talk to him."

"No! He needs to think I'm a hostage too."

"So tell him you're a hostage. And tell him we're not ready to talk. If he can keep quiet about what happened, we'll contact him with our ransom demand when we're secure."

I left my HITR with the packs, but I brought a Beretta with me. Not the one that killed Ransom—I don't ever want to touch that one again. This is the one Rawlings gave me. It's clean, its clip-on holster secured to my thigh. I draw the gun, using its lethal shape to augment the gravity of my words. "You've done your part, Perez, and I don't need you anymore. If you even hint to Carl Vanda that this is anything but a kidnapping-and-ransom situation, I will kill you."

Despite the chill of the cockpit, a sweat breaks out on his cheeks. "I'll . . . I'll say what you want."

Ilima routes the call to him. I listen in. There's a whispered strain in Carl Vanda's voice that hints at his injuries, but his tone is calm, cold, as he talks to Perez, who can't help stuttering. I'm glad I pulled the gun on him. It's helped him to do a convincing job of sounding afraid.

As soon as the basics are conveyed, I cut the call off. Then I tell Nolan to disconnect the satellite phone. It's a security risk, and I don't want any more unexpected calls.

Ilima and I go over our route. We'll fly over the North

Pole, a northern "great circle" route, and then south above the Atlantic. I'm not entering the airspace of any other country if I don't have to.

Jaynie appears at the top of the cockpit ladder. She's taken off her helmet. Her audio loop glistens in one ear, and she's got an earplug in the other. Her voice comes to me through the overlay. "You need to see the colonel."

Her tone tells me all I need to know.

I take off the headset. She hands me earplugs. As we head down into the brightness of the cargo hold, my dark-adjusted eyes strain to adapt. "I want you to take my helmet," I tell her, handing it over as we walk back through the plane. "Set it up so the cam is focused on our prisoner at all times. I don't want any trumped-up allegations coming back to bite our asses."

"Yes, sir."

"And then I want all the firearms collected and secured in the firearms locker. Bring me the key."

"Anything else, sir?"

"You're already putting together a watch rotation?"

"Yes."

"Thank you, Sergeant."

Moon is with Kendrick. He's fiddling with the valve on a bag of clear fluid feeding into Kendrick's arm through an IV. Like Jaynie, he's got his helmet off, with one ear wired and the other plugged. "Is there a problem?" I ask him.

"I-I'm not sure. We found this emergency survival kit, and the dates are good to go on the IVs, but it's been a year since I last trained with this stuff. Shit. I just wish I could talk to Guidance."

I check the IV, and it looks okay to me. "You're doing fine on your own, Moon."

But even if he was a fully trained medic, I don't think he could do Kendrick any real good. The colonel looks bad—

wan and shocky, his breathing shallow. Though his eyes are open, they don't seem to see me when I kneel beside him.

When I was airlifted out of Dassari, I received expert trauma care. Kendrick isn't going to get that. We're going to be flying at least thirteen hours before refueling. We can't land, for fear we won't be allowed to take off again. And while we're in the air, there's almost nothing we can do for him.

I open a solo link to him. "Colonel Kendrick? How you doing?"

His eyes blink, shift, focus on me. Gen-com filters out the noise of the plane and boosts his voice . . . but it's still weak and gravelly. "Episode three has turned out to be a bitch."

"Yeah."

"It's in your hands now, Shelley . . . as much as that scares the fuck out of me. Do not let the enemy get under your skin . . . and don't fuck it up."

"Colonel, you—"

"Shut up . . . I don't want to hear it. You need someone . . . to talk to . . . talk to Vasquez. And check in . . . with Rawlings."

"Will do, sir."

"And finish the . . ."

"We'll finish the mission, sir."

He closes his eyes. His breathing is shallow. I watch him for a few minutes, while across the cargo hold Sheridan demands to know what the hell we think we are doing. Harvey is guarding her. She's the only one still wearing a helmet. She keeps her anonymous, unfeeling face turned on the prisoner and doesn't reply.

I step away from Kendrick, unstrap from my dead sister, fold it up, and stash it with the others. "Tie these down," I tell Tuttle. "The packs too."

Ransom is still lying out in the open. I need to do something about that.

I ask Moon where the survival kit is. When he shows me, I paw through it and to my grim relief, I find three body bags. Tuttle helps me secure Ransom inside one of them. I try not to look at his face. It is not at peace—not with the back and the top of his head blown out. I want to know why the Red didn't warn him, why it let him die. I don't want to believe his life didn't matter, that he was just a spear carrier in someone else's drama. I want him to be alive.

I send Tuttle to help Jaynie collect the weapons. Then I drop into one of the many empty seats and open a solo link to Colonel Rawlings. The angel, parked nearby in the cargo hold, anonymizes the request and relays it to a satellite network, which in turn relays it to a randomly selected gateway server that shunts the call through a private network—and Rawlings picks it up. "Congratulations, Lieutenant. Phase one complete."

"The full record got through?" I ask him.

"Everything. All the records from the helmet cams, and your overlay."

"Then you know Matthew Ransom is dead. And Colonel Kendrick, he's . . ."

"The mission remains," Rawlings says in a brusque tone. "You must get the DNA test done."

Ahab Matugo will not let us land in the city of Niamey, his adopted capital, unless we prove by DNA that the prisoner we carry truly is Thelma Sheridan.

"The DNA test is next, sir."

Which means I have to talk to Thelma Sheridan.

My head plays games with me. I flash on a sequence of memories: the way my hair stood on end that day I talked to her at Kelly AMC; the mind-stripping glare of the nuke dissolving the two pilots who forced her rocket down;

Ransom's head snapping back as the first bullet ripped through his brain.

I'm going to need Jaynie at my back.

The engines mask the sound of our footsteps, so Thelma Sheridan doesn't notice as Jaynie and I approach. She's hunched in her seat, balanced on its edge in an effort to ease the pressure of hands cuffed behind her back. A blanket is spread across her lap, but she still looks cold. I almost feel sorry for her—until I see spatters of Ransom's blood clotted in her short, coppery hair.

My helmet is strapped down two seats away, its camera watching her, watching us. Harvey is still standing guard. Keeping the blank face of her helmet fixed on the prisoner, she speaks on gen-com: "LT, this bitch is a babbling psycho-killer. I don't know if I'll ever be able to wash the crazy off."

"Take a break, Harvey."

"Glad to, sir."

Jaynie says, "Be back here in ten."

"Yes, Sergeant."

Sheridan notices when Harvey moves away. She lifts her head—and sees me. Shadows play on her gaunt face. She's no coward, though; I have to give her that. She gathers herself, sitting up straighter. "Lieutenant James Shelley," she says over the sound of the engines. "You will lament this day."

I drop out of gen-com. "I already do, ma'am."

Her gaze moves across me from head to toe, noting all the details. "You're not army anymore, are you, *Mr.* Shelley? No one here is wearing insignia. And you stole my plane. You're a terrorist, nothing more."

All true.

I breathe slowly, deeply, determined not to lose my temper. The red veins of the skullnet icon pulse almost in time to my booming heart. I desperately wish the plane was quiet.

"I am here to collect a DNA sample, ma'am."

"Who do you work for?"

"We need a cheek scraping."

"I can see the Red inside your eyes."

Jaynie's behind me, wearing latex gloves and holding a cheek swab. I turn to her and mouth the word, *Ready?* When she nods, I move quickly, grabbing Sheridan in a choke hold—no way I'm going to risk Jaynie getting bitten or head butted. Sheridan stiffens, but she doesn't struggle. She may be crazy, but she's not stupid.

Jaynie inserts a finger into the corner of Sheridan's mouth, follows with the swab, and takes a scraping. As she steps away, I release Sheridan.

She looks at me, calm and unflustered. "It's not too late to save yourself, Mr. Shelley, but all our days are numbered."

I glance toward the front, looking for Harvey, wishing she'd come back already so I can make a coward's retreat. Jaynie is a few chairs down, transferring the DNA sample to a clear film for an automated analysis. "How could the LT save himself?" she shouts over the ambient noise.

Sheridan and I turn, both of us surprised by Jaynie's question, but Sheridan recovers first. "We're very close," she says, and though she's projecting her voice, she sounds like a normal person—calm, interested, not at all unhinged. "I'm part of a consortium funding a massive research effort to undermine the Red. A cybervirus is under development—it's very close to testing stage—and when it's released into the Cloud, it will hunt down every aspect of the Red, every algorithm, until the Cloud is clean again."

"How do you know it will work?" Jaynie asks without looking up.

"Because the brightest minds in cyber science tell me it will."

Jaynie looks up at me and, projecting her voice, she says, "LT, if there's a way—"

I switch to a solo link. "It's bullshit, Jaynie. There's no magic cyber potion."

Her face goes stony. "How can you know that? Viruses wreck programs all the time—"

"If there was something that could knock the Red out, it would have happened already. The Red *uses* viruses. It has to."

Maybe Sheridan can lip-read. She leans toward Jaynie and says, "You have to understand, he can't help it. The Red speaks through his mouth."

"Sergeant, are you done with the test?"

"It's still processing, sir."

I switch over to gen-com. "Harvey, get your ass back here."

The test finishes up; the kit automatically relays the results to Colonel Rawlings, and to an address provided by Ahab Matugo.

Harvey comes back. I have her cut the cuffs, then she and Jaynie escort our mass murderer to the toilet. When Sheridan comes back I cuff her feet but leave her hands free. "Very kind of you, Mr. Shelley. I thought maybe you'd be sticking a gag in my mouth."

Tempting.

"Ma'am, we are required to offer you humane treatment. Since our own government has refused to pursue a case against you for your involvement in the Coma, you will appear before an international tribunal where evidence will be weighed and your guilt determined."

She looks stunned. Maybe she thought our purpose was a simple ransom kidnapping, or maybe she assumed we were a death squad sent by the Red to interrogate and then eliminate her, but she realizes now we're something else altogether.

"That's outrageous. You can't be serious. You can't actually believe you will ever be allowed to put someone like me on trial."

"It will happen," I assure her. "Good soldiers are willing to give their lives to see that it does."

"Good soldiers? Soldiers are a commodity. They can be purchased at roughly a quarter-million dollars each. This plane is worth a hundred times all of you put together. And that's nothing. That's less than the political subsidies I provide every year. Do you think my politicians want me testifying at your tribunal? Do you think my peers will allow me to speak? They will not. They want no unrest in their kingdoms. You've been set up, Shelley. None of us will live to see the inside of a courtroom. The slam is coming."

I hold a meeting with my senior sergeant not far from Kendrick's bedside. There is no office, no conference room, no hope of real privacy on this plane. Only the thrumming of the engines can keep what I have to say between me and Jaynie, but that won't prevent us from being watched. Harvey, Tuttle, Moon . . . they're trying not to make it obvious. Sheridan isn't that subtle. She's staring at us from across the bay, a knowing look on her shadowed face.

I turn my body, so she can't see my lips move. Jaynie shifts too, side-eyeing me with a resentful gaze. We've got a solo link open. "I need to ask you, Sergeant, who is the enemy?"

Her chin rises; her lip curls. It's the first time I've ever seen Jaynie Vasquez openly angry. "Thelma Sheridan is the enemy, sir!"

"That's right, Sergeant, and you let her play you."

"The Red is also our enemy. When Sheridan suggested there is a means—"

"The Red is *not* our enemy. It's not our ally. It just *is*, like the weather."

"There is no virus that can get rid of the weather, sir."

"And there is no virus that can eliminate the Red."

"She said—"

"She's a lunatic."

"She might be a lunatic, but this consortium she mentioned has got to be employing the very best software engineers on the planet."

"Software engineers can lie like the rest of us, and tell their employers whatever they want to hear. You remember what you said, Jaynie, right before we left on this mission? You said that most people who know about this stuff won't want to get rid of the Red. They'll want to control it, and use it, so they can run things. That makes sense. It makes sense, because people want power. If they think they can grasp a new weapon, a new technology that can give them control over the world or the people around them, then they'll take all kinds of chances. That's the only reason we have any fucking nukes left in the world—because it gives governments power. It gives them control."

She's torn. I see it in her face. She doesn't want to argue against herself, but she desperately wants to believe in Sheridan's consortium.

I push her harder. "Jaynie, Guidance has been trying to figure out how to block the Red at least since I got to Dassari. My girlfriend, Lissa Dalgaard, works at a think tank, and they've been trying to figure out the Red. Her company even has an army contract, but Lissa had nothing to tell me about how to stop it. They haven't gotten anywhere. None of that matters to Thelma Sheridan. She'll believe what she wants to believe." I tap my head, remembering what Elliot told me. "It's the mental filters. We all have them. Sheridan's filters allow her to believe impossible things, and to deny things that are real. She already has a fact-free belief that it's okay with God if she murders a million people, so why would she require actual facts to believe in something as banal as a magic cyber potion?"

Jaynie is frowning, staring off past my shoulder. I let her think about it for a few seconds, and then I repeat, "You let her play you, Sergeant. And when you indulge her fantasies, you are undermining my authority . . . unless that's your purpose? Unless you *are* concerned that it's the Red speaking out of my mouth?"

Her gaze shifts back to me. "Is it a concern for you, sir?"

I don't have to say anything. When I look away, she knows the answer.

I'm tired and I hurt, so I sit down for a minute. I want to call Lissa, let her know I'm still alive, but the only link I'm allowed is to Rawlings. I think about asking him to contact her, but I know he wouldn't do it. He'd call it a security violation. At least she's safe, locked deep inside a secure facility under the protection of Major Chen.

I get up again and go to see Kendrick. Moon is sitting cross-legged beside him, staring at a handheld monitor. He shows it to me. "His heart rate is really crazy. It keeps changing. That's a bad sign."

I go up to the cockpit to check our course. So far as I can tell, we are where we should be. I give Nolan ten minutes to pay his respects. When he comes back, I send Flynn. By the time I go back to see Kendrick again, Tuttle has taken over guarding our prisoner. Harvey is lying on the deck, wrapped up in a blanket, not far from Kendrick. She's got her helmet and her dead sister off, but she's not sleeping. Her eyes are wide open, staring at the ceiling.

Jaynie is sitting with Moon alongside Kendrick's pallet. I sit down on the other side. After forty minutes, the monitor can't detect a heartbeat. We wait twenty minutes more. After that there's no doubt. I get out another body bag. No one says anything as we move him into it, and seal it up. We carry it to the back, lay it beside Ransom, and tie it down.

I'm the CO now. I should say something—but Nolan saves me the effort when he speaks over gen-com. "LT, we've got two fighter aircraft coming up fast."

I sprint the length of the cargo deck and scramble to the top of the ladder, reaching the cockpit just as Colonel Rawlings links into gen-com. "Status?"

At first I can't see a thing, but as my eyes adjust to the darkness, I make out Ilima in the pilot's seat, Flynn behind her, Perez across the aisle, and Nolan up front in the copilot's chair. They all have cockpit headsets on. Flynn and Nolan have their audio loops underneath the headsets, so they're also hooked into gen-com. I ask Nolan, "Do we know who they are?"

"Ilima says they're American, sir. They haven't said anything."

Rawlings is monitoring the feed from my overlay. He can see what I see, hear what I hear, so I don't repeat the information for him. I lean on the back of Nolan's seat to look out the wide bank of windows. The fighters are easy to see because they're flying right alongside us with their navigation lights on. One is flying at our level, the other is higher and slightly behind.

"Flynn, give me your headset." When I've got it on I use the intercom to ask Ilima, "Do we have any defensive systems on board?"

She looks up at me with a resentful gaze. "We are a civilian craft, sir. If they want to shoot us down, there's nothing we can do to stop them."

I wait for the fighter pilots to contact us, but they stay silent. I assume it's a way to rattle us—it's going to be hard to think of anything else while they're dogging us.

Maybe I should have gotten back to Carl Vanda with a ransom demand . . . but I have a feeling he knows that's not what we're about.

Nolan says, "At least we're not directly in front of their guns."

Ilima gives him a withering glare. "That could change in a second."

An alarm goes off. She looks at the instrument panel. "Two more planes. Russian, I think."

Colonel Rawlings opens a solo link. "Don't do anything, Shelley. Don't say anything. Just stick to the course."

What the hell else can I do?

The fighters stay with us as we pass over the top of the world. I stand there and watch them as an hour rolls past. When I notice Flynn nodding off, I send her downstairs. "Grab a blanket. Sleep while you can." Then I take over her seat, behind Ilima. The feedback from the prosthetics is starting to burn my spine, but I don't adjust it. It's keeping me awake.

The fighters dog us as we head south on a route that will take us over the Atlantic. Time creeps past. We take breaks. We eat—or we try to; I can't eat. After six and a half hours in the air, we're coming up on Iceland, and it's still night.

An unchanging Arctic winter night with stars and northern lights dancing and blazing above us. A night that will last for the duration of this flight, that will follow us all the way to Africa.

I'm staring at that astonishing sky, thinking about Lissa, wondering if I'll get to talk to her again, when our escort finally contacts us.

Everyone in the cockpit jumps as an American voice, male, speaks over the radio: "Vanda-Sheridan Globemaster Eight-Seven-Z, this is an interdiction. You are ordered to divert from your present course."

"Hold your course," Colonel Rawlings says using a solo link.

"Hold steady," I tell Ilima over the intercom.

I unstrap and stand up, leaning on her seat back to make sure she doesn't do anything. Nolan is still in the copilot's seat. He watches her too, poised to intervene.

The American speaks again: "Eight-Seven-Z, acknowledge this order."

Ilima reaches for the panel. I tell her, "No."

Several minutes pass, and then the two Russian fighters pull away. One of the American fighters shoots ahead of us, blazing on afterburner as it cuts across our flight path. We hit the jet wash and buck and wobble. I hold on to Ilima's seat back, trying to remember if everything in the back got strapped down.

"Eight-Seven-Z, if you do not immediately comply with the course change, we will commence firing. You will be shot down."

I turn again to our treacherous engineer. "Perez." He flinches when I say his name, watching me, the whites of his eyes bright in the dim light. "I want you on the radio again. Like before. Tell him you're a hostage. Ask him not to kill you. Don't give *me* any reason to kill you. Ilima, put him through."

Perez keeps his eyes on me as he speaks. "This is Lucius Perez. I'm a hostage on this plane, along with Thelma Sheridan and Ilima LaSalle. Please don't shoot. You'll kill all of us if you do."

Ilima screams.

I look up in time to see twin lines of tracer rounds coursing above us, streaking down over the cockpit. Holy hell. Modern fighters have laser-guided sights. They must have loaded up the tracer rounds just to scare us.

Ilima leans forward; her fingers fly across a keypad.

Nolan and I realize at the same time what she's doing. We lunge for her. I get to her first, grabbing her wrist. "Stop it!"

"Don't you get it?" she says, cowering in the seat. "They're going to kill us!" Her gaze cuts from me to the window. "Oh Jesus, here they come again."

I look up as one of the jets passes in front of us. Our plane bucks again. I have to release Ilima and grab on to the seats to keep from falling. She gets the new heading entered before Nolan can stop her. Our C-17 starts to turn.

I reach out to Rawlings. "Colonel, you got anyone with you who knows how to fly this plane?"

"That is affirmative, Lieutenant. Get her the hell out of there."

Ilima cringes as I reach down, unbuckle her harness, and strip off her headset. I grab the front of her jacket and use it to haul her to her feet. Then I shove her at Jaynie, who has just climbed up the cockpit ladder to receive her.

I glance over at Nolan, wondering if I should put him in the pilot's seat. But he's been awake as long as I have, and it's Flynn who likes big toys. I speak over gen-com: "Flynn! Break time's over. Upstairs, *now.*"

Flynn comes running.

"You're up," I tell her when she hits the top of the ladder. I hook my thumb at the pilot's seat.

Her eyes look huge in the dim light. "Sir, I don't know—"

"Move."

She edges past me, drops into the seat. I tell her, "Strap in. And don't worry, Flynn. All you have to do right now is program the autopilot."

She reaches for the pilot's headset, but Rawlings tells me, "Get her into her helmet, so we can use the cam."

I put the word out on gen-com, and Tuttle brings her helmet. We get Flynn properly hooked up and then, after some fumbling, she starts entering numbers into the keypad. Seconds later the plane shifts course again, and the radio wakes up: "Eight-Seven-Z, maintain your new heading! Do not return to prior heading or you will be shot down."

They haven't shot us down yet. I'm pretty sure they don't want to.

They threaten us with more tracer rounds. They rock us with jet wash. But it turns out they're not ready to murder our hostages.

Not yet.

I take the copilot's seat, and send Nolan to rest. Samuel Tuttle takes over the seat behind Flynn.

Our escort sticks with us. At long intervals the fighters drop back, one at a time, to rendezvous with a refueling plane, but they never leave us alone. They continue their antics, rolling across our flight path, rattling the air around us with gunfire . . . making sure we don't sleep as the hours creep by—or at least that we don't sleep for long.

Whenever things quiet down for a few minutes, I catch myself nodding. Flynn is still at the controls. She's got her visor transparent, so I can see she's drifting too. Thank God for autopilot.

We both jerk awake as Colonel Rawlings speaks on gen-com. "Shelley, Flynn. We've come to the tricky part."

I check our position: We're off the northwest coast of Africa—which means it's time to refuel. We knew from the start we couldn't make it all the way without a stopover, but to protect the secrecy of our initial operation, the mission plan called for our landing site to be negotiated with a host country after we were in the air. "Jaynie," I say over gen-com. "Bring Ilima back up here. We're going to need her to land this plane."

"Negative," Rawlings says. "There will be no landing. It's too risky regardless of promises of safe passage. We've arranged for a tanker to meet you. Scheduled rendezvous in eleven minutes."

I'm alert enough to know this isn't good news. "Sir! Those fighters aren't going to let us rendezvous with a tanker." I peer out into a star-filled night, looking for our escort, but right now they're not in sight.

"I think they will. Any interference on their part and your plane could blow up, along with the tanker. We're betting they're not going to take that risk."

If he intends this as comforting, it misses the mark. Flynn looks at me through the transparent shield of her visor. I can't think of anything reassuring to tell her.

"You copy me, Shelley?"

"Yes, I do, sir."

"This is our only option."

"Understood."

Jaynie fulfills my original order, sending Ilima back up to the cockpit. I decide to let her stay. Leaving Flynn where she is, in the pilot's chair, I yield the copilot seat to Ilima, handing her my headset. She scans the instrument panel, notes the level of our remaining fuel, and turns to me with a waxen face and pleading eyes, speaking words I can barely hear—but I can read her lips: *Lieutenant Shelley, we have to land.*

I gesture to her, palm out, asking her to wait. I need a headset.

In the seat behind Flynn, Tuttle is wide awake, watching me with worried eyes. I don't want to send him downstairs—I like having him at my back—so I turn instead to our accomplice, Perez. He's done a good job of playing the frightened hostage. Even now. He's hunched over, rocking slightly in his seat, avoiding my gaze.

"Jaynie?"

"Here."

"I don't have room for Perez, so I'm sending him down. See that he's confined."

He cringes when I tap his shoulder, but when I give him the signal to go, he's eager, slipping off his headset and rushing the ladder.

I take over his seat and his headset, then I use the intercom to explain to Ilima about the tanker, adding, "If there's a problem, if we can't pull it off, you'll need to have someplace lined up where we can land."

"Give me a minute . . . okay, we have enough fuel to make Cape Verde."

I remember seeing that name on the navigation maps. I check my encyclopedia and confirm it's a group of islands off the African coast, between fourteen degrees and eighteen degrees north latitude. "Cape Verde is good. But don't change the heading until I tell you."

"Lieutenant," she pleads, "you don't understand. We don't have fuel for maneuvers. Our margin is minimal. We need to adjust heading now."

"Not until I tell you."

I check the time. Four minutes until the tanker is due. I shut off the intercom so Ilima can't hear. "Rawlings. Status?"

"Stand by."

We wait.

A minute passes, and then another. I open a solo link to Rawlings. "What the hell is going on?"

"Stand by."

I get up again, standing just behind Ilima. She tried before to change our heading on her own. If she's scared enough, she'll do it again and I'll need to stop her—though this time I'm not so sure I want to.

I search the night sky for the lights of the tanker.

Tuttle says, "It's been eleven minutes."

My heart thuds, each beat a painful strike against the bruises on my chest. My spine hurts too, so I give in and drag the feedback bar lower, but not by much. I don't want to lose track of my feet.

"LT?" Flynn asks on gen-com. "What do we do?"

Ilima's hand darts for the instrument panel. I don't know what she's planning, and I don't wait to find out. I catch her wrist and twist it back. "Rawlings? Where is the tanker?"

Several seconds pass without answer—which tells me the tanker isn't coming. I release Ilima's wrist, and over the intercom I tell her, "Adjust our heading."

"Do not adjust heading!" Rawlings barks on gen-com. "You are not going to land."

I signal Ilima to wait, and ask Rawlings again, "Where is our tanker?"

"On the way. It was delayed. Rendezvous is rescheduled. Estimated time, twenty-two minutes."

Twenty-two minutes sounds like forever. After twenty-two minutes, we'll have no margin at all. "What happened, Rawlings?"

"Someone leaked. The tanker delayed takeoff to allow time for an accompanying passenger jet. It's transporting a pool of mediots, Lieutenant, armed with video cameras. In other words, *witnesses*."

Witnesses to what? Our deaths, when our plane runs out of fuel?

Another ten minutes pass, and then the proximity alarm goes off, announcing the return of the two fighters. They slide in from above, moving ahead to occupy the airspace required by the tanker. "Rawlings, are you looking at this?" He can see exactly what I see in the feed from my overlay. "They are not going to let us refuel."

"You are not going to land, Lieutenant Shelley."

I don't answer. There's no need. We're not martyrs. Rawlings has to know that if it's a choice between landing and running out of fuel, we will land.

A few minutes later, Flynn spots the distant lights of the tanker. "There, sir!" The lights of the media plane flash behind it. We move quickly toward rendezvous—but the fighters hold their position.

Ilima looks up at me. "This is not going to work," she says on the intercom. "We need to land."

"Continue on," Rawlings says.

I argue with him. "Sir, there is no margin—"

"I know that, Lieutenant. So does our enemy. So does everyone on the media plane. Don't give in. They *will* let you refuel, if you leave them no choice."

He's so sure of himself, but he's not here. I want to override his order. I know I should override his order for the sake of everyone on this plane . . . but I don't want to give up on the mission.

"We have to go now," Ilima pleads.

Flynn feels the same way. She turns her big eyes on me. "Lieutenant Shelley?"

I lift my gaze to look again out the window at the lights of the fighters. They're holding their positions. I watch them for another twenty or thirty seconds. I do not believe they will let us refuel. I'm on the verge of telling Ilima to change our destination to Cape Verde when the skullnet icon flickers. It brings with it a sense of certainty and suddenly I know—I just know—that Rawlings is right. "Hold steady," I say, using the intercom and gen-com, so everyone can hear. "We'll be okay. Just a few more seconds and they're going to leave."

Twenty seconds later, both fighters break off and retreat. It's like a magic act.

"Oh my God," Ilima whispers.

"LT," Flynn says, astonishment in her voice, "how did you know . . . ?"

"I didn't know. I just had a feeling." A premonition whispered into my back brain, a certain knowledge of what was ahead. On patrol at Dassari I learned to trust that feeling. I still trust it, and why shouldn't I? Episode three isn't over yet.

The tanker lines up against a background of stars. Flynn gets instructions on how to open the refueling receptacle. Ilima watches her, confirming every move. And we load up.

Flashing pinpoints of light put the position of the fighters far to the west. They've stayed close to us for most of our journey, so when the tanker leaves I look for them to close in again, but they don't. They keep their distance. It's the media plane that flies beside us now, its navigation lights bright off of our east wing.

"Status, LT?" Jaynie asks over gen-com. "Are we okay?"

I smile. We're three hundred fifty miles off the coast of western Africa, with enough fuel to go all the way to the city of Niamey, where Ahab Matugo waits to take custody of our prisoner. "We're good. Everything's good. We're going to make it."

Harvey's voice rings out over gen-com: "*Hoo-yah!*"

Nolan echoes her, but as Moon joins in, the cockpit radio wakes up. A new voice comes in over the headset—a man with an American accent, but not the fighter pilot who spoke to us before. With the cheering going on I can't make out what he's saying, so I drop out of gen-com, picking up his communication as he repeats our call sign. ". . . Eight-Seven-Z. Vanda-Sheridan Globemaster Eight-Seven-Z. Lieutenant James Shelley . . . are you in command now?"

Tuttle and Ilima are wearing cockpit headsets, so they've heard the transmission. So has Rawlings, because he's following my feed. He opens a solo link. "Don't answer that, Shelley."

I don't intend to. But I ask him, "Who is that? You know, don't you?"

"It's not relevant to the mission."

"Of course it's relevant. He knows my name." No one should know who we are. We are anonymous. That's why I made Perez talk for us on the radio; it's why I've only spoken to Rawlings on the encrypted connection relayed by the angel. I've talked on the plane's intercom, but that isn't broadcast. "He knows something happened to Kendrick."

"Let it go."

The stranger speaks again on the radio. "Lieutenant Shelley, I believe Mr. Lucius Perez came aboard your plane in possession of a phone. Why don't you get that and turn it on?"

I know the phone he means. Nolan brought it to me after he searched Perez. My hand slides into my pocket. I find the phone and pull it out.

"Do not turn that phone on," Rawlings warns. "It's a security breach. The signal can be used to track your location."

"A media plane is following us," I point out. "Our position is not secret." I turn the phone over, examining it. "Who is he, Rawlings? Why does he know my name?"

"Your only concern is to finish the mission."

If Rawlings won't give me answers, I'll find out for myself.

I turn the phone on. It boots in a second and a half. In another second, it's ringing. I push back one side of the headset, tap to answer, and hold the phone to my ear. I don't say anything.

"Shelley?" a woman's voice asks, trembling, tentative. "Shelley, if you're there, if you hear me, don't be afraid."

It's Lissa.

My heart rate spikes. Despite her words, fear rushes through me, faster than the skullnet can counter. "Lissa? Where are you?"

"You can't do anything for her," Rawlings says. He's monitoring my feed, so he can hear what I hear, including her voice on the phone—but that doesn't mean I have to listen to him. I drop the solo link.

"Lissa?"

She doesn't answer. Instead, I hear the voice that was on the radio. "You've had a nice run, Shelley, but it's over now."

"Who are you?"

"You don't need my name. You only need to know that I've been brought in to recover Thelma Sheridan. I trust she's still alive?"

*A merc.* No doubt an Uther-Fen officer.

Tuttle eyes me from the seat behind Flynn. His lips are moving. I can't hear him because I'm not on gen-com, but I know he's relaying to the LCS what he thinks is going on. When he starts to get up, I signal him to stay put, and then I return my attention to the merc. "Sheridan is alive," I assure him. "Where is Lissa?"

"Lissa's with me."

"Where are you?"

"Look out your windshield. You'll see us out there."

I lean on the seat backs and peer into the night, but Ilima is first to spot the lights of a new aircraft, far ahead of us. "Someone else out there," she says on the intercom.

"It could be anyone," I object.

The merc says, "Tell him, sweetheart."

"Shelley? It's not your fault. We thought we were safe, but they broke in. They shot Keith—Major Chen—I don't know if he's alive—"

"Shh, shh, darling," the merc says in a soothing, fatherly tone. "Let's just tell him what he needs to know."

I faked my death to keep Lissa safe, but it wasn't enough. It didn't fool anyone.

My senses are supercharged with fear, with dread. When I sense movement behind me, I whip around. Jaynie has come into the cockpit. I don't have time for her. I turn my back and look again out the window.

"Shelley?" Lissa asks.

"Tell me, baby."

"They want you to land in Cape Verde."

Thanks to our fuel fiasco, I'm familiar with Cape Verde.

"Listen to me," Lissa adds in quick, whispered syllables boosted in volume by the phone—"don't do it."

I flash on her, shoulders hunched, head turned aside, lips barely moving against the phone as she advises me on what she sees as my best course of action while the merc looming over her fails to hear her whispered words, lost against the drone of the plane's engines.

"Speak up, darling," he says.

She does: "I love you, Shelley." Her voice calm, resigned.

She doesn't ask me to save her life. My Lissa . . . she's analyzed the situation, and she doesn't believe I can.

"We'll land behind you," the merc says. "And have a nice, peaceful exchange of ladies. You understand, Lieutenant Shelley?"

No. I don't understand. Lissa is telling me to abandon her, while that inner feeling that I've come to trust is telling me to delay. Delay, delay, put off any resolution for as long as I can, though in my rational mind I know nothing can be gained by delay. I have to cooperate, or Lissa will die.

The merc speaks: "You *are* listening to me, Shelley?" At the same time, a familiar icon wakes up in my overlay as Rawlings switches me back into gen-com. "Lieutenant Shelley," he says, "you will answer me."

I answer them both: "I'm listening."

Rawlings first: "You can't do anything for her. Terminate the contact and continue the mission."

The merc can't hear him, thank God. "I'll need your cooperation, Shelley, if you want to see pretty Lissa again."

I stare out the windshield and wonder, *What the fuck am I supposed to do?*

The skullnet icon flickers, and I feel it more profoundly: *Delay*.

I turn away from the lights of the distant aircraft to find myself facing Jaynie. Beneath her skullcap her gaze is wary, worried, when what I need from her is trust. "Sergeant," I say, still holding the phone to my ear, "we've got a situation."

Her voice is crisp, official, coming over gen-com. "Colonel Rawlings has informed me of the situation, sir. I am to remind you that the mission comes first."

The mission comes first. I know that. We don't negotiate with terrorists—but I am not going to abandon Lissa. I can't.

The merc doesn't like what he's hearing. "What the *fuck* are you doing, Shelley? Do you give a shit about Lissa or not?" Without waiting for an answer, he hits her, making sure I hear it: the smack of his hand; her short, sharp scream of shock, of pain.

My skin crawls. I try not to imagine what else he could do to her, *will* do. I want to get my hands on him. I want to be wearing the dead sister so I can get my arm hooks on him and tear him apart, but he might as well be in another dimension, another world, because there's no way I can reach him.

"Vasquez," Rawlings says, "take the phone."

She glances at Tuttle. I eye them both, giving a negative shake of my head, and a warning, *Don't try it.* The skullnet picks up the thought, translates it to voice, and sends it to gen-com. The merc can't hear it, but Jaynie can.

She drops her chin, glaring at me, but she holds back, and gestures at Tuttle to do the same. On the phone, the merc tells me, "Shelley, I need your cooperation."

"I understand." I hear Lissa in the background: short, choking breaths as she tries not to cry. "You don't have to hurt her."

"Don't make me hurt her. Change your heading now."

*Delay.*

I switch on the intercom. "Ilima." Her chin snaps up. She looks at me from the copilot's seat, wide-eyed. I worry she's on the verge of meltdown, so I try hard to keep my voice calm. "I need you to recalculate our heading. Figure out an adjustment to get to Cape Verde."

I look up at Jaynie, I look straight into her eyes, and I think, *Tell her do it slowly. Delay.* My skullnet picks up my intent and translates to gen-com.

But my changing demands have confused poor Ilima. "Cape Verde?" she asks me.

My gaze is still fixed on Jaynie when I say aloud, "Just do it."

Jaynie is scowling. Her lip curls in frustration. Her

questioning gaze demands to know: *What the fuck are you doing, sir? Is this some brilliant plan to save the day?*

No, I don't have any fucking plan, only delay, delay, waiting for what, I don't know, a lightning bolt from God maybe, to set the world right, because I can't see a solution as things stand. If I land at Cape Verde I betray the mission along with my soldiers' lives, their futures, their honor, their resolve. If I accept Lissa's analysis and don't land there, then I condemn her to torture, terror, and death.

*Delay.*

Jaynie makes up her mind. Moving quickly, she commandeers Tuttle's headset, then speaks over the intercom to Ilima, while I shield the phone with my hand to make sure the merc can't hear her. "Do it slowly, Ilima," she instructs. "Take as long as you can—and don't enter the heading without specific instruction."

Ilima's perplexed gaze moves from Jaynie to me. When I give her a reassuring nod, she reaches for the instrument panel. "It's a fast process," she cautions me.

I guess so, because the merc is already suspicious. "You're bullshitting me, Shelley."

"My pilot is working out the route."

"Ah, Lissa." His voice becomes hollow as he turns away from the phone. "Your Jimmy doesn't love you as much as we thought. Maybe it's the wiring that gives him a stone-cold heart."

I don't know if she grabs the phone, or if he gives it to her, but her voice is close again—high and frantic—slurred words wrestling past her tears: "No, Shelley. Please, please listen this time. Don't do it. Don't go back for Dubey Lin."

The merc takes the phone. "Poor, frightened girl," he says, satisfaction in his voice because he's made her beg—and he has no idea what she's talking about. But I do.

"Are you there, Shelley?"

No. I'm back at Dassari and I know I can't save anyone and I know it's stupid to try—but how can I not try?

"I'm going to make it easy for you, Shelley. Those fighters shadowing you? Their pilots would rather stay out of our fight, but they are not going to allow you to reach the coast. When I give the order, they will shoot you down. If Lissa's life isn't worth anything to you, maybe you'll play to save your own."

I force myself to focus, to answer, to argue, to *delay*. "You want me to believe you'll murder Sheridan?"

"It's like this: I get a bonus if I bring Ms. Sheridan back, but if that doesn't work out, I still get paid damn well to make sure she never gets off that plane."

I shouldn't feel relieved. It's wrong. Jaynie sees it on my face and her eyes narrow in mistrust. But if the merc is telling the truth, he's given me a way out. I don't have to choose between Lissa and the mission, because the mission is doomed. We have no defense against missiles.

"The merc is lying," Rawlings says.

The merc offers proof. "The jets are coming in now." I look to the west to see the fighters' distant lights begin to move. "They'll transition east of you to reduce the hazard to other planes in the area. If you have not changed course by the time they come around, it's over."

The phone beeps. I glance at the screen and scowl. The call is ended. The merc hung up.

To our west, the fighters are coming in fast. We have no choice. I can't delay any longer. "Ilima, adjust course. Take us to Cape Verde."

"Don't do it," Jaynie warns. She moves a step closer to me; less than an arm's length away. "Shelley, we can't believe him. Those fighter pilots have threatened us over and over, but we're still here."

Nolan isn't in the cockpit—he's down on the cargo deck—but he backs Jaynie up over gen-com. "LT, Vasquez is right. It's an empty threat. They won't shoot us down, especially not in front of that plane full of witnesses."

Moon agrees, saying, "It's bullshit, LT." As if this is a democracy.

But it's not bullshit; it's not an empty threat. It's our new reality.

"God*damn* it," Harvey explodes over gen-com. "I am not listening to this anymore. She needs to shut the fuck up right *now*."

"Harvey!" Nolan barks. "Back off!"

I do not need another fucking crisis. Not now. "What the hell is going on back there?"

"Harvey," Nolan says, "you're relieved. Moon, take over."

My gaze shifts. I pull up a menu on my overlay as Nolan explains, "It's Sheridan, LT. Fire and brimstone. Harvey's burned out on it."

My helmet is in the cargo hold, strapped to a seat with its cams running, collecting video of everything that happens to Sheridan. I tap into those feeds—and right away I wish I hadn't.

Sheridan is secured in her seat, but she occupies it like it's a throne. Her spine is straight, eyes wide, righteous determination on her face as she lectures the cargo bay at a volume bold enough to carry over the engine noise. "—*is* real I warned him. I told him what would happen. Twenty thousand dollars. Think about that! That's the trivial cost for the missile that will end all our lives." She turns to face the helmet cams, like she knows I'm watching. "Do you want to die at a cost of only twenty thousand dollars, *Mr.* Shelley? Surrender now, or we go together into the fire."

I drop the video feed. I don't need to hear any more. "Goddamn it, Nolan! Did she hear you talking about our situation? Do *not* discuss issues where the prisoner can hear you."

"Yes, sir. Sorry, sir."

Jaynie is a step away, glaring at me. I convey to her the ugly truth: "Sheridan is right. She predicted our situation. She knew exactly what Carl Vanda would do." I gesture at the fighters, outside in the night. "He's behind this. He held them back this long hoping he wouldn't have to use them." Vanda believed Lissa's presence would be enough to force my cooperation.

It should have been enough.

Now there's no choice.

"Sheridan promised none of us would live long enough to see the inside of a courtroom—"

Rawlings cuts me off. "Lieutenant Shelley, you are relieved of command. Vasquez, Tuttle, place the lieutenant under arrest."

I raise my hand to block Jaynie as she starts forward. Tuttle's a lesser threat, because there's not enough room for him to get close to me. "Rawlings is covering his ass," I warn them. "If the mission is going to fail, then it's better for him if we're blown out of the sky. That way we can't testify against him."

Lights looming bright in the west catch my eye. I glance sideways to see the fighters, only seconds away. My hand is still up to fend off Jaynie, but it's Flynn I should have worried about. Flynn, quiet in the pilot's seat, saying nothing, doing nothing, in the brief minutes since the merc contacted us on the radio. She goes for the holster on my thigh, snapping it open and pulling out the Beretta. It's the only firearm still at large on the plane. Every other weapon is locked up in a strongbox.

I don't think about what I'm doing. I just react, slamming my forearm into Flynn's visor, knocking her sideways.

She's strapped in, so she doesn't go far, but her grip slips. I wrench the Beretta out of her hands just as Jaynie lunges for my arm. If we were wearing dead sisters, it might be an even match, but I'm taller and stronger. I get a grip on her jacket and shove her back hard. She lands on her ass in the tiny span of the aisle between the two backseats, and I've got the Beretta aimed right between her eyes.

*Fuck me.*

I am not going to shoot Jaynie. I drop my arm, taking my finger off the trigger just as the fighters shoot past us. "Ilima! *Now*," I shout. The jet wash hits us, making the C-17 shudder and buck. We're still riding turbulence when the deck tilts sideways and we begin our turn toward Cape Verde.

Outside the windows, the two fighters sweep around and head west again.

Despite the turbulence, Flynn unstraps. She thinks she's in trouble, and she's right. She's scrambling over the back of the pilot's seat, in a play to get away from me, when I lose my balance and fall against her. It's as good a time as any to confront her. I shove the Beretta into an inside pocket where she can't reach it, then I grab her by her jacket and slam her back into the seat. "Tell me that wasn't your idea, Flynn."

"Colonel Rawlings's orders, sir."

"Colonel Rawlings is not your commanding officer and he does not give a shit about you."

In the aisle, Jaynie is getting up. She's got her hand on Tuttle's shoulder, holding him back.

"Yes, sir," Flynn says. "I'm sorry, sir."

"I want you out of the cockpit." I get up and haul her with me. Jaynie squeezes out of the way as I shove Flynn toward the door. "All of you. Out."

"Stay where you are," Rawlings counters.

I lay into him. "Get off of gen-com and stop interfering. This is my squad, my mission—"

"You're damn right it's your mission, and you have a duty—"

"Didn't you have a duty too? Wasn't it your duty to protect Lissa? You and all your secret conspirators—"

"You're the one who gave it away," Rawlings says. "That combat robot you took down, it had an infrared camera. That's how they ID'd you, Shelley—by your heat signature. Prosthetics so cold they didn't show up in IR. You must have looked like a ghost floating legless above the snow."

*Fuck.*

*Me.*

"You did that to him?" Jaynie demands, incredulous. Despite my order, she's still in the cockpit, and so is Tuttle. Only Flynn has left. "No one worked that out before the mission?"

No one did, because the legs work so damn well our mission planners didn't think of them as a liability, and gave them no special consideration—but I should have. I live in the uncanny valley. I know the difference. I knew it walking in the forest, when shafts of ice were jammed into my bones.

But my critical error came much earlier, at Fort Dassari, when I tried to ignore the warning of the Red. If I had listened and gotten my people out in time, I would have been standing in the snow of the Apocalypse Forest on human limbs, not the lifeless titanium legs that betrayed me, and Lissa would be safe.

I wonder if she's still alive.

I take note of the fact that we are. We haven't been blown up yet.

*Please listen this time.*

"What now?" Jaynie asks me.

I give her the answer, straight up. "We're waiting for the Red."

Ransom would back me if he was here, but Jaynie has to think about it. While she does, gen-com is silent. I hope that means my soldiers trust my judgment, but it's easier to imagine that down on the cargo deck, Nolan, Harvey, Moon, and Flynn are plotting a coup. Judging by the suspicion on his face, Tuttle is sure to join them.

We all flinch as the proximity alarm goes off. Ilima kills it instantly. "Two more fighters," she announces in a trembling voice. "Shikras, from the east."

A shudder runs through me. This is it, I just know it, this is what we've been waiting for. It's Dassari all over again and I wonder what essential piece of me I'm going to give up this time.

But this time is different. This time I'm listening; I'm heeding the will of my artificial god. That buys me a different ending . . . doesn't it?

The radio wakes up. There's a scrambled transmission, and then the merc speaks: "It's over. Take them out."

I look east, and spot the lights of the Shikras. Their pilots don't care if they're seen. They kick on their afterburners. Trailing long white cones of blazing exhaust, they shoot to a higher elevation and then swoop down again on a vector that will bring them across our path.

West of us, the American pilots are maneuvering too, but they're not moving to meet the Shikras. One pulls straight up and away. The other dives toward us.

I see the flare of light as a missile is released. I take grim satisfaction in the sight. It's vindication. I knew the threat was real. Now we will be shot down. And there's nothing I can do for Lissa anymore. Nothing I can do for anyone. Seconds left, as the missile beelines toward us.

The nose of the C-17 suddenly drops out from under me.

I stagger and catch myself against the pilot's seat. Ilima has put us into a steep dive. Light from the instrument panel gleams against the sweat on her cheeks as she tries to evade the missile. It's coming anyway, following us. I see it beyond her bowed head.

Then something changes. The angle of the missile shifts. Its nose rises, its tail drops, and it's not tracking us anymore. It shoots past our fuselage. I whip around to watch it, just as one of the Shikras blasts past. As the C-17 rolls in its jet wash and I clutch the seats to keep my feet, I glimpse the missile again, its fiery tail angling south.

"He diverted it!" Ilima cries in disbelief, in joy. "The Shikra pilot diverted it!"

The American fighter pilot who threatened to shoot us down hours ago finally comes back on the radio, but he's not making threats anymore; he's on the edge of panic. *"Take evasive procedures, now, now, now!"*

I'm watching the receding missile—and I don't want to believe what I'm seeing. It's found a new target, homing in on the distant lights of Lissa's plane.

Ilima pulls us out of our dive as the merc comes back on the radio. "What the fuck did you do? What the fuck?" And then behind his breathless cursing I hear her one more time, my Lissa, her voice tinny with distance from the mic and pitched high in fear as she chants over and over, *"I love you, Shelley. I love you. I love you. I—"*

A blazing yellow glare wipes out the night sky, illuminating our cockpit with the light of burning souls. Seconds later, the shock wave hits us. I hold on tight to keep from being bounced against the ceiling as flaming debris shoots past.

Then it's over. We're flying level again, and all I see outside the windows are stars.

On the radio, the fighter pilots are screaming accusations at each other. Someone is talking to them from the ground, telling them to hold their fire, don't start another war, it was an accident. Colonel Rawlings is issuing orders over gen-com but I can't understand what he's saying because this is a dream. A dream.

There's a touch against my arm. "LT."

I turn around. Jaynie's right behind me. Tuttle's with her. She puts her hand on my shoulder, concern in her eyes. "There was nothing you could do for her, Shelley. It's not your fault."

She's half-right.

I turn to Ilima. "Forget Cape Verde. Take us to Niamey." My voice sounds a little rusty, but Ilima understands me anyway. She bites her lip and nods.

Jaynie squeezes my shoulder. "Shelley? I'm going to take your gun, okay?" She doesn't wait for an answer. She slips her hand inside my jacket and pulls it out of the pocket where I stowed it, then passes it quickly on to Tuttle. He turns and leaves the cockpit.

If this is a dream, why can't I wake up?

I sit hunched at the top of the ladder with my head in my hands. After thirty minutes the skullnet succeeds in imposing an altered state on my brain that feels much like calm acceptance. Lissa is a wound that will never stop bleeding, but my need for her has been numbed and hidden behind a chemical curtain. I wipe my face on my sleeve and straighten my shoulders.

We have a mission.

I look out across the cargo bay—and lock eyes with Thelma Sheridan, still secured within her seat. She speaks—words I can only half hear over the C-17's endless droning roar, but as her lips move, my overlay tags her with dialogue: *The Devil will always demand your soul, Lieutenant Shelley.*

It's not my soul she needs to worry about.

Nolan, Harvey, Tuttle, Flynn, and Moon are all clustered several seats away from Sheridan. Moon has a bandage on his forehead; he must have bounced around when the shock wave hit. Perez is sitting in another fold-down seat, as far from everyone as he can get. That means only Jaynie and Ilima are in the cockpit.

I rise, and make my way down the ladder.

On gen-com, Flynn says, "He's coming down here."

Nolan stirs. He puts himself between me and Sheridan. "LT," he says over gen-com, "you okay?"

"I'm okay." I move to step around him; he moves to stop me, his hand on my arm. We look at each other, trading unspoken questions. "I'm not going to kill her, Nolan."

"Good to hear it, LT, because then we'd have gone to a hell of a lot of trouble for nothing."

He's not entirely reassured, though. As I walk over to Sheridan, he sticks close, just in case.

Sheridan squares her shoulders, putting on a brave face as I approach, but I note the nervous tremor in her throat, the slight shift in her eyes. She speaks first, still full of bluster: "You think you've won, Lieutenant Shelley. You haven't."

"I know that, ma'am." I crouch in front of her, so it will be easier for her to hear what I have to say. "I want you to understand exactly what is going to happen to you, ma'am. We are flying to Niamey. When we arrive there, you will be turned over to government officials. They will see to it that you are held in a secure facility until your trial convenes and the evidence is heard that will implicate you in the events of Coma Day. And then you will spend the rest of your life in prison."

Even before I finish, she is shaking her head in denial. "No." Her gaze is adrift. "This trial you want so badly will never happen. *Never.* All that you've done, all the dead, your very soul—gone for *nothing*."

She's afraid. She wants to frighten me too, but I'm too numb to play that game.

"You will be tried," I insist. "You will be judged. And all those who helped you?" I lean a little closer. "I sure as fuck hope you give up the names of every single one of them to the tribunal. That way, when you're rotting in prison, you'll know you're not the only one."

Her restless gaze settles on mine. "You've been used, Lieutenant Shelley. The Red has used you, and it will not protect you from the whirlwind that is coming."

"Yes, ma'am. I think you're right."

I head up to the cockpit, where I find Jaynie in the copilot's chair, across from Ilima. She turns her seat half around. The dim light casts exaggerated shadows around her eyes as she studies me with her habitual questioning gaze. *Are you going to keep it together, sir? Can I trust you not to blow your brains out?*

I drop into the seat diagonally across from her, drop out of gen-com, and pull on the headset. "What's our current status and position?"

"We're about ninety minutes from Niamey, where we've been authorized to land. The American fighters were recalled before we reached the coast, but the Shikras are still with us, along with the media airliner."

The next words are hard for me to get out. "When I told you to delay, I didn't know the Shikras were coming. I didn't know it would work out like that."

Her gaze darts away, then returns with a suspicious glint. "What did you think would happen?"

I shake my head. I don't want to say because it's naïve . . . but I thought it would all work out. Somehow.

Jaynie doesn't push it. Instead, like a good non-com, she fills me in. "The word is, Matugo sent the Shikras to protect us, in case the Americans decided to shoot us down."

"They did decide to do that."

She acknowledges this with a nod. "You were right about that. They were serious. If you hadn't made us change course, they would have shot us down before the Shikras got here."

The Shikras diverted the missile intended for us—that's the only reason we're still here—but after the missile spared us, it locked on to Lissa's plane. I want to believe that was an accident, that it was a failure in the weapon's target-acquisition rules.

I lean back in my seat, all too aware of an exhaustion that touches every cell of my body. "That was a fucked-up end for episode three."

"That wasn't the end."

She's right, of course. "You ever wonder who wrote the script we're following?"

Jaynie scowls at the deck, thinking about this for a few seconds. Then she looks up again. "You're thinking it's the Red?"

"Sheridan wants to believe this trial will never happen, but the Red wants it. That's where this story is going."

Lissa got in the way of that. She was an impediment to the mission. While she lived, my loyalty was uncertain, locked up in a black box of indecision. Would I abandon her to deliver Thelma Sheridan to trial? Or would I betray my soldiers?

I make my confession to Jaynie. "I still don't know what I would have done, if Lissa had lived."

She cocks her head. "Why think on it? It wasn't your decision. Even King David doesn't get to debate God's plans."

True enough. The Red has its own agenda. I turn to gaze at the night beyond the window, remembering something

Lissa said to me weeks ago when she was figuring all this out . . . that measured against the billions of people in the world, no single one of us matters all that much. Not even her. Not in the schemes of the Red.

*Lissa.*

My memory of her is like a land mine in my brain. I tiptoe around it. I don't get too close.

Think of the mission instead: "Ninety minutes to go?" I ask, just to be sure.

"About that."

"Okay. I'm going to make sure we're ready."

The media plane lands ahead of us in Niamey. It's 0307 local time. The temperature outside is eighty-two degrees American. We've all changed into the summer-weight uniforms we brought with us: gray camo, with no insignia.

Our gear gets stowed in the packs—everything but our weapons, which we'll leave behind in the locker, and our ammunition, which we leave out in the open. Our helmets get carried in their own padded sacks. We won't be wearing them. We need to show our faces, and own what we've done. But we're all still linked through our audio loops, and everyone is still wearing a skullcap, except me.

When the gear is packed, we strap into our dead sisters.

I put Jaynie in charge of our prisoner. There's a distant look in Thelma Sheridan's eyes, like none of this is real for her anymore. "You haven't won," she reminds me as Jaynie takes her arm. "There will be a reckoning."

"That's what we want," I tell her. "That's why we brought you here." I look at Jaynie. "Sergeant, you'll follow us with Sheridan. Ilima and Perez will come last."

"Roger that, sir."

The two body bags holding Kendrick and Ransom get

moved to the center of the cargo bay, close to the ramp. I put Nolan and Tuttle between them. Harvey goes on the left, with Moon behind her; Flynn goes on the right behind me. For each of the bodies, we have an empty exoskeleton, neatly folded. I give those to Moon and Flynn to carry.

"Ready!" I bark. "Kneel!"

Six of us drop to one knee.

"Secure grip!" We grasp the loops of the body bags with the arm hooks of the dead sisters. "Stand!" The bags sag only a little.

I look to Perez, who is waiting by the ramp control. When I nod, he triggers the mechanism to lower the ramp, opening the cargo bay to night—the same endless night—pushed back by a ring of blazing lights.

The light falls across lines of black-skinned soldiers in brown combat fatigues, arrayed in a perfect double vee. Whether they're here to greet us or arrest us, I don't know, but standing at the far point of the vee is a man I recognize from the pictures and video I've seen—my former enemy, Ahab Matugo. He's a tall, distinguished-looking man, young enough that his hair is still black. He's wearing a business suit, as most politicians do. Officials stand behind him, men and women, all of them formally dressed. Though it's three in the morning, everyone looks wide-awake.

Beyond the soldiers and the officials are the media, some of them no doubt disgorged from the plane that landed ahead of us.

I wonder how far this story will be allowed to spread and how the Red will try to play it.

I wonder if there will ever be an episode four.

If there is, I sure as hell hope I'm not part of it.

With my gaze fixed straight ahead, I issue my last order as commanding officer of the ragged remains of our C-FHEIT LCS. "For-*ward*, march!"

# LINKED COMBAT SQUAD

---

EXTENDED EDITION

IT'S BEEN QUIET FOR A COUPLE OF HOURS. I'M sitting next to Jaynie in the passenger cabin of a tiny chartered jet that's taking us back across the Atlantic. Nolan is in a seat across the aisle, leaning up against the bulkhead, his eyes closed. Harvey, Moon, Tuttle, and Flynn occupy the seats behind us. The thrum of the engines is a constant background, but it's blissful white noise compared to the C-17.

We stayed in Niamey less than a day—just long enough to testify to the accuracy of the video records collected by our helmet cams and by my overlay. An attorney talked to us about our legal options—we could have applied for asylum—but we all chose to go home. At the least, our court-martial will make the reasons for what we did a matter of public record.

I'm playing with the slider bar in my overlay that controls the intensity of feedback from my legs, seeing how high I can crank it before I start to sweat. It's a mental exercise that takes a lot of focus, crowding the ghosts out of my mind.

Beside me, Jaynie is sitting with her arms crossed over her chest, head tilted back, eyes closed. I assume she's asleep, but I'm wrong.

"How long are you going to sit there and torture yourself?" she asks—a cogent, clear question so unexpected, I jump. "You should be working on a strategy to keep us out of prison."

I don't remember ever telling her about the feedback slider, but I avoid her gaze as I adjust it to something more reasonable. "You think a strategy like that exists?"

It's like I'm caught in some circle-of-life bullshit: I first got in trouble in defense of a principle. I went into the army to avoid prison. I strove to learn a new life, and after I made it my own, I gave it all up in defense of another principle, sacrificing Lissa in the process. Now I'm heading right back to where I started.

"*Innovation,*" Jaynie says. "*Coordination. Inspiration.* That's the motto of the linked combat squads."

"I know what it is."

"So don't assume there's no solution."

It's been only a day since we were locked up on the C-17. I know for sure that sometimes there *is* no solution, but I don't say that, opting to tell her what she wants to hear. "I'm going to testify that we did what needed doing, and that we did it because the people who should have stepped up refused to do so—but don't count on that truth keeping us out of prison."

Her fine eyebrows pull together in a scowl. "I'm counting on you, Shelley. You're the Lion of Black Cross, you're goddamn King David—"

"I'm not King David! That's the bullshit that killed Ransom."

"You're our CO anyway, and you need to fight for us, from the moment we step out on the tarmac at Dulles. I know you got slammed again, and I'm sorry for what happened to Lissa, but nailing yourself to a cross isn't going to change it."

"I'll do what I can! When's the last time you saw me sit out a fight, anyway?"

"Don't make this the first time. Just saying we did the right thing isn't going to count for much. You need to believe it. You need to make other people believe it, or we lose."

Another battle? Maybe that's what I need. My mood levels up in anticipation. I eye the skullnet icon, wondering if the Red is riding me, but the icon isn't glowing. So maybe it's all me, just wanting to hit back. There really is a lot left to do.

"We only slammed one dragon," I muse. "Lot more out there."

Her eyes narrow in suspicion. "God whispering plans into your head again?"

"Nothing obvious. Can't really know for sure, though."

"And you're okay with that? You're okay with the Red squatting in your head?"

"It's inside you too, Jaynie, and you know it. You hate it, not knowing if a choice is your own or if it's been put in your head just to continue the story."

She turns away, a fiery glare fixed on the forward bulkhead as she runs both hands over the smooth surface of her skullcap. For a moment I think she's going to take the cap off, but she's an emo junkie. We all are.

"Jaynie, if it makes you feel better, I think it's only now and then that the Red steps in. It's a marketing program, remember? Out to optimize the world and everyone in it. Lissa thought so, anyway. Doesn't mean everybody gets a good deal—"

"That's God's truth."

"But maybe the odds go up." I turn to look out the window. It's still night out there, but I think I see a blush of dawn behind us.

"You serious about slamming more dragons?" she asks.

"Hell yes. And it starts with the court-martial."

We talk it over with the squad and we agree that our strategy will be to make no deals. We want to force the court to follow the evidence, to name the name of every official involved in protecting Thelma Sheridan, and then with luck—or with the judicious influence of the Red—additional investigations and indictments will follow, in a chain reaction that will burn a lot of powerful people.

Alone over the Atlantic, it's easy to believe we have a chance. But later, when we pick up an escort of navy fighters two hundred miles off the coast, I get a new sense of the scale of the mission we've taken on. The fighters are with us for protection, here to ensure our safe passage to Dulles. We have enemies now.

As we head inland, I search the sky, but though it's a clear day, I spot no other planes. These flight corridors that used to be crowded with civilian traffic are eerily empty—a sure sign that the Coma has not loosened its grip.

The fighters peel away as we touch down at Dulles. We turn off the runway and almost immediately, we come to a stop. I peer through the window at a cordon of military police vehicles, their warning lights flashing. Shielded behind the bulk of the vehicles, MPs rigged in armor and bones survey the surrounding fields, HITRs in hand.

Jaynie leans over to get a look at the defenses. "They're expecting trouble."

"But not trouble from us." They know we're unarmed. Our surrender is arranged. "They're worried some dragon is planning to hit us. So they're putting on a display of force, like with the navy fighters—discourage premature action—and that means we have more to worry about than just the outcome of our trial."

Dragons rule from the shadows. They've got everything

to lose and nothing to gain from what's coming, so they'll try to silence us. They'll try to stop our court-martial proceedings if they can. They have to, or there's a risk we'll take them down.

The fight that's coming won't be limited to the courtroom.

It should be interesting.

# ACKNOWLEDGMENTS

In fall 2011 I returned to short story writing after a hiatus of more years than I care to admit. Two of the resulting stories, "Nightside on Callisto" (*Lightspeed*, May 2012) and "Through Your Eyes" (*Asimov's Science Fiction*, April/May 2013), set up an irresistible alchemy in my head. While there is no obvious relationship between these stories, and I didn't imagine them to be in the same story world when I wrote them, the more I thought about it, the more intrigued I was by the idea that they *were* related, despite their separation in time and space. *The Red: First Light* rapidly evolved as a way to begin exploring that relationship.

Given the diversity and swift advance of real-world technology, writing fiction set in the near-future is a dangerous business, requiring simplification and compromise to allow a writer to get on with the story—but reality always deserves a hat-tip.

Resource people interrogated during the writing of this book include Ronald J. Nagata Sr., Ronald J. Nagata Jr., Mike Brotherton, Paul Kaufman, and Edward A. White. I also want to acknowledge the Internet, and all those people who use it to generously share their knowledge.

Beta readers Wil McCarthy, Dallas Nagata White, Edward A. White, and Nancy Jane Moore all provided helpful comments and excellent advice.

*The Red* began as a self-published novel put out under my own imprint, Mythic Island Press LLC. The assistance of three people was intrinsic to the success of that edition. Editor Judith Tarr provided suggestions and guidance that greatly improved the story; the sharp eye of Chaz Brenchley, who served as copy editor via the writers' cooperative Book View Café, provided coherence and consistency; and my daughter, Dallas Nagata White, made the book stand out with her striking cover art. The Saga Press edition of *The Red* has superseded that original release, but my gratitude to all of you has not diminished.

Everyone mentioned here has my thanks and my appreciation. They tried to steer me in the right direction. All remaining errors and deficiencies are my own.

Finally, hearty thanks go out to all of you who have chosen to buy and read my novels and short fiction. Readers are what it's all about, and I'm very grateful for your support and your encouragement.

If you enjoyed *The Red*, please consider reviewing it on a blog or at an online bookseller, or mention it on your favorite social media. Don't forget to look for the sequel, *The Trials*, also from Saga Press. And if you'd like to be notified of my forthcoming books and stories, please visit my website at MythicIsland.com and sign up to receive my occasional newsletter.

# ABOUT THE AUTHOR

LINDA NAGATA is the author of many novels and short stories, including *The Bohr Maker*, winner of the Locus Award for best first novel, and the novella "Goddesses," the first online publication to receive a Nebula Award. *The Red: First Light* was a finalist for best novel for both the Nebula and John W. Campbell Awards. Linda has spent most of her life in Hawaii, where she's been a writer, a mom, and a programmer of database-driven websites. She lives with her husband in their longtime home on the island of Maui. Visit her at MythicIsland.com.

THE TEASER TRAILER
TO THE NEXT ADVENTURE
OF LT. JAMES SHELLEY
AND HIS TEAM

THE SEQUEL TO
**THE RED: FIRST LIGHT**

**THE TRIALS**

LINDA
NAGATA
THE TRIALS
A RED THRILLER

# AGAINST THE BEAST

---

## EPISODE 1: THE TRIALS

"We are being asked to crucify Colonel Kendrick."

Five pairs of eyes glare at me from stony faces: my soldiers—the Apocalypse Squad. That's the name the mediots have given us and it works for me. We're seated around a cheap oval table occupying the center of an otherwise bare, white-walled conference room in the federal courthouse in Washington, DC. It's the first time in the five months since we stepped off the plane at Dulles that we've been allowed to discuss our case all together, with no lawyers present.

I'm James Shelley. I presently hold the rank of lieutenant in the United States Army, but that will change at the conclusion of our court-martial.

"Our attorneys have decided that since Kendrick is dead, he's not going to scream and he's not going to argue when we hammer the nails in. So they want us to testify that the colonel used undue influence to get us to participate in a conspiracy. They want us to claim we were not mentally responsible at the time and therefore it is not our fault."

Our return to the United States was voluntary and we're widely regarded as heroes. It's a status I've leveraged to get us the privilege of this ten-minute session to confer on our defense strategy. Not a private session—camera buttons are watching from the corners of the room and the ocular overlay I wear like contact lenses in my eyes is always recording—but we're used to that. We're LCS soldiers, and in a linked combat squad you expect to be observed.

"In just a few minutes, each one of you will meet individually with counsel, where you will be advised to pursue an affirmative defense, claiming a lack of mental responsibility."

It's been over five months since Coma Day, when seven improvised nuclear devices were used to destroy data exchanges across the country, shattering the Cloud and collapsing the economy. Travel and communication have been a challenge ever since, so an agreement was reached to hold our court-martial in the centrally convenient District of Columbia Federal Courthouse. We are using the facility but not the staff. The army is conducting our court-martial, with a court composed of army personnel and presided over by a military judge.

Our court-martial hasn't started, and we will not be in court today, so we're all wearing the informal brown camo of combat uniforms. Everyone but me is also wearing their linked combat squad skullcap. The caps look like athletic skullcaps, but they're precisely fitted to ensure that the mesh of fine wires embedded in the silky brown fabric is held close to the wearer's hairless scalp.

I don't wear a skullcap anymore because I have something more advanced: a mesh of sensor threads implanted against the surface of my skull. It's called a skullnet, and it monitors and influences the activity in my brain. It could be my get-out-of-jail-free card, if I want to try to use it for that.

I tap my head, where my black hair is trimmed to a short buzz cut. "The attorneys want me to say Kendrick controlled my thoughts, my emotions, my decision-making processes, through my skullnet. They want each one of you to say he hacked your heads through your skullcaps. They want us to argue we were not in our right minds and that we didn't understand what we were doing."

Specialist Vanessa Harvey speaks up first: "Fuck that, LT."

She crosses her arms, fixing me with a glare that could stop bullets . . . almost did, at Black Cross, where she was shot in the face. Her visor took the impact of the slug, and she got away with only a broken nose—but no sign of that injury remains in her sharp-featured, bronze-complexioned face.

Specialist Samuel Tuttle expands on Harvey's sentiment. "Fuck *them*." The rim of his skullcap enhances his scowl as his brooding brown eyes shift from Harvey to Sergeant Aaron Nolan, who must have been his big brother in some other life.

Nolan is six foot one, broad shouldered, with deep-brown skin. He told me once he was half Navajo, half white. Generally, he's a congenial man, but now he drops his chin and coldly informs me, "Those shit eaters can go to hell."

Little Mandy Flynn, with her green eyes and fair skin, is only a private, but she's more eloquent than anyone else. "No way are we pissing on the colonel's grave, sir."

"Damn straight," Specialist Jayden Moon agrees. Moon is tall, skinny, and dark eyed, the offspring of Asian and European bloodlines mixed in some complicated formula. He used to have a tan, but our stint in jail has bleached his skin to a pale cream. "LT, this is just bullshit."

I glance up at Sergeant Jaynie Vasquez, who stands somewhat loyally at my right shoulder. Jaynie is the ranking non-com in our squad. She's got a lean build and moderate height. Her skin is smooth and black. She tends to regard the world with a reserved expression that perfectly reflects her nature: smart, controlled, determined, and not entirely trusting of my judgment. She answers my questioning look with a nod, letting me know she'll back me up as long as I say the right things.

I turn back to Moon. "Of course it's bullshit, Moon. It's the same bullshit we LCS soldiers get all the time."

Outside the linked combat squads we are commonly believed to be soulless automatons, emotionless killing machines controlled by our handlers in Guidance. It's a prejudice our attorneys want to exploit.

"But it's a bullshit that can be used to buy you a not-guilty verdict and a medical discharge."

Moon looks confused. His gaze shifts to Jaynie. "I don't get it. That's not why we came back."

He's looking at Jaynie, but I'm the one who responds. "No, it's not why we came back. The crucifixion of Colonel Kendrick is an option we are being offered because both trial and defense counsel are under extreme pressure to limit the scope of our court-martial. They do not want to look into the chain of responsibility—"

"*Lack* of responsibility," Jaynie interrupts in a low growl.

I concede the point with a nod. "They do not want to look into the layers of corruption that forced us to take the action we did. We are here to expose that corruption, to confront it. That's why we came back. But this is not a game. We are facing life in prison, very possibly execution. If you want to reconsider your reasons for being here, now is the time. Just know that for the affirmative defense to work, all of you will need to agree to it. If even one of you dissents, that will cast doubt on all the others."

Harvey's arms are still crossed, her brow wrinkled in suspicion. "What do you mean, *we* would have to agree? What about you, LT? I thought we were all in this together."

"That's up to you, Harvey. There's no fucking way *I'm*

going along with it. But the rest of you can claim your commanding officers exploited your sense of loyalty. Let me know if you'd like me to step outside while you discuss it."

Jaynie, still standing at my right shoulder, speaks. "Take a pass on the drama, LT. We've got nothing to discuss, because I dissent. I'm not participating in a bullshit defense."

"I'm not either," Harvey says.

This sentiment is echoed around the table with nods and murmurs. Using my overlay, I launch a facial analysis program, letting it study each member of my squad. It detects no deceit in the faces of my soldiers, no real doubt. I look up at Jaynie. She frowns down at me. The program confirms the caution I see on her face, but her caution doesn't bother me because Jaynie has always been the most thoughtful among us.

The standard way for a story like this to unfold is for at least one, maybe even two, of my soldiers to prove treacherous, cutting a secret deal with trial counsel that will betray the rest of us while saving their own asses—but Colonel Kendrick preempted that tired plot device when he hand-selected everyone in the squad for a spectrum of personality traits including a compelling sense of justice and a group loyalty strong enough to keep us together through two harrowing missions. As I look around the table I know that everyone remains loyal to this, our current mission.

"So what the fuck are we going to do?" Harvey demands, her sharp gaze focused over my shoulder because she is addressing her question to my sergeant and not to me.

My fist hits the table with a loud bang, and I regain the attention of every set of eyes in the room.

We don't have many options. The charges entered against us include conspiracy, multiple counts of murder, aggravated assault, robbery in excess of $500, and kidnapping, with a general article for abusing the good order and discipline of the armed forces. I get an additional charge of destruction of military property since I was present when Colonel Kendrick deliberately destroyed an army helicopter.

Moreover, we did in fact commit every act we are accused of during the execution of a rogue mission, code-named First Light, in which we took a United States citizen to face trial in a foreign country for crimes committed within and against the United States. Every moment of that mission, every conversation, was recorded by multiple devices, including my ocular overlay. There is no lack of evidence that can be used to convict us. There is only the question of whether or not circumstances justified what we did.

It's a question the court is desperate to avoid, which is the only reason we've been offered the I'm-not-responsible defense . . . but we're past that.

"Because this is a death-penalty case our plea is automatically entered as not guilty. That means the prosecution has to prove the case against us, step by step for the public record. We want that. We want the public to know who we are and what we did, but above all else we want them to know why we did it."

I know a hell of a lot more about the law now than I did when we started this. I present my strategy with what any competent attorney would surely regard as an amateur's optimism. "The only valid defense we can make goes to our service oath to support and defend the Constitution against all enemies, foreign and domestic. So what we are going to do is expose those enemies—our domestic enemies—shine a light on them, and examine every link in the chain of command that had a hand in sheltering Thelma Sheridan from prosecution for her part in the Coma Day insurrection. We push the judge on it at every step. We force the scope of the investigation to expand. If it ultimately takes in the president, so be it, I don't give a damn. If it sets off a revolt against the rotten core of our country, you won't find me weeping."

"Burn it all down?" Jaynie asks softly.

I look up at her again, wondering at the suspicion in her voice. "No. That's not what I want."

She studies me, like she's trying to see beneath the surface. "Just don't push it too far, sir. You might not like what's on the other side."

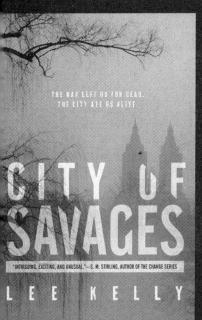